An epic of the colonial frontier is completed after nearly a century.

George Washington, Frontiersman was first printed only in 1994, by The University of Kentucky Press, and this is the first mass market edition.

Zane Grey's first three novels were about the frontier in his native Ohio, including his first novel, *Betty Zane*, then *The Spirit of the Border* and *The Last Trail*. Late in life he returned to that setting and those times to complete the saga, but the novel was not published in his lifetime. Zane Grey's completion of his multi-volume work, with the return of popular characters, such as Wetzel and the Zane family, is a singular event.

ZANE GREY

GEORGE WASHINGTON, FRONTIERSMAN

A TOM DOHERTY ASSOCIATES BOOK
NEW YORK

GEORGE WASHINGTON, FRONTIERSMAN

A Forge Book
Published by Tom Doherty Associates, LLC
175 Fifth Avenue
New York, NY 10010

www.tor.com

Forge® is a registered trademark of Tom Doherty Associates, LLC.

ISBN: 0-812-57923-2

First Forge edition: February 2001
First mass market edition: February 2002

Printed in the United States of America

0 9 8 7 6 5 4 3 2 1

Contents

Introduction

George Washington, Frontiersman is the last of Zane Grey's works to be published. When Grey died in 1939, about two dozen full-length manuscripts were found in his home in Altadena, California, that were regularly published in the years ahead. Even as short a time ago as the 1980s, stories were still being uncovered that were attributed to this prolific author. Thus, it could very well be shortsighted to claim that the presentation of *George Washington, Frontiersman* "closes the door" on his work. As far as I can determine, however, there will be no more Zane Grey manuscripts.

Grey began his literary career (he had been a dentist before going into writing) in 1903 with the publication of *Betty Zane*. He followed this work in 1906 with *Spirit of the Border* and *The Last Trail*. These three novels made up the Ohio River trilogy. *Betty Zane* dealt with settlers (among them, Ebenezer Zane, Grey's great-grandfather) going into the Ohio River Valley, around Ft. Henry, which is today Wheeling, West Virginia. Highlighted in this work was the desperate and heroic run of Betty Zane across enemy lines to get much-needed gunpowder. *Spirit of the Border* was a brutal account of the relationships (or lack of them) between the white settlers and the Native Americans. Frontiersman Lewis Wetzel was a main character in *Spirit of the Border*, as were Jonathon Zane and renegade Simon Girty. The third of this series, *The Last Trail*, represented a "pacified" frontier, at least in comparison to what had gone before.

George Washington, Frontiersman fits well into the motif of the Ohio River trilogy. In fact, its events and placements were largely the settings for *Betty Zane, Spirit of the Border*, and *The Last Trail*. Many of the same characters populate all four of these books: Lewis Wetzel; Betty, Ebenezer, Isaac, and Jonathon Zane; Daniel Boone; Christopher Gist; and several Indian chieftains such as Shingiss, Half King, and Scarrooyaddy. It was, in a way, fitting that Zane Grey's first publication, *Betty Zane*, and his last publication, *George Washington, Frontiersman*, should deal to such an extent with the same subject—bringing, as it were, "full circle" his lifetime interest in the Ohio River Valley. Though he went on to fame with nearly a hundred romantic novels of the American West, he never forgot his own Ohio Valley roots and the exploits of his forebears.

As a youth (he was born 31 January 1872 in Zanesville, Ohio), Grey had been an inveterate reader. He claimed practically to have memorized Charles McKnight's *Our Western Border*, which inspired many of his Ohio River stories. He also read biographies of George Washington and Washington's diary, in addition to numerous accounts of General Edward Braddock's defeat in 1755. He kept notes, but he also had a prodigious memory for what he had seen and read. Thus, in 1938, when he set about to write *George Washington, Frontiersman*, he did not have to research it to any great extent, for he already had his materials.

In writing *George Washington, Frontiersman*, Grey used a method that was somewhat awkward to him: dictation. Through the years he had been used to writing in longhand, with a pencil, on a lapboard over a Morris chair that he always took with him on his travels. In 1937 he was fishing on the Umpqua River in Oregon when he suffered a debilitating stroke. It took the better part of a year for Zane Grey to recover at least some of his faculties. He could walk and speak—somewhat more slowly than in the past—but could barely use his right arm. His mental faculties remained intact, and he seemed bound and determined to finish the last two novels he knew he had in him. Thus, he hired several secretaries and dictated *George Washington, Frontiersman* and his very last novel, *Western Union.*

Western Union, of course, went on rather quickly to publication, because his publisher, Harper's, wanted to maintain the "Zane Grey image" of that particular time. Other manuscripts left behind at his death more readily fit the "image" of the romantic West of the late nineteenth and early twentieth centuries than *George Washington, Frontiersman*, a novel that went as far back as the middle of the eighteenth century. *George Washington, Frontiersman* was not the only Grey novel whose publication was slow in coming. It was not until 1977 that Harper's decided that the "image" would not be fatally injured by publishing *The Reef Girl*, a novel about the South Seas presented to the Harper's editors in early 1939, a few months before Grey's death. Also in this regard, one could mention *The Westerner*, brought out for the first time in 1977 by Belmont-Tower Books, and *The Rustlers of Pecos County*, published in 1980 by Ian Henry of Hornchurch, England.

It is only in our own time that editors have begun to let Grey speak for himself; this changed editorial attitude surely explains why versions of some of his novels have been reissued, showing how he originally wrote them. *Thirty Thousand on the Hoof, The Maverick Queen*, and *The Vanishing American*, for example, were written in the twenties, with quite a bit of sexual and ethnic explicitness (though it would be considered rather tame in our own time), which had been deleted by editors before publication.

George Washington, Frontiersman is a work of fiction that definitely fits the general description of a "historical novel." In a historical novel, the major characters are real; events, generally, are "real" too, except that sometimes an author will expand or contract an event to suit his literary needs, and also create a character or two that are composites of several different people. Personalities are usually magnified in the historical novel beyond what they are in typical biographies or history books. A sense of people and their times can be conveyed by historical novels sometimes quite as well as—or better than—traditional learning methods. One thinks of Irving Stone's works in this regard, especially with Dolly Madison, Rachel Jackson, Sigmund Freud, and Eugene Debs. Or Gore Vidal, who so frequently pushes his action ahead by imaginary conversations between and among his principal characters; one particularly thinks of *Lincoln* here. Grey, then, in *George Washington, Frontiersman,* is not writing history, though it is history. It was a tribute to his versatility that he could connect the frontier novel and the western novel to such an extent.

Through the years, Grey was scorned by critics for creating faulty characterizations. He frequently painted characters much larger than life and gave them attributes that no mortal human being could have. He did not indulge in this practice, however, as much in *George Washington, Frontiersman* as he did in several of his other novels. He did not give George Washington, George Fairfax, Daniel Boone, Patrick Henry, Christopher Gist, and General Braddock roles that would have been impossible for people of their experience to fulfill. He did not have to invent most of his characters in this book (although there were a few purely fictional people such as Michael "Red" Burke), and perhaps the restraint of the various historical accounts of the people and events contributed to these muted characterizations.

Though Grey created superhuman characters in his works, he was generally credited, even by the most skeptical critics, with beautiful descriptions, aesthetically and geographically true in almost all their details. This was certainly the case with the Ohio River Valley of which Grey speaks in *George Washington, Frontiersman.* One can only marvel at Grey's knowledge of the valley, after being physically separated from it for over three decades. Grey *knew* the Ohio River Valley; and he was able to put into the mouths of his mostly authentic historical characters words that exemplified their roles in the history of this country.

Good historical novels will not credit a story when it is generally known to be false. Thus, the cherry tree story is not a part of *George Washington, Frontiersman*, although there is a hint of it when young Washington is given a tomahawk as a present. There are still enough differences among historians—professional and otherwise—about Washington's relation with Sally Fairfax to prevent laying the rumor of his love for her to rest. Thus, the story remains open to conjecture. Grey presents the Fairfax story as one of the central motivating factors in the life of young George Washington—thus, I let it stand, not seeing the point in eliminating it in a historical novel.

Washington's surveying trips with Fairfax, first into the Shenandoah and then into the Ohio River Valley, are factual, as are all the Indian chieftains he met along the way. These, and the trips he subsequently made for governor Robert Dinwiddie of Virginia, laid the foundations for his relationships with numerous woodsmen, who generally wanted to settle permanently in the wilderness, and frontiersmen, who maintained an itinerant life—foundations that served him well when battles occurred. Grey captures the spirit of George Washington during his young years as both a woodsman and a frontiersman, a person who liked peace but savored battle. As Charles W. Eliot said in *Four American Leaders*, "Washington was roused and stimulated by the dangers of the battlefield."

George Washington was twenty-three in 1755 when he was made an aide-de-camp to General Braddock in the campaign to wrest Fort Duquesne from the French. Washington was by this time an accomplished frontiersman, both in real life and in Zane Grey's novel. He knew people like Christopher Gist, Daniel Boone, Captain Jack the Black Hunter, Lewis Wetzel, and many others who participated in the debacle of Braddock's Field. It is well-known by anyone with an interest in history that Braddock's defeat could have been avoided if he had been willing to listen to the advice given to him by people like George Washington and Daniel Boone. Hundreds of young soldiers had to die because of the obstinacy of this one British general. Most of Washington's "corps" at Braddock's Field came off unscathed, proving beyond doubt that frontier warfare was vastly different from that experienced in the Old World. Grey, in any novel he ever wrote, never came off better in his descriptions and delineations of Braddock's Field than he did in *George Washington, Frontiersman.* He shows here an uncommon historical astuteness in bringing these events truly alive.

After the French and Indian War ended in 1763, the focus in colonial America, and in Grey's novel, turns to difficulties between the various colonies and the mother country. High-handed bureaucracies, the wish for increased taxes, and the unwillingness of the British Parliament even to discuss equitable representation brought on one crisis after another. George Washington's friends had been telling him for some time that a crisis was on the way between the colonists and the mother country. He never quite believed it until the French and Indian War ended. Then he saw for himself that the clash was not inevitable but highly predictable. *George Washington, Frontiersman* ends where it should, with the highest honor to that time in Washington's life being conferred upon him: commander in chief of the revolutionary forces. All his life he had served the British crown, and only reluctantly did he come to the point of gainsaying that authority. Once the break was made, however, he did what he had done throughout his life: he gave it his all. Though the novel ends with Washington accepting the commission, the reader, almost by instinct, knows the rest of the story.

In preparing this manuscript for publication, I decided early on to do certain things with it. First, I thought it best for Grey's work to speak for itself as much as possible. I did, however, write the first three manuscript pages of the novel, for some pages were missing from the typescript that was made back in the 1930s, and I have "filled in" one or two other missing pages. Second, I let certain words and expressions stay intact, for they were written in a time when they were more acceptable than in the early 1990s. Such words as "Injun," "nigger," "darky," and "blackie" have never been acceptable, but they were more in use during the 1930s than in the 1990s, and I want the reader to remember that this book was written in 1938 and not 1993. Third, my student assistant, Matthew Lunsford, and I–in the manner of many of Zane Grey's other novels–provided titles for the chapters. We thought providing titles would encourage readers, especially young readers, to read the book. And, fourth, although I let Grey speak for himself, I did find it desirable to write a few endnotes. I did not want to clutter up the pages of the novel itself with endnote numbers, for I feared this would be intrusive; therefore, I adapted a device used by William Safire in *Freedom:* I list at the back of the book the page numbers of and notes for passages that might require some explanation. I did not do this to the extent that Safire did in *Freedom* but enough, I hope, to clarify certain points.

I am indebted to many people for helping me edit this novel. My assistants at Western Kentucky University, Wendy Lear Shuffett, Todd Crowe, Tracy Kirkwood, Matthew Lunsford, and Steve Walters, did fine work, and I appreciate their help. Western history department secretary, Trena Wilhoit, helped considerably, as did secretary Liz Jensen–who typed the final draft–and her staff. Dr. Loren Grey, Zane's son, was, as usual, cooperative, friendly, and helpful. I do, of course, take responsibility for any errors in the editing of this book. It is fitting that Zane Grey's last novel appears ninety years after the publication of his first novel, *Betty Zane*, in 1903. My great hope is that Zane Grey fans around the world and readers of historical fiction will relish this book, the last work ever to be published by famed author of western novels, Zane Grey.

CARLTON JACKSON

Young George Washington

The two men stood on the porch looking out into the cold Virginia night, conversing softly. "Well, Augustine, you are about to become a father again. How do you feel about it?"

"Humble, I suppose," Augustine replied. "Though Jane and I had children before she died, this child is Mary's first, and we have many plans for him. If it's a boy, we plan to call him George, after our sovereign."

"Ah, things will become different–quite different–I'll wager," said the other man, "between what you know of English royalty and what your George will know. You never were much of a hand to talk politics, and you seem not to care a hoot what becomes of these American colonies. If it is a boy, I predict that he will grow into a man who will take an interest in our conditions here. It would serve you right if he turned out not to be so loyal to the king he is going to be named after. But I will not bore you any more with such chatter. . . . We must talk and think of what a beautiful night it was last night. And that great white screaming comet that paled all the stars—how magnificent! This man Halley who calls himself an astronomer, his father boiled soap, made himself wealthy, and this son sees a comet—when was it? 1682—and predicts that it would show again seventy-six years later. By jove, he was right! It occurs to me that we won't either of us live to see the next one."

A Negro slave girl came running out upon the porch and cried, "Massa Washington, Massa Doctor, the time has come."

Four tranquil February the twenty-seconds passed over the Bridge Creek plantation, adding years to Augustine's life, new cultivated acres to his plantation, and numbers to his slaves. Mary was fond of commenting on her young son's precociousness. "He's very much different from the others," she said often to her patient husband.

"And what do you mean by different?" asked Augustine, smiling.

"Oh, he's much larger than most boys of that age," she returned earnestly. "He has a violent temper. Runs away into the woods every chance he gets. They found him stark naked on several occasions. Seems to hate his clothes and to be washed clean. He does so many queer things like squatting on the ground and watching a hole. There are so many things, all normal I think, but different from what I have observed in other children."

"Mary, that is not so different from other boys," observed her husband thoughtfully, divided between amusement and gravity. "He's your only child, and it's quite natural that you should imagine little George is reserved for some special and noble place in the world. I hope so. We will need great men in the troublesome times ahead."

"Augustine, you are always predicting a dark future for the colonists. Nothing has happened to worry us since George was born. We are certainly better off, and you have more leisure than ever. In fact, too much leisure. I think you take Lawrence hunting and fishing too often, and I am worried because little George shows undue interest in those idle pursuits."

"Mary, the best foundation for a youth in this country is to learn the ways of the woods and water. American boys will be dependent on their guns and fishing poles for a living. I would be very glad if George took to the woods like an Indian. There is much to learn from the Indians."

"But we hear more and more all the time about the growing hostility of the Indians and their fraternizing with the French. I certainly don't want George learning anything from those red men."

The oldest son Lawrence entered the big sitting room, bringing with him the odors of the woods. He was now eighteen years old, a tall, sallow young man, not robust and strong.

"Mother, what do you think George has been doing?" he asked in a pleasant voice.

"Oh, gracious me, I have no idea," she returned in excitement. "Tell me."

"Well, it appears that George's slave, William, turned his back a moment, and George made off into the woods. When William found him he had fallen into Muddy Slough. It was quite deep water, but what do you think? The young rascal didn't drown. Maybe he was too fat to sink. Maybe he held to some bushes or something. William was too frightened to observe what kept him up. He fished George out and fetched him back home. I saw them when they came past the barn. George was a sight to behold but not in the least concerned. He's a great youngster."

"I fear he must be punished," murmured Mary, as she left the room.

"So you think your little stepbrother is a great youngster?" inquired Augustine, with keen eyes on Lawrence.

"I certainly do," returned the young fellow heartily. "I always was fond of George, and lately I have been paying more attention to him. He interests me more than my own brothers. When he gets a little older I will surely make a chum of him."

"Lawrence, that's fine," said the father feelingly. "Only don't wait. He's big enough now to learn the ways of outdoors. His mother will not approve and surely she won't allow us to take George on any camping trips, but begin to teach him what you can. Precocious or not, he's not quite old enough for his letters yet, but a youngster is never too young to get his first lessons in outdoors."

"Father, that boy is old for his age. He stole my fishing pole and hid it in the bushes. When I taxed him about it, he did not commit himself, but when I found it, he frankly said he put it there. George is clever and deep, but he's honest."

Mary paused in the spacious dining room and gazed at the picture of her father which hung above the mantelpiece: a noble picture of a man whose stature equaled his qualities. She had always been convinced that little George looked more like her father than anyone else. And it had been her secret prayer that he would inherit those qualities which her parent had possessed. During the prolonged months while she waited for George to come, her imaginative and dreamy nature had come to have full sway. She did not believe that she was unduly foolish or sentimental; yet there was something she felt but could not explain. Her own mother, and other women who had confided intimately with her, had related natural ambitions and hopes for their offsprings; however, no one she knew had ever been so possessed before the birth of her child with the fantasies and songs of her inmost soul which seemed to have had their origins in the convictions that her son had been born for an unusual and great life.

The few timid overtures she had made to her husband that might have led to full confession had always been inhibited by his amused tolerance and convictions of his own about his son. He wanted George to be a hunter, fisherman, planter, and a good subject to the King. Mary believed secretly that, loyal as the colonists were, the time would come when they would want to make their own lives and their own state, but she had never dared speak her mind.

She went out across the yard and looked everywhere, calling George. She finally found him at the woodpile, busily tearing it down. He was a sight to behold: soaked from head to foot, with a bloody scratch on the back of his leg. Along with Mary's serious thought about him, she felt a thrill at his size and energy. At the moment he had none of the handsome attributes which she took so much pride in.

"George," she called severely, halting behind him. "What are you doing?"

The urchin ceased tearing at the sticks of wood and turned around. He had wiped the mud from his face, but it was still streaked and stained. "I'm chasing a chipmunk," he replied.

"Did it occur to you that the chipmunk might have a nest in there and might have young oncs?" she asked.

"I didn't think about that. I jest wanted to ketch him."

"Well, George, you may desist in your play and listen to me. I do not need to be told that you have disobeyed me and fallen into Muddy Slough."

"Mother, I didn't promise I wouldn't fall in, an' William took me."

"How did it come that William let you fall into the water?"

"It was my fault, Mother. I said I'd sit still while he went for fishing worms. An'—an' I didn't."

"Why didn't you?" queried his mother reprovingly.

"I don't know. I saw a little turtle, an'—an' then I forgot."

"You slipped in the water, of course, and then what happened?"

"I held to the bushes an' waited for William."

"Did you cry out—call for him?" she inquired wonderingly.

"No. I wasn't scared."

"George, you will have to be punished for this," she cried.

He gazed up at her with clear apprehensive eyes. Then he dropped his head.

"You understand, of course, that William will have to be punished too."

"But he didn't do nothin'," protested the lad.

Mary, hands trembling, broke off a switch from a nearby bush. She had never punished George before. He watched her with steady, unflinching eyes.

"George, if you promise not to do it again, the punishment will not be so severe. Will you promise?"

"Mother, I promised before an' I did it anyhow, so I won't promise."

She laid hold of her unresisting boy, and, with her heart mounting to her throat, she switched him over his bare leg. As she had never done this before and was under stress, she must have struck harder than she had any idea. He grew stiff under her hold but did not resist or cry out. When she saw welts coming upon his legs, she desisted.

"Now, sir, do wash yourself and put on clean clothes. You are to stay in the house, but you will not get any supper tonight."

As she let him go, he ran off swiftly around the back of the house. It was then as she stood holding the switch, remorseful in spite of herself, that she heard him hollering. That relieved her somewhat for it was her opinion that children who did not cry when they were whipped were not normal. As she turned to go in, she saw William dart from behind the shed where evidently he had watched the performance, and the fleeting glimpse she had of his face showed that he was frightened. She would consult Augustine about what kind of punishment to mete out for William. What she did not feel at all right about was the punishment she had given George, and this caused her concern. Probably she would not be able to repeat it, and the incident showed her that George had passed babyhood and was fast growing up.

William was not the only witness to that unprecedented switching near the woodpile. Lawrence, too, had spied on the scene. It recalled to him the many switchings he had endured when he was that age and older. He was particularly intrigued by the way little George had manfully taken his licking. But, presently, when Lawrence had made his escape from his hiding place into the house, he was suddenly brought to a standstill by George's lusty yowling. He was glad none of his brothers and sisters were around to enjoy George's pain and grief, and he began to feel a little sorry himself for the youngster. After all, if George had taken the punishment without a whimper, it would have made the boy seem unnatural.

Lawrence went into his room and waited a while until George's caterwauling had subsided. Then he tiptoed to the door, and, knocking, he entered. He found the youngster seated on the floor, dirty and ragged, with his long locks hanging down over his head. Tearstains had added further to his forlorn aspect. George had a leg turned around and was rubbing the back of it where little welts ran across the calf. Lawrence was shocked to see blood. George's mother must have whipped him cruelly. Slumping down on the floor beside him, he said, "George let me see? Oh, does it hurt?"

George looked up as if he thought that question was silly.

"Of course it hurts, but the thing to do is to think that it doesn't," said Lawrence.

"How's I gonna—do that?" sniffled George.

"It seems funny, but it can be done. . . . This is a bad scratch, George. It'll have to be bound up. I first thought Mother's switch had cut it out of you."

"I cut myself there—when I fell in. . . . And Mother whipped me right over it. It hurts—something awful."

"Sure it does; you forget it. I'll tie it up for you and help you wash and change your clothes, and then I have something wonderful to tell you."

George did not show any interest and went on tenderly rubbing his leg until Lawrence wiped the blood and the dirt away and tied up the wound.

"Young man, I'll bet you will be interested when I tell you. Where's some of your clean clothes? Here's some. . . . Where's your towel? Here it is, and almost as dirty as you are. George, did you know that Indian boys are cleaner than you are?"

"Injuns!" exclaimed George, looking up.

"Yes, but of course they don't wear very much. Stand up now till I fix you. And, listen, I don't think Father will punish you. A man doesn't think it's so bad when a boy falls in the water or gets dirty and soils his clothes. Mother is very particular about such things. She insists on you and your brothers being little gentlemen all the while. I told Father about your stealing my fishing pole and that you wouldn't deny it. He doesn't think you are too young to learn something about the outdoors. So I am hoping to take you in hand. Every day we'll do something. We'll fish Muddy Slough and Ridge Creek and then the river. I know a great deal about hunting and fishing, and all about the birds and squirrels and snakes and turkeys and everything in the woods, and I'm going to teach you."

Long before Lawrence had gotten that far in his information, George had forgotten his pain and that he hated to have his face washed and his hair combed and was standing erect, tingling all over, with his large eyes shining, fixed raptly upon his brother.

"An' Injuns!" he burst out.

"Yes, Injuns too. We may see some now and then, but, George, most all the Injuns now are bad Injuns. We'll have to be pretty careful when we go far away into the woods."

"An' will I get to go campin' out with Father an' you?"

"Sure you will, someday, when you have learned a lot and can better take care of yourself."

"An' can I have a fishin' pole of my own?"

"I'll give you that small one you stole from me on condition you'll never steal anything again. Promise?"

"I will, promise," replied George solemnly.

"And soon as you learn how to use it, you shall have a knife, and then someday a tomahawk."

"An Injun hatchet?" rejoined George breathlessly.

"Yes, someday. It depends on how much you learn and how much you mind your teacher. You shall have a bow and arrow someday and then, when you get big enough, a gun."

This was wholly too much for little George, who was speechless. Lawrence considered the moment as definitely establishing a new relationship with the youngster. Young as George was, he had something that drew Lawrence to him.

He wasn't afraid and he wasn't deceitful and he had always looked up to Lawrence as someone to worship.

When Lawrence had made George presentable again they were called to supper. "Now, George, you go to Mother and tell her you're sorry and that you'll never do it again." They went into the dining room and there, before the other children and his father, George approached his mother and without embarrassment or timidity made his plea to her. And Mary, quite surprised and touched, looked from George to her husband and then back again to tell George that, as he had made amends, he could have his supper. There were some curious looks and snickerings from George's half brothers which were detected by the father, who straightaway stopped them. Lawrence observed, however, that George did not notice the conduct of the other children. They had supper and then Lawrence took George for a walk out along the creek.

Lawrence Washington, owing to weak lungs and a constitution that required building up, had divided his time between schooling and living in the open. He began little George's education, and there was never a day that they were not out somewhere in the forest or along the streams. George proved such an apt pupil that there was nothing too little for Lawrence to call his attention to and explain and study. The youngster asked questions that were far beyond Lawrence's knowledge of natural history, but Lawrence religiously tried to reply in some way to every query. George was going to be a most desirable companion in the wilderness. Sometimes in a whole afternoon he did not say anything at all. He had a marvelously quick eye and his ears were as keen as a deer's.

After they had been fishing for days and days and Lawrence had expected the boy to lose his interest, he found that time and experience only added to the lad's obsession with natural and exciting things. George learned rapidly, but his emotional temperament was equal to his attention. He did not forget instruction but he could not resist impulsiveness. While they were fishing, he would sit motionless on a log or beside the bank, and, although absorbed in watching his fishing line and float, he never missed the flight of a wild duck or the swoop of a hawk or the drumming of a pheasant deep in the woods or the ripple of a breaking fish or any of the sights and sounds that one would suppose so young a boy would not catch instantly. When a fish bit, he never could wait for the right time to jerk, and, therefore, more often than not, he would miss the hooking.

"Wait until your float bobs under," advised Lawrence, time and again.

But George did not soon learn the art of waiting. When he did hook a little fish and it escaped, it was impossible to assuage his grief, and, if he hooked one that stayed on, he invariably threw it back over his head into the grass or bushes. And when he did catch one, he would put it on a string and back into the water where he watched it until Lawrence called him again.

The time came when George required a new and stronger fishing line and of course a larger hook. There were good-sized catfish in the streams, and sooner or later George was going to hook one of them. Lawrence thought that he certainly did not want to miss that occasion.

The boy seemed fair to make a better hunter than fisherman. He followed along after Lawrence through the woods and in his bare feet made no more noise than a mouse. He learned to see and be careful where he stopped. He could see snakes and frogs as quickly as they saw him. Poisonous snakes were not numerous in that country, but it was wise to be cautious. He never developed a desire to kill snakes, but he would watch them as long as he was permitted. Birds in their nests with eggs or young ones fascinated him. But he did not rouse any of them. On the trails it did not take him long to tell the difference between deer tracks and raccoon or cat tracks. Lawrence had a dog that they often took with them, and George became familiar with dog tracks. When Lawrence went after wild game, he always put George on the back of one of his gentle horses. He taught him how to ride bareback.

On the occasions when Lawrence could not go with George, William accompanied the boy. William's job was to take care of the lad he called master. When they went fishing, William carried the poles, the bucket, the bait, and the lunch. On the return from a successful fishing trip, however, George insisted on carrying the fish he had caught and sometimes brought a live one home in the bucket to put in the watering trough by the barn. Before the summer was over he had a lot of little fish in that trough and spent hours watching them.

During these months George grew like a weed. He lost his pudginess, and though he did not get thin he grew tall for a youngster his age. Augustine was happy over Lawrence's tutelage of the lad, and his promise of growing to be big and strong and an outdoor man. He even persuaded Mary of the good that was being accomplished and how much George was improving in every way.

When Indian summer came with its melancholy days and the coloring of the leaves and the purple haze in the glades of the forest, and when the afternoon stillness was seldom broken by anything but the plaintive notes of a bird, then Augustine knew that soon they would be taking their camping trip into the woods. Although Lawrence thought it would be all right to take the youngster with them, the father decided against that for another year. Some of their jaunts would be quite far into the forest and might possibly be too much for the lad. But Lawrence averred that George could outwalk him. The lad would not be in the way at all, and, aside from being an asset to the hunts, he would be a source of great fun. Nevertheless, the father decided against it because of George's youth.

Not until Augustine had made arrangements to take the first hunt did he tell George that he would have to stay home. And then he found what this prospect had meant to the boy. His disappointment was so keen that Augustine almost relented. That night, appeasingly, hiding something behind his back, he approached George and said, "Lad, I have something for you that you have waited for for a long time."

"What?" cried George, his large eyes trying to peer through his father.

Whereupon Augustine brought into view a bright little tomahawk.

"Oh, my Indian hatchet!" burst out George, trying to keep from snatching it out of his father's hands.

"There! Be careful what you chop with it," admonished his father.

2 Young George Sees Indians

George had two other possessions very dear to him. One was a little red coat made like that of the British soldiers, and the other a fringed and beaded buckskin shirt fashioned after those used by frontiersmen. George liked the buckskin one better. His father had always encouraged him to wear the red coat and play that he was one of His Majesty's soldiers. But in making a choice now there was not the least indecision. George put on the buckskin shirt and his little feathered cap.

Then he sallied forth, brandishing his hatchet. Outside, William waited for him.

"Whar yo gwine, Massa Gawge?" inquired the Negro apprehensively.

"I'm gonna kill Injuns," replied George, and made straight for the woods.

William followed him, feebly protesting. George chopped at everything that came within his reach. Evidently the little tomahawk was strong because George took solid thumps at different objects. He chopped at the barn door, which elicited a louder protest from his guardian. At the edge of the yard where the garden began there was a certain beautiful little tree standing all by itself. That was Mary's special cherry tree which, time and again, he had been admonished not to climb or even touch. As it was forbidden fruit, it had a fascination for George. When he walked around this slender tree, eyeing it with his deep-set eyes and brandishing his tomahawk, William burst out in consternation, "For de Lawd's sake, Massa Gawge, you leave dis tree alone. If we touched dat, yere mudder'd skin us alive. Look dere, see the marks? Somebuddy has scratched dis tree."

"I don't remember if it was me," replied George dubiously, and then turned away through the orchard for the woods.

Once gaining the bank of the creek where the timber began George had unlimited opportunity for the use of his hatchet. He chopped at everything.

"See that, William? My hatchet is sharp," he said.

"Massa take care you don't cut yoreself."

George began to stoop down and glide cautiously from tree to tree, peering out from behind each one and motioning his follower to keep silent. They proceeded in this fashion until they came to the bank of the creek.

"George, if yus lookin' fer Injuns, they ain't none heah so close to the plantation."

"Yes, there are, William, I can see them over there on the other bank."

William, impressed by his companion's sincere and fearful statement, peered long from behind his tree and at length said, "Wal, ah shore cain't see none, but if yu see any, we better run back."

"I'm gonna chop one's head off—just like this," declared George, picking up a dead stick and whacking the end off of it. "William, how do Injuns scalp white men?"

"Dey run der knifes around the top of their haids an' tear the scalp off."

"I wouldn't like that," returned George thoughtfully. "I'll have to watch out for my scalp. When I get big I'm gonna hunt Injuns—bad Injuns."

"Massa Gawge, ah's heared there ain't nothin' but bad Injuns."

"Father says there's some Injuns good friends to us white folks."

"Wal, mebbe it was that way once, but the redskins are gettin' bad 'cause the white folks are takin' more and more of their lands."

The restless George wanted to walk across the creek but was dissuaded by William, whereupon he retraced his steps through the woods, now and then vigorously swinging his hatchet. When they returned to the yard, George again was evidently seized by some almost irresistible thought and regarded the beautiful cherry tree more ponderingly than ever. This time William dragged him away. At the back of the house they encountered George's father who had evidently been watching them.

"Father, my little hatchet cuts everything," declared the lad. "When you take me camping, I'll chop all the firewood. When will you take me?"

"I told you, son, perhaps next year."

"But that's such a long way off," protested George. "Won't you take me sooner?"

"I might if your mother would let you go. We'll ask her. Let's go in the kitchen, George, and find something to eat." They were surprised in their enjoyment of a pie by George's mother.

"Augustine!" exclaimed Mary. "What an example you show your young son! Did you steal my pie?"

"I am afraid that I cannot tell a lie about it."

"George," began his mother severely, "if you must take after your father, be sure to get his good traits. He has a few. You see that he tells the truth."

"Mother, I'll try," returned George, "but can't I go camping with father soon?"

"Not until you are a little older."

Sorrowfully George ate the last of his pie and then picked up the little hatchet which he had laid on the table. His temper got the best of him for he wielded his hatchet as if he would like to strike something in his disappointment.

"George, your shirt is all soiled," complained his mother, "and your hands are filthy. How often have I told you not to eat with dirty hands? And if you must brandish that tomahawk around, go outdoors where you can't do any damage. And be a little Indian!"

"All right, mother," returned George, leaving the kitchen.

George and William had been told of the depredations of Indians in the outlying districts and had been admonished to confine their outdoor activities to the Washington plantation. For days on end they obeyed and kept within sight of the house. George did not forget, but as days passed he grew less fearful. He was infinitely curious. As they tramped along the river or sat on the bank, he was always peering under the trees as if looking for something. The movements of squirrel, however, or ruffed grouse or even a deer were somehow not as satisfying as they had once been. And every day they tramped a little farther into the woods.

One October day they had poor luck in all their favorite fishing holes along the river and they wandered up Bridge Creek deep into the forest to find untried and better fishing grounds. The creek ran shallow and rippling in many places, forming deep pools and bends, and they found one place they were loathe to leave. The afternoon waned.

"Massa Gawge, you's had the bestest fishin' ever, an' we betta be goin' home," said William.

"Let's ketch one more," replied George. "Maybe I'll get ahold of another big one."

"Spose it got dark? I ain't shore you could find the way home."

"I could, even if it got dark."

"Wouldn't you be scairt?"

"As long as it's daylight, I think I wouldn't be, but mebbe . . ."

"What's dat?" whispered William. "Ya heah dat?"

"Yes, William, I hear it. Splashin' in the water. Jest round there," whispered George, in reply. "It wasn't no turkey."

"Reckon it was a deer, but let's hide."

They crawled back from the bank of the stream and crouched in the cover of some low bushes and peered out, up the stream with bated breath. It was coming near sunset, and there were both light and shadow upon the water. The splashes became more distinct, until it was easy to distinguish them as footsteps. Then followed a disturbance in the willows along the bank scarcely a hundred feet from them, and all at once the willows parted to show the dark naked form of an Indian cautiously peering out, gazing up and down the creek. He stepped out into the sunlight, a live powerful form, darkly bronzed. He carried a rifle in one hand and a heavy sack in the other. It dragged in the water as he stepped. He wore buckskinned leggings and there was a tomahawk sticking in his belt. Around his shoulder was a string holding a powder horn. His lean head was shaved except for a little tuft of hair on the top, where he wore a feather. As he faced toward the boys his dark features and glittering eyes showed plainly in the light. He had a malignant and deadly look. Two other Indians followed closely after him, each carrying rifles and sacks; and it was evident they had been on a foraging trip to one of the plantations. With quick steps in the shallow water, almost noiseless, they crossed the creek to part the green foliage and disappear.

For what seemed long moments George and William crouched behind the bushes, motionless with staring eyes fixed upon the opposite bank and ears strained for rustlings in the brush and snappings of twigs. But they heard no more sounds.

"Massa Gawge," whispered William, "Them was bad Injuns. They been stealin'."

"Aw! Weren't they–just wonderful?" whispered George.

"They was turrible, boy, an' we shore betta be gettin' out of heah."

Securing their string of fish they set out for home, William in the lead following as best they could the way they had come. Every few steps they stopped and listened. After going some distance downstream, in the opposite direction from which the Indians had gone, they began to feel safer and hastened their steps. At last they got on the river trail and made better time. It was dusk when they emerged from the forest and made their way toward the plantation.

"Massa Gawge, if we tells yore fadder we shore won't get to go fishin' any more," said William.

"We won't tell unless he asks us."

"Wal, he'll want to know," returned William, " 'cause we never come home this late before, an' we shore went a long way."

"With this big string of fish, we won't have to talk much," responded George.

It chanced that Augustine and Lawrence had not returned from their journey to town, and George's mother did not question them. She said supper would not be ready just yet, that William could clean their fish and George make himself presentable. So it happened that they were not questioned about their adventure.

In the succeeding days as the weather grew colder, the frost came and the leaves began to fall; when George and William went hunting with Lawrence or his father, George grew more and more filled with a bursting desire to tell about the Indians they had seen. At last George told Lawrence and in that way Augustine came to know.

"George, you should not have gone so far nor waited so long to tell me," reproved his father. "This forces me to postpone your camping trip, perhaps for a long time."

"But, father, we couldn't help it if the Injuns came along. An' we kept them from seein' us," protested George.

"I know, George, and the fact is that Indians are liable to come right close to the house these days. I'm not sure that they would harm you but they might. And you be very careful when you are out of the yard. Don't forget that a good woodsman sees everything first."

In time the Indian scare passed and William and George confined their activities to the plantation and nearby river bank. Once or twice a week Lawrence took George into the woods with a gun and perfected his use of firearms, so that at that early age George was unusually proficient. Long before George was given his first schooling he was used to the woods and water and had been given full rein to the primitive instincts of his ancestors.

One summer day, when William and George were returning from the river, they saw a big column of black smoke rising above the plantation, and, running into the clearing, they saw that the house was on fire. Arriving at the scene they found the Negroes and Lawrence and his father carrying things from the house. It was a time of great trouble and grief. George ran here and there and when he tried to run up the porch into the house Lawrence put him back and said his possessions had been carried out. Mary and the other children had not returned yet from a visit. George was compelled to stand by helplessly while the men kept at the work of salvaging until the flames forced them to desist. Then they stood around and watched the Washington homestead where George and his father had been born burn to the ground.

Kindly neighbors on an adjoining plantation took in the homeless family. Next day Augustine and Lawrence drove to Fredericksburg and soon sent word back to have the slaves bring the household goods they had saved and all their possessions together with the stock, and for the family to be ready to follow when they were called for. In due course they were sent for, and little George never forgot his first long ride on top of a big wagon down the country lanes and along the forest roads to their new home.

Mount Vernon was not so wild as Bridge Creek, but the plantation was girded by the woodland and waterways which George loved so well. The level fields and grassy hills soon made up for those that he had lost. His grief soon wore out in the warmth of new friends and new places to explore, new fish to be caught, and forests where there were no Indians nearby. Belvoir, the estate of the wealthy Fairfaxes, was not far from Mount Vernon, and, in young George Fairfax, George found his first intimate friend and comrade, outside of his slave William. Young Fairfax was six years older than George, and at once took a great interest in the lad and helped him in his first perplexing ABC lessons. It was here at Mount Vernon that Mary took up the serious matter of George's education along with the other children. Here George also learned to play marbles, to fly kites, to play games called stone tag, King and I, stool-ball, and also base ball. Mary always insisted that the boys play a game called Scotch hoppers which she claimed would be very beneficial to their health and growth. Morning lessons began by Fairfax or one of the other youngsters saying,

> "He that n'er learns his ABC
> Forever will a blockhead be."

And George, being the youngest, was expected to complete the verse by quoting,

> "But he that learns his letters fair.
> Shall have a coach to take the air."

Lessons in the morning and games in the afternoon–and of course the trips to the woods or streams with William whenever these trips could be sandwiched in–made the weeks and the months fly. As George had been an apt student in woodcraft so he was also in mastering his ABCs and into the more intricate problem of reading and writing.

One day, more than a year after George began his momentous pursuit of education, an incident occurred which was to prove how far he had really advanced. William entered with an important look, and, flourishing a package and a letter, he announced, "Massa Gawge, heah's a letta an' a package for you–all from the post."

"A letter! And a package!" exclaimed George excitedly. "It feels like a book. Oh, Mother, will you read my letter to me?"

"Son, why not open it yourself? You read very well, and while your first letter may be important, it shouldn't be beyond you."

George tore open the letter with trembling fingers. And scanning it with great animation he called out, "Dick Lee has written me. Oh, I hope I can read what he says."

"Well, why not try?" suggested his mother, smiling.

Whereupon George began laboriously to read:

> "Pa brought me two pretty books full of pictures he got them in Alexandria they have pictures of dogs and cats and tigers and elefants and ever so many pretty things cousin bids me send you one of them it has a picture of an elefant and a little Indian boy on his back like uncle jo's sam pa says if I learn my tasks good he will let uncle jo bring me to see you will you ask your ma to let you come to see me.
>
> Richard henry Lee."

"That is very well, George, only you read it as if it were one sentence. Let me see Dickey's letter. . . . Oh, I see. Here are a good many words, some of them misspelled and no punctuation whatever. Now, George, when you answer Dickey's letter, you be very careful to punctuate it properly."

"Oh, Mother, I can't get that punctuation right," expostulated George.

"Well, it is time you are learning."

"Mother, may I go over to Dickey's next week? An'—and may I ride the colt?"

"George, you're big enough but not old enough to ride that colt. He's wild. Wait for a year or two. Get Uncle Ben to go with you or William and ride your pony Nero. Now, while you're so keen about it, you write to Dickey and bring me the letter."

George labored so long over that letter that his mother dismissed the other children and sent them out to play and left George there with his problem. He eventually brought it to her with a hesitating yet hopeful manner.

Mary took that letter and complimented George on its neat appearance.

"Mother, I wrote it over again and again," he said.

"I hope it will sound as good as it looks," she said, and proceeded to read:

"Dear Dickey,

I thank you very much for the pretty picture book you gave me. Kick asked me to show him the pictures in it; and I read it to him how the tame Elephant took care of the master's little boy, and put him on his back and would not let any body touch his master's little son. I can read three or four pages sometimes without missing a word. Ma says I may go to see you and stay all day with you next week if it be not rainy. She says I may ride my pony Nero if Uncle Ben will go with me and lead Nero. I have a little piece of poetry about the picture book you gave me, but I mustn't tell you who wrote the poetry.

G. W's compliments to Dickey
And likes his book full well,
Henceforth will count him his friend,
And hopes many happy days he may spend.

Your good friend,
George Washington."

"George, this is very good indeed," said Mary, folding the letter. "It will more than do for you reading and writing lesson today. Now, let us take up with arithmetic."

In any event it was hard enough for George to concentrate on anything mathematical, and today the effort seemed quite futile.

"Dickey's letter reminds me that I ought to get one from Lawrence. I knew I had been looking for something to happen. That's it. Why did Lawrence go to the West Indies and why doesn't he write?"

"You'll get a letter eventually," replied his mother quietly, "and if you do not, he will be coming home soon."

"I miss him so much," said George feelingly. "I can never go so far into the woods with William–and I've never had that camping trip that I was promised."

However, Lawrence did not come home soon, and it was a long time before George got the hoped-for letter. Then it would have been better had he not heard at all. Lawrence had gone to the West Indies to benefit his health. Apparently he was not well at the time he wrote and said nothing about coming back.

Eventually a message came to Augustine informing him that Lawrence would arrive on a certain day. George was restless and preoccupied during the interval of waiting, and when the day did come he was hopeless for lessons or play or anything else but parading to and fro on the porch gazing down the road. When at last Lawrence appeared on a galloping horse, his red uniform nonplussed and excited George very much. Running down the road to meet him, George waved his hand, and Lawrence, halting the horse, helped George climb up behind him. George thought his half brother looked wonderful in the uniform, and he was happy to see Lawrence so bronzed and apparently well. But he could not voice his feelings. Lawrence, however, had a cheery and affectionate greeting for him, and, as he rode on toward the house, he put his left arm back and held George close to him.

Lawrence was welcomed by the family and, turning his horse over to a slave, entered the house with the family all clinging to him. At lunch Lawrence began to speak of the West Indies, and when he spoke of the war there between the English and Spaniards, his father significantly changed the subject, evidently not wishing the children to hear. But that night in the sitting room Lawrence was relating his adventures: "And Admiral Vernon had captured Porto Bello, but the Spaniards preferred to revenge the blow. Then there was the terrific siege of Carthagena when the troops attempted to escalade the citadel. But the ships could not get near enough to throw their shells, and the scaling ladders were too short. Then—"

"Wait, Lawrence," interrupted Mary, "you can tell us later. Here comes George."

George entered then and his impetuosity and the flare of his big eyes betrayed that he had heard something not intended for his ears.

"George, it's your bedtime, isn't it?" suggested his mother.

"Aw, why can't I hear about the war?" George asked. "Why can't I hear what Lawrence's captain's uniform is for? Did he wear that in the tobacco business in the West Indies? Lawrence, I'll plague you until I get it, and I promise you that I can tell as exciting a story as you can about the West Indies."

"All right, George, come out with it," replied Lawrence, with interest.

Augustine intervened and inquired where in the world George could have heard an exciting story about the West Indies.

"I didn't hear it. I *read* it," retorted George. "Lawrence, all the slaves in New York banded together and planned to burn the town down, murder all the white people, and set up a black king. Everybody got terribly aroused and outraged. Lots of white people were killed and lots more slaves were killed."

"Yes, indeed, George, that actually happened," admitted Lawrence, "but on a smaller scale so far as the West Indies were concerned. You would have been scared, wouldn't you, if you had been there?"

"No, I don't get excited over nothing, and I wouldn't been scared, because I would have known it wasn't true. Somebody thought up that talk and told it to somebody else, and then somebody told it to somebody else until they all got excited."

"Where did the West Indians come in?" asked his father.

"Oh, I forgot that. They took fifty slaves from New York and sent them to the West Indies and sold them there."

"Well, George, now that you have carried off the honors by telling a more exciting story than Lawrence, I think you had better go to bed," said Mary.

"Don't I have to go to bed every night without this one night?" protested George stubbornly. And when his father waved him away, he reluctantly said good night to his half brother and left the room.

3

George Falls for Sally

There came a sunny day in May which was almost equally as momentous for George as when he had expected Lawrence to come home. This was to be the occasion of George acting as host for the first time to a number of his young friends. He had not had much patience with his mother's insistence that part of his deportment as host had to be rehearsed. He claimed that, as he was nearly eleven years old, he was no little boy any longer and should be permitted to act for himself. Notwithstanding this, it was evident to his mother that this morning he was unusually perturbed, and she suspected that it was due to the coming of little Sally Cary, the youthful reigning belle of that district, for whose favor all George's boy friends had vied and to which he himself secretly had strived.

The four boys and their little queen assembled on the front porch. Sally was a trim and bewitching girl with shining golden hair and dark blue eyes, audacious and challenging. She carried herself with an air of distinction, and love of conquest glowed like a light upon her lovely face. George, as usual, hung in the background longing to address her as the other boys were doing but not having the courage. George Fairfax, the eldest of the group, a handsome patrician lad, appeared to have the boldness and confidence the others lacked. He playfully elbowed his cousin Harry out of the running and he said, "Sally, I'm the oldest here and the best horseman, and I claim the first chance to show you how well I can ride George's pony."

"You can't ride any better than I," retorted Richard Henry Lee.

Sally turned her bright eyes from these boys to George Washington and said sweetly, "George, it is for you to say who gets the first try."

"I—he—Fairfax ought to have it—I think," stammered George, blushing like a girl because he secretly would have liked the chance himself.

George Fairfax pointed out toward the meadow where William appeared leading a spirited black pony that evidently he had to hold in. "George, that is a fine-looking horse. Come on, let's all go out."

"He looks pretty wild to me," said Richard.

"Why, Dickey, he's as tame as can be. I could ride him myself," returned Sally, with a sly glance.

When they reached the rail fence adjoining the field, Sally indicated that she wanted to climb it, and Fairfax, being too gallant and quick for the others, helped her to a perch on the top rail.

"Massa Gawge," burst out William, "dis heah pony shore is a hawse. Nothin' like yore old Nero. He's nearly pulled my arms out. 'Pears to me, he's never been rode."

"Uncle Ben says he's safe enough," replied George anxiously. "He's just skittish. I've been on him several times."

"Ah shore wouldn't call that ridin' him," replied the Negro, "you all better look out."

Sally stood erect upon the fence, the better to look imposing, and with a roguish devil shining from her blue eyes she announced, "The wilder he is, the more I will accord the victorious rider. Come, knights, which of you will venture first? I promise to marry the one who wins."

"Sally, then you will marry me, which I always intended you to do," declared George Fairfax.

"Oh, no she won't, Fairfax, she'll marry me. I can best you any day," grandly contradicted Richard.

Harry good-naturedly waived any intentions of climbing on that wild-eyed pony and contesting for the first place in Sally's affection. She gave him the disdainful look of an outraged princess and turned the battery of her eyes upon George Washington.

In the interval, then, William burst out with great seriousness, "Wal, ah aint worryin' either about her marryin' me 'cause ah shore am goin' to stay off from de back of dis pony."

Fairfax took the bridle away from William and with elegant action mounted into the saddle and gave the pony a slap. Almost at once something remarkable happened. The pony got his head down and, arching his back, he began to bounce up like a rubber horse, giving young Fairfax a precarious seat in the saddle. In her excitement Sally fell off the fence. Fortunately she fell into the thick grass and was not hurt nor suffered any ill to her pretty dress. George helped her to her feet. The other boys were yelling at the top of their lungs, in a fiendish glee at Fairfax's efforts to stay with that pony. William had been most certainly correct. The pony was little but he was mighty. He bounded around on the turf like a cork on a rough sea. He sent Fairfax bobbing skyward and finally unseated him so that Fairfax came down upon the pony's haunches. And the next buck sent him hurtling through the air to alight on his head and shoulders and have the breath knocked from his body. While William went to secure the pony, the other boys helped the discomfited Fairfax rise to his feet.

"The—the stirrups—didn't fit me," said young Fairfax miserably.

The boys kindly refrained from any comment and managed to keep straight faces, but Sally, evidently disillusioned and disappointed, remarked rather satirically; "George Fairfax, you didn't fit the pony. Come on, Dickey. You can ride him."

Meanwhile William had returned with the horse and said, "Massa Gawge, ah shore advise against these proceedin's. If Massa Fairfax had lit his head on a rock, he'd shore not have much sense left."

"I'll ride him or die," declared Dickey valiantly, and taking the bridle from William, he leaped into the saddle. It was manifest that Dickey meant to profit by Fairfax's mistakes, and he wrapped his long legs about the pony, and hanging on to the saddle with both hands, he yelled thrillingly, as if he meant both to dare the pony to do his worst and that Sally would now see some great riding. But alas for his vainglory! The pony went through some new gyrations and finally reared up on his hind legs and fell over backwards against the fence knocking Richard off and bruising him severely.

When the youngsters had gotten Richard to his feet and had ascertained that he was not badly hurt, William brought the pony back to them. "Massa Gawge, ah told you an' ah tells you again."

George made no reply, and he looked pretty grim when he took the halter away from the Negro. His intention was evident in the bold flare of his deep eyes and in every line of his sturdy figure. Sally now came forward with red spots suddenly appearing in her white cheeks, and she said, "George, I'm sorry I egged the boys on. I'm ashamed of myself. Please do not attempt to ride this pony. He's a wicked little beast."

Shy as George was, he mumbled that he had not forgotten her promise. Then he bounded into the saddle and got firmly settled before the vicious pony began his mean tactics. When first he began to buck, he almost unseated George; then he tried rearing but George jerked him down and hung on. For a space he tore up the turf all around, and then it was noticeable that his violent exertions began to lessen. Then the pony bolted into a run. This was all well for George for he was a splendid horseman, and with so much at stake he excelled even his best. The pony tore down the field and across and back again. Then in desperation he began to plunge once more and to kick and to bounce up on four stiff legs and in every way endeavor to get rid of his rider. But George stuck on.

The pony had the bit between his teeth but likewise George's teeth were grimly set. What had begun as play now became deadly earnest. Pictures from Ivanhoe flashed through his vivid imagination. He was riding for his princess and the exalted mood of that wonderful action. With Sally watching, staring with wide dark eyes, waving and cheering, he gave no thought of the frenzied pony. He drove him round the field, up and down and across, and goaded him to his desperate utmost, until finally back in front of his young guests George was brought to his senses by feeling the pony suddenly break and sink under him. He slipped out of the saddle as the pony sank gasping and then stood horrified while his friends ran to his side, with Sally clutching his stiff arm, all of them silent and aghast, as they saw the pony choke and die.

Not until after his guests had gone did Mary speak to George about the tragedy.

"Oh, Mother, I am terribly sorry," cried George in distress. "I didn't think—I didn't think! I ought to have known—that—that he might . . . but I was furious. I was furious with Fairfax and Dickey and—and with Sally. She wasn't to blame but she made us—she made us want to beat one another. . . . But to *kill* the pony—that is more than I can bear."

"That is distressing, George," returned his mother. "If I had come out sooner I would have stopped you, but I was with your father. He's had another attack. Nothing to worry you, perhaps, but you had better run after the boys and stay with Fairfax or Dickey for supper. Come home early."

"All right, Mother" returned George soberly, as he wiped his eyes. "I hope father isn't sick. Is Lawrence with him?"

"Yes, he is now. It was he who saw you through the window. 'George is running that colt to death,' he said. And he was very angry. So that is why I think you'd better avoid seeing him until he gets over it."

George rushed out of the house and, what with the dimness of his eyes and the confusion of his mind, he stumbled off the porch and almost fell headlong. His first instinctive action was to rush back into the woods, but, remembering that he had been told to go to the Fairfax's, he changed his course and ran down the road. He had no intention, however, of going to his friend's house. He wanted to be alone. Things were in a terrible state. A mile or more down the road he leaped the fence and made across the fields toward the woodland and the river.

He felt distressed about his father having another sick spell. There had been more than one of these spells during the last month and, as a terrified George had seen the doctor shaking his head seriously to his mother, he thought there was reason to be concerned. Then his pitiable blunder in riding that spirited young colt to its death—that was distressing and unforgivable—and that Lawrence was provoked with him was something not likely to be shaken off.

George reached the woods that skirted the banks of the Potomac and here he went gliding into the silence and the sunlit glades of the forest. From long habit of play he fell naturally into the slow, watchful, stealthy step of the woodsman. Playing the game of hunting Indians, as well as the pursuit of woodland game, had developed his naturally keen sense of sight and hearing until little escaped him. And here, having entered the forest burdened by more trouble than he had ever before known, he was not long in making the discovery that there was something about going into the loneliness of the forest that worked subtly upon his feelings.

He struck the river trail and, following it, walked a mile or two to the west, and then, finding a beautiful wild spot where he had been before, he sat down to meet as best he could, his problems. They would not stay steadfastly before his consciousness. A bird or an animal or a fish would always interrupt his meditation. The river was broad here, and on the far shore there was a dense forest that extended as far as the eye could see in either direction. There was a lulling hum of insects in the tall grass, a crow cawed somewhere from a distant hill, a hermit thrush sang his melancholy song deep in the woods, and these were all the songs that disturbed the deep stillness. Many as were the times he had been alone in the woods, this time stood out significantly. He guessed that he was getting older. When he was little he didn't have troubles. And now he felt some nameless comfort in the wilderness around him.

Fear for his father gradually softened. Even if his father did have a sick spell he would sooner or later recover from it. The matter of him riding the colt to his death was more difficult to dispose of because he could not excuse himself. It was an accident. It might have happened to anybody. Maybe the colt was not as well and strong as they had supposed. George had always been taught a lesson through his mistakes along the river and in the woods. His mistake in regard to the colt was something that he could not condone, but at last he understood it. And he would never repeat it.

That blue-eyed Sally Cary was to blame. But he reproved himself of that accusation. Sally couldn't help being pretty. And she certainly liked her own way, but profound as her commitment had been, she could hardly have meant it, yet George had a deep, burning, stultifying consciousness that he hoped she did. He dismissed the perturbing Sally from his mind. Lastly, his mother's admonition about Lawrence being angry with him did not frighten him here in the woods as it had done when he fled from the house. He had merely to be honest with Lawrence and tell him how it had come about that he had been so thoughtless and cruel and that he would never do it again.

These pondering thoughts and conclusions were far from being closely connected in George's mind. He paid more attention to the sensations that came to him from the surrounding trees and glancing waters and the live things and the westering sun. But when dusk began to creep under the trees and his troubles were alleviated, if not wholly overcome, he arose to take the trail back home with the knowledge that he had been helped by his lonely hour on the river bank.

That was the wonder which made him thoughtful as he stalked swiftly homeward down the trail. Countless times George had gone into the woods with childish and then boyish griefs, but he had not known before what seemed clear now—that there was something comforting and revealing under the shadow of the great oaks and sycamores that he had never found any other place. It was a wonderful thing to find out. He believed he could learn more in the woods than by studying at home. Not about history or countries or wars or business, things that grown-up men made such a fuss about, but he could learn more about what he really loved, about the nesting and mating of birds, about the living creatures that made the woodland their home, about how to seek and find and do in the wild environment that seemed a natural home for any man whether red or white.

Dusk finally darkened the trail, but George's eyes were so keen and so accustomed to the shadows that he walked as swiftly and well as if it were daylight. When at length he emerged from the forest, the moon was rising in the east, and there was a silver light blanketing the hills and fields, the broad expanse of the Potomac, and the long line of forest. This hilly Mount Vernon country was more beautiful than the flat landscape around Bridge Creek, and this night it was brought home to George that he really loved it and that in time he might cease to pine for the old homestead.

Quietly as George made his way to his room he did not keep Lawrence from hearing him. When he lighted his candle Lawrence entered, not quite such a forbidding figure as George's imagination had conjured up.

"Son, you've been gone a long time," began Lawrence. "Did you go over to Fairfax's?"

"No, Lawrence, I went into the woods along the river."

"You look pretty white and peaked. I see it's been rather a bad time with you. I'm sorry. You needn't worry overly much about Father. We had the doctor, and Father's resting easier now. George, these attacks of Father's don't mean so much now but someday–"

"Oh, I understand," murmured George, "but it's good to know he's all right now."

"Now, George, I want to talk to you about killing that colt on his feet. It was a brutal, stupid thing, and I am amazed at you. You have always loved horses and you have seemed to get along well with them and you've certainly become a good rider. In this country, whether you become a planter or a surveyor, which work you have shown interest in, or a soldier, you will always have to do with horses. I can imagine situations where riding a horse to death is excusable even if deplorable. But in your case–in fun–just to show off before some of your boy friends, and that pretty blue-eyed little minx–that's hard to forgive you for."

"Lawrence, I know, and I don't ask you to forgive me," returned George humbly, and though he felt so ashamed his cheeks turned scarlet, he could not hang his head or remove his eyes from the sharp glance of his half brother. "All the same I want to try–to tell you how I came to do it. I wouldn't blame anything on a girl, but, you see–the boys were bragging, Sally sat up on the fence like that princess in Ivanhoe–and she said she–she'd marry whoever rode the colt. And the colt threw Fairfax on his head–and Dickey on top of the fence hurting him pretty badly, and Harry refused to get on the colt, and I–I must have been crazy. It just happened, that's all. I'm terribly sorry and I'll never mistreat a horse again."

"Fine! That's good talk, George," replied Lawrence, slapping him on the shoulder. "I didn't suspect the girl in the case. Then there are always extenuating circumstances. Well, Son," he concluded with a broad grin and a twinkle in his gray eyes, "you certainly won the joust, and are you going to marry the princess?"

George was visibly shaken. Evidently the jocular query struck deeply into him and made him realize what he had not dared put in words. "I–I hadn't . . . Lawry, I'm afraid I would–if I could."

"Aha! I guessed your secret. Well, you're rather young yet and probably there will be several other princesses who will throw down the gauge to you. Maybe father will send you to England as he did my brothers. Then you'll see some real princesses. But remember, George, faint heart never won fair lady, and that Princess Sally will have many a knight tilting for her favor."

4

George Makes a Choice

Time passed; the months had wings. George continued to grow like a weed. He won praise from his mother for progress in his studies. He distanced William in their favorite pastime of fishing. The time came when he could outwalk Lawrence in the woods, and Lawrence frankly admitted that George had absorbed all his wood craft and had found some of his own. But they never went on that camping trip his father had promised; in fact there were no more camping trips. Augustine grew less active as the days passed.

George never forgot anything, and he never outgrew his shyness. He and Fairfax grew from playmates to be the closest of friends. Lawrence, who announced that he was going to be married to Fairfax's sister, Anne, brought George and Fairfax into more intimate association. Sally had gone away to school in Philadelphia, and that certainly relieved George, though he pined in secret for sight of the bonny lass and the trill of her voice. It was remarkable that George and Fairfax never talked about the girl, not since that distant day when

George had ridden the colt to death, and Sally had promised to marry the victor.

One day George was visiting Fairfax and shooting in practice in his yard when William, George's slave, came galloping up on a horse to call out, "Massa Gawge, get yore hawse an' foller me quick," and he turned to gallop away.

"Fairfax, that can mean only one thing. I must go," declared George, and, running to his horse, he mounted and galloped away while Fairfax yelled after them, "Hope it's not bad news!"

George urged his horse to full speed, and before they reached the Washington plantation he caught up with William. "What is it, William? Father–" called George.

"Mass, I shore sick. . . . Yore father–is dyin'."

George entered his father's room, the last of the family to get there. He saw his father propped up in bed, and a strange, dread pang settled upon his heart.

He hurried to the bedside fearing to look at his mother, taking hold of his father's hand. "I'm sorry, Father–I hope . . ."

"George, do you remember–I never told you about your ancestors as I promised?"

"Yes, father, but never mind now. Someday."

"I think I'd better tell you while I've time. . . . George, you remember the old homestead at Bridge Creek, I'm sure, because you and I loved it best. You were born in the same room where I was born–in that very house. My family lived there for seventy-five years. How sad it was the old house had to burn! It was built of solid oak and would have stood another seventy-five years. Your great grandfather . . ."

"I know. John the emigrant," replied George.

"Yes. He came to Virginia in 1657," replied Augustine, with a pleased smile at George's memory. "From England, of course. The first Washington–they spelled the name Wewsyngton then–came to England with William the Conqueror. His name was William D. Hearteburn."

"Yes, I remember," replied George softly, "and Father, tell me, am I English or am I American?"

"You were born here in America, of course. That makes you an American but always British."

"Please go on, father," George urged, as Augustine paused in his weak voice and seemed to be groping in the past.

"For two or three hundred years the Wewsyngtons were either knights in shining armor who fought for chivalry or they were clergymen cloistered in the service of God."

His father stopped again, his mind wandering, and his eyes glazing over while he held to George's hand.

"It had four rooms and a large attic that I played in—and so did you . . . the very steep roof which I used to climb and low hanging eaves and two large chimneys . . . the big fireplaces with their oak fires in winter. It burned down, George, it burned down—the old homestead." Closing his eyes, his low voice trailed away to nothing. Then George sobbed as his mother put her arm around him and led him from the room.

Lawrence presently came into George's room and said to his mother, "It is all over. . . . George, don't take it so hard. It's natural, and I'll be a father to you."

"But you're to marry Anne Fairfax—and you'll move away—or we'll have to leave Mount Vernon," sobbed George.

"Lawrence will live here, George, and wherever we go, you may come to visit him as often as you want," said his mother. "It makes a break in our lives. I have been expecting it and am prepared. George, bear up under this as bravely as you can. Come, Lawrence, let us leave him alone."

Lawrence inherited the Mount Vernon property from his father and at once proceeded to repair and remodel it into a more spacious and comfortable house. Mary would have been welcome to live there, but she preferred to take a small plantation some miles distant. George and some of his half brothers moved there to farm it and make a living as best they could. Besides George and the others she acquired several pupils from the adjoining neighbors, and this helped in making ends meet. For the young people the time was divided between work and study, and for George his beloved activities in the outdoors were confined to a few hours in the late afternoon or evening. Mary taught her pupils with earnest and persistent energy and purpose. She would read to them in this wise.

"Tell us about others who came to the colonies."

"Well, there was Ponce de Leon, a companion of Columbus, who landed in Florida. He was an old man seeking the legendary fountain of youth. He took possession of the land he explored in the name of Spain. And another Italian, Verrazzano, under Francis I of France, explored the whole coast from Nova Scotia to the Carolinas and called it New France. But we must get back to our reading. 'Be not hasty to believe flying reports, to the disparagement of any one.' "

"Mother, tell us what is to become of the colonists?" inquired George thoughtfully.

"Goodness only knows," replied Mary impatiently. "George, I must say you are a poor example to the other scholars. And you the oldest too!"

Mary's one fault to find with George's farming was that she often caught him leaning on his hoe, motionless as a statue and pondering something she could never get him to tell. Nevertheless, George, as much as he disliked farming, and however his beloved woodland lured so closely by, always managed to get the work done. George continued to grow big and strong, and, under the stress of the studies imposed upon him, the labor and privation, the nature that called to him so deeply, and the haunting memories of Sally Cary, his character developed. During the travail of this youthful period of his life there were many calls upon him to control his temper and his natural propensities for the moods his mother had so striven to correct. There were English-Americans in Virginia who had begun to look down on the white people who labored in the field, but members of the aristocratic Fairfax family were not among them. George Fairfax had been George Washington's devoted friend; though during this interval, they did not see as much of each other as formerly, the bond of friendship was still there.

During this time George saw very little of Sally Cary. Twice during this period when she came home from school George met her each time when she was surrounded by friends, and outside of speaking eyes there had been little contact between them. More than ever she reigned as the belle in that growing community. From these two occasions George returned home beside himself with he knew not what, impelled and haunted by emotions only the solitude of the woods could relieve. Without daring to give a name to this distemper, he strove manfully to put out of his mind the beautiful image of this girl whom he divined could not be for him.

So the years went by, and at length Mary acknowledged proudly and sadly that George had acquired all the schooling that she was capable of giving him. She had long talks with him about his future, and Lawrence often importuned George about what lifework he was going to undertake. George could never give any satisfactory answer to these anxious queries. In the depths of his heart he had instinct and feeling which he did not voice. First he thought he would rather be a frontiersman. The wilderness to the north and west of Virginia called for exploration and settlement.

At rare intervals George had listened to conversations at the tavern in Mount Vernon where backwoodsmen and soldiers talked about the vast Ohio River Valley and the French and Indians who were getting too friendly with each other to suit the British. He sensed vaguely the great events that were to occur on that wonderful waterway.

Then the life of a woodsman, a hunter, called to every pore of his being. But he could not go against his father's wishes and his mother's eloquent unspoken pride and hope for his future; he could not become a hunter just for the sake of hunting. When he grew old enough, he might become a British soldier and enlist with King George's forces in America. This prospect appealed very much to George; yet whenever it came up there was something that hindered it, something that had to do with events about to be, something that vaguely yet deeply stirred him. At these times he was always confronted by the fact that he had been born on American soil, that he was as much an American as the Indians he pitied and liked despite their evil reputation.

One day when George went to visit Lawrence, a Man Of War was anchored in the Potomac in front of Mount Vernon. It made a brave, soul stirring sight to George as he gazed down the sloping green to the line of noble trees on the bank and the broad Potomac glistening there under the bright sun, the huge gray ship swinging at anchor, the sails being reefed, and the sailors scurrying over the vessel. All about that ship was memorable of the great English nation, with its powerful grip on the American colonies. The thought flashed into George's mind—why not be a midshipman?

Lawrence stood beside George and watched the boat being lowered from the ship to bring some officers ashore at the Mount Vernon landing. "They're good friends of mine—officers who were with me in the West Indian campaign. They're going to visit us for a while, and I wish you would come over often."

"Lawrence, will you speak to them for me," burst out George eagerly, "about getting me a midshipman's warrant?"

"I've already talked to mother about that, George. She would not stand in your way, but she doesn't want you to go to sea. She had strong objections which she could not explain to me. I think it would be a fine job for you, and I envy you. It makes me think how good a sea voyage would be for me right now. I am not well."

"Well, Lawrence, I'm sorry," responded George, "but I remember when we lived at Bridge Creek you were always outdoors, you were stronger—and somehow happier."

"Yes, George, I was. The Indian life suited me as well as it did you."

Lawrence went to greet his guests and soon the officers were reminiscing jovially over wine and rum punch. George stayed timidly in the background but did not miss a word of the conversation. Once when the officers laughed heartily over some escapade of the past, George joined in with the laughter. They glanced at him, hardly noticing him, and then were quickly absorbed in their tales of the siege of Carthagena once more. As the glasses were emptied, George ran eagerly to fetch more wine and rum punch, and when he returned the men were talking about Admiral Vernon. Timidly he announced to the roomful of officers, "Mount Vernon is named after Admiral Edward Vernon."

The officers looked at each other and, as though at a signal, all guffawed loudly. There was a brief, tense, silence; then Lawrence said, "Yes, George, that is exactly right." When his officer friends perceived the severe look in Lawrence's eye, they nodded their assent.

Excusing himself, Lawrence walked to an adjoining room, beckoning George to follow.

"I have obtained the consent of your mother for you to enter the navy," he said.

"You haven't really, Lawrence!"

"Yes—and don't mind what just happened; they are just taking advantage of the fact that you have never been to sea."

"I don't mind at all, Lawrence. Some day soon I will take similar advantage of them. When do I leave?"

"Mother is coming for lunch tomorrow and you leave directly after."

"Lawrence, I can hardly believe it, and I can't thank you enough—but is it really true?"

"Definitely true! William Fairfax and I together arranged for you to receive your midshipman's warrant and uniform which you will get also tomorrow after lunch."

"Half brother, brother, father," said George, grasping Lawrence's shoulder affectionately. Then, overcome with happiness and excitement, he walked out alone into the night.

Next morning, George Fairfax called at Mount Vernon for his sister, Anne, and to say goodbye to George.

"Father asked me to tell you that if he has been of any small assistance to you in this respect, he is highly pleased." Fairfax told George. "And as for me, I'll rather miss you, George—you out on the high seas tracking down the haunting spirit of Captain Kidd, while I—"

"I know, Fairfax, while you will be doing a dull job of surveying. But I always did think that you exaggerated the dullness of surveying—I even think you will be lucky to come back with your scalp."

"George, you are either a liar or a gentleman or both, because if you thought that there was so much excitement in surveying you would not let me go alone—you would come with me."

"If it were not for the sea, Fairfax—"

"I know, George. Well, come on, Anne, we must be going. I think I see your mother's carriage coming way down the road, George."

A few minutes after Anne and Fairfax had left, Mary's carriage stopped in front of Mount Vernon.

"Mother," shouted George, bounding to meet her. As he took one arm and Lawrence the other, Mrs. Mary Ball Washington, looking graceful and dignified, stepped down from the carriage.

"Come into the house, mother," Lawrence invited her.

"No," she replied, "not just yet. First I would like to have a look at George's new home on the sea."

"It isn't on the sea, mother," George said, "it's just on the Potomac, at present anyway. But soon—just as soon as I get aboard, out we will go to new adventures."

"And to a career," she added, "at least as glorious as Lawrence's."

"There's an odd note in your voice, mother," said Lawrence.

"You think that, Lawrence. You always have, and I guess you always will. But what you forget is, although I am only your stepmother, you are your father's son every bit as much as George."

"I'm sorry, mother. I guess that if there is any difference between us, it's that we vie with each other in our love for George."

"Come on, you two," insisted George. "Let's go down to the landing. I must be off."

"Go along, son, and may God be with you. And furthermore," said his mother as she cleared her throat, "don't come back until you have made a man of yourself."

"Yes, mother."

"Or half a man, anyway."

"Yes, mother," George repeated, adding, "but you almost seem glad to be rid of me."

"Well, and why shouldn't I?" she replied. "You're old enough, aren't you, to go and make a way for yourself? Then do it, and be off with you. Here—" she gave him a quick kiss and walked up the path toward her carriage.

"Goodbye, Lawrence."

"Goodbye, George, and luck be with you," his brother answered, adding hastily, "and now I think I'd better help mother back to her carriage," and walked after her.

"Mary Ball Washington, you're crying," said Lawrence, as he reached her side. He waited for a humorous retort, which was not forthcoming.

Lawrence hesitated a moment and then, begging her to excuse him, he ran toward the Mount Vernon landing. George was there about to step in the boat that would take him on board the ship. His eyes had a far-off look and he seemed in a daze. But at sight of Lawrence his face changed. "Lawrie! You oughtn't to run like that. What's the matter with you? I almost believe . . . Don't you want to go to sea?"

"Why—certainly—I do," replied Lawrence, in a strangled voice.

"Then why are tears streaming down your cheeks?"

"I guess that's because—your mother's crying too."

"Well!" cried George ponderingly. Then snatching up his bag he strode up from the landing and made for his mother's carriage. She was sitting there with stained face, and when she saw him her waving hand dropped. George stowed his bag away in the carriage and, leaping in beside her, gazed at her searchingly. Nothing could have been said more poignant than the look in her eyes. Without a word he tore off his cap and threw it high over his left shoulder into the air.

"Gracious! George! Whatever do your strange actions mean?" pleaded Mary.

"Mother, I'm turning my back forever on the sea."

She could only cling to him, mute, not daring to accept this blessed transformation.

"William, drive home," cried George, with a ring in his voice.

Presently, as the carriage rolled away from the landing Mary waved to Lawrence who stood looking up at them. He too waved exultantly.

"George dear," she began, wiping her eyes, "sometimes you make wise decisions. I am sure this one is. I have been against this from the first, but I did not want to influence you. The sea holds nothing but waves and whales, and perhaps an Atlantis, so far buried. Even if it ever existed, you would not find it in a thousand years. You belong to the land. You love that little plantation of ours. It means home. You labored over your crops. You made a success of your tobacco even though your heart was not in farming, but this right about-face of yours must have been predestined. Your farming is only a means to an end. Then you will have your beloved forest—your communion with Nature—your outdoor life which I never again will say one word against."

"Yes, mother, my sudden change was an inspiration, perhaps more than that. Our land looms great now as never before."

It was late afternoon when they reached the plantation, and while Mary hurried into the little house, George got out his baggage and then proceeded to help William unhitch the horse. "Hyar you Gawge," called the Negro. "What for all dis mean? Why'd you fling yorc cap that way? Aint you never goin' off to sea? To fight wid de Spaniards off down dere in de South?"

"No, William, I'm not going to be a sailor," replied George. "I've come back to the land. I'll be a planter—a fisherman—a hunter—and if my dream comes true, a frontiersman of the Colony."

"Yes suh, Gawge, I don' just savvy but dat shore sounds good to me," declared the Negro. "Ah shore don't cares what keeps you as long as you stays home, an' we can run wild in the woods again."

"William, we're going out into the woods right now."

"Do tell! Marse Gawge, you shore have a wild look. I reckons it's the same as that one you had when you come home from the Fairfax's last time. You shore was in love den."

"William, you do say some intelligent things. You've opened my eyes more than once. I didn't know it, but I was in love. When I came home from Belvoir and I'm in love now! With the earth, the trees, the grass, the flowers, everything that breathes here at home. . . . Put the horse away, William, and never mind about following me now. I am going in the woods to be alone."

5

George Fights Red Burke

Upon returning home George decided to divide his time between plantation work and riding into town five days every week to attend school. That was not an easy decision to make because it was bound to cut into his rambles into the forest, and they were hard to give up even in little measure. But he did it, consoling himself with the thought that when he was done with school then he would have ample time for his wilderness pursuits.

George took his school duties seriously and was pleased to be in contact with young people his own age. There was one pretty girl in whom he became very much interested, and before long he found himself yielding to his secret fascination, for he never spoke to the girl, except to the extent of writing verses to her under the title "Lowland Beauty." This was a kind of pleasure to him which he had not yet analyzed, and, as far as that was concerned, he did not think as deeply about his studies or the affairs of the district as he did about his experiences in natural history. But he worked hard in school because that was his natural aptitude about anything that he undertook, and he had the satisfaction of being among the several leaders of his class.

"I have read the essays on freedom, which you handed in," said the teacher to George's class, "and I find that there are two extremes in the conceptions of freedom brought out in these essays. I think both of them ought to be read. The first is by Michael Burke. Michael, will you read what you have written please?"

Michael Burke, the redheaded bully of the school, shuffled to his feet, grabbed his paper from the teacher's hand, and read with an insolent grin: "Freedom to me means, one, to scalp all Indians; two, punch anybody that gets in your way; three, whip all slaves, even though they didn't do anything, because it's fun; four, trap a wolf and then don't shoot him–let him die slow and first tear off his tail, hack off his left paw and just before he dies burn out both his eyes, using a red hot poker."

"And now we shall hear George Washington's essay," said the teacher as Michael Burke finished.

"This is called 'Freedom of the Press,' " explained George, "a term which means a great deal to the colonies and to the world in general. I believe the phrase is an excellent one. I did not make it up. I wish I had.

"Many years ago, in 1735, a lawyer named Andrew Hamilton defended a poor printer. The printer was John Peter Zenger who was on trial for publishing false, scandalous, and seditious libels against the crown. Zenger was a German American that nobody knew.

"The German Zenger was kept in jail for a long time, until his trial came up, but he kept editing his paper from his cell, because his beautiful wife came and helped him.

"The speech of Mr. Hamilton's that won the trial should be quoted here, even though it may be longer than my essay.

" 'The question before the Court and you, gentlemen of the jury, is not of small or private concern; it is not the cause of the poor printer named John Peter Zenger which you are trying: it is the cause of LIBERTY and the FREEDOM OF THE PRESS.

" 'The liberty, both as exposing and opposing arbitrary power by speaking and writing Truth.'

"What this means is, a person should always be allowed to write and speak the truth, and that is what the trial of John Peter Zenger proved. So here's to Mr. Zenger, the German printer who died last year."

"And now that we have heard both of these essays," said the teacher, "you will agree that Michael Burke is a wolf and a ruffian, and that Master Washington wrote well of freedom."

"Michael Burke is a wolf—a big red wolf," one of his friends whispered to him, mimicking the teacher, and Burke grinned, well pleased with his reputation.

Upon leaving school that day George's dreamy sense of being pleased with himself was disrupted by sight of several boys, among whom was Michael Burke, evidently waiting for him at the corner of the commons. They did not appear to be intending to play games, and George, being quick in intuitive reactions, saw that they were going to waylay him. As he neared the group his quick eye took in the signs of mischief and excitement on their faces and something more than that in Michael's coarse features.

"Well, George, you did yourself proud today in your essay and we thought we would wait to congratulate you," said Michael blandly.

"Thanks, that's very kind of you," replied George drily, not in the least deceived by Michael's apparent sincerity.

"Yes, you're mighty good at writing essays, but when it comes to verses you're just simply awful," declared Michael, with a taunt in his voice.

"Verses!" exclaimed George, halting short, conscious of a sudden swelling heat within. "What do you know about my verses?"

"Fact is, George, we know some of them by heart. They're so funny that we just can't get over them."

The storm gathered inside George. He knew what Burke meant. He was shocked when he remembered that he had left some of these verses to his Lowland Beauty in his desk in the schoolroom, yet on the instant he thought more about his threatening reaction to the theft of his poems than to the shame and ridicule.

"Red, why don't you quote some of his poems for him?" suggested one of the other boys.

"Great idea, Dick. Here goes. 'Poor restless heart/Hounded by cupid's dart!' 'Ah, woe is me that I should love conceal/ Long have I wished, and never dared reveal.' "

Burke's companions yelled their glee, and one of them said, "Red, you sure are eloquent."

George stood motionless, overcome by the swift bursting gush of hot blood that swept like fire over him.

Michael tauntingly began again to speak. "George, I'm not so poor myself as a versifier. How do you like this? 'George loves a girl who is his foe/She pities not his grief and woe.' I gave those verses to Lucy. We figured that you did not have the nerve to give them to her yourself."

"Burke," exploded George, in concentrated passion, "to steal my verses was a low trick, but to give them to Lucy–that was despicable." And with all his strength George launched out his big fist and struck Michael's grinning red face with a sudden blow. The blood squirted out, and Michael went down with a thud and lay prostrate and limp. He had been knocked senseless.

The other boys made an outcry and knelt beside him, lifting his head and calling to him. George sustained a horrified shock. He had never before struck anybody like that. He had not known his own strength. He had an impulse to join the boys in their efforts to revive Michael, but the fury of his temper still held him in powerful grip and he strode away toward home without ever looking back. He had been so furious that he forgot his horse. Hurrying back to the pasture, he secured his horse and, saddling him, rode at a gallop homeward. The violent exercise and the cool wind worked upon his anger, and by the time he reached home he was composed and bitterly regretted the incident. Lawrence had driven over to get something from George's garden, and, when opportunity afforded, George related the encounter with Michael.

"Mike Burke!" rejoined his brother. "I know that lad. He's not much good. One of the Burkes killed a man in a questionable manner. I think you need not make so many excuses for yourself. In view of the fact that Lucy will be made ridiculous, your action was chivalrous to say the least. I venture to predict that you will not be insulted that way again."

"I really had not thought of Lucy's reaction," returned George thoughtfully. "It's pretty embarrassing—maybe for her too. I hope she doesn't make fun of me."

"George, if I know girls, she will be delighted that she evoked such eloquent poetry from the shy and dignified George Washington," said Lawrence, with a laugh.

It was George's fortune next day to meet Lucy at the schoolhouse. Evidently she had waited for him, and he had arrived purposely late. George was conscious of a sudden dismaying emotion, and he had all he could do to hide it. Lucy's pretty face was stained with a blush, but her dark eyes had an earnest soft light.

"George," she said, "here are the verses that Michael gave me. They belong to you. I read them, of course."

"You—I—Lucy, I hope you were not offended?" stammered George. "I was only in fun. You see—you're the prettiest girl here—and you sort of inspired me."

"I didn't make fun of you, George, and I think those boys are horrid. What's more, I saw you knock Michael down, and I was as tickled as I was scared. I don't care what the boys do—or what the girls think."

"Thank you, Lucy," murmured George.

"Don't feel badly about it," she whispered, with an arch look, and then, as if frightened at her boldness, she fled.

George methodically unsaddled his horse and turned him loose. Then he slowly made his way toward the schoolhouse. Here was something he had not calculated. Lucy's sweetness and kindness somehow disturbed him. He liked her the better for her championship, and he would like to go on with a romance so amazingly started. But George's impulse died a violent death along with his poetical instinct. The other scholars were too plainly interested in what might develop between him and Lucy. The incident made George shyer than ever.

More than ever, George kept to himself, and, what with study and work at home and the long twilight walks along the river, he hardly knew where the time went. Since his fight with Burke he had kept to himself more than ever at school, but when Burke left school it released George from a tension that he had never lost while the red-haired bully had been present. George had taken up surveying as his most serious study at school. This had been prompted by his friend Fairfax and by the fact that it might well become a valuable vocation, one that would take him into the woods. Toward the end of that year he had an opportunity to test his knowledge. George liked the surveyor's work and showed much aptitude. Lawrence was pleased with his work too, and, as he had acquired some pieces of land around Mount Vernon and farther afield, he offered George odd jobs when his farm-work permitted.

One day, with William carrying the instruments, George went to survey one of Lawrence's pieces of land. The tenant was a Dutchman who spoke with a strong accent.

"Young man, I have took this piece of ground, and you'd make me very glad if you'd measure the lines correct so I'll know right what I'm renting."

"I'll certainly do my best, Mr. Schmidt, and I think as the job is not at all complicated, that I can promise a correct survey."

While George got ready to run his line he became aware of an attractive Dutch girl hanging around and making sheep's eyes at him.

"Massa Gawge, yo-all can see powerful good in the woods, but your shore are blind as a bat when there's any girls around," said William.

"Well, William, you're right, but it's not because I haven't sharp eyes. It's because I'm afraid. Who is that girl, William?"

"Ah reckons she's a bonded girl, Massa Gawge."

As it chanced, a horseman approached who turned off the road and halted near the group. It was none other than Red Burke.

"Hello, George. I see you have taken up surveying. I'll wager you will be leaving school soon, same as I did. We have something in common—love of freedom. I'm taking to the hills. I don't like the restraint put upon us here by the English. Strikes me if you were honest you'd say the same thing."

"Red, I love freedom as well as any man," returned George ponderingly. "If I were compelled to give up my hunting and fishing, I don't know what I'd do. But a man must work. I can very well do some surveying along with plantation labors."

"Haven't you heard any of the talks about the dissatisfaction of the colonists?" inquired Burke.

"No, and I advise you not to think too much about it yourself."

"Washington, you're not showing much of the spirit of old John Peter Zenger as you are credited with feeling," returned Burke scornfully. "We all thought you'd turn out to be another Andrew Hamilton."

With that, Red Burke turned to the Dutchman and demanded to know who the girl was and what she was doing there.

"She's a bonded girl I had come from my modder country."

"She's not English then," interposed George.

"No, she's from my modder country," explained the other. "She's Dutch and five years she be free."

"Washington, why not put some of your essays on freedom into action?" queried Burke. "Maybe you mean to free the lass yourself. Maybe you want her yourself?"

As George stood up straight and sharp from his task, Burke rode over to the girl and, holding out his hand, he said, "Hop up. I'll give you a ride."

With his assistance she readily climbed up behind him. Then he spurred his horse and rode him in a fashion meant to unseat the girl and give her a tumble. But he could not loose her. She held on tight. Then Burke rode back and halted his horse before the Dutchman. "I'll give you five pounds for her," he said peremptorily, "and if you don't take it, I'll ride off with her anyway, you damn Dutchman."

"Ha! Five pounds is more better than nothing," replied the Dutchman. "You give it me, and you can took the girl."

"It's a bargain, only that's five pounds I owe you," called out Burke, as he made ready to ride away.

"Mr. Measure Man," cried the Dutchman to George, "your friend. He say he go way with my girl and no give me five pounds."

George took a few quick strides up to Burke and, laying hold of the girl's arm, gave her a pull. She was evidently frightened and slid off so hurriedly that she almost fell into George's arms.

"Burke, you'd better clear out," said George sharply. "Your morals are as bad as your habit of playing dirty tricks."

During the ensuing months the one great worry on George's mind was the gradual decrease in Lawrence's health. Finally when the family doctor advised a tropical trip to ascertain if a sea voyage and a hotter climate would not benefit Lawrence, George declared that he would go with him. Leaving his mother and William to run the plantation, George packed his brother on board a schooner and took him to the Barbados. There they rented a little cottage high up from the sea, and while Lawrence appeared to improve during the long bright days and the warm nights, George sat on the porch and watched the white sails out on the blue or listened to the roar of the surf and dreamed boyhood dreams all over again. Sometimes in the early morning he gathered shells along the beach. That came to be his one pleasurable diversion. Sometimes on moonlit nights he patrolled the shore listening to the melancholy roar as the waves dragged back the pebbles and found almost the same rapture in the lonely shore that he had known in the wilderness.

He waited on Lawrence, read to him, encouraged him, and did everything possible toward the recovery, which the invalid seemed to be approaching. George was happy and relieved to see that his brother was getting so much better. The long hours dragged sometimes, and he was not much of a hand to write. He just waited and prayed for Lawrence's ultimate recovery.

Then smallpox broke out on the island. For some time George kept this from Lawrence, but eventually he found it out.

"George, this epidemic is getting serious. I've been told by several Englishmen and one native. Now, I'm getting better but I'm not well enough yet to go home, but you had better catch the first schooner for America."

"Oh, Lawrence, I don't think I need to go until you can come," remonstrated George.

"But you might contract smallpox."

"Well, I suppose there's a chance, Lawry, but what of it? I could stand it."

"George, I want you to go," declared Lawrence, pale and determined.

"I'm sorry, but I won't do it," replied George gently. "I won't leave you here alone. But I will say that if you improve so much that you can travel alone, I will go."

That was all there was to the argument. George remained, and he did fall victim to smallpox. In the hut some little distance from where Lawrence stayed he shut himself up and fought the disease. His good constitution and his willpower kept the disease at bay so that it did not attack in its most virulent form. A native woman took care of him and brought reports of Lawrence's continued improvement which cheered him and upheld him till the smallpox had run its course.

When he was over it, George found Lawrence so much improved that he considered it safe to leave him, and so he journeyed home alone. He believed that his half brother was far on the road to recovery, and he did not regret the smallpox scars on his cheek which kept him from smiling and which marred his face the rest of his life.

Not very many weeks after he returned home, George received a letter from Lawrence which conveyed the glad tidings that he was well and coming back on the next boat. When at last the message came out to the plantation that Lawrence had returned, George made haste to ride in and welcome him, only to learn that life's vicissitudes can be ironic and real. Lawrence had died suddenly upon arrival at Mount Vernon.

Fairfax and Sally Cary rode over to attend the funeral, and even Sally's loveliness and graciousness did not make an impression on George's grief-shocked mind. He never had a moment alone with her. Riding home the moment he could get away, he put his labors aside and took the trails in the woods. From early morning until late at night he kept to the silence of the woodland. And there, as once before nature had assuaged his sorrow, he managed to meet the loss of this more-than-beloved brother. He did not even know for days on end that Lawrence had left the Mount Vernon estate to him, and also a beautiful valley some distance from Philadelphia which Lawrence had acquired and which he called Valley Forge. At that time George did not care anything about the great estate. He importuned his mother to go back there and live but, as she refused, he left the plantation to the care of others.

There was plenty of work on his own little plantation but he left that too, to be looked after by William, and, with autumn coming on, the golden lonely days that he loved, he took to the wilderness in earnest, with all the future before him, and he felt that the wilderness would surely claim him for good.

6 George Goes Surveying across the Blue Ridge Mountains

George found the wilderness around Valley Forge much to his liking. There was an old log cabin on the place, which would require plenty of work if he was ever going to make it habitable. His first visit there was really camping out, something that he had always longed intensely to do but never until then had been able to do. His needs were few and, with the fish and game so easily procurable, he indeed fared well. He worked at tasks until tired, then took his gun into the woods. As there were Indians all over that country he exercised care in his ramblings and, if he ran into any Indians, he made sure he saw them first. Vigilance in the forest had become second nature to him.

He relaxed that vigilance only when he was hidden away in some deep nook or on some high hill where he could listen and watch with a feeling that he was alone and safe. Without really dwelling upon it, he found that the loss of Lawrence had, during his sojourn there at Valley Forge, insensibly become bearable, and that his daily and nightly contact with solitude had soothed his inclination to morbidness.

The habits George had incurred during his youthful experience in the woods and along the waters had been mostly those of observation. His watching and listening had become instinctive, if they had not been that in the first place. Everything pertaining to the woodland was intensely interesting to him. The ways of the birds and wild creatures had become an open book to him, and he found that they were always presenting a new page for his study. He loved all phases of nature—the sunrise at dawn, the dew on the grass, the melody of birds and the fragrance of flowers, the dank odor of the lowlands along the stream, and the dry tang of the deep forest, the wind in the tree tops, the white fleecy clouds that sailed across the blue, the sultry summer afternoon, the muttering of thunder in the distance, the gathering of storm clouds, flashes of lightning and showers of rain, the deep pervading silence of the deep forest, the sound of running water, the white stars blinking at night, the soaring full moon radiant in the sky and blanching all the landscape with silver light, or late in its last quarter a grotesque crescent, orange-hued and sombre, sinking to the west—these and numberless other aspects all around him seemed to have become a fixed part of his life and a joy and thought-provoking manifestation which were almost all-satisfying at this time of his life.

But George found on this first visit to this property that his leisurely and dreamy sensorial perceptions were increasingly pierced by a thinking and pondering curiosity. He was just as apt to think what effect these influences would have upon his future as he was to wonder at the increasing awe of the universe. His reading the last few years had quickened his mind. An intelligent young man could not love the forest and its denizens as well as he had come to without it being revealed to him that there was no death. The individual perished, but the species prevailed. This was just as true of man as of plants and wild creatures in the forest. And if that were true, the universe that he peered into so curiously, lying at noondays trying to pierce the blue above him, was without beginning and without end. It was pondering on these things that brought to George early in his life the inevitable sense about Omniscience.

It was wonderful to settle in his mind some of these perturbing questions. But even so, and thinking more deeply all the time and learning from a communicable spirit, he divined that his future would take care of itself. His dreams and delights seemed to gather life and strength from these deductions.

When at length a messenger came from George Fairfax importuning him to return at once on a matter upon which they were in accord, George reluctantly packed his few belongings, and, taking his rifle, rode away from Valley Forge toward home. There were seldom-used roads and trails by which he traveled, mostly through the woods where he saw wild creatures at every turn. A long horseback ride was for him almost as productive as a walk. He liked to go slowly and take his time. But when at length he got into more settled country, he put his strong horse to frequent trot and pace, and when darkness came that first night he made camp by a brook and enjoyed the experience so much that he was loathe not to prolong it. Halting at taverns the two succeeding nights, he arrived at his plantation late the next afternoon and the following day rode over to Belvoir to consult with Fairfax.

Naturally his thought reverted to Sally Cary, and he wondered if she had returned from school. He was divided between a longing to see her again and a fear that he should not do so. But George found himself inconsistent in his feelings, for he was terribly disappointed to find that Sally had not returned.

The news George Fairfax had for him was more intriguing and important than he had supposed. He had an opportunity to do some extensive survey work.

Lord Fairfax, brother of young Fairfax's father, had come from England to live his life in Virginia and had gained possession of considerable wild land which it was his intention to survey into manors. George and his friend Fairfax were to be supplied with proper equipment and assistance to survey these lands in the wild country on the other side of the Blue Ridge Mountains. Young Fairfax was far better fitted to undertake this arduous and dangerous mission than his young friend George. He was six years older than George and an experienced surveyor with several years work behind him, part of it being the northern Neck Line and later considerable work in the Shenandoah Valley.

George rode back to Mount Vernon to see his mother and acquaint her with his good fortune while Fairfax attended to the details of their supplies and pack horses. He arranged to call for George at Mount Vernon in a day or two.

George's mother was delighted to see him and at the prospect of having him home for a while, but her face fell when he revealed the nature of his new job.

"George, I do not like that at all," she complained. "Over the Blue Ridge Mountains! In that wild country full of hostile Indians and animals! Why on earth did Lord Fairfax pick out land over there?"

"Mother, he is convinced that our colonies here in America will grow, and he wants to be in advance of the renewed travel from England and the prospects of settlements growing larger. I understand he wants these manors to be something comparable to the great estates in England."

"But it's a bad idea," returned his mother. "Suppose many colonists do come, suppose settlements do increase here in America, it will mean only more restraint and taxes imposed upon us."

"Well, mother, that's a new angle on colonization in America," responded George thoughtfully. "Certainly Lord Fairfax hadn't thought of that, and I had not either."

"Besides, for you to become a backwoods surveyor, probably fighting as much as you survey, does not fit in with my—"

"With your what, Mother?" queried George, as his mother paused, at a loss for words. "With your old dreams about me and the great place you expect me to fill here in America?"

"Something like that, George," she admitted.

"Mother, I believe this new job is a splendid augury of my future. There is nothing as important to this new country as the uninhabited wilderness. I too have visions."

"But you will be in danger from Indians," she protested.

"That is what Fairfax says. But we will not be alone. We can engage a trustworthy guide and frontiersman if necessary. George Fairfax himself is well capable of taking care of himself in the wilderness, and if I am not capable also, as I feel that I am, I will soon learn to be."

"Whatever is intended to be, will be," said his mother resignedly. "I see you have set your heart on this work, and I will withdraw my objections, but promise me you will be more actuated by a surveyor's duties than in running wild over the Blue Ridge."

George remained with his mother for dinner and then rode back to his plantation. He had some pleasure in telling his slave William that they were going on a journey that had all the elements of camping, hunting, and fishing.

"Massa Gawge, what for you gwine traipsin' over there in that Injun country?" queried William, with vast disapproval. "You'll shore get yore hair lifted yet. Ah's gwine to hang on to my scalp."

"William, I never heard of an Indian scalping a Negro," said George, laughing.

George had often been perplexed by the need of carefully choosing what articles he would take with him on a trip, but this one being a long prospect, he was hard put to know what to leave behind and what to take. He picked out one article and then eliminated it. In the end his pack contained more clothing, fishing tackle, and ammunition than he could possibly need—all of which proved he was still a boy and looked more at the prospect of adventure than actual labor.

The following morning George Fairfax arrived early with his two pack animals heavily laden in charge of two mounted Negroes. In short order, George had William bring out their packs. They mounted their horses, and soon the little cavalcade was headed west. They crossed the Occuquan Ferry and took an old road that passed Quantico from which they pushed on west to George Neavil's place, where they arrived near sunset having traveled around forty miles. Neavil lived at an important crossroads, one of which the party was to follow north to the falls of the Rappahanock. At Neavil's they met James Genn, a county surveyor for Prince William County. Genn was an experienced wilderness surveyor. He had already the year before surveyed Lord Fairfax's south branch and Greenway Court manors. Young Fairfax's job was to subdivide these manors which Lord Fairfax intended to let go.

Genn was a rugged type, and although he did not wear buckskin he struck George as being a frontiersman. He was a bluff, hardy fellow. "I'm sorry I can't take this here trip with you," he said, "but you won't have no trouble finding places with this here map I drew for you. And if you do get lost you can get back on the trail all right; fact is, through the Blue Ridge you can't very well get off the trail. That's what's bad about travel over there. You're pretty sure to run into some Injuns, if not on this side of the Blue, then after you git over there. I advise takin' plenty of tobacco an' likker and some little gim cracks or other with you to use to make friends with most Injuns. Wal, if you'll set down here now, I'll go over this map with you."

"Genn, I'd heard the hostile Delawares and others were more to the southward," spoke up Fairfax, with concern. "I've talked with hunters who lived in Williamsburg. Some of them have ventured far over the Blue Ridge, and I understood the roughest mountain trail and the really great danger was in that country west of Williamsburg."

"Wal, Fairfax, you've heard right about the rough country," returned Genn. "The mountains air a tough proposition down there. I know a man named Zane who lives in Williamsburg now. He lived with the Quakers for a while in Philadelphia. Came to this country with William Penn. He had an idea of exploring west of the Blue Ridge and settling down there somewhere along the Ohio. That was a great idea of his, but pretty dangerous these days. Zane has four or five sons, all wild youngsters who took to the woods like ducks to water. They'll probably open up that western country."

"Genn, that *is* an idea," responded Fairfax thoughtfully. "Are some of our colonists thinking about breaking new ground in free country, out of the jurisdiction of King George?"

"That's precisely what is in the mind of these youngsters," returned the surveyor solemnly. "What could you expect? They have been born here. They have the example of that carefree, happy hunting life of the Injun. They'll grow up to be frontiersmen answering only to laws and rules of their own."

Fairfax turned to George with a singular bright gleam in his blue eyes as if to try to find corroboration of his thought in the eyes of his friend. What had been but vague and illusionary now seemed to become fixed in their minds, and without exchanging a word they seemed to understand each other. If anything, George was more impressed than his older friend. They bent over the table and listened intently to Genn while he went over the map with them and emphasized this point and passed lightly over others, ending by repeating his caution about the Indians. When he was gone Fairfax said to George, "My friend, I've let you in to more than I bargained on. But do you remember how we used to talk about the wild woods and the bad Indians and bears and camping out under the trees?"

"Fairfax, I do indeed recall all of those talks we used to have," answered George warmly. "This job seems to be an answer to my prayers, if not them, certainly to my dreams."

"Perhaps you won't be so keen after you've had a little real experience of wild life," returned Fairfax. "I'm glad I packed plenty of liquor because I anticipated just this. The other articles we can procure here."

The following morning bright and early they were off and soon struck the Shenandoah hunting path, an Indian trail going into the mountains. George could not remember as thrilling a morning as this. Before they had ridden far, the mountains began to take shape and loom out of the gray morning mists, and when the sun came out warm, the mountains stood up slope after slope and dome after dome, shading from dark green to the blue for which they were named. They found a winding path where the ascent was gradual and where soon the height of the ridge was lost behind the looming slopes.

It was George's first experience in the mountains. He had always loved the hills and had lost no opportunity to climb the few near where he had lived, but they were nothing compared to these bold wild mountains ranging in every direction, some of them seamed and scarred, showing gray where the rocks cropped out, and craggy cliffs overhung the Shenandoah. George saw so many deer that he soon tired of counting them. Birds of various kinds were abundant, squirrels chattered in branches above the trail, and crows called from the high places. Once he saw the swoop of an eagle that he marked as the finest spectacle that he had yet added to his observations. He kept a sharp outlook for eagles after that and finally saw one sailing high in the blue over one of the mountain peaks. His majestic motion without the slightest movement of wings showed how this great bird was master of the air. When at length the eagle bowed his wings and shot like a thunderbolt down and down and down to disappear beyond the mountain top, he conceived that what he had seen represented the very essence of freedom. That moment marked George's birth of love for the American eagle.

The trail crossed the river here and there where the horses splashed over the stones and halted knee-deep to quench their thirst and to go on and climb out again to the winding trail. It was all so new and exciting to George that he rode along in silence, gazing and gazing as if he would miss nothing of this wonderful ride, listening to the sound of falling water and the wind in the pines.

About noon high up somewhere, Fairfax finally consulted his map at what he said was the highest point on the trail; they halted to rest the horses and to eat. It was George's sharp eyes which picked up fresh moccasin tracks in the dust, and he noted the embers of a little fire. Fairfax searched around them and found other tracks which he concluded must have belonged to a small party of hunting Indians who had crossed the trail at that high point.

William intently hung upon Fairfax's words, and finally burst out, "Wal, Massa Fairfax, Ah's done powerful relieved. Ah dreamed dat my hair was gonna be lifted on dis ride an' Ah's been seein' Injuns behind every tree."

After refreshing himself with meat and drink, George trailed the Indians a little way into the forest. After he got beyond the trail in the green aisles between the whispering pines the task took on an entirely different color from what he had started in fun. He gazed all around, listening, and peered into the dense shade, and when he divined that this trailing of savages was something that he would presently take up in earnest, he turned and went back to his companion. They resumed their journey and soon crossed the divide and struck the descent where the travel was a great deal easier on man and beast. Going down, George found the prospect more beautiful and pleasing than the ascent. There were places where he looked down the precipitous slope into the white and gold river, and others where, from a turn in the trail, he could see a long way down the valley toward the other side of the Blue Ridge.

They rode miles through the forest where the view was obstructed by foliage and they came out into the open to find the green slopes sheering up to the dim rounded blue summits. For part of that afternoon's ride Fairfax let George take the lead, cautioning him to see Indians, if there were any, before they saw him. But many as were the flashes and glimpses of unusual things along the trail that caught George's eyes, not one of them proved to be a redskin. Hour after hour they rode down the zigzagging trail until toward sunset it leveled out into comparatively open country. They arrived before dark at Captain Ashby's cabin where they were welcomed most heartily.

When George came to make his second entry into the diary that he had begun to keep he jotted down the main brief facts without any comments and added, "Nothing remarkable happened." As he wrote this and mused over it, he thought that was how Genn and Fairfax would have regarded the trip and reported accordingly. But for his intimate, personal self the trip had been remarkable. The ride had been so full of beauty that he felt he would keep the pictures in his mind always. The blue domes of the mountains, the long winding trail, the shining Shenandoah, the sight of deer crossing the river, and his first black bear ahead on the trail, these brought some nameless solace to his hungry heart. And when would he ever forget finding that Indian moccasin track in the trail, and the bursting thrill which followed the discovery?

The following morning they rode up four miles to the beautiful country called Green Way Court where Lord Fairfax intended to establish his residence. The land along the river was exceedingly rich and fertile and the beautiful sugar trees captivated George's eye. From there they went down the river a dozen miles or more to the home of Captain Isaac Pennington, a notable plantation growing grain, hemp, and tobacco in abundance. Here they surveyed some land on what was called Kate's Marsh and Long Marsh.

During the surveying adjacent to Pennington's property, Fairfax had occasion several times to fetch George out of his dreamy contemplation of the beautiful country around him and the grand looming blue slopes of the mountains.

"George, come out of your trance," he said once.

And at another time when they were running a pretty knotty line, Fairfax laid aside his instruments and, wiping his heated face, remarked dryly to his friend, "George, this is a surveyor's job that I have gotten you. Certainly I appreciate how you revel in this wonderful country. I do myself when the work is over. Would you like to take time off to have a little hunt in the woods, or catch us some fish for supper?"

"I certainly would, Fairfax," responded George heartily, "but of course, I wouldn't take time off if you granted it. Only I implore you to be a little human. This is all simply grand to me."

And still at another time when both Fairfax and George had forgotten George's delinquency, he was hauled up short from his trancelike obsession with a particularly beautiful vista by his superior's caustic words.

"George, that ecstatic smile of yours reminds me of how I saw you look shortly after the last time you saw Sally Cary."

"Oh! I—I'm sorry, Fairfax," stammered George, the red showing bright through his tanned cheek. But the blush was not for his tardiness but for Fairfax's sly hint of his infatuation for Sally. That was a secret George imagined lay hidden in his own breast. Here he was brought up with a shock wondering if his friend had guessed it. "Fairfax, I promise you it shall never happen again."

Next day they were caught in a rain and had to return to Pennington's place. When the rainstorm cleared away, they returned to work and stayed at it until night. Pennington gave them a small cabin to sleep in, but, to George's surprise, Fairfax, without comment, spread his bed outside under the trees. George, as much as he loved the rain, decided to take his repose inside. The bench where he proposed to put his bed had only a thin mattress of straw. George made his bed thereon and he could see out under the trees to where the firelight cast shadows upon Fairfax and the sleeping Negroes. It looked very comfortable out there, but George was too tired and sleepy to get up and quickly went to sleep. During the night he was awakened by a burning sensation which, after some little conjecture and investigation, he found to have been made by an army of lice and fleas which had encompassed him. In great chagrin he got up, and, biting his tongue to keep from yelling that Fairfax had played a trick on him, he went outside, shook his blanket, and beat it over the woodpile until his arms ached. Then he remade his bed out in the open and, having not yet had his sleep or rest, was soon lost in slumber. George slept rather late but was further discomfited by being awakened by Fairfax who touched him gingerly with his boot.

"Hey, Admiral Washington, it's time to get up," he called.

"Surveyor Fairfax, are you fearful of contamination of some kind that you disturb me thus with the tip of your toe?"

"Ha! Ha! Ha!" roared Fairfax. "Would you mind telling me why you made such an uproar last night? Slapping your blanket on that log like pistol shots! Roaming around quite shamelessly in the nude! And thus quitting your comfortable bed under cover."

"George Fairfax, you have not yet outgrown your propensity to play tricks. I'll watch you in the future and when occasion comes, I will reciprocate," replied George menacingly.

Then followed days of hard work in rain and shine. On the fourth day they traveled thirty-five miles to Barwick's plantation where they found the river in such a flood that they could not cross. They camped at Warm Springs where they enjoyed several days' rest. George indulged himself to the utmost in his outdoor pursuits, and the time passed swiftly. Another day they swam their horses across the river into Maryland where they reached Charles Polk's place. The rain continued, and they found traveling very uncomfortable and work impossible. There was a woodland road between Polk's and Cresap's Camp which was upward of forty miles in length and the most miserable boggy road that Fairfax claimed there was in the whole world. Another flood in the river detained them at Cresap's that day and the next. Cresap, who was a hunter and a woodsman, advised them to stay at his place until he returned from a trip down the river. According to Fairfax, the hunter was concerned about something which he did not divulge.

That afternoon they were very much surprised and quite apprehensive over the arrival of a band of Indians, about thirty in number. Fairfax said that most of them were Delawares and that they had been on the warpath. Again it was George's sharp eye that detected a bloody scalp on the person of one of the Indians. If there were more scalps in the party, neither George nor Fairfax could locate them.

The Indians were distinctly unfriendly. The chief, a gaunt savage of middle age, almost naked, belted with tomahawk and knife and carrying an English musket, could speak but little English. Fairfax knew enough of his language to make himself understood, and he explained what they were doing in the country and that the anticipated arrival of white men there to trade with the Indians would be to the tribes' benefit. Gifts of tobacco and a knife mollified the chieftain to some extent, and other gifts divided among the Indians rather toned down the hostility. Then to make sure, Fairfax brought out his liquor. The chief yelled, "Fire water!" and that manifestly won his good offices and that of his men. Fairfax was careful to retain some liquor, hoping that what he gave them would be sufficient. It did not take very much of that strong drink to put the Indians in a good humor. Too much liquor, Fairfax averred, would tend to rouse the vicious in them.

The Indians built a fire and cooked the venison they had brought with them and settled down to stay a while. Fairfax ascertained that they had some business with Cresap, and Fairfax and George wondered if that had anything to do with Cresap's departure. The Indians made short work of the liquor that Fairfax gave them and demanded more. This had to be forthcoming and Fairfax assured them that it was all he had. It was not enough to intoxicate them but they grew noisy and merry and cut all kinds of antics the rest of the afternoon and at night replenished their fire and began to dance. One of the Indians stood up and harangued the others as they sat around watching the dancers. They had a pot full of water with a skin stretched over it and a gourd with some stones or beads in it, and these they banged and rattled at a great rate. Several of the Indians kept drumming and rattling until all the other Indians were dancing. They kept this up for hours.

This was George's closest contact with hostile savages so far. Naturally, he as well as Fairfax, had been frightened at first but as that wore off they watched the Indians dance with great interest. Sometime in the morning the Indians all fell asleep and when daylight came they were still so deep in their slumbers that Fairfax thought it would be a good plan to take advantage of the situation and get out of that vicinity. To that end they hurriedly made their way to Patterson Creek over which they swam their horses in a swift current full of driftwood. Not until they had put fifteen or twenty miles behind them did they stop for camp, and they kept anxious guard that night fearing the Indians might follow them. But to their relief they were not pursued and went on with their surveying.

What with earnest work, wild turkey hunting, and the hospitality extended to them by the farmers and planters who sparsely settled that country along the river, George found the days multiplying and his experience mounting equally with the unfailing delights as well as with the vast knowledge his keen mind accumulated. George earned the praise of Fairfax as far as his work was concerned, and soon they were rivals in the thrilling game of wild turkey hunting.

7

George Returns Home and Meets the Zanes

Upon the return of Fairfax's surveying party to Fredericksburg, the little party split up, Fairfax with his Negroes returning to Belvoir while George went to Mount Vernon to stay with his mother for a while, sending William out to the plantation to bring back a report of how things were there.

Reluctant as George had been to give up that fascinating life in the backwoods, he was very glad to return home. His mother was not well, and his presence gave her relief and comfort. He suspected that worry more than anything else had worn upon her. She was amazed and delighted with the change in him, but it was not that he had grown taller and had lost more than a stone in weight during his hard riding and hard work. She did not commit herself, being reticent as usual in regards to George, though he believed that the change she divined had been mental. He related in detail his adventures, making sure to gloss over the many real hazards he had passed through successfully.

The reports that William brought back from the little plantation were so eminently satisfactory that George had a vision of well-being if not prosperity. He sent William back with instructions, among which was to acquire another laborer to help him. As for George, after a few days of solid rest and comfort, he became aware that it was necessary for him to keep active. He took long walks and rides and hauled in logs from the woods, happily chopping them when he had a huge pile in the yard. He remembered that at a very early age he had become proficient in the wielding of a hatchet, and it was but a short step from that to handling a heavy axe. His hands were calloused and hard, his big muscles like steel, and he had a long reach and a quick eye. The woodpile grew apace. When he had split and cut for an hour or so, he piled the pieces of different lengths neatly in rows intending to stack up cords of each dimension.

While engaged in this strenuous but pleasurable pastime, he revolved in his mind his experiences over and beyond the Blue Ridge Mountains and what they had opened up to him. He had always known, of course, that he loved the outdoor life, but the planters and the woodsmen he met out on the Shenandoah had put ideas into his head. It would be an ideal existence if he could combine the work of an explorer and a surveyor and a planter all in one.

Often he thought of the surveyor James Genn and what he had told about the Zanes and their interest in the Ohio Valley beyond the mountains. The father of these Zane boys had vision. It was conceivable that a river as great and broad and surely long in proportions would have a wonderful future in America. Ohio, too, with its vast wilderness and its numerous Indian tribes would be a marvelous factor in developing provincial America. If there was one thing George would have loved more than anything else, it would be to explore that wilderness with kindred spirits. He wanted to meet these Zanes and talk with them about the Ohio River Valley, and as he was now a surveyor, to let them know that he was open to any kind of proposition. This thinking of George's was in line with his old dreamy habit, only it was more ambitious, more in keeping with his development as he approached manhood.

There was one thing that Genn had put into his mind which was disturbing and which he had tried vainly to dispel. And that was the restless, freedom-loving spirit of these young Zanes. If it were true of them, it must be true of many other youngsters who had been born in America. How significant it was that Fairfax had looked at him with flashing eyes but had never said a word about how Genn's information had affected him! George put aside that disturbing thought for the present. Now that he was a property owner and realized intimately the enactments of the British laws, it might have been easy to fall in the habit of mind of dwelling too deeply upon that magic word freedom. Out in the wilderness with Fairfax on that long trip George had realized as never before what freedom really was.

George was interrupted by the clip-clop of hoofs and the sound of wheels in the yard, and he awakened to the fact that he had been standing there for he could not tell how long leaning on his axe and thinking. He looked up to see that a carriage had halted in front of the house and that two young ladies had alighted with sprightly steps which gracefully swayed their voluminous skirts. George recognized his brother Lawrence's wife Anne, who had gone back to live with the Fairfaxes, and her companion, none other than Sally Cary. The same Sally, yet somehow vastly different! The blood rushed back to George's heart and made it pound audibly in his ears. What with his work and adventures, the latter weeks of his wonderful wilderness trip, he had almost forgotten Sally Cary. But here she was, changed, taller, a beautiful young woman advancing with elegant poise and a glad light in her dark blue eyes, proving to George with a sinking sensation of calamity that no physical adventure in the wilderness could ever be a rival to her. In a moment he succeeded in managing an outward composure, and he would have advanced to meet them had they not gaily waved him back.

"George, don't leave your wood pile," called Anne gaily. "You look very picturesque. We saw you as we drove in and stole this march upon you."

"Hel-lo, George," added Sally, in her slow tantalizing voice he remembered so well. "It's ridiculous to ask how you are. You bronzed giant! Fairfax told us about you, but really in my wildest dreams I did not expect you to look like this."

"Well, Anne, this is indeed a pleasure," replied George, as he shook hands with his sister-in-law, and then turned shyly to greet Sally, over whose little gloved hand he bowed. "Sally Cary! I'm glad—to see you. It must be a year or more—since you—since I saw you last."

"Yes, indeed, George. It is more than a year. And that time seems to mean a good deal. I'm sixteen years old next week—quite a grown young lady, and have come home for good."

"That'll make everybody happy I'm sure, Sally. You'll go in the house, of course, and see mother. She'll be delighted to see you both."

"I want to see mother and so does Sally," returned Anne, "but our visit is mostly to hear about your adventures. Fairfax has excited our curiosity to a high degree, and then Sally has a most urgent request to make of you."

"Indeed I have," corroborated Sally, laughing with a roguish twinkle in her eyes as she looked up at George. It brought back to him her old arch imperiousness and the fact that she always had her own way. He felt that he was in for it.

"Oh—you have? That's—interesting," he stammered. "Suppose you girls go in to see mother. I'll finish stacking my wood and come later."

"George, did you chop all that pile of wood this morning?" queried Sally.

"Yes, all that and more. I've already stacked half of it."

"Mercy! How big and strong you are. I think I'd like to stay out here and watch you."

"Well, in that case, Sally, I will have to abandon my labors and take you in to see mother."

As George led them up the curved path to the steps, he was tinglingly aware of Sally's small hand on his arm, while she flung question after question at him. One of the servants was leading the carriage away and others were waiting expectantly on the porch. Then Mary appeared at the door, white apron over her dark dress and her handsome face beaming with pleasure.

"Mother, here are two bewitching young ladies come to visit you," said George. "Pray take charge of them while I make myself look less like a backwoodsman."

Then followed the gracious greeting and affectionate embraces in the midst of which George escaped to run to Lawrence's room which had always been kept for his use. First he sat down on the bed to try to realize what had happened. He felt all the old feelings that Sally had always aroused in him magnified a hundred fold. How sweet and lovely she was! Quite grown up—quite the aristocratic young lady! He caught his breath as he recalled the warm glad light in her blue eyes and the pressure of her little gloved hand on his arm. Sally was home—home to spread devastation as of old among the boys of her set.

He was glad, but he felt how little he had ever counted in her sphere. He had not in the least calculated upon a contingency like this. But she was here and there was no help for it. It seemed there was nothing for him to do but to hide his mysterious and ridiculous sentiments and be the friend he had always tried to be. Yet he was conscious of a vast difference in the situation now. Sally was home for good, and she was no longer a young girl.

He was the master of Mount Vernon and of a vague future that called insistently. He hurried to remove the stains of labor from his person, and, making himself presentable, he went out to find his visitors upon the shaded porch having tea with his mother. George was very glad she was present, for that would make it easier for him. He took a seat with them at the table, and Mary poured him a cup of tea and presently they were all chatting familiarly as old friends who had been separated some time. George divined that the suspense, the poignancy of that meeting had its rise in his own sensitive temperament. He probably felt things stronger than most people. Presently Sally set down her cup, and, turning the challenge of her blue eyes upon George, spoke directly to him.

"George, before I make this most urgent request of you," she said sweetly, "I want to hear about your trip over the Blue Ridge. You know how Fairfax likes to talk and how impossible it is to believe him. Did you really have a band of Indians come to your camp—murdering redskins with scalps—and were you frightened out of your wits when they got drunk and danced the whole night long? I want to hear about everything. Did one of those woodsmen really interest you in that wild country? Was Fairfax lying when he told the funny story about you going to sleep inside an old cabin that was full of vermin? And that you almost tore the place down when you awoke to find yourself violated? Did you swim your horses across flooded rivers and particularly did you save Fairfax when he was hanging onto his horse's tail in fording one of the bad streams and got crippled by a kick?"

"Well, Sally, suppose I let you see my diary?" queried George, hoping this expedient would keep him from narrating their adventures, and when the girls clamored to see it he left them and returned with the little book.

"Girls, there's nothing very much in that diary," said Mary. "George used to be good in writing essays, but when it comes to telling stories even of his own adventures, I think he slights them."

"George never was one to blow his own horn," returned Sally, as she took the little book and began avidly to read the designated pages. The perusal did not take her long and her rapt expectant face fell. "George, this is like the notes you used to write when you were a boy. Nothing but dates and figures. Didn't *anything* happen to you such as Fairfax claims?"

"Yes, Sally, things happened to us," returned George, with a short laugh, "but I did not think it fitting to put my feelings about them in my diary."

"Why not? You're too modest. How do you know that this diary will not become a precious document someday?"

"Sally, that is rather far-fetched and illusionary."

"Tell me the truth then about those several things that I mentioned," she appealed.

George, despite his shyness and his reluctance to talk about himself, could not resist her eagerness and something in her beautiful eyes made him believe she was indeed interested in him and what had happened to him. So he began to narrate the outstanding happenings of their trip into the wilderness and, once having launched himself he grew interested in the telling, and even if he slighted his own feats he augmented Fairfax's, and altogether it made a thrilling story.

"Thank you, George," said Sally, with a deep breath, when he had concluded. "I'm glad for once that you've vindicated Fairfax. He said you were a wonderful fellow in the woods, and he thinks the world and all of you. Your story was tremendously thrilling. Why, just look at Anne! She is actually pale. Sometime I will coax you to tell me more."

"Sally, I fear that's about all," rejoined George. "When I take another such trip I'll have more to tell, and possibly a better story."

"Are you taking another one of those mad jaunts?" queried Sally, quickly, her eyes shadowing with thought.

"Indeed I shall. The first chance I get. Didn't Fairfax tell you that?"

"No, he didn't. That was the only thing he was vague about. . . . Now, George, here is the main reason why I came over to Mount Vernon. My birthday is next Friday, a week from this Friday. I will be sixteen years old. You know that is quite an ancient age for a young lady to reach in this colonial America. They are going to give a party at Belvoir for me to celebrate my birthday and my return home. And I want you to come."

"Oh, Sally, that'll be fine—for you!" exclaimed George, "But much as I would like, I don't think I could come. You know I was never much on the social things, and I haven't any clothes that are respectable."

Sally regarded him with speaking eyes while his mother burst out, "Nonsense, George. You have a dark suit as good as new. Only the other day I saw it, and your shoes and stockings."

"That's true, mother. My one good suit is very well as far as condition is concerned, but I've grown fully four inches taller since I had that suit on last."

"That's unfortunate if it's true," reported Sally, blue eyes intent on him. "If you really wanted to come—to do me honor at this important time in my life—you'd find a way."

Anne interposed in her sweet way. "Oh, George, you must come. Every one of our old playmates will be there. It would not be such a happy occasion without you."

Sally fixed him with accusing inscrutable eyes and tilted her chin proudly, an action that he remembered so well in her. "I'm asking you, George, to *please* come to my party."

George would have liked to have gotten out of it, but with his mother and Anne so solicitous and with Sally gazing at him with hurt, proud eyes, he had to make the promise. Whereupon they were all happy and Sally was particularly gay again. They did not remain long after that. George ordered their carriage around and saw the ladies into it and bade them goodbye. Then he turned to look up at his mother who stood on the porch.

"Mother, what in the world shall I do?" he asked, in dismay.

"Very simple, my boy," she returned, with a smile. "Ride to Williamsburg and buy some new clothes. You'd prefer your horse, I think, to the stage from Fredericksburg, and while you're at it remember that you are a planter's son. You are surely destined to wear more than buckskin."

The rest of that day was a blank to George. Restless and uneasy, dismayed and intrigued by turns, he puttered around the plantation trying to put his hand to some useful task.

Once he set out for Williamsburg, however, finding himself in the saddle again with the open road ahead of him, his uncertain mood changed, and he began to forget fateful possibilities regarding Sally Cary and to take interest in his trip. It would have been hard for George to be unhappy while on horseback. He rode his horse, Roger, which was almost as comfortable as riding in a rocking chair. The road to Williamsburg was familiar to him as he had been over it a year or more before and once when he was some years younger. He was like an Indian in never forgetting places that he had seen or ground that he had once been over. The old habit of absorption in sensorial perceptions settled down upon him, and the hours passed by as swiftly as the miles. He stopped for the night at a wayside tavern, and very early in the morning, before sunrise, he was on the road again. That day was like its predecessor except that the way led through more plantations. He passed vehicles of various kinds on the road and met the same coming from other directions. And he also met a stagecoach, the driver of which hailed him cheerfully.

Toward the close of that day when he was not far from Williamsburg and was congratulating himself on the excellent time he was making, he came to a ford of a little river that he remembered—only now it was in flood and no longer a little river. There was a string of pack animals crossing in the rear of a large canvas-covered wagon, and from the other direction there was another wagon heavily laden approaching to pass them. The swift water was up to the haunches of the mules and considerably over the hubs of the wagons.

Hearing the drivers halloing to one another and detecting a note of alarm in their voices, George halted at the brink of the river to survey the scene. He grasped at once that both drivers were trying to stick closely to the road, manifestly fearing to get into deep water off either side. When they came abreast of one another, the horses evidently became frightened, and there was considerable plunging on the part of the team and shouting from the men. George saw the driver of the canvas wagon leave his seat to hold back his plunging horses. As there was an imminent collision, George hurried Roger into the river, and they made the water fly as he made fast headway. Then came a crash, loud outcries, and a furious splashing, but neither wagon was turned over. George saw, however, that the driver who had left his seat was thrown into the water, and, as he did not make any commotion, George concluded that he had been stunned. At any rate he was floating down with the current. George spurred Roger off a direct line. He found the water swift but not deep enough for swimming, and, by dint of urging the horse to furious action, he succeeded in reaching the young man and, grasping him by the coat, held his head out of water and dragged him ashore. There George dismounted and saw that he had rescued a young fellow not many years his junior. He was conscious and apparently not badly hurt. Presently he sat up and said gratefully, "Thanks, mister. I got a bump on the head. Must have stunned me."

"I'm glad you're not hurt. At first it looked pretty serious."

"That fellow Stover hogged the road. He ran right into me."

"Well, he appears to be all right now, for I see he has got past your wagon. Luckily there seems no more damage done. The driver of that pack train is holding your horses."

The young man yelled to the pack driver to lead his horses on to the shore. George mounted again and followed the young man to the junction of road and river, and they both waited there until the double team of horses came splashing ashore hauling the dripping wagon. Then the young man turned to George. He was a handsome, dark-faced, dark-eyed lad, well-built and clean cut. "My name is Isaac Zane. I'm a son of Ebenezer Zane. He will want to thank you for saving me. May I ask your name?"

"George Washington of Mount Vernon at your service," replied George, smiling as he offered his hand. "If you are one of the Zanes I heard about up in the Blue Ridge Mountains, I'll certainly look you up."

"Well, Mr. Washington, we are the only Zanes in Williamsburg, or in America for that matter," replied the youth, smiling. "What did you hear?"

"Nothing much, only very interesting to me. That you Zanes were great woodsmen and interested in the wild country beyond the mountains."

"We are indeed. My father is discontented here. I'm sure he'll be very glad to meet you."

They parted then and George rode swiftly on his way pleasurably meditating upon the prospect of meeting the Zanes. It was after dark when he reached the town, and, arriving at the Red Lion Tavern, he turned the horse over to an attendant, and, on having removed the stains of travel, he sat down to a good dinner, conscious that the trip he had taken under protest bade fair to turn out entertaining and profitable. He became interested in his fellow diners, and, after the meal, he repaired to the main room of the tavern, which was fairly well crowded, and lounged about listening and watching.

George listened to various discussions, some of them quite heated and outspoken in criticism of government policies. George listened to these with a quickened consciousness that it was only of late that he had become vitally interested in more than just the love of American land and wilderness. The freedom of this beloved America of his was being questioned, openly in a public tavern, and it was disturbingly thought-provoking. The tavern keeper remembered George, but no one else there knew him and he did not intrude upon anyone. He went to bed quite soberly cognizant of the fact that he was more than a planter, a hunter, and a frontiersman in the making, he was an American and not an Englishman.

Next morning after breakfast he sought out the one tailor in Williamsburg. He picked out the various goods for his suits and got measured for them, and, by dint of much eloquence and by offering more than the regular price, he secured the promise of having them ready in three days. After that he had nothing to do but kill time. Indeed Williamsburg was interesting enough to a backwoodsman, and he did not anticipate any tediousness in passing the time. He made at once for the wharf. There were three English ships in, one loading to depart that day and the other two just arrived. Therefore, the wharf was a beehive, and profoundly intriguing to George.

His first reaction was a melancholy remembrance that he had been obsessed with the idea of becoming a sailor and that he had renounced the opportunity to sail as a midshipman. He knew then that the sea would never claim him as a merchant sailor or as a naval shipmate. He spent hours there and hardly knew where the time went.

He remembered at length that one of the things he wished to get while in Williamsburg was a new small bore rifle such as backwoodsmen used, and with which a wonderfully accurate marksmanship could be attained. The gunsmith showed him one that was new and finely finished, in fact, the finest rifle that George had ever seen. It had a small stock and a tremendously long, heavy barrel, and it fit George perfectly. He purchased it and all the accoutrements that went with it, even down to a supply of powder and ball. He also bought an oilskin sheath that fit around the stock. Thus laden and sure that nothing he could have purchased in Williamsburg could have pleased him so much, George repaired to the tavern and took his purchases to his room.

There, like a boy, he fondled them and tried everything, and was elated at how steady he could hold the rifle, and dwelt thrillingly at what deadly execution he would do with it.

That night at dinner he made the acquaintance of travelers from England and exercised his gifts of being a good listener. Some time later, as his new acquaintances departed, he was approached by a distinguished-looking man of medium height and powerful build, with a dark, deeply lined face, piercing black eyes, and white hair.

"Sir, may I inquire if you are Mr. George Washington from Mount Vernon?"

"Yes sir, that is my name," replied George.

"My name is Ebenezer Zane. I am the father of the boy whose life you saved. I hasten to assure you of my gratitude and that if I can be of any service to you while here, pray command me."

"Ebenezer Zane? The pleasure is mutual, I assure you. To meet you Zanes was one of the pleasurable anticipations I had in mind before I got here."

"Indeed, Mr. Washington, that is interesting. Let us sit down and talk over a bottle of wine," responded Zane courteously, as he waved George to a table nearby. This man's speech was punctiliously correct, with just a slight accent that was not English. It was very evident that he was to the manner born. "Where, may I ask, did you ever hear of us Zanes? Certainly we are the only Zanes in America."

"Recently I was on a surveying trip across the Blue Ridge mountains. Out there I met a surveyor named James Genn who instructed me where and how to run some lines on Lord Fairfax's property. Among other interesting things Genn told me that he knew you, that you had a wonderful idea of locating far west of the Blue Ridge in the Ohio River Valley. That you had a family of remarkable boys, all keen woodsmen and longing for a freer life, far away from these provincial restraints. I always inclined to those very things myself and naturally I was interested."

"You speak of Lord Fairfax. Is he any way related to you?" asked Zane.

"Not at all. I don't even know Lord Fairfax. He is the uncle of young George Fairfax who is a friend of mine and with whom I did the surveying. We were brought up together."

"Washington, have you any inclination toward politics?"

"None at all," responded George, quite surprised. "I took up surveying because I love the woods. It is my ambition to be a frontiersman."

"That might be an admission that you are not wholly a slave to King George's rule," replied Zane, with a wry smile. "That's enough for me. I would not presume to question you further."

"I want to meet your sons," said George frankly. "I imagine we would be as alike as peas in a pod. My inclinations have been restrained or I would be as wild a hunter as any of your sons could possibly be."

"My eldest son Ebenezer returned from a lamp tramp into the wilderness. He took only his dog and was gone for months. He returned with vivid stories about that wonderful

Ohio River Valley. A fertile, rich, marvelously productive country. He dwelt a good deal upon a magnificent island called Wheeling which he discovered in the Ohio River. He met Indians there. They are friendly now to the whites but will not always be so. Ever since his return I have planned to bring together some hardy young men like my sons and go to this Ohio River Valley and start a settlement. But the time is not ripe just yet. My sons are about your age. Ebenezer may be a little older. You seem to be matured quite beyond that age. But he, and Silas, and particularly Jonathon, are still, I fear, too young and too wild to undertake this dangerous enterprise. I shall wait a little longer, possibly as little as two years, before undertaking this trip."

"Zane, I am bold enough to say that I believe I would like to go with you," declared George.

"You would be welcome," responded the other. "You are a kindred spirit. There are many such now in America. By the way, have you heard anything about me?"

"Only what I told you."

"It might be well to tell you a few facts," went on Zane. "I am Danish. I was exiled from Denmark, not for anything criminal, nor my politics. I came to America with William Penn and for some years lived with the Quakers in Philadelphia. I could not stand them, or perhaps it would be better to say, they could not stand me, and I came to Williamsburg. Here I met an English girl of fine family and superior education. We had four sons and one daughter. Elizabeth is now five years old. My wife died several months after Betty's birth. Too soon, alas, for her to begin to educate the little girl as well as she did my sons. When she died that was an end of the restraining influence that had kept me anchored. As I could not get along with the Quakers in Philadelphia, so I cannot get along with these English here in this province. There are too many laws, too many restrictions. The taxes are exorbitant and unjust. I will not endure them much longer."

"I understand, Mr. Zane, and I sympathize," returned George earnestly, "but, surely, matters will not be helped very much and certainly only temporarily if you do make a home far from here. King George's hand will reach out and clutch as far as any of his subjects go."

"Washington, I do not share that opinion," returned the other, his fine eyes narrowing so that they shone piercingly like fiery slits. "I see into the future. I have not brought up my sons to respect this present regime. May I ask, Washington, just how far would you be in sympathy with my sons?"

"I don't know," returned George ponderingly. "That's a moot question. My father was born in America but he never complained of British rule. My friends, the Fairfaxes, are the same. I've heard my mother complain many times about the hardships she laid to the taxes. It's a question I cannot answer now. But I *do* know that the free life of a frontiersman appeals powerfully to me."

"Washington, you do not need to say more," replied Zane. "You are too young to see this political state in its appalling perspective, but the time will come when you too, with all the young Americans, will rebel."

George regarded the older man with unfeigned amazement and concern. "Rebel? Zane, that is speaking aloud more than I have ever thought. American colonists rebelling against English rule! It is hardly conceivable."

"It *is* conceivable. That will come home to you before many years. The English will have to fight the French and the Indians, and when they conquer them, if they ever do, then they will have the colonists rising against them. It is inevitable. This grand country will be free—free as the savages which now rule it. But pray do not let my opinions disturb you. We can talk of it again during your sojourn, if you care to. I have enjoyed this bottle of wine and this discussion with you, and I want you to meet my sons and my little daughter tomorrow or any time while you are here. And so, good night."

"Good night, Mr. Zane. It has been most interesting to meet you, and I look forward with great pleasure to meeting your family."

* * *

After a day George was taken to the home of the Zanes. They lived on the outskirts of Williamsburg in a little gray house fronting the bay. There were schooners and ships riding at anchor, and they, with the white sandy beach and the wheeling gulls and the gentle surf that lapped the sand, made a picturesque outlook from the little porch. The moment George met the Zane boys he knew that their father was right when he said they would be kindred spirits with him.

Ebenezer resembled his father and was an athletic youth somewhere approaching George's age, quick, bright, eagerly responsive, and a most agreeable young fellow. Silas was the next son, and the third was Jonathon, a lithe, dark-faced and dark-skinned youth of thirteen, quiet, soft-spoken when he did speak, and noticeably much older than his years. Isaac was a boy of ten, and Elizabeth, the daughter, was a lovely roguish-eyed girl of five. She had dark rippling hair, dark piquant eyes and a pretty face that won George at once. During his visit that day with the Zanes she passed from aloof to shy, from shy to interested, and thus to such friendliness that she hung around George while he was talking with her brothers. His discourse with the brothers, especially Ebenezer, was almost altogether concerning the wilderness beyond the Blue Ridge. If George had been keen before about this Ohio River Valley, he was entirely obsessed when Ebenezer completed telling him about it. He took the brothers to the tavern for dinner that night and visited them again the following day.

This time he met a remarkable youth who came in with Jonathon, named Lewis Wetzel. This young man was singularly handsome; built like a wedge, broad-shouldered, with muscular frame betraying itself under his buckskinned garments; and dark as an Indian, with glittering black eyes and long black hair that hung down his shoulders. He looked the epitome of a wilderness youth. He hardly spoke one word during the time he stayed there and hung in the background, quiet and aloof. After he had left with Jonathon, Ebenezer explained.

"Lew Wetzel is only fifteen years old, but he looks far older. Only a few years ago, he and his brother Martin were returning to their farm from a hunt and they found the cabin burned down, father and mother and sister and baby brother murdered, ravished, scalped, and horribly mutilated—the work of savages. Those brothers swore sleepless and eternal revenge upon the whole Indian race. They have already killed several Indians. When we all go to take up our homes in the Ohio River Valley, we will want the Wetzel boys to go with us."

"That accounts," mused George thoughtfully. "I understand him now. The most remarkable young man I've ever met! What a frontiersman he will make."

All too soon, George's new suits and other purchases were carefully packed, and he was ready to ride away on the following morning. When he bade goodbye to the Zanes and assured them anew that their meeting would surely be productive of future friendship and association, it was little Elizabeth who particularly was reluctant to let him go.

"Bye, Mista Washington. Come see me again."

"That I shall, Betty Jane," replied George. "I hope I can come before you go away to school, and when you grow up you will travel across the great Blue Ridge Mountains to your new home on the Ohio River. I am going there too, you know, and we will meet again. Goodbye."

8 Red Burke Causes Trouble at Sally's Dance

George might have spared himself his great concern about the long horseback ride and sojourn in Williamsburg and the slower return, for he got back to Mount Vernon two days before Sally Cary's much-heralded party. He met people who were invited and got acquainted with them on his return trip. And the party was almost the sole topic of conversation at Fredericksburg and Mount Vernon. For his mother's edification, George tried on his suit, white ruffles, buckled shoes, and all. "Well, Mr. George Washington," his mother said, "I always thought that Sally was in love with you, and now if her girlfriends do not succumb to you in that array, I shall greatly miss my guess."

"Rubbish!" exclaimed George, his face reddening, and he would have left his mother had she not detained him.

"Young man, now for a dancing lesson. You were always slow and awkward about dancing, but now you will have to learn some steps." And patiently and persistently she took him in hand and stuck at the task until he protested that he was exhausted and that he would hate it if she did not let him off.

"Now, listen, George, I think the best dance for you is the minuet. It suits your stately presence and dignity, but you would have to have your wits about you. Dancing is supposed to be fun. I think the gavotte is beyond you at present. I'd advise you, however, to stick to the Virginia reel. You do very well in that."

"Mother, I would like the reel if I could hang on to my partner all the time, but you know in that dance, part of it is done alone. I'll be frightened at that."

"The first few turns might be awkward for you, but take my word for it, you will get along in that well enough to suit even Sally. And goodness knows, she's particular."

George had his usual long walks and once he rode out to his farm; nevertheless, uppermost in his mind was Sally's party. And when he dubiously interrogated himself he found that it was not so much the party that concerned him, but that he must dance with Sally, and in conclusion he deduced the matter down to the embarrassing fact it was Sally that was on his mind. He appeared to be reverting to the old familiar moods of his years gone by, only now there was a difference in his thought. He just could not understand himself and ceased trying to.

The night of the party came all too soon, and he was glad indeed that it was a clear, lovely night and not too warm. His mother went with him, and William drove the carriage. George was relieved that the appearance of his vehicle could not be closely observed after dark. He had been vastly concerned about his own appearance, failing to check his elation, but was frankly outspoken about how handsome and aristocratic his mother looked in her new black silk.

"William, I prefer that you drive slowly," said George, as they left Mount Vernon.

"Dat's just what Ah'd like, Massa Gawge," replied the Negro, "Ah'm sort of afeerd of dis off hawse."

"But, George, why drive slowly?" protested Mary. "We're rather late now."

"I'd rather get there late."

Slow driving or not, they arrived at Belvoir all too soon for George. The big mansion was brilliantly lighted and the bright moon washed the spacious ground and garden. They fell in behind several carriages going up the driveway, and George had a last few minutes to compose himself. Their turn came presently, and George, assisting his mother out and up the porch steps, found himself in the midst of murmuring voices and gay laughter and the sound of low music. Through the wide door streamed bright lights. George had a glimpse of color and movement inside, and then he and his mother were met by Mr. and Mrs. Fairfax, Lord Fairfax, and lastly Sally's aunt with whom George had always been a favorite. Sally's parents were in England. Next to meet them and take charge of Mary was George's sister-in-law, Anne. She certainly did credit to the Washingtons, and George made her a graceful compliment; he thought how sad it was that Lawrence could not be there.

"Anne, will you take pity on me and be the first to dance with me?" asked George appealingly. "I'm sadly in need of instruction and practice."

"Oh, George, have you forgotten that I am a widow?" she replied merrily. "But we might slip out on the back porch and risk it."

Anne led his mother away, and George was left alone. For a moment he stood uncertainly surveying the animated and beautiful scene and finding pleasure in it despite his dread. Most dancers were in the large room beyond that in which he stood. His eager glance searched here and there, seeking out Sally with the thought that as much as he wanted to see her, he was relieved that he would not have to pay his respects immediately. But he did not see her until the music stopped and she came floating in her billowy white gown, so poised and elegant and lovely that he caught his breath. Indeed she was no longer little Sally! As she met him with outstretched hands, her face radiant with gladness, he felt astonishment that the small regal head came up to his shoulder.

"Oh, George, I'm so glad you came," she murmured, and squeezed his hands. "I know you promised, but I feared—never mind, you're here."

"Sally, it was hard to get here," said George, bending over her hand, "but it's more than worth it. I congratulate you upon your advanced age of sixteen, and you look lovely."

"Thanks, George, that's wonderful coming from you," she returned archly. "You are rather staggering yourself. I hardly recognize my giant frontiersman."

"I see you are the same old Sally. I suppose everybody in the world is here."

"Indeed yes, including one of my old admirers, Red Burke, and your former sweetheart, to whom you used to write verses."

"Sally, you can't mean it?" ejaculated George. "Red Wolf—and Lucy? But she was never my sweetheart."

"Oh no! But you were never one to tell. Lucy is engaged now to Tom Farrell of Fredericksburg, but that should not keep you from paying some attention to her. I imagine you won't be so glad to meet Red Burke again. Frankly, George, I did not invite him. *You*—you are the only old friend that I personally asked to come."

"Red Wolf won't bother me," said George. "I'd like to talk to Lucy, though, only wouldn't I have to ask her to dance?"

"Certainly you will," Sally retorted gaily. "But don't pay her too marked attention and dance too often with her, for I'll be jealous."

George could only stare at her, quite speechless at the potentialities she brought up.

"George, I've saved four dances for you. What do you think of that?"

"I'm overwhelmed, Sally, but the only one that I will dare risk—that is to get out on the floor—is the Virginia reel."

"That's fine. You can have the next dance following this one about to start. That will be a Virginia reel, and I venture to hope that after I have danced that one with you, you may appreciate my partiality in saving you more dances than anyone except Fairfax."

"Oh, Sally, I do appreciate it. I'm simply overcome. But you know me. Can't we sit out those others dances—or perhaps take a walk outside?"

"Perhaps we can," she replied, blue eyes intent upon him. "I must leave you now. Remember the next dance after this. I'd like you to pay your respects to all our old friends—even to Red Burke. It's *my* party, you know, George."

She left him then and glided away, a vision of loveliness, he thought, that on this night had marked him for calamity. Yet she had been more than gracious to him. That could have only one meaning, he argued. Then as the music commenced again, George began his rounds of the room, greeting those people whom he knew and who were not dancing, and, having begun this social duty on behalf of Sally, he discovered that as soon as he forgot himself and his shyness there was something warm and moving about greeting old playmates. Dickey Lee was especially glad to see him.

"George, my fiancée is dancing with Fairfax," said Dickey. "I want you to meet her. Fairfax, the sly dog, has already danced twice with her. She's French, lives in New Orleans, and, when I point her out to you, see if you don't think she's just as lovely as Sally. You're about the only young man I won't be afraid of."

"Dickey, that's a doubtful compliment."

"Look here, George, here's an old flame of yours, Lucy Grimes. She's dancing with young Farrell from Fredericksburg."

And just then as the couple indicated whirled toward them, George looked full into the sweet face that once had inspired him to poetry. It did seem so long ago, yet it wasn't long, only she had grown up and so had he. The stabbing pang in his heart must have been for those boyish fancies and poignant emotions now dead and gone. She flashed him a look of recognition and gave him a dazzling smile while the scarlet tinged her cheek.

Then a rough hand touched George's arm and a voice just as rough struck familiarly upon George's ear. "Howdy, George Washington."

It was Red Burke, handsome enough in a bold way, grown to man's stature and somehow as bold and unlikeable as ever. Yet there was no discountenancing his virility and handsome presence. George shook hands with him, and they exchanged greetings.

"Ah, George, there is your old inspiration, Lucy," said Burke, his white teeth flashing in his dark face. There was amusement in his dark eyes and satire in his deep voice.

"Yes, Red, I have already seen her," replied George. "Lucy has realized her early promise by growing into a beautiful girl."

"It's my idea she has outgrown her promise. Washington, I have not forgotten the crack you gave me over that girl. Do you remember?"

"Well, Red, I've forgotten all unpleasant things. Life is hard enough without treasuring old slights and troubles—and mistakes."

"I don't share your noble sentiments. I've never forgotten nor forgiven that knockdown you gave me when I wasn't looking," returned Red Burke, with a snarl.

"No?" returned George mildly, as he eyed his old enemy. "Red, if your memory was as good as you boast of, you would recall that you were looking squarely at me when I hit you."

Burke shrugged his shoulders and moved away, and Dickey Lee called him an insufferable cad.

"Dickey, let's go have a drink."

"That's an offer and an opportunity not to be missed—with you," replied Dickey, and arm in arm they adjourned to the sitting room where they were served among other gentlemen by the Negroes. "George, what are you going to do with yourself?" asked Dickey, with interest. "Fairfax and Sally have told me all about your surveying work back in the woods. I fancy that would just about suit you. But, George, it is not big enough work for you."

"Big enough, Dickey? Say, if you knew how hard it was, you'd call it big."

"You ought to go into the military."

"You mean an English soldier serving in King George's army here in America?"

"Well, yes, for the present. You would learn the soldiering that you and I and all us young Americans are going to need," returned Dickey enigmatically.

George was reflecting upon that rather singular remark from his old friend and was about to make a serious query when the music outside stopped again and Dickey saw his sweetheart. Whereupon he dragged George into the ballroom and presented him to a beautiful, slender, dark-eyed girl who held to Fairfax's arm.

"Oh, it ees Monsieur Washington," she cried, with a delightful accent, and a bewildering smile, as she gave her hand to George. "Dickey an' Monsieur Fairfax, they tell me so—so many wonderful things. I so delight to know you."

George returned the compliment. They exchanged some repartee, and then Fairfax intervened to say, "Friends, excuse me. This next is to be a Virginia reel. George, you are going to dance it with Sally, and Dickey, of course, will have Marie, and I've got this with Lucy Grimes. We'll all get together."

"Well, Fairfax, I feel that I will do better with old friends around me in the dance. I'll get Sally, wherever she is, and meet you here."

It pleased George to find that Sally was trying to locate him, and, when he told her that they were going to dance in the reel with Fairfax and Dickey, she was delighted although she whispered that Fairfax was a terrible tease and that as he and Lucy were probably the best dancers present he might poke a little fun at George. When they came to take their positions in the reel, George found that he and Sally were third from the end and that, much to his distaste and concern, Red Burke was next to them, his partner being a tall, handsome brunette whom George did not know. But when the dance started and they began going through their steps, the rhythm of the music and the gay atmosphere, the bright lights and colors, and particularly Sally's entrancing presence, the dance of her dark, arch eyes and the way she squeezed his hand, went to George's head like wine. And he found himself dancing without thinking about it, giving up to the thrill of it all.

Then it appeared they were in the middle of the floor and George was whirling Sally, when all of a sudden something happened—some misstep or some jostling, and George went plunging to the floor all his long length, carrying Sally with him. She appeared to fall right upon him almost enveloping him in her voluminous skirt. An instant lying prostrate George heard the shout of merriment that went up on all sides, and confusion crowded out the pleasurable sensations he had been feeling. He and Sally appeared to be intricately tangled up. He heard her laughing and her face appeared to be somewhere near his although it was hidden behind her skirt.

"George, for heaven's sake," she whispered, and at the same time giggling, "do something. My skirt is over my head. I must be a spectacle to behold. Please exercise some of your frontiersman gifts and rescue me."

In a daze, George got up on his elbow, freeing his right arm, with which he brushed aside folds of Sally's gown. To his horror he discovered that his actions had exposed Sally's extremities, the beauty of which only magnified George's appalling predicament. Thinking seemed to be impossible for a moment. Sally moved to her knees and, slipping, fell with her face right close to George, so that her lovely rounded cheek like a rosy pearl lay almost against his lips. In another instant he had kissed it, felt the soft cheek grow hot under his lips, and suddenly as she jerked away he saw that her face was scarlet. From the circle of spectators crowding around them there arose a delighted gleeful shout. Then Fairfax and Dickey were helping them to their feet and Lucy was smoothing down Sally's gown and everybody was laughing and talking at once.

"I'm—awful—sorry, Sally!" faltered George, beside himself. "Please—excuse me!"

"Oh, George," cried Sally. "Don't go. After all, we don't care. If only you had not—"

George tore away from her, and breaking through his friends he made for the door leading out onto the porch. He gained it and got outside when Sally, like a white avalanche, caught up with him.

"Here, you big Indian," she cried, in a pleading voice, half-stifled by laughter, "don't leave me to bear the brunt of it all."

"Sally, please let me go. I must have been crazy. I couldn't face them now."

"George Washington, it *was* crazy of you," she protested. "If you *had* to kiss me, why in heaven did you do it there?"

"I don't—know," moaned George, distracted, "but please forgive me."

"Forgive you! Of course I forgive you," she whispered. "But it's done. Come, go back with me. Let's make the best of it. Don't break up my party."

Thus, George, finding himself appalled at the conflicting tide of emotions that swept over him and almost powerless under her sweet pleading and clinging hands, halted there incapable of a decision at the moment. Fairfax and Dickey came through the door out on the porch and Lucy and Marie followed. Next to join them was Sally's brother, Richard Cary, a tall and fair young man recently come out from London.

"Fairfax," he drawled, in a cool pleasant voice, "shall I call out Washington and kill him for disgracing my sister or will you do it?"

"Dick, don't be silly," cried Sally, with flashing eyes. "It's embarrassing enough for George without making it worse."

"George, of course Dick was only in fun," intervened Fairfax. "It didn't disgrace Sally. I take it the little minx liked it, but if anybody should be called out and shot it is Red Burke, and George you ought to do it."

"Red Burke!" ejaculated George, startled out of his discomfiture. "Call him out? What for?"

"Fairfax, *don't tell* him," burst out Sally.

"Why, of course I'll tell him, Sally. George, Red Burke deliberately tripped you. I saw him stick out his foot. Everybody saw it but you."

"That's right, George," added Dickey Lee. "It was a trick of a black-guard. If you could have seen his face as you and Sally went plunging down in that mess, you'd certainly do more to him than that day after school."

"I'll kill him!" exploded George, all in an instant prey to that terrible temper which had been his from childhood. He stood there glaring back into the ballroom, his big fists clenched, all his being subjugated to a rushing, stinging, bursting flood of blood.

"Washington, I will take pleasure in being your second," spoke up Richard Cary.

Then followed a tense silent moment in which the faces of the young people blanched and Sally's wide eyes darkened and dilated. "Heavens, don't talk of a duel!" she cried breathlessly.

"Sally, I think George should call him out," protested Fairfax. "I don't know who invited Red Burke here tonight, probably Father. But it was a blunder. Red should not have come here. He has a bad name in the colony. He ought to be taught a lesson."

Sally got between Fairfax and her brother and George. "Leave this to me," she said, with a ring in her voice. "Dick, you and Fairfax were always keen for a fight of some kind, but you're not going to provoke George into one over me. Even if Burke did intend an insult we do not have to take it as so. To be sure, I can't deny that George kissed me. Anyway, *I* liked it. And I don't care what anybody thinks. Only, this is going to end right here. Brother, you go inside and leave me here with George. Fairfax, you and Dickey take the girls and leave us alone."

"All right, Sally, we'll go. I'm sorry I upset you, but Red Burke should be dealt with," said Fairfax stiffly, and turned away with the others.

"George, come away with me out of sight of all these people," said Sally, taking his arm, and she led him away to a shaded end of the long porch where there was a bench comparatively secluded for the moment. "George, I know Red Burke tripped you, and honestly I would like to see you shoot him," she whispered earnestly. "But I won't have a duel. I won't have you fighting over me. Particularly I don't want you to run the chance of being killed."

"Sally, it's almost too much to stand," returned George.

"I know how you feel—so sensitive about dancing and to be made the butt of a trick like that in a crowd, to be made the laughingstock of all those present. But I beg of you. Do not call Burke out."

"Will he not make light of you? Will he not talk about you in every tavern and gambling place in the country?"

"Like as not he will, but what of it? You heard me declare myself to Fairfax and the others. I said you kissed me and that *I* liked it. I should scold you for doing it in such a place and at such a time. If you wanted to kiss me, why did you not wait until out here? Certainly I should have liked that better."

That Sally had boldly confessed that she liked his kiss and that she sat there beside him holding his hand in both hers and looking so sweet and distractingly eloquent and appealing had the power of allaying George's fury to the point of his becoming somewhat like himself again.

"Sally, you're not going to ask me to go back in the ballroom?" he queried.

"Really, perhaps that would be too much," she admitted softly. "I won't exact it. But I cannot stay out here with you any longer. Will you promise me that you will not seek a duel with Red Burke?"

"Sally, I'll consider what you say," responded George slowly.

"But that will not be enough, George," she protested. "I would not be able to sleep, not to say being able to enjoy the rest of my party."

"I'm terribly sorry, Sally, but I can't promise you."

"Oh, I am disappointed in you, George. Is there anything I can do that will change you, for my sake, George? It wasn't the accident, the—the tripping you up that was so bad. The thing that was so—so, I don't know what, was you forgetting yourself and kissing me there—while we were tangled up on the floor. Just think of that! You must have wanted to kiss me terribly, didn't you?"

"I—I—I always wanted to, Sally."

"Well! In all our lives you've never asked me. Why didn't you if you felt that way?"

"I don't know."

"George, I think it's sweet to know that you have felt that way all these years, but it's rather late in the day now. Still . . ."

She leaned towards him, her eyes wide and dark, her face white and lovely in the moonlight, her lips coming closer and closer, alluring and irresistible. He felt drawn by a magnet. With his breath halting, his heart beating high in his throat, George bent to her lips, and in that long sweet kiss her cool tremulous lips suddenly took on a tenseness and fire. Abruptly she moved back from him. "Oh!" she whispered. "I—we—where are we drifting? But I'm not sorry, George. Only make me a promise. Please do not decide to fight Burke before you see me again."

"I can promise that," returned George haltingly.

"Then meet me tomorrow, early afternoon, halfway down the road to Mount Vernon. You know that grove of oak trees back up from the river? I will ride down there. Be sure to come. I'm sorry I have to go. Good night."

George sat in the shadow, wrapped in tumultuous emotions, overcome by the significance of her words and the wonder of her lips. He could not get beyond them. And all his thoughts whirled wildly about them. He walked out into the grounds. The full moon was white overhead, and the broad landscape and the silver-blanked river wore a glamour of enchantment. Mockingbirds were singing sweetly from the dark trees and the fragrance of magnolia blossoms was heavy on the air. He walked for some time under the trees and at last decided to return to the house to find someone to tell his mother that he was going home.

9

George and Sally

Once having set out down the road with his long stride, George soon found his mind clearing from the bewilderment and exultation that had obsessed him. Yet he realized that he was still a long way from composure. His habit of mind during the last several years had gradually tended toward a pondering, brooding consideration of things, analyzing and working them out to arrive at clear, sound judgments.

The hour was still before midnight and the moon had begun to slant toward the west; a perfect night to walk. He imagined that sleep would be far removed from him for many hours. His good fortune had been to meet Anne on the front porch and to give her a message for his mother that he was going home, that she was not to worry, or hurry home after him.

First and foremost of the rational thoughts that came to him was the one concerning Red Burke. His blood still leaped at the thought. His natural inclination was to see Burke, insist on an apology, and if it was not forthcoming to thrash him soundly. And then of course if Burke insisted on meeting him, there would have to be a duel. But George had not dwelt on this problem long before he realized that for Sally's sake and his mother's he would not provoke a duel with his old enemy. Sally's appeal to him, her frightened eyes, the way she betrayed something that must have been fear for his life, the clinging touch of her hand, and lastly the kiss that had been his undoing seemed to be factors too great and too all-satisfying to be resisted. His anger then and the temper of which he was ashamed had brought about Sally's importunity. It had transported him. He certainly would not fight Red Burke. Instead he vowed to put away from him all the enmity he had felt for this old schoolmate.

It was almost as if he felt gratitude instead of resentment, for Burke's action had precipitated Sally's betrayal of her—George could hardly dare to whisper it to himself—her love for him. But that dread of Sally's for his life—that betrayal that had been so productive of so much joy to him—was so overwhelmingly sweet to George that he could not resist the temptation to hold back a little while the fact that he would not compel Burke to meet him in a duel. Even at that moment George felt that he was doing something small, perhaps ignoble, but he had starved so long for Sally's affection that he surrendered to a lover's deceit.

It was a relief to have that one serious side of the situation settled and done away with. Then he reverted to the wonder of hopes and dreams that naturally crowded upon his conviction that Sally really loved him. Thoughts of the future, however, of bringing Sally to Mount Vernon as his bride, profound and beautiful as they were, simply would not stay before his consciousness. He must wait until the morrow, till his meeting with Sally, when that momentous question must be decided.

There was nothing left then, it seemed, but the insidious return of the tempestuous emotions that had beset him earlier in the night. So, as George plodded down the road, time and distance were naught. It was a long walk, something that he had not taken on foot since his boyhood days. But tonight it was far too short. The moon slowly sank toward the west, and, as it lost its brilliance, the stars came out again to shine white above him.

All the other factors of a moonlight night that George had loved so well were tremendously magnified. The Potomac, like a broad silver meandering ribbon, floated steadily into the distance, the booming of frogs along the shore seemed melodiously long and full, a flock of ducks' winged, whistling flight over the moon-blanched water, streaking out of sight; across the wide river in the woods mockingbirds sleepily burst into night song, a deer bounded out of the brush and, trotting into the middle of the road, stared at him a moment with great long ears erect and then leaped away with a frightened snort; the gray rabbits nibbling the grass along the road hardly noticed his passing, and, on the moment of his thinking these things, a shooting star appeared, turned from white to blue, and vanished, leaving a white filmy trail in its wake. It was a lonely road and there were no sounds except the few natural ones that enhanced the silence. The night was too beautiful, life too unbelievably glorious, the future too dazzling to be anything but a dream. Yet deep in his consciousness, in that divining moment, George Washington had a revelation that his dreams would all be true for him.

Nearing Mount Vernon he turned around several times to see if his mother was coming, and the last time far up the road he saw the horse and carriage moving darkly against the fading moonlight. It occurred to him then that he would rather not see his mother until after he had met Sally. Therefore he entered the house and, going upstairs to his room, undressed without making a light and went to bed. Presently he heard the carriage, and then his mother entered the house, and when, sometime after, he heard her gently push open his door, he pretended to be asleep. She called softly to him, but he did not answer. She went away and left him with thoughts that precluded sleep. He did fall asleep, however, to dream wild and whirling dreams, one of which awakened him in the gray of dawn. He arose and put on his riding garb and a new fringed and beaded buckskin coat he had brought from Williamsburg. Then he went downstairs and out into the kitchen where he got himself a cup of coffee and some breakfast. It amused George mildly that he could fall for the prosaic habit of eating when he was in the throes of a great passion.

It was just daylight when he went out, and there was a lovely and ethereal rosy effulgence in the east. George sat on the woodpile and watched the sun rise in an enchanting burst of glory. He was grateful in that moment that he had been born with a love of nature, and that his father and Lawrence had helped its free rein develop in him, and that the last year with his first real dangerous venture into the wilderness, that love had grown strong, full-blooded, contending always with selfish instinct and worldly doubts that he could not escape.

Then he took to the trail along the river, wading through flower-bespangled and dewy wet grass until he got into the woods. Here he lingered from one noble old tree to another, pausing to look down familiar sunrise-flushed vistas yet which had never been so pure, so ineffable, so beautiful. Long streamers of gray moss that waved across the path he caught with a gentle and loving hand and pressed them against him and wound them about him.

The woods were alive with flashing colorful birds, gay with their morning play and work. He watched everything with keen translucent eyes that took on the golden glow of the morning. He buried his face in the dewy fragrant honeysuckle that lined the trail; and he had a touch or a look for every living thing in the woodland. Nature seemed prodigal with its perfumes and colors, with its melody and the loud pounding of woodpeckers in the tops of trees. George strolled on and on, lingering in familiar spots that seemed to have added something new and profound to their comforting presence. He lay on the grass of the riverbank staring up through the treetops; he gazed and gazed out over the green gliding stream, not conscious of a single thought, yet revelling as never before in what was so great a part of his life. It was his good fortune that morning to see young rabbits, young squirrels, young fawns, young birds, frisking and free, all intent on play and the business of eating.

As the sun began to get high and warm, George turned to retrace his steps, finding that time had enhanced all which so marvelously intrigued him. He must go back to the pasture and get his horse and ride out down the river road to meet Sally. That wonderful fact was behind every thought, every observation he made during his walk, every touch of leaf and flower. What Sally had meant to him always, what she was now going to be, seemed to have solved the mystery of his absorption in natural things. It was love, and love was the meaning of life, and life in that revealing hour was intangible, divine, and everlasting. Seeing and feeling there in the solitude of the woodland, George knew that there would be no end to the inscrutable and loving ways of nature nor to the good and noble in life. No matter what ever happened to him, even if this glorious dream of his was to come to naught, he could never lose the strength and the beauty that had come to him on that exalted morning.

Since early afternoon, George had waited in the oak grove for his rendezvous with Sally. She was late, but that was nothing. He knew she would come. Sally never decided anything or promised anything that she did not fulfill, and the more time he had the more he could gloat over the sweetness of this meeting and the better be prepared for it.

The oak grove stood on a knoll back from the river, reached by an old logging road that was now overgrown by grass and weeds. He could see the placid shining river and the rolling green and gold landscape for miles. The road toward Belvoir was in plain sight for a long way, and every moment George's keen sight fastened on the green notch where the road disappeared in the woods. He stood beside his horse, walked a few paces in the shade, went out to look again and to do this over and over. He had thought so much and felt so much in the last twenty-four hours that he did not see how it could be possible for him not to be calm, yet he knew it was going to be difficult for him to practice that innocent deceit upon Sally, even for a moment. But he would try.

Then his sharp eyes caught sight of a horse and rider emerging from the green notch where the road led into the woods, and he sustained a tremendous thrilling shock. And he stood there trembling, his gaze riveted to that swift oncoming horse and the dark small form of Sally. They were coming like the wind. She could ride and evidently she was on one of Fairfax's fastest horses.

Swift as they were coming it seemed long before he saw Sally distinctly, her bright hair streaming in the sunlight. Evidently she had not donned a riding habit; perhaps she had run off from Belvoir without letting anyone see her. But there she came, almost below him now, hauling in the spirited horse and gazing up toward the oak knoll. George stepped out from the shade of the big tree and waved his scarf at her. She saw him and waved back. Soon she turned off the main road and came trotting the black horse up the gentle hill toward the giant oak where George awaited her. Her disheveled hair blazed in the sun, and her wide eyes appeared almost black in her white face. Her cheeks were flushed. George thought that if there ever had been any moment in his life that equaled this one, he could not remember it. He whispered to himself, "She is coming—my love, my sweet!"

Sally came trotting her horse up to him and called out gaily as the nettlesome animal went past George into the grove. In a few more paces she got him stopped, and George, running forward, came abreast of her. He laid one hand on the bridle and with the other met Sally's little gloved hand so eagerly proffered.

"Oh, what a run!" she cried, in sheer joy. "I sneaked away, bribed Fairfax's hostler to let me have his fast horse. And here I am, Oh, joy!" She leaned toward George, her eyes bright, her red lips parted, and offered them as if to be kissed was the simple natural thing to do. As George met her with a kiss that had all his concentrated emotion behind it, she yielded to it for an instant, then broke away from him with a little incoherent cry and a scarlet wave to cheek and temple.

She recovered almost instantly, leaving her hand in George's and gazing down upon him.

"George, let go his bridle," she said. "I think he'll stand now. If he doesn't, I'll get off. But I ought not stay long."

"Good, Sally. You look bewitching in that blue gown. So you sneaked away without putting on a riding habit?"

"Yes, I did," she retorted, "and you should be greatly honored. I never met anyone this way before in my life."

"Well, Sally, neither have I," replied George composedly, "and I never kissed *any* girl in my life."

"Fie, George Washington," she returned banteringly. "You don't expect me to believe that."

"It is the honest truth, Sally. I'll wager you can't say as much—at least about the kissing."

"That would be telling," she responded brightly. "But I will say you seem a very apt pupil. Stand back, George, and let me look at you. My giant frontiersman! How big you are. I am quite confounded. And you've donned a new buckskin coat for my edification. It was like you to wear that."

"It's new and rather large for me. That's what makes me look so big."

"You look some other way too," she replied, fixing him with an intent and speculating gaze. "Not so gay and joyous as I had expected. Evidently a rendezvous with Sally Cary has not meant so much to you."

"Sally, it means more than I can say."

"But why so solemn, so pale?" she queried apprehensively.

"I would have been joyous enough even for an exacting little coquette like you if it had not been for the serious and unfortunate circumstance last night."

"Oh, George!" she cried. "Haven't you forgotten that?"

"Have you?"

"No! No! No! I couldn't. They wouldn't let me forget it. What a time I had with all of them! They plagued me unmercifully, and I overheard Dick ranting about your calling Burke out. I couldn't sleep. I got up early and hardly resisted the desire to ride over here the first thing. . . . George, why do you look at me like that?"

George dropped his eyes for fear that Sally would detect his insincerity and find out too soon that all he wanted was to see what she would do and say if she believed he was going to fight Red Burke. "Sally, I—I don't know how I look. I wish I could forget—that affair, that I could give myself up to the sweetness of this meeting, but—"

"George!" she cried frantically and reined her horse closer to him where she leaned over and put a hand on each shoulder. Her eyes, now darkly dilated, peered into his imploringly, growing more intense as she gazed. "But—but—what do you mean? Surely you are not going to fight Red Burke. You promised me."

"Sally, I did not promise you more than that I would wait to see you again before I made up my mind."

"You've made it up, George Washington," she cried tragically.

"Sally, I—I am afraid I have," he stammered, trying to feign dark intent, but what he really meant by that was that he had made up his mind to ask her to marry him. And he would not be able to contain himself much longer.

"Oh—George. I should have told you before. . . . But when did I have a chance?"

"Why—about our despicable one-time schoolmate, Red Burke?"

"Well, while you and Fairfax were away on your surveying trip, Red Burke came home and during my short visit here he annoyed me very much. Then he followed me back to Philadelphia, and—and I saw something of him there."

"Sally, this is amazing. You mean you met Burke—that you didn't rebuff him?"

"Oh, I'll be honest about it," burst out Sally, evidently disconcerted and remorseful. "I flirted with Red—the same as I used to when we were kids. Only that's no excuse for me since I grew up. Red is a handsome brute, and he is fascinating to women. My friends in Philadelphia—one or two of them carried on with him. I flirted with him—led him a dance, but when he became offensive I drew the line and was disgusted with him and myself. Then his real nature came out. He's a beast!"

George was searching her telltale face with piercing eyes. "Sally! Did he insult you?"

"He certainly did. He more than insulted me before I got away from him. I never saw him again until last night. During that quarrel and what precipitated his jealous fury was that I threw your chivalry and gentle breeding into his face. I said his actions would be impossible to you, and that if I told you how he had treated me, you would horsewhip him within an inch of his life."

"And you, Sally Cary, expect me *now* to let him off?" queried George passionately.

"Of course I do. He's not worth your laying a hand on," replied Sally, just as passionately. "And that brings me to the reason I have confessed this. I'll never forget him. He snarled like a dog. He swore he would disgrace you, insult you, force you to fight him. And he would *kill* you! That explains his tripping you up last night and making a fool of us right in the middle of the dance."

"Did you tell this to Fairfax?"

"I didn't dare. I haven't told anybody but you. You're the only person I can trust. I should have written you from Philadelphia. I thought of it but hesitated. It hasn't been easy to confess, George. Now you will understand why I have been so distressed for fear that you would fight Burke."

George had no answer for her and stood leaning against her saddle, his big hands closed tight and his dark face somber and inscrutable. He thought that to refrain from shooting this fellow or at least horsewhipping him would now not be so easy as it had been. Sally read his silence and his somber face to mean that he was set upon this duel. She watched him a few moments in growing fear and then burst out.

"George, listen—listen, I beg of you," and her voice was tremulous and strained with the effort to control herself. "I see this thing from all sides. I don't overlook your side or Fairfax's either, but to call Red Burke out is wrong, foolish, and risky. It's not worth it. From my side it would be a very grave mistake. It would ruin me. And if he killed you or seriously wounded you—then it would be worse. My family is an old and proud one. There has never been one single blot on our fair page. George, if there is one Virginia gentleman who can be intelligent enough and big and noble enough to sacrifice his esteem for the sake of a girl, you are that man. I will never speak to Red Burke again. Please give me your word of honor that you will turn your back upon him."

Still George did not speak or lift his bowed head. Whatever conflict there had been within him was over, and he had won. And at the moment it was utterly impossible for him to put an end to her brave, honest, and impassioned appeal.

Evidently his strange attitude distracted Sally. She put her arms around his neck and, pulling his head up against her, she gave vent to her fear and grief. "Oh, you big stubborn Indian, can't you see? Won't you be generous? Please be noble, George, like you used to be when you were a boy. I'm to blame for this. I've been a little fool. I implore you, George—my old boy sweetheart—give in to me. Can't I do anything to move you? My wish used to be law to you. Last night—on the porch there—you were not so cold and strange as you are now. I will kiss you again—and more. I would do anything in the world, George, to keep you from this disgraceful affair. If I could—if I were not bound—I—I'd throw myself at your head. I'd really be what perhaps I am at heart. Please—please, for God's sake—for my sake—give in to me!"

"Sally, I am listening, with all my heart, I'm listening," responded George, his voice thick and broken. "It is so sweet to listen that I could go on forever, but I cannot endure your distress. I give you my word of honor that I will not fight a duel with Red Burke over you."

"Oh—George," she whispered and collapsed on his shoulder, weeping.

"Sally, don't give way like that," appealed George, holding her tenderly. "Let me set you back in the saddle? This horse is liable to bolt any instant and scatter us all over the place." He tried gently to disengage her arms from him so that he could place her upright in the saddle, but his efforts were in vain. She clung all the tighter. Her fragrant hair tumbled across his lips. He felt her hot tears on his neck. He tried again incoherently to stop her weeping and her clinging to him, then suddenly he gave up to the surge of his own emotion. He pushed back the bright hair from her face and lifted it, tear-stained and convulsed, within reach of his lips. He kissed away the tears that welled from under her shut eyelids and was aware that her weeping ceased and she seemed to stiffen tightly in his arms; then as his lips closed passionately on hers she sagged a limp weight in his arms. Once having yielded to his lifelong hunger for her kisses he could not be satisfied. That she responded to them was as certain as the fact that he stood there in the shade of the great oak, supporting Sally in his arms.

She was the first to awaken from that trance. She stirred in his arms and whispered huskily, "George, let me go! Oh, I beg you. We are mad! I am mad—to forget myself like this. Please let me go. I never dreamed . . . Oh, you'll never forgive me."

"No, I never will forgive you for hiding this from me," he whispered happily.

"George! Let me go. Put me back in the saddle," cried Sally sharply.

He complied rather haltingly, wonderingly, and set her straight in the saddle again, but he held one of her hands in both his. And he gazed up at her. The flushed lovely face had grown strangely pale and her blue eyes were straining intensely at him. "We forgot ourselves," she whispered, her voice low and rich with emotion. "I'll not regret it but—"

"Darling, there is no occasion for regrets," he replied simply. "I have loved you all my life."

"But, George—don't you *know*?" she queried, her free hand going to her breast which rose and fell with her agitation. Her eyes burned down upon him.

"Know?" he echoed happily. "I don't know anything at this moment but that I worship you and—you must love me."

"Yes, George, I do love you. I never knew how well until now. But—"

"There you go again with another but. I tell you there are not any buts."

She wrenched her hand from his and covered her face for a moment and murmured, "Oh, what have I done?"

"Sally," he burst out, suddenly stung, "you act—and speak very strangely. I could not help but think after last night that you cared for me and today, surely *you*, Sally Cary, must love me a little or you could not have acted this way."

She uncovered her face, her eyes were like great wide stars shining through tears. "George, I love you more than a little," she replied softly. "If it were not for that, I would not have a shred of self-respect left. Still I am terribly guilty to yield as I did—to let you—"

"You speak in riddles," he returned hoarsely. "What *do* you mean?"

"I pray that you will forgive me, but I'm afraid you never will. Much as I love you, George, I love Fairfax more."

He stared up at her and let his shaking hands slide from the saddle, and he stepped back, mute, with the conflict within his breast suddenly ending a paralyzing shock.

"George, I thought you knew. You should have guessed. You are the only one in all Virginia who doesn't know. Last night I promised Fairfax to marry him."

10 George Makes Peace and Goes Surveying in the Wilderness

It was a day in mid-November and George lounged in his favorite spot high up above a little stream and valley in the deep forest back of Valley Forge. The afternoon sky was dull and the leafless forest gray and severe, streaked with the dark trunks of trees. Dead brown leaves floated down the stream; a few bits of color showed down low in protected spots where the frost had not reached. Through the forest came a long, low wail of wind that was the knell of autumn.

Against the trunk of the pine tree beside George lay two fine haunches of venison and a wild turkey, whose golden plumage was sadly disheveled. And the rifle had a different aspect. The brown metal had been worn steely white in places, and the polished stock was scratched and stained. George had become a hunter.

In these wild jaunts through the forest he had found peace. He was not the same man. All his deep knowledge of nature seemed to have clarified, and he found that as he could judge things in the forest so strangely he could apply his thought and judgment to other things besides hunting. But his future still held aloof; the call which he had vaguely anticipated still held itself in abeyance.

George got up and, shouldering his game and gun, addressed himself to the long wilderness walk home. He started early in the afternoon and reached his plantation before dark. He had chosen to be alone at Valley Forge, and, as work of any kind had been a blessing to him, he took pleasure and pride in his household tasks.

Night found him sitting in his rude armchair before an open fireplace. It was cool enough at night to make the blazing sticks and red embers exceedingly pleasant. As a child he had longed to have campfires, and now as a man he looked into this fire. He saw a dearly remembered face and a nameless future. George happened to open the knapsack on the table, and his hand came in contact with a little book. It was his sadly neglected diary. He opened it, and, holding it to the firelight, he read over a few entries. It dropped from his hands, and he mused. What was a diary for? And as he had learned to answer many momentous questions, he found this one easy to record. A diary was a chronicle of dates and events which its author wished to remember. The absence of recording so many vital things that had happened in his life the last six months was explained by reluctance to speak of intimate and personal things as well as the profound and sad assurance that he knew he could never forget them.

George reluctantly decided that the time had come when he must stay with his mother a while at Mount Vernon and look after the affairs there and on his little plantation, and then find out what he was going to do. If he were ever to find any happiness it would be in the outdoors. To him it seemed far from being a lazy, futile life, yet he found responsibilities with his aging mother and his half brothers and the property Lawrence had left him, not to think of the most important—the strange calling footsteps on his trail, these mysterious voices of the future.

Next morning George was ready to go home. He stowed away his few utensils and cleaned up his living room. When he was about ready to go and hunt his horse, the sound of hooves arrested him. Peering out the door he was astounded and thrilled to see a familiar horseman, no other than his lifelong friend, George Fairfax.

"Hello there, old frontiersman," came the cheery call from Fairfax. "Lucky I am to catch you home. I've been here twice before."

"Hello yourself, Fairfax," returned George heartily, a warmth stirring in him, adding a deep ring to his voice. "So yours were the tracks I discovered in my yard? Get off your horse. I am very glad to see you."

Fairfax complied and came forward swiftly, yet plainly restraining himself, and offered his hand with apparent diffidence. He was quite pale and evidently under the stress of emotion. The two old friends met on the porch, and, clasping hands, they looked long into each other's faces. What constraint there had been on Fairfax's part wholly vanished. George found himself free of any feeling whatsoever except gladness to see his boyhood friend.

"Well, Fairfax, it's good to see your face," declared George. "Let's sit down. I'm sorry I can't offer you a drink or even a smoke. I'm all out of supplies. I've two haunches of venison hanging there, by the way, and you are welcome to one of them."

"Thanks, George," replied Fairfax. "That'll come in very handy for Sunday dinner. We have not yet had any game meat this fall."

"So you have been here twice before, Fairfax?" queried George, as he sat down in front of the other. "Must be important?"

"Yes, indeed it is. At least this time," returned Fairfax frankly. "It's a mighty fine commission I have for you—which I'll speak of later. The other two times I came were from purely selfish and personal motives."

"Fairfax, nothing you could come to me for could be selfish."

Manifestly Fairfax could not at once broach the subject close to his heart. "George, you're looking wonderful. I never saw you so big and thinned out. Sally was indeed right when she said 'Go and find that big Indian.' "

"Sally?" echoed George blankly, and the name was like a stab in a healed wound.

"Yes, Sally," returned Fairfax, swallowing hard, and the eyes he bent upon George held an honest and earnest glow. "Ever since—Sally and I were married—she has importuned me to come to you. Of course I have wanted to come on my own account. George, it's been hard as hell to come over here and it will be harder to say what I want to, but it oughtn't to be. Sally says it would never be . . . We know you have been terribly hurt. Sally has never forgiven herself for—for . . . George, we've been like brothers all our lives, and Sally has been a sister to you. Cannot we resume the old happy relation?"

"Indeed we can, Fairfax," responded George warmly. "There's little need of saying much. It appeared I loved Sally always, and I was such a child of nature that I lived within my thoughts and never knew what was going on truly in the world about me. There is absolutely nothing for me to forgive. It has been a privilege to call you friend and certainly it was wonderful for me to love Sally. If I had crazy dreams that could not come true, that was my misfortune. I took to the woods, Fairfax, as of course you see, and I have come out the better for it all."

"Yes—I see!" choked out Fairfax, wrestling with powerful feeling. "I'm ashamed that Sally knew you so much better than I. You make it easy for me, old friend. For the rest, there is no bad news at all. Sally and I are very happy. We get along marvelously. There has never been one bitter drop in our cup of sweetness except—this fear for you—that we had lost you."

"Fairfax, neither you nor Sally have lost me," returned George gravely. "In truth you have gained as much in friendship and love as I have gained in my lonely months out here. You can tell Sally that. And I will tell her. Afterwards let us never mention this long break in our intimacy."

"Thank heaven! You make me happy, George. I would like you to tell Sally yourself."

"Well, I could do that today if you're as good a rider as you used to be," said George. "I have only to catch and saddle Roger."

"We have all day," returned Fairfax, "and now that the troublesome knot is untied and I can tell you presently my important mission for you, I'd like to mention one or two things. George, you went back to Williamsburg right after Sally's party last spring. I know because I've been there myself and talked with Ebenezer Zane. He said you wanted his sons to take that trip into the Ohio River Valley, and he claimed they were too young yet. He said that you were a changed man, much different from when he first met you."

"Yes, that is true. I would have been glad to go into the wilderness with the Zane boys."

"And—later," continued Fairfax hesitatingly, "you went to Fredericksburg, didn't you?"

"Who said that, Fairfax?" asked George easily.

"Nobody said it. I've just thought it, and Sally swore she *knew* it."

"Indeed. As a matter of fact, Fairfax, my memory is a little hazy—no! I don't mean hazy, I mean that I have obscured many of the incidents that now seem so long past. But why are you and Sally so curious?"

"I'm certainly glad to tell it," declared Fairfax, with a ring in his voice. "Not long after you were in Williamsburg that time there was an incident which happened that caused considerable gossip and yet was never cleared up. No one but Sally and me and possibly her brother Dick ever connected you in any way with the incident. Some man who was never recognized dragged Red Burke out of a brothel in Fredericksburg and horsewhipped him almost to death. He was cut to ribbons, and he will wear the scars to the end of his days. We thought—that you might have ministered that just punishment to our old schoolmate."

"You did, Fairfax? I suppose that's natural for you and Sally," returned George coolly, looking straight into Fairfax's eyes. "Sally always regarded me as a knight riding abroad to redress human wrongs. But I say! What thrilling news that is. What a justifiable retribution!"

"George, I always had my doubts," rejoined Fairfax, evidently baffled by George's open-faced nonchalance. "I thought it must be some man jealous of Red Burke's well-known appeal to women, good or bad, but Sally swore she *knew* it. I'll never forget her when we first heard it. She raged up and down the parlor like a tigress. She was radiant—magnificent. I never saw her so lovely. She said 'George Washington did that! He broke his word to me—no, not that, for he only promised not to kill Red Burke. I know he did it. Something tells a woman sometimes. And I forgave him for it and love him more than ever.' "

"Fairfax! Did Sally say that?" returned George, a little huskily, and a dark tide of red tinged his bronzed cheek. "Well, it was only natural, I suppose, and if she persists in having me a hero I can stand it. Now, Fairfax, we must think about riding on, but first, tell me your important mission."

Fairfax regarded his old friend in wonder and admiration. Manifestly he had been answered in the negative, but that had only convinced him all the more. He made a gesture as if to wave aside something that, however thrilling to him, was distasteful to George.

"George, we've got another big surveying job to do," began Fairfax. "It is to run some lines through property that Lord Fairfax has recently secured, and after that there will be government surveying to do and very probably a great deal of it."

"That's good news indeed, Fairfax," responded George, with strong interest. "I will be glad to brush up on my surveying. I have run a lot of straight lines with my naked eye through the woods these last few months. I suppose Lord Fairfax's holdings will be beyond the Blue Ridge. When do we start?"

"Right away. We had better hurry to get the work done up in the hills before winter sets in. But before we start it's my duty to tell you that there is a bunch of Indians running amok in that section. I don't know what tribe. I tell you this, but I fancy it will not make the slightest difference to you."

George heard his own pleasant laugh for the first time in months, and that was his answer to Fairfax's information. "What does Sally think about you going off with me into the wilderness where there are bad Indians?" he asked.

"Sally doesn't know about the Indians," returned Fairfax soberly. "She made a strong enough objection on my going without knowing that. As a matter of fact, she objected to you going just as strongly."

"In my case it is of little moment," rejoined George, "but I don't believe you ought to go."

"That worries me too, George. But I am keen to have one more last trip into the wilds with you. I think we can be too smart for the Indians. With your eyes and ears and my experience, I think we can safely go. One thing I forgot to say, we'll run less risk if we go alone. We're not afraid of hard work, and our Negroes are not good woodsmen."

"That's sound judgment, Fairfax. I'll saddle my horse and we'll be ready to start quickly."

Once having started for Mount Vernon, putting their horses to a brisk trot, the friends had no opportunity for conversation. George's mind was full. He was glad indeed that Fairfax had come to him and that the old relation had been resumed, surely deeper than ever. And George was astounded and likewise elated to find that he could hear about Sally and speak of her and face the certainty of meeting her again without any repetition of the grief and dread that he had overcome. For the rest, he actually thrilled at the thought of seeing Sally again. As long as he could not have her he was happy that his best and, in fact, his only friend should be her husband. Soon Mount Vernon was in sight, and presently he and Fairfax reined in at the stable yards.

"Now, George, I'll ride on home as I have many things to do," said Fairfax. "And you will be busy too. Then you have your mother to console not only for your long absence lately but for this new adventure. And, believe me, I don't want to be around when you tell her. Sally is enough for me. So bring one pack horse. I don't need to tell you to pack light, and plan to take dinner with Sally and me tonight at seven."

"All right, Fairfax, I'll be there. Goodbye."

Mary was overjoyed to see George. She told him that she had been expecting him for days. "George, I knew you would win over your trouble, but knowing you and your father—the nature of your strong feelings—I thought it would take longer and I did not expect you to come back looking so splendid. Why, George, you're a man! And handsomer than you ever promised to be."

"Thank you, mother. You are certainly very flattering. But I am afraid you will not be so happy when you learn that I am going away with Fairfax on another surveying trip into the mountains."

"I think that is fine for you, but Fairfax—why, he's married! And Sally confided in me that already she had intimations of a wonderful event sometime next year."

"Mother!" exclaimed George, aghast, conscious of a queer sensation within, and he gazed at her with awe.

"Yes! What could you expect? It's natural and it's just fine, but I would be against Fairfax going. As for you, this surveying of yours will lead to something bigger. The colonies are growing. More and more plantations and manors are being taken up on the edge of wild country. There is a good deal of unrest and dissatisfaction along the seaboard. Until it wears out—which it will never do—and comes to a head, I'll be satisfied to have you in the woods."

There it was again, that strange disturbing voice whispering of the future. George had no reply for her, but the thought probed curiously into his mind. In the succeeding hours he got rid of it. There had to be consultations with his mother as to Mount Vernon affairs and instructions to give William on running his farm out in the country. And then it was pleasurable to listen to his mother's gossip. Much as she had known and felt over his loss of Sally, she gave no hint that it had occurred to her. She did not even give him any advice about how to conduct himself with Sally. In fact, the several times that she fell to serious conversation it had to do with increased taxation and other perturbing restraints placed upon the colonists directly from England.

At sunset George was packed and ready to leave, and, bidding a cheery farewell, he mounted, took the halter of the pack horse from William, and set off for Belvoir. As he trotted leisurely down the road, he could not help but recall the moonlit night he had walked home from Belvoir and the state of his mind that seemed incredible to him now. The sun was setting behind the oak grove where he had met Sally that day.

It was late November now. What leaves remained on the oaks were sere and brown, and the barren fields stretched out gray and monotonous toward the bleak forest. There was a cool wind blowing, and it sighed among the treetops. It took some time after he passed the oak knoll once more to regain his poise and know that everything was all right. He reached Belvoir just at dark. The house was brilliantly lighted as usual, and through the door that was flung wide open a broad yellow and red light streamed out upon the grass. Fairfax, Sally, and Anne were all there welcoming him in unison. George answered their welcome with a cheery greeting, and, dismounting, turned his horses over to a servant and was led into the house. He suffered a little pang of remorse to see how happy his arrival had made Fairfax and Sally and especially Anne, and that extended even to Fairfax's mother and father. They all talked and talked, and George as usual listened. Not until he was seated at dinner did he venture to look across the table at Sally. He appreciated a difference in her, yet he could not define it. If anything she was lovelier than ever, and she gazed at him with her challenging eyes with just a little wonder and perhaps a shade of disappointment. Twice she remarked how wonderful he looked and once she said he was more a big Indian than ever.

After dinner they repaired to the sitting room where George was hard put to keep his mind open to all their points of view about this and that. Mr. Fairfax wanted to talk politics; Dick Cary shot a few sly digs at George, and, finding him impervious, tried to interest George in what the young men of the colonies were thinking. Mrs. Fairfax was not favorably impressed by her son's proposed trip into the wilderness, and Sally came right out forcibly and declared with flashing eyes that this would be the last trip for Fairfax into the mountains. At length Fairfax put an end to the animated discussions by asserting, "George and I will be saying good night. We have to get up at four o'clock in the morning. We have a forty-mile ride to make, and we'll need all the rest we can get. We will not be seeing you in the morning so I pray you, make your farewells now."

When it came George's turn to say goodbye to Sally he found her the same at maneuvering things to suit herself. She dragged him away, and, holding both his hands, she told him with rich, deep emotion in her low voice that she was proud of him, that she had never been free from worry about him. "George, it's so wonderfully good to see you, to know that you have come back nobler than ever—my Indian frontiersman as never before! Remember this, George, when you come back, I will have the finest girl in Virginia for you. That I owe you. . . . And that I promise, despite the horrible jealous pangs that I shall have to endure."

George bent over to kiss her hand, knowing full well that she had the same power, that she was the same Sally, that her speaking tear-filled eyes and the softly tremulous lips that she upheld were as alluring and attainable as ever. But he was stronger. He was glad of the test. He rejoiced in the knowledge that Sally was safe in the love and protection of his best friend.

"Goodbye, Sally," he said composedly. "I'll take care of Fairfax. Do not worry about him. And I shall remember that you promised to get me a sweetheart. She must be a Virginian—and certainly like you, if there be another."

Sundown the next day found the two friends at the end of their forty-mile jaunt, on the edge of rough wild country, happy as two boys at their old camp tasks. Next day after an even longer ride, they reached Crenshaw's on the Shenandoah, and there the news was forthcoming that it was more hazardous than Fairfax had affirmed to go into the Blue Ridge country. Crenshaw was comparatively new to the country, having taken up his nest on the river since George and Fairfax were out that way, and he was deeply concerned about the Indians. George listened quietly to the trader and later questioned other men at the post and then some of the slaves. He did not form any opinion on the moment.

Next day he met a hunter named Bidlow who happened to mention, among other bits of information, that he had met two of the Zane boys and young Wetzel on the other side of the Blue Ridge. The boys were not communicative. Young Lew Wetzel particularly was reticent and plainly not sociable. He wore a scalp lock at his belt. Bidlow said these wild youngsters had been coming in from a long tramp in the wilderness and what little they did say about Indians was thought-provoking. It was then that George formed his opinion that Fairfax and he must be exceptionally vigilant upon their surveying venture. Neither this hunter nor anyone else at the post could tell to what tribe these hostile Indians belonged.

The following day the two young surveyors resumed their journey into the mountains. Then for a couple more days they met no person on the lonely trails after which they stopped at Ashby's and another time at Cresap's where they were relieved of some apprehension about the Indian scare. Ten days of concentrated riding and surveying, camping out most of the time, without one untoward incident happening, led Fairfax to declare that all this talk about Indians beyond the Blue Ridge was probably idle gossip. George shook his head somberly. "I don't think so, Fairfax. I can't explain my feelings. It's sort of a prolonged presentiment, not readily explained. Only we'll keep up our vigilance and pray that our good fortune continues."

About noon the next day when they had advanced the line of Lord Fairfax's new manor farthermost to the West, they were confronted by a stalwart backwoodsman who frightened them by stepping noiselessly out of the bush with the silent step of the Indian.

"Howdy, young fellars," he said genially. "I heard you were in these woods and I've been hunting you up."

"Howdy, yourself, hunter," responded Fairfax, rising. "My name's Fairfax and this is my partner, George Washington. Who are you?"

"I'm Captain Jack, the Black Hunter," returned the other. "Likely you have heard of me."

"Yes, Captain Jack, I have heard of you," returned Fairfax, offering his hand. "But not this trip. Who told you we were in these woods?"

"Some Injun friends of mine two days back."

"Indians? We haven't seen any—not even a moccasin track."

"Wal, they see you all right. I reckon they felt friendly towards you or the story would have been different."

George stood there listening intently to this talk and studying the remarkable presence of this hunter. He was almost as tall as George and big in proportion. He wore the coonskin cap and buckskin garments of the woodsman, but in this case the buckskin shirt, pants, and leggins instead of the usual gray or yellow were a peculiar striated black. This color had been wrought on the buckskin, George's scrutiny elicited, no doubt by red hot charcoal and it was as much a burn as a discoloration. Captain Jack was a man still under thirty, handsome and smooth-faced. He carried the hunter's long rifle and belt with tomahawk and knife, and around his shoulder he wore a powder horn and buckskin bullet pouch.

"You boys must come with me to my cabin," the hunter was saying. "It's not far from here. It's pretty lonely there for my wife and kids, and whenever I can, I fetch in visitors."

"Well, Captain, we'll be glad to go with you," responded Fairfax. "Our work is done here and we have too long a ride to our next camp to make this afternoon, so your kind invitation fits in nicely."

They soon had pack animals and horses ready and followed the Black Hunter through the woods. He had said his cabin was nearby. But evidently, distance with him had little meaning. They followed Captain Jack miles through the forest.

They came at length to a clearing, part of which was an actual glade, and, when Fairfax burst out enthusiastically that it was the prettiest place he had seen beyond the mountains, George heartily agreed with him. Through the center of this green glade, still only little affected by the frost, a shallow clear brook ran noisily, and under giant sycamore trees there was a neat log cabin and from the stone chimney curled a column of blue smoke.

As they approached the hut several children ran to greet them. A fair-haired boy with several bright feathers stuck in his unruly curls bounded up to their host, swinging a toy hatchet. A tiny girl, who had been playing "hut" in the front yard with crude wooden figures for dolls, dropped her toys and toddled down the path after her brother.

The older children worked industriously around the house, carrying wood, mending the fence, hauling water. But one by one, as they saw their father approaching, they dropped their tasks and ran to meet him. He greeted them all heartily and introduced them to George and Fairfax with great pride.

Captain Jack's wife was waiting for him in the doorway. She was a beautiful young woman with an aristocratic air— the kind of woman one would expect to find on a wealthy plantation rather than in this frontiersman's crude hut. Her face glowed with pleasure as she greeted her husband and his friends. They all went inside with her while she finished preparing the dinner.

As she bent over the stove George and Fairfax caught sight of the calico border of her petticoat. Fairfax leaned over and whispered to George, "It's the Covent Garden crossbar pattern."

"How do you know?" whispered George.

"Sally has one like it."

"My knowledge in such things is very meager," responded George, with a laugh.

They spent a pleasant time with Captain Jack and family, made friends with the lonely children, fished in the creek with the eldest boy, and that night had a wonderful dinner and slept under the roof. Next morning they were up and packed early. "Captain Jack, I've been wanting to ask you," inquired Fairfax, "aren't you afraid of the Indians here?"

"No. I'm not," replied the hunter, "but that's because I'm the Black Hunter. So far they have been friendly with me and respected my efforts to make a plantation here in the woods."

"It would probably be a good idea for us to blacken our buckskin suits," said George pleasantly.

"It would indeed. At least in your case, Washington. I see you have the earmarks of a frontiersman, but your friend Fairfax here wears clothes that came from London, if I know anything."

"They did, Captain Jack," laughed Fairfax. "I used to wear buckskin, but my young wife objects to it. Says if I have buckskin clothes lying around I want to get into them and go hunting."

"Where are you going to camp tonight?" queried the hunter.

"I know just where it is and how to get there," Fairfax replied. "I imagine this brook runs into the Sycamore creek, and somewhere near the mouth of that creek there's an open savannah. There's a bunch of big pines and a jumble of rocks where I want to camp."

"I know the place," replied the Black Hunter. "There's a new cabin there now. A settler named Hawkins has recently moved in. He's an old hand in the woods and like me is not afraid of Indians. But that's a pretty risky place he's taken up. It's right at the forks of the Indian trail. Hawkins aims to cultivate a large plantation there, and it sure is a fertile spot with little or no clearing to do. He has friends south on the Potomac, and he expects to have them join him."

"Is there a trail that leads to this Hawkins's place?"

"Yes, there's one of mine easy enough to follow if you look sharp. Come with me."

About midafternoon Fairfax and George emerged rather suddenly from the forest into a wide open area where brown high grass waved in the wind; they spied the clump of pine trees and the jumble of rocks which was their objective.

"There's the cabin, George," said Fairfax. "It surely is a fine location. I wonder why Lord Fairfax did not get possession of some of these parklike opens?"

"Hold on, Fairfax," called our George sharply. "I see Indians. There are several on foot—one on horseback. See, through the trees?"

"By jove!" ejaculated Fairfax. "You're sure right. This doesn't look so good."

"It doesn't. They see us, and if those gestures are friendly, I miss my guess. . . . They're running away! That Indian on horseback is yelling. They probably think we are not alone."

"George, that's a hostile move, if I ever saw one," returned Fairfax.

"Then the only thing to do is to ride post haste up to the cabin and see what's what. Hawkins will be there. I hope we arrive in time."

With that, the surveyors dropped the halters of their pack animals, and, spurring their horses, they galloped down to the cabin. Doors and windows were barred. George's quick eyes took in the body of an Indian lying before the cabin. Fairfax rode round the cabin and returning yelled, "Hey there, inside! We're white men—friends—the Indians have run off, but they'll probably come back. Let us in."

"You bet they'll come back," George said. His keen glance was fastened on the edge of the savannah where the Indians had been joined by several more. "Get off, Fairfax. We're in for it."

Fairfax complied, and with rifle in hand he fronted the cabin and called louder that they were white men and friends.

Then they heard the drop of a bar inside the cabin, and the heavy door swung in to disclose a young pale-faced woman with rifle in hand.

"Come in," she called. "You're just in time."

"Fairfax, give your horse a slap so he'll run in among the trees," said George, and then he turned to the door. "Young woman, are you Mrs. Hawkins?"

"Yes," she returned. "My husband expected these Indians, and he rode off for help. He ought to be back soon. Thank heavens you came," she said fervently.

"Did your husband shoot that Indian?" inquired Fairfax, as they entered the cabin.

"No. I did that. It's a wonder you didn't hear the shot," she replied. And she dropped the bar in front of the door.

"Are there any portholes in this cabin?" asked Fairfax.

"Yes, one at each end, there. They can't surprise us and they can't very well destroy this green cabin. They can't do much damage before my husband gets back here with help."

"Well, they're coming," declared George, peering through the small porthole at his end of the cabin.

"Let them come," said Fairfax grimly. "We've got three rifles and two pistols. George, how many Indians in that bunch?"

"Let's see. Five—six—six Indians all now on horseback," said George. "The cunning red devils are circling so they can come up behind the house where we can't get a shot at them."

George saw the swift riders come on apace, sweeping to the left, just out of rifle range. They were naked to the waist. Each of their sleek heads was shaved except for a tuft of hair which held a feather. They brandished guns and tomahawks, and, even at a good distance, George made out their dark lean features, repellent and sinister. Then they passed beyond his range of vision. It developed presently that there was a little boy and girl in the cabin, who had been hiding under the table. The pretty little girl was scared and speechless, but the boy, somewhat older, had flashing eyes and his red hair stood up like a mane.

"Mother, we're all right now," he said resolutely. "We can hold them off until Daddy gets back."

George's sensitive ears awakened to a strange sound. He heard the tread of moccasined feet on the roof. "Fairfax, some of them are on the roof—hear that? By thunder, they're coming down the chimney!"

"If it isn't true!" corroborated Fairfax incredulously. "What do you make of that? Pretty foolhardy, I'd say. We can take care of all the Indians that come down that chimney."

"They acted like they were drunk," spoke up Mrs. Hawkins.

"The fire is still smouldering," observed George. "Our redskinned visitor is liable to burn his feet. Fairfax, if I can believe my ears there's more than one Indian coming down that chimney."

Just then there came a rattling from up in the chimney, and some small pieces of rock fell into the fireplace followed by a rushing sound, a cloud of yellow and black dust and soot which puffed out into the cabin, hiding the fireplace from sight.

"Look out, Fairfax!" called George, and, clubbing his rifle, he backed away from the cloud. Then followed a scraping sound and a solid thud. A dark body rolled out into the room and leaped erect. It was an agile savage, brandishing a tomahawk, peering as if half-blinded through the smoke, blackened of face from his contact with the chimney. Appearing demonical, he let out a wild yell, which was answered by smothered yells from the chimney. George swung his clubbed rifle, and Fairfax fired his pistol. They both hit the savage at the same time, and he sank to the floor like an empty sack. The cloud of dust and soot thinned out. "Fairfax, stand ready. There's more of them. They must be stuck in the chimney."

"I'll fix them," declared the young woman. She seized the feather tick from her bedstead, dragged it to the fireplace, and, ripping the cloth, turned the spilling contents right upon the smouldering fire. There was a tiny blaze, then a loud puff, and roaring flame and smoke went up the chimney. The yells and frantic sudden sounds that issued from the fireplace attested to the celerity of the Indians in crawling back to escape. Shrill yells from the remaining Indians had a note of alarm, and then the rapid sound of beating hoofs followed by rifle shots proved that Hawkins and his rescuers had arrived.

George ran to his porthole in time to see one Indian running swiftly on foot and beyond him three mounted Indians galloping swiftly for safety. Rifles cracked again, and one of the Indians pitched off his horse into the high grass. Then came a pounding on the door and a hoarse voice, "Well, open if you're there; open the door!"

The young woman ran and, swiftly letting down the bar, pulled in the heavy door. A stalwart man in buckskin saw her with sudden leaping gladness in his haggard face. "Are you all right?"

"Yes, I'm all right, and so are the children. But I don't know what would have happened if these men had not arrived."

Washington Receives a Commission and Meets Christopher Gist

One late December afternoon several days before Christmas, George Washington and Fairfax arrived at Belvoir as rugged and ragged as two backwoodsmen could well be, happy to arrive home safe and sound and congratulating themselves on their labors and the way they had surmounted all danger and obstacle.

Washington refused to go in, saying that he must hurry home to see his mother, but Fairfax would not let him go until he had promised to bring his mother over for Christmas dinner. Whereupon Washington turned his weary horse and pack animal back onto the river road and traveled the last few miles to Mount Vernon. The afternoon was overcast and gloomy, with a chill wind blowing from across the river. The Potomac presented an unusual sight, being ridged like a washboard in choppy green and white ripples. The trees were bare and the fields brown and the moaning wind presaged a storm and bore a cutting edge that hinted of snow. But the weather was mild to Washington after having traveled ten days in snow over the Blue Ridge Mountains.

He was thinking that he would be glad to have a little rest at home before returning to work, this time without the companionship of Fairfax, on a surveying job farther afield and more hazardous. It would be good if he could spare the time to ride down to Williamsburg, but in lieu of that he hoped to get word from the Zanes and also instructions for his next surveying trip. The horses were both footsore and weary, and Washington dismounted and walked the last mile or so to Mount Vernon, arriving at dusk. He had unsaddled his horse and was unpacking the other when William and another slave discovered him, and their happy shouts were echoed by Negroes from the house.

Washington hurried into the sitting room, and the cheery log fire in the grate seemed to throw him a warm welcome. His mother was there, having read aright those cheery calls from outside, and she met him with outstretched arms and shining eyes.

"My son! You great ragamuffin! You bring the smell of smoke and the woods. Oh, how glad I am to see you. I knew you would come before Christmas. I've never lost you for one single day."

"Home again, Mother darling," replied Washington, hugging her. "If you are as happy as I am that will be mightily more than I deserve. You look as sweet and fresh as the day I left. Well, you'll have a lot to tell me, and I hope it will take you long so I shall not be called upon to recount all that happened to us."

"Gracious, I've heard enough!" exclaimed Mary. "Sally read that letter of Fairfax's which told how your lives were saved by a feather bed. I rejoice that you still wear that mop of tangled hair which was always my pride." She ran her hands lovingly through his hair and spread aside the long locks as if to assure him how sadly they had been neglected. "George, your scalp would be a great prize in any Indian chieftain's wigwam. But it will never adorn one!"

"Mother, there you go again with one of your old prophecies," returned Washington gaily. "They are always happy auguries. It's comforting to know that with all your mystic powers you have never predicted a dire disaster."

Washington met his growing big-eyed brothers and promised them stories that would make their hair curl. They had a joyous dinner, after which Washington and his mother sat before the sitting room fire for hours while she talked and he listened. He escaped from being compelled to narrate any of his bloodcurdling adventures. The next day was a busy one during which Washington went all over the plantation and then rode out to his little farm with William to see what state of affairs existed there. He was well pleased. William had proved himself to be a valuable overseer. The yield of tobacco that season was Washington's first large one and would prove profitable. He decided to postpone riding to Valley Forge until after Christmas. The next day Washington alternated between devotion to his mother and some important tasks and a few hours of rest. That night at dinner he remembered the Christmas dinner engagement at Belvoir.

"Oh, George!" exclaimed his mother, disappointed. "I looked forward so happily to our Christmas dinner together and alone."

"Well, Mother, I'm sorry. I promised. Fairfax would be hurt, and I'll wager Sally would ride over here after us. You can have another Christmas dinner for me."

"You need a good many wholesome dinners," she retorted. "You may be as big as a hill but you're as thin as a lath. Of course, I'll be glad to go over to Fairfax's. Did it ever occur to you, my son, that Sally, married woman as she is, who will be a mother in June, would like to have you dangling after her as you did when a boy?"

"No, mother, that never occurred to me," he replied, with a laugh. "But if it is true, it's pleasant to contemplate."

"I don't know about you, and certainly not about Sally," she said dubiously. "But what to wear at a Christmas dinner with the Fairfaxes?"

"That doesn't worry me at all, mother. You always look most gracious and distinguished, but what worries me is something to give Sally for Christmas. I've a gift for Fairfax that will be very acceptable, one of Lawrence's few remaining bottles of wine. But what on earth to get Sally?"

"Son, I can take care of that," rejoined his mother. "I have some lovely old lace that even Sally Cary would not elevate her dainty nose at."

"Good! You have saved my face, dear mother."

Once again Washington drove up to the stately house at Belvoir where the bright lights sent cheery rays into the gloom. The old Negro butler admitted them. A Negro maid led Mary upstairs, and Washington was ushered into the large warmly colored library where Fairfax met him. They were soon joined by Fairfax's father and Lord Fairfax, and greetings of the season and toasts were offered by both Lord Fairfax and his brother to these young and successful surveyors. In the quarter of an hour before they were called to dinner the conversation was wholly about the adventures of the young men.

Soon then they repaired to the brilliantly lighted dining room with its decorations of pine and green and red wreaths. Anne Washington came in with George's mother, and Mrs. Fairfax came in with Sally. Washington was prepared for the old familiar thrill and in this case with a succeeding pang. Sally looked lovelier than ever in her elaborate gown, and her radiant welcome and that of Anne and Mrs. Fairfax left Washington quite speechless and almost breathless. He had a melancholy thought of how much his life in the wilderness cost him.

It was a merry, happy Christmas gathering. Then they sat to dinner. It was a considerable repast, and, after the hard fare that Washington had been used to for months, he feared he would do himself harm. After dinner, as they all sat around the bright fire, Washington found that his friend Fairfax had made him a hero in all their eyes. And as for Sally's eyes, they were so wonderful that Washington could only withstand a fleeting glimpse into them. But despite Fairfax's exaggerated claims and the importunities the ladies directed at Washington, he managed to escape, committing himself to Fairfax's encomiums. Washington laughingly put off one question after another, sometimes agreed modestly with a smile, and at others denied Fairfax's outrageous flattery.

Later Sally, with one of her clever pretexts, led him out of the room into the dimly lighted ballroom where she halted before him to gaze up at him with bewildering eyes. "George, do you remember what happened right on this spot?" she asked.

"I certainly do, Sally," he replied ruefully. "Here is where my one ambition to be a fine dancer went into eclipse."

"George, I wanted to get you away by ourselves—of course, to be alone with you a minute, but mostly to thank you for saving Fairfax's life," she said, her rich voice earnest and low. "In there you denied all Fairfax said. That's like you, of course, but this one thing is particularly dear to my heart."

"Sally, what particular thing do you mean?" he asked.

"Oh, I know it's true. Fairfax would not lie about a thing like that. It was when, that night you got lost and had to make camp exhausted and unable to go on farther . . . Fairfax said he was awakened by something strange, the fire had burned down low, the wind moaned, the forest seemed so wild and inhospitable, he heard a rustle and raised himself to see a hideous savage kneeling over him with uplifted tomahawk . . . and—and then . . . do you remember, George?"

"Sally, I'm not likely to forget that. The most terribly poignant moment of my life."

"But you saved him!" burst out Sally passionately, her eyes flashing dark in her white face.

"Sally, perhaps I ought to admit that. I must have saved Fairfax," replied Washington ponderingly. "But his reactions to peril are instant and wonderful. He's as quick as lightning. He might have rolled out from under that Indian's tomahawk and have shot him without any intervention of mine."

"Oh, George," she whispered softly. "You who cannot tell a lie!"

"Well, Sally, it happened this way. It was salvation for me as well as Fairfax. I crippled that Indian and gave Fairfax time to grasp his gun and kill him. The other Indians creeping towards me were frightened and, rising out of the grass, they ran. I think I winged one of them before they got out of sight and—and that is all."

"That is quite enough, George Washington," murmured Sally. "I flatter myself that I have at last got a meritorious admission from you. Now, Fairfax is never going to leave me again on one of those wild trips. Later I will try to persuade you to do the same, but that is probably his last narrow escape. I love him very dearly. We have everything—or soon will have everything to live for. And I want to—I must thank you."

She was clinging to him now, her face upraised, more enchanting and devastating than ever before.

"Sally, to see you like that is thanks enough. It makes me very happy," returned Washington gravely. "Let's return to the others before—before you go back to your schoolgirl days."

"What can I do to thank you?" she flung at him with sweet fire.

"Sally, I'm quite—concerned—about what you *might* do."

"Oh, merciful heaven, how I wish I could have two husbands."

"Sally! Well, you can't," returned Washington, managing a rather hollow laugh. She was beyond understanding at that moment. He felt impelled to think with lightning swiftness, as if there was as much at stake as that night when he had saved Fairfax's life.

"George, do you remember the night of my party? When we were alone on the porch?" she went on softly, her voice no longer steady.

"Yes, I remember, Sally. That made up a thousandfold for my shame and anger. But, my dear, this moment does not call for anything like that. You two are my dearest friends. I love you both. It seems that ever since I was a boy when I came to love something or somebody I just went on loving them. And so it will be forever."

"Thank you, George Washington," she whispered, suddenly relaxing. "I might have known you would talk like that. It is one reason why I have always loved you. But I will reward you or be shamed forever. George, I promised you a sweetheart. A beautiful Virginia girl of blood and race—one who will take my place and make you happy, one who could appreciate your greatness. To my shame I confess that I could not do it; during your absence I met two Virginia girls, more deserving of you than I ever was, but I was too little—too miserable—too much a jealous little cat to keep my word and win one of them for you. But I shall do it yet. I swear to you. I must find you a sweetheart or I can never be happy."

Washington returned to his surveying work. He secured a middle-aged woodsman named Andrews as a helper and with two trustworthy Negroes they spent the winter in the lowlands of Virginia running lines for the government.

As soon as the snow melted off the trails over the Blue Ridge, Washington led his little company over the well-remembered trails to work left undone the year before. He was to meet Captain Jack again and to be advised by that hunter either to get out of the country or spend half his time keenly on the lookout for hostile savages. Then followed brushes with the Indians, several narrow escapes, a fight which they won but in which they were all wounded, and long weeks in the forest surveying their line. Life in the woods satisfied him. He was doing good work, saving his wages, exercising all the woodcraft he had learned, and every day adding to his store of knowledge about how to preserve his life in the wilderness.

In a fight with wandering savages of an unknown tribe, one of the Negroes was wounded and the other one killed. They hid in the deep recesses of the forest until the Negro could travel and then took him back to Fredericksburg. This time Washington journeyed to Williamsburg to make his report to the Governor, and incidentally to see the Zanes. He grieved to learn that Ebenezer Zane, the father of this interesting family, had died and that his eldest son had gone off alone on an exploring trip to the Ohio, leaving word to his friends and brothers that when he returned this time he would lead them to a wonderful country in the west. After returning to Mount Vernon, Washington found awaiting him a letter from Silas Zane. Zane stated that when Ebenezer returned to Williamsburg he was ready to go with him to the Ohio Valley, and if Washington was available, he would gladly take him along. Meanwhile, Silas went on to say, he had been traveling in the eastern provinces and when he did have the pleasure of meeting Washington again, he would have a great deal to tell him about the ferment that was growing in the breasts of the colonists.

"There it is again," mused Washington, as he reread Zane's letter. "I don't want to know what it means, but it is evident that the life and work I have now is more to be desired than to become a slave in this colony."

On his next trip over the Blue Ridge he inquired at every post about his friends, the Zanes. But he could not obtain knowledge of their whereabouts. It occurred to him then that in six more months when his contract expired he might take the Zanes' trail and follow it to the Ohio. A hunter who could trail a savage in the forest would have no difficulty on a white man's track. This was a fascinating thought that persisted in Washington's waking and sleeping hours. When he returned he took care not to mention it to his mother.

One more long trip still farther afield finished the work that had been allotted him. It was with regret that he ran the last line and worked out his last figures in that wonderful wild country beyond the Blue Ridge. He wondered what he would have to do when he returned to Mount Vernon. He would like to stay home with his mother for a while. There was much grafting of fruit trees that he wanted to do and other improvements on his slowly prospering plantations. It would be good to get relief from this constant vigilance, from the necessity of seeing or hearing savages first, from the rough work and hard fare and sleeping with one eye open. He had been almost continuously in the forest for two years, and he thought, if he did say it of himself, that he would be a good man to join the Zanes on the Ohio. And so, with these thoughts in his mind changing and augmenting, he turned back over the Blue Ridge, down to Fredericksburg and so on back to Mount Vernon.

His mother, welcoming him home even more joyful than usual, almost in the same breath acquainted him with the news that Governor Robert Dinwiddie of Virginia had heard of his fine work in the mountains, that he had an important commission for him which called for all the intelligence and diplomacy of an English gentleman as well as the hardihood and daring of an Indian frontiersman.

When Washington arrived in Williamsburg and was promptly ushered into the presence of His Excellency Governor Dinwiddie of Virginia, he, with difficulty, contained himself and did not let curiosity and strong anticipation interfere with calm and dignified demeanor. He had divined that this was to be an important interview for him, and the courtesy he received at the hands of Governor Dinwiddie's aides verified his conviction. The Governor was a large man with florid countenance, shrewd eyes, and graying hair, and his bearing was one of military authority. He greeted Washington affably and took him in with a speculative glance.

"Mr. Washington, I have sent for you to discuss a very important mission which I want you to take to the commandant of the French forces on the Ohio River. It is a dangerous mission. If you are interested we will discuss it further."

"Your Excellency, I am very much honored in your sending for me, and I may say that I am very deeply interested."

"Good! That is what I have been led to expect," returned the Governor with satisfaction. "Some time ago you were recommended to me by the late Ebenezer Zane who was my friend and who has furnished me with much information about the country beyond the Blue Ridge. I have also heard from Lord Fairfax and the government surveyor James Genn. I could not ask for any better guarantees of a man's ability."

"Thank you, sir. I am indebted to them."

"Very well then. We will go on." Here the Governor consulted papers on his desk. "The lands upon the River Ohio in the western parts of the Colony of Virginia are so notoriously known to be the property of the Crown of Great Britain that it is a matter of equal concern and surprise to me to hear that a body of French forces are erecting fortresses and making settlements upon that river within his Majesty's dominions. These are the bare facts. My information is meager. But I have learned and certainly you will appreciate that this mission calls for a man who is first of all a frontiersman and then a man of sound judgment, keen intelligence, and a faculty for making friends with the Indians. England is going to have trouble with France, in fact, is having it now, and there is great likelihood of a war over this Ohio Valley. The Indians are going to side with the French, at least some of the tribes will. Have you any opinion on that matter?"

"No, sir. I have found the Indians amiable in a good many instances."

"You have done your surveying under hazardous circumstances?"

"Yes, sir. It would not be strictly true to say that it was not dangerous, but we managed to get the lines through all right."

"Lord Fairfax writes that over a period of two years you outwitted the Indians, evaded them or fought them, and that sometimes you have had to kill Indians to save your scalp."

"Your Excellency, I would like to deny that last, but I cannot honestly do so," returned Washington seriously.

"Your surveying work in Virginia was child's play compared to this frontiersman's mission that I want you to undertake. Will you undertake it as Major George Washington, as onc of my Adjutant Generals of the Dominion?"

"Your Excellency, I accept with gratitude and will serve you with all the ability I have."

"Good, Major Washington," returned the Governor. "Your mission is to proceed to the Ohio River and complain to these French forces that they must withdraw. You will learn all possible as to the extent of these French forces and where other French forces are located down the Ohio River and the Mississippi as far as New Orleans. The need of making friends of the Indian chiefs is cardinally important. You will learn all you can about the tribes in Ohio and about the country round and about the Forks of the Ohio. It may be necessary for the English forces to erect forts, and you will be required to pick out strategic points. You will take the necessary equipment, engage French and Indian interpreters and what men you will need to serve you as helpers, including the best frontiersmen you can find. Your pay as major will treble what you earned as a surveyor, and if you are successful in this undertaking there will be advancement for you."

Washington, with his commission and instructions, bowed himself out of the Governor's office and, thrilled as never before in his life at the prospect ahead of him, hurried to the Zane homestead where he hoped to find some of the boys. He regretted deeply that he would not be able to thank their father, Ebenezer Zane, for having put this great opportunity in his way. He found only the younger boys, Isaac and Andrew, at home. Silas was touring the colonies on a mission about which the boys were mysterious. Ebenezer and Jonathon with the Wetzels were on a protracted hunt beyond the Blue Ridge, and Betty was at school in Philadelphia.

"We're waiting patiently, Mr. Washington," said Isaac. "When Ebenezer comes back this time, we'll pack up and make for our new country on the Ohio. We don't like it here."

"Well, boys, I am going to learn something about this Ohio River," returned Washington, "and it is possible that I will run across your brothers or at least hear about them, and if so, I will send you a letter. In the meantime, if Ebenezer comes home soon, please tell him that Governor Dinwiddie has appointed me to visit the French and Indian forces on the Ohio and inform them that they must move out of his Majesty's Dominion. They may mean war."

"War!" echoed the boys, in unison. "Will the colonists have to fight the French and Indians?"

"No. That will be for his Majesty's soldiers, but I am sure many of the colonists, especially the hunters like you boys, will be asked to volunteer. And if I am called upon to find volunteers, I will certainly remember you Zanes and the Wetzels."

Washington took the stage for Fredericksburg and, the same day he arrived, engaged Jacob Vanbraam as his French interpreter. He was still under middle age, and his supple and wiry frame indicated his athletic prowess. He was a famous swordsman. With this man, Washington traveled to Alexandria and from there to Winchester where he bought horses and equipment, camp duffle and utensils, and a goodly lot of supplies. Then they proceeded up the Shenandoah over a trail familiar to Washington which was now called the New Road.

The weather was cold and in part rainy, and the two men had a hard and uncomfortable trip as far as Wills Creek. Washington knew men there he could engage to accompany him, and he very much desired men who would be trustworthy as well as experienced. As luck would have it, Washington found his two Indian trader acquaintances, Currin and Macguire, at home and very glad to go with him. They recommended two hunters, Stewart and Jenkins, as the other two helpers they would need. On the following day with this company of men fully armed and equipped, Washington left the settlements and struck out into the wilderness. He still had to engage his guide, and, according to the traders, he would surely find the right man when they arrived at the Monongahela settlements.

They traveled by plantation roads where available and soon left those for the Indian trails. It was a method of travel that Washington liked best. They rode leisurely through the forest and up the open valleys, camping where sunset found them. But for the frequent rains, the swollen streams they had to ford, and the scarcity of game, the riding and camp tasks would have been pleasant indeed. But outside the actual time spent in the saddle, it was work. The November wind and frost had whipped the trees bare, and the colorful beauty of the foliage that Washington loved was wanting. Nevertheless, Washington began at once to learn what was available from his men and to spend many hours pondering how he would handle the situation when he got among the French and Indians on the Ohio. Sometimes in camp, Washington took a lesson in swordsmanship from Vanbraam, and he often rode beside one of the traders where he passed the long hours on the trails by learning what Indian languages they knew. His old habit of acquiring knowledge and storing it up began now to be an important adjunct to his new work.

When opportunity afforded Washington would ride off the trail and climb an eminence from which he tried to get a view of the country. They were traveling away from the Blue Ridge that daily grew dimmer in the distance. He was keen to get his first sight of the Allegheny Mountains about which he had heard a great deal. He did not expect that his present mission would take him into the Alleghenies, but he was sure to get a sight of them.

Washington had been informed that Christopher Gist, the best-known frontiersman in that country, might be met on the trail coming from Monongahela, and for that reason he clung to the main trail. He could hardly have been more vigilant than was his habit, but one day when they halted about midafternoon to make some much needed repairs of a pack saddle, Washington took his rifle and slipped along the trail looking for wild turkey or deer. He had proceeded about a mile from camp when he espied a big turkey gobbler that walked into the trail and then stood motionless, his long head erect and his wonderful plumage shining in the sunlight. The turkey was suspicious so Washington froze in his tracks and raised his rifle so slowly and cautiously that the wild turkey did not catch the movement. Then the rifle froze for an instant and belched forth its red and yellow contents. The turkey flopped over, buffeted the ground and brush with its huge wings, and then lay still.

Taking pride in that excellent shot, Washington began to step off the distance. His strides were long, and when he had counted two hundred, his sharp eye caught a movement ahead on the trail. Again Washington froze in his tracks. He had been trained to take instant heed of any unusual movement in the forest. This might have been the flash of a bird, or of a buck's tail, or a gray animal of some kind, but Washington did not think that it was. After a moment of keen peering ahead he stepped off the trail to reload his rifle. That accomplished, he once more began to move along the trail with his keen eyes wavering like a compass needle, and again he saw that flash. It was gray in color and either belonged to a deer or a hunter in a buckskin. It might have been an Indian. Washington stepped behind a tree and peered cautiously out. He saw the gray thing again, just a tiny bit of moving color, and this time he would have sworn that it was made by the leg of an Indian or a white man.

Without more ado Washington slowly thrust his rifle from behind the tree, and, cocking it, he got ready to shoot. An instant later he saw a gray hairy object protrude from behind a tree some yards beyond where his turkey lay in the trail. He did not stop to think beyond the fact that if it belonged to a human being it was an ominous action. Drawing a quick bead on the object, he fired. Almost simultaneously with his shot came the report of a similar rifle and the bullet from it glanced off the barrel of his rifle and went spang into the forest. No Indian could shoot that well. That shot had come from a white man.

"Hello, there!" shouted Washington lustily.

"Hullo, yourself," came the loud reply.

"White man, what are you spying on me for?"

"I reckoned you was doing the same to me. And you shot a hole through my coonskin cap."

"Well, what did you stick it out for? I'm George Washington, surveyor. If you are Christopher Gist, I'm looking for you."

With those words, a tall, buckskin-clad figure stepped from the green out into the trail and the owner of it called, "Wal, you was looking a little too darn sharp to suit me. I'm Gist all right, and I've heard a lot about you, young fellar."

They advanced along the trail and, meeting at the point where the wild turkey lay with his colorful feathers spread everywhere, shook hands. Washington saw a rugged and hardened frontiersman, a man between forty and fifty whose dark weather-beaten face and clear gray eyes impressed him favorably at first sight.

"I heard at Wills Creek you were coming from the Monongahela settlements, and I was looking for you," said Washington. "But I expected to meet you on a horse."

"Wal, I travel a good deal on shank's mare," returned the other. "Hawses are very well, but they get you in trouble easy in this Injun country. That's a fine gobbler you shot. I heard your rifle and I reckoned there was a Injun-hunter along the trail. Where's your camp?"

"About a mile back," replied Washington, and, picking up the turkey by the feet, he flung it over his shoulder. "Come back to camp with me and have dinner."

"What might you be wanting of me?" inquired Gist, as they walked abreast down the trail.

Washington briefly told him about the mission on which Governor Dinwiddie had sent him and that he very much wanted the services of Gist as guide and comrade on that precarious journey along the Ohio. Washington went on to say that if Gist's return to Wills Creek was important he might return along the trail and catch them before they got to the Monongahela.

"Wal, Washington, I reckon I can about face and go right along with you," returned the frontiersman thoughtfully. "I've nothing to do at Wills Creek that can't wait. I'm employed by the Ohio Company in more than one capacity and going right along with you fits in with it. Fact is, I'll be glad to go with you. Of course you have horses and supplies with you?"

"Yes," returned Washington, and proceeded to tell about the men and equipment he had with him.

"Know them all," said Gist, "except Vanbraam. And you couldn't get no better men. You'll need them too. The French are in strong force over in the Ohio country and they've got a lot of the Injuns on their side, and winning more all the time. If Dinwiddie wants to drive them back, he'll have to send an army and it's got to be a big one, for the Frenchmen have learned from the Injuns how to fight in the woods, and they'll take a lot of licking."

"I am afraid of that very thing," replied Washington ponderingly. "I needn't say how glad and fortunate I am to have you come along with me. You shall be well paid, and if my fortunes are in the ascendant, as something persuades me they are, it will be a very profitable connection for you."

On the remaining walk down the trail to camp Gist held forth about the Ohio River Valley, its marvelous possibilities, of what an empire there was in the making, and that the few hardy pioneers who were venturing into it had vision and were men of heroic mold. Listening to the backwoodsman talk, Washington could not help but congratulate himself on the good luck that had attended him. Gist was the oldest and most experienced frontiersman Washington had met. And now, with his party complete, the prospects ahead were thrilling in the extreme. Here was a woodsman who traveled light like the Zanes and the Wetzels and Captain Jack. He had a small knapsack over his shoulder, a powder horn and bullet pouch, and in his belt a tomahawk and knife. They arrived at camp, and the welcome his men gave Gist further made Washington appreciate the frontiersman. As the sun sank they had dinner and then talked beside the camp fire. One of Washington's men, Stewart, put a question that had been on Washington's lips. "How about Indians between here and Monongahela?"

"Wal, I ain't seen none, and all the tracks on the trail have been pretty old. None of them made since this rainy spell set in. I reckon we won't see any reddies before we get to the settlement."

"And how long will that take us?" asked Washington.

"Wal, I walked it in three days, but you ain't likely to make it that fast riding hawseback. Let's say four days, comfortable."

On the second day from the meeting with Gist the trail came out on the Monongahela River. It was not as broad as the Potomac, but it was the same deep and slow stream meandering between densely wooded banks and, as Washington had heard, a splendid waterway for canoe travel. The Allegheny River, Gist said, was about the same size but was a swift and turbulent stream coming down out of the mountains to meet the Monongahela at what they called the Forks, the source of the great Ohio.

"The Forks is whar the English want to build a big fort before the French do it. You never in your born days saw such a grand place for a fort, and it will be needed for the war that's coming and later for the pioneers that are going to troop into Ohio."

It was well that Christopher Gist was not only an experienced frontiersman but loquacious and glad to talk as long as anybody was interested. They kept him up late that night, and, when Washington went to bed under the trees with a warm camp fire near at hand and the raindrops pattering off the swaying branches and the moan of wind overhead, he had it come home to him stronger than ever that his wildest dreams were going to be realized. He would need all his knowledge and a sagacity to cope with the physical obstacles and all he could learn from such men as Gist, with intelligence that he prayed would come to him, to carry Governor Dinwiddie's mission to a successful outcome.

Next day they made upwards of twenty-five miles along the river trail through such dense timber that Washington welcomed the few times that they got out of the shade. It was not a pleasant ride by reason of the dark sky and the squalls of rain and bitter wind, but the exercise kept Washington warm. He had always thought he was a good walker himself, but this frontiersman had anyone beaten that Washington had ever known. He was tireless, and on the trail as he led the way he was taciturn and gave all his faculties to the forest ahead. Next day they had spells of open country, and there, being met by snow squalls, Washington was wishing they were back in the forest again. The streams that fed the Monongahela were flooded, and it was hardly possible for the men to ford them without getting wet.

When late in the day, on November fourteenth, they rode into the outskirts of the settlements, it was none too soon for

George Washington. The rude clearings in the forest which left dead trees standing, ghastly and bare, and the crude huts, larger log buildings, and canvas tents here and there, wholly without picturesqueness let alone beauty, were nevertheless a welcome sight. The columns of blue smoke that curled aloft were indications of shelter and warmth and good meals and for the time being were a guarantee of protection. Farms and plantations spread out on both sides of the Monongahela. It looked like a rich and fertile country, and its promise was great. All that was needed here were willing hands and hearts. And as to that, Washington was greatly surprised to find this outpost on the edge of the wilderness as populous as it was. Gist guided them to a tavern where they were made comfortable and their horses and equipment taken care of. A wholesome but plain supper was placed before them after which Gist led Washington out to see the post and to meet some of the men stationed there. Washington's men followed, all deeply interested in this growing settlement.

The trading post was run by a man named Daniels, a hearty, bluff Englishman comparatively new to the country and one evidently with means enough to have built himself a large log cabin post. The spacious room was full of merchandise and had a huge open fireplace at one end where pine logs now blazed and at one side a drinking bar before which were lined a motley crowd of men. Washington stayed in the background and listened to Gist and Daniels and his own men as they mingled with the crowd.

There were several coureurs de bois present, and Washington was particularly interested to hear Vanbraam converse with them. He had read about the exploits of these Canadian canoeists all over the lake country and the St. Lawrence waterway. A number of colonists came into the post having heard of the new arrivals, and their welcome to Washington and his party were proof of the gladness that pioneers showed to newcomers. There were soldiers and frontiersmen in their picturesque garb and also a group of Indians, who kept aloof in the background. The chieftain was a man of commanding presence, and he wore a rich and beaded costume. Washington wanted to make the acquaintance of these Indians when occasion afforded it.

One of the colonists, a young man named McKnight, appealed particularly to him, and they talked for some moments and planned to further their acquaintance on the morrow. McKnight, whose family lived in Monongahela, was keenly interested in Washington's mission. They were from New York and had journeyed west to give themselves to the pioneer life. McKnight frankly spoke of his servitude in the New York Colony and wanted no more of it. He was another of that slowly growing number of discontented colonists who had revolution in their hearts even if they did not let it pass their lips. Washington wondered about that rapidly augmenting number and what it foretold for the future.

McKnight insisted that Washington should have a drink with him, and they proceeded to the bar. Here, Washington came into close contact with several roughly garbed backwoodsmen, only one of whom had a smooth shaven face. He was a tall man striking in his soiled and stained buckskin and in addition to the knife and tomahawk in his belt there was a pistol. Washington never forgot a face, and he had seen this man somewhere. He might once have had prepossessing features, but now they were sodden and coarse from dissipation.

When this man turned to look squarely at Washington there followed a blank, stultifying moment after which Washington recognized him. He was none other than Red Burke. Washington was astounded, and then as he met the baleful glare in Burke's hot, dark eyes, he sensed that old fiery thrill along his veins. It was manifest that Burke recognized him now, and it was pretty certain that he had recognized him on their last meeting in Fredericksburg. Washington sensed untoward events. McKnight ordered their drinks but before they were served Burke shoved his way between two of his comrades, saying in a loud voice, "Men, here's a fellow I know." Then confronting Washington, he added, "Howdy, George. I heard you were coming to this country. You're ambitious, but you won't last long out here."

"Hello, Red Burke," returned Washington calmly. "That remains to be seen, but I don't take your remark as friendly."

"Friendly, hell! You'd be crazy if you did. I haven't forgotten. God knows I haven't any reason to be glad to see you, but I am. If you go on wild-goose chases here to make friends with the Indians, I'll get even with you."

"Burke, if you feel that way about it, why not try it now?" suggested Washington, with a coldness that belied the burst of heat within.

At this juncture Christopher Gist joined the party, and if he had not heard Burke's nasty speech he could easily tell by the man's face that he was angry at Washington. "What's this, Washington?" he asked quietly. "Do you know this Red Wolf?"

"Gist, I'm sorry to say that I do know him. I went to school with him. His name was Michael Burke."

"Wal, his name out here is Red Wolf. What air you spoiling for, Red?"

Burke sneered at Gist and moved his blazing eyes upon Washington. "I was just glad to meet my old schoolmate and rival, George Washington."

"Wal, he's *Major* George Washington now, in his Majesty's service," retorted Gist.

"To hell with that!" cried Burke harshly. "He's milk-sop George Washington to me! Sally Cary could have been his sweetheart! Writer of lovesick verses to Lucy Grimes, but never had the nerve to kiss her—which was easy enough for us other boys!"

"Burke, shut up," replied Washington hotly. "You mention the name of those girls again, I'll do worse than whip you with a blacksnake whip!"

"You will like hell," retorted Burke savagely. "Not out here!"

As Washington lunged at Burke, the sturdy Gist intervened and came between them, careful to face Burke. "Look hyar, you damn renegade," he rasped, "Major Washington can't fight the likes of you. You are an outcast from the colonies. Now git out of hyar with your backwoods pards!"

"Gist, you can bet your life Washington has not heard the last from Red Wolf!" hoarsely replied Burke, and turning back to his comrades he led them away toward the door of the post.

"Renegade!" ejaculated Washington, his gaze coming back to Gist. "What do you mean?"

"Wal, it doesn't sound so good," returned Gist. "Your old schoolmate is one of the white men whose gone Injun out hyar on the border. There's lots of them. It's not generally known that Red Wolf is hand and glove with the several tribes of Injuns not friendly to the whites, but I know it."

"Renegade! Michael Burke fallen to that low estate," returned Washington, profoundly moved.

"Wal, it's true, and I reckon true of better men than Burke," replied Gist, "and it ain't good news for us. I don't know if he's friendly with the French yet but that would be easy if he's thick with the Hurons. You'll hear of Red Wolf again, Washington, and when you meet I advise you to see him first. You've got Injun eyes, Washington, you saw me first. As this hyar coonskin cap of mine shore testifies." And taking his cap off, he grimly ran one of his big forefingers through the hole that Washington's bullet had made.

"You mean he'll ambush me on a trail, if he can? An Indian trick!"

"Exactly. I reckon he was as scared of you as he was mad. You had a fight with him once?"

"Yes, indeed I had, Gist, and I shall live to rue my bad temper," returned Washington soberly.

"Wal, Washington, quick temper ain't such a poor asset out here on the border. You've gotta have spunk and do things quick. Come over hyar and meet my Injun friends. They belong to the Oneida tribe. This chief is Black Hawk. Scarrooyaddy is another Oneida chief. He's a great friend of the whites. He speaks English and will be of great help to us, but he ain't hyar now. Call your interpreter. I reckon you'll like the old chief's daughter. All the young white men hyar at the post have been keen about her, and I could never see that it done them any good. Your friend Red Wolf is thick with a lot of these Injuns, but he never got nowhere with the Oneidas."

12 Washington Meets the Oneida and Delaware Tribes

Washington went with Gist, accompanied by his interpreter Vanbraam and young McKnight, to be presented to the Oneidas. He had noted the chieftain before, though not at close hand and now found him to be an imposing figure, with a dark, stern-lined face. The young daughter, Winona, whom Gist had called a squaw, struck Washington with most agreeable surprise. He thought Indian princess would have been a more felicitous name to call her. Her buckskin garb set off her lithesome figure to advantage. He had not seen many young Indian girls, and this one was exceedingly pretty. She had a small regal head crowned by hair as black as coal dust, her piquant face was a sort of dark golden tan, and her dusky eyes, which she kept shyly half veiled with downcast lashes, were very beautiful. Washington shook hands with her, and the little hand which he gallantly bent over was a further surprise to him. He had supposed squaws' hands were large and calloused from labor, but this girl's hand was small, and, though it was supple and strong, it was not hard. When the chief asked through the interpreter what the Major's mission was in that country, Washington found himself called upon for the first time to choose his words carefully.

"I have been sent by the British government to make friends with the Indians and to warn the French to get out of the Ohio River Valley."

The chief then asked what Indians, and Washington replied any and all Indians who wanted to keep the peace with the whites and be on friendly relations.

"The Great White Chief cannot take the Indians' land and then expect to be friends," said the Oneida.

Major Washington agreed and assured the chief that he in all his personal relations with the Indians would promise full compensation for any injustice done to them. The chief replied that the Oneidas and some of the other tribes were friendly, but the Hurons had become hostile and the Shawnees and the Mingoes had gone over to the French. There was bound to be war. Washington, finding that he had favorably impressed the chief, grew wary in his replies and was careful not to promise anything that he could not keep. He let it be plainly seen that his sympathy was with the red man. He desired Black Hawk to understand that the English would be fairer to the Indian tribes than the French.

Washington's rather long speech was slowly delivered and eloquently spoken, and toward the end he saw that the Indian girl had forgotten her shyness and was watching him with great dusky eyes alight with wonder and interest. Black Hawk asked the Major to visit the Oneida encampment on the Monongahela, and Washington promised to do so. He would have promised in any event, but he was not oblivious to the fact that the Indian girl's dusky eyes were nothing if not alluring. The pleasant and interesting conversation was rudely disrupted by a coarse sarcastic voice: "Hey there, George Washington! I wouldn't miss the chance to send Sally Fairfax word that you're keen after an Indian squaw."

Washington actually jumped with rage at that insolent taunting voice. Red Burke with his comrades was passing the group, and the leer on Burke's face was not possible to overcome. Washington made at him but was prevented by McKnight who seized his arm and by Gist who stood in front of him. That enabled Burke to pass on, and his hollow mocking laugh came through the door as he departed.

"Hold on, Major," interposed Gist. "It wouldn't do for you to follow those men outside."

"Major, that renegade is certain to come to a bad end," spoke up McKnight. "He's been hot after Winona, but the girl's father would have none of him. As a matter of fact, we all admire that Indian girl. I confess to a weakness myself. Winona understood what he said to you, and she certainly saw what you would have done to Red Wolf if we had let you go. Look at her! If you want to see a pair of blazing magnificent eyes, look!"

But Washington did not look. He was still in the grip of passion. Bowing to the Indians and excusing himself to his friends, he left their presence and sought his room. Composure came to him presently, and he was grateful to Gist and McKnight for preventing him making a spectacle of himself. He was astounded at the way his temper ambushed him, and the thought came to him that out here on the border life was going to be primitive, and if it were to be preserved, dignity and forebearance would have to go by the board. In the future he would avoid Red Wolf, but he had a premonition that ultimately that would not be possible. How his taunting jibe had galled Washington! He had no doubt but that Burke would keep his word and write Sally that her old friend had succumbed to the charm of an Indian squaw. At length, blowing out his candle, he went to bed. And the aftermath of his wrath was indulging in pleasant remembrances of the Oncida maid. Washington mused that Pocahontas might have been like that. If she had been anything like Winona, he certainly did not blame Captain Smith. The inference to be gotten from McKnight was that the Oneida chieftain's daughter was as good as she was beautiful, and Washington, pondering the strange hidden phases of character that he could never be sure of himself, ruefully acknowledged that it would be just as well for him not to see that Indian girl again.

The next morning after breakfast, Washington applied himself with tremendous interest to a rudely drawn map which Gist placed before him.

"Major, this hyar is a map of Ohio beyond the river. Of course it's not anyways accurate, but in a general way it will give you some idea about getting that big country clear in your mind. You know Virginia used to be part of Ohio and far to the west there isn't much known about Ohio."

Gist went on to say that the vast and fertile Ohio wilderness was the home of numerous powerful Indian tribes. Along its southern and eastern border ran the broad river. The name Ohio was Huron, and it meant Great. The Hurons believed that the Ohio ran straight on to the Gulf. Cornplanter, the chief of the great Shawnee tribe, occupied a large part of Ohio not far south of the Forks of the river. Far across the wilderness to the southwest lived the Miamis. The Mingoes and the Oneidas lived in eastern Ohio. The Wyandottes, one of the most powerful and hostile tribes, occupied central and northern Ohio. Their chief was a great warrior named Tarhe, meaning Crane, which appellation had been given him because of his great height. Pontise, the Ottawa chief, ruled his tribe in the Auglaize river country. He was one of the wise chieftains with whom the English and the French and the colonists would have to deal. There was a tribe of Cherokees in the extreme south, but not much was known about them in the white settlements around Monongahela.

"Major Washington, that ain't naming all the tribes," went on Gist, "but that numbers most of them. You'll think Ohio's sure full of redskins. Wal, it is, but it's a big country, on vast forest land cut up by many rivers, some flowing north into the great lakes and the others south into the Ohio."

"Gist, I fear I am somewhat stunned," confessed Washington. "If some of these tribes align themselves with the French—"

"Wal, they ain't no ifs about it. They have done it," interrupted Gist.

"Then how will England ever drive the French out of the Ohio Valley?"

"My guess is that they ain't a-going to do it very soon. English soldiers can't fight these Injuns, and the French that have worked down from Quebec have been so long used to this country and the Injuns that they fight like the Injuns. Scarrooyaddy agrees with me that his Majesty's army will get hell licked out of it a few times first off, but of course England will win eventually."

"You've mentioned Scarrooyaddy before. Tell me about him."

"He's an Oneida chief, not so high in rank as Black Hawk. If we could take him with us on this mission, it would be good for us, but he ain't available."

"Can you mark on the map where the French forces are located?"

"No, I can't, but we will find out when we get down on the Ohio."

"Is there any reason why we should not go on at once?" asked Washington.

"Wal, nothing I know of except high water. As the weather gets colder the rivers will run down."

That afternoon Washington's company, not to be daunted by bad weather and rough travel, proceeded on down the Monongahela and made camp some miles from the settlements late that afternoon. The next afternoon they reached the mouth of Turtle Creek where a man named Frazier had an Indian trading post. He put Washington's party up for the night. He owned quite an establishment and there were a number of Indians present and several white men in his employ. Frazier imparted some disturbing information that had not yet reached the Monongahela settlement. Messengers had gone down the river to carry news to the traders that the French general, Paul, who had been sent to build a fort at the junction of the Allegheny and the Monongahela rivers, had died and that the French soldiers were going into winter quarters to wait till spring before building the fort. This would be called Fort Duquesne.

"We are not getting here any too soon," observed Washington. "I wonder if Governor Dinwiddie had any conception of the magnitude of the mission upon which he sent me?"

"Hell no," returned the frontiersman. "Nobody has any idea of what's going on in this country until they get hyar."

They discussed the many angles of this disturbing news until a late hour. Frazier was not at all optimistic about the success of Washington's enterprise. "If you can win over Half King and some of the other Indian chiefs, it will make the stand stronger. But I don't believe the French will get out of the valley."

Next day Turtle Creek was pouring a muddy flood into the Monongahela, and Washington decided to obtain canoes from Frazier and to send Currin and Stewart to transport the baggage down the river to the Forks. Washington and the rest of his men followed the river trail with the plan of swimming their horses across at the most favorable point. Gist picked out a ford some miles from Fraziers' post and here they took to the river. It might have been a good ford at low water, but at this stage it was hardly passable. Vanbraam was swept from his horse and was rescued by Gist and Washington only after persistent, hard work. Jenkins and Macguire luckily made the ford without wetting their powder and had their rifles available in case of necessity. Washington got soaked to the skin with the cold muddy water, and the priming of his rifle and pistol was even spoiled. Fortunately his powder horn did not leak. He was, however, most miserably cold and uncomfortable on the rest of the ride down to the Forks.

The two traders had made camp at the Forks, and a bright camp fire and hot meal were very much to Washington's satisfaction. He allowed his wet clothing to dry on his back, and he made the best of the trader's good supper. It was still some time before sunset, and Washington, studying the two rivers and the point of land at their junction and the birthplace of the broad Ohio, was deeply struck with the picturesque location despite the leafless trees and cold dreary landscape. In his mind's eye he envisioned a fort on the triangular height of land above the rivers. There was enough big timber on that point to erect a large fort and the log cabins that would be sure to follow. It would have command of the Allegheny River as well as the Monongahela which ran up to the English settlements, and there was deep water at the confluence of the Monongahela and the Allegheny which would be suitable for any kind of water transportation. The Allegheny was a swift, turbulent stream at this season, and it came tearing down from the mountains carrying driftwood upon its yellow current. At the mouth the rivers were broad and ran nearly at right angles. It was a most wonderful sight and Washington wondered that the French had not already taken advantage of it, and he was disgusted with the English for being so lax in this regard.

"Major, we'll rest hyar tonight and dry out," Gist was saying, "and tomorrow we'll go on down the river. We'll let the traders take the baggage down the river in the canoes and we'll stop at the camp of the Delawares where my company intends to erect a post. Shingiss is the chief of the Delawares. He is a friend of mine, and he is sure to like you and be favorably impressed by your mission."

That night Washington wrote quite at length in his diary.

> Besides a fort at the Fork might be built at a much less Expence, than at the other place.
>
> Nature has well contrived this lower place for Water Defence; but the Hill whereon it must stand being about a quarter of a Mile in Length, and then descending gradually on the Land Side, will render it difficult and very expensive, to make a sufficient fortification there.—The whole Flat upon the Hill must be taken in, the Side next the Descent made extremely high, or else the Hill itself cut away: otherwise the Enemy may raise Batteries within that Distance without being exposed to a single Shot from the Fort.

It rained hard that night, but Washington lay warm in his blankets in his tent and enjoyed the patter and drum of the rain above his head. He was conscious of excitement and the difficulty of controlling agitation roused by the growing importance of his mission. He had to bear in mind the dangers of the expedition, but that took second place in his mind, and in fact he reveled in it. Already his little contact with the border had made him speculate on the great problem the Indians would have here on the Ohio frontier, and, beyond this mission of his, whether it was successful or not, he would have much to do with that country. It was intriguing to think of traveling down the broad Ohio in canoes or on a raft down to the island the Zanes had told him about; he wondered how far it was and if they were already there. Sleep did not soon visit his eyelids. He thought of undeniable romance of the Ohio Valley. He thought of Sally and of the ordeal of childbirth she would have to bear soon, and he wished he could tell Fairfax what his marvelous prospects were. He thought of the renegade Red Wolf and tried manfully not to curse him, and the last image in his fading consciousness was of the dusky-eyed Indian princess.

Gist had them out at daylight the next morning. It was clear and bright, but the November air was nipping and there was white frost on everything. Washington's hands were numb when he got to the fire to warm them. He made as hearty a breakfast as any of the men.

"Major, we'll send the traders down the river in the canoes after they paddle us across again to the Pennsylvania side. I reckon you won't be sorry to start the day's ride in dry buckskins."

"Indeed I shall not," averred Washington heartily. "Buckskin is a joy to wear, but when wet, it is abominable."

"I dried out your rifle and pistol and reloaded them. We'll ride through some rough country today before we get to the Delaware camp, and we'll see something to shoot. Possibly a redskin or surely a bear; there are lots of bears along the river at this time. They're fattening up on berries and acorns before going into their winter quarters."

Washington went across in the first canoe, and, climbing the high bank, looked back across the Monongahela and the point of land that separated it from the Allegheny and then out at the broad Ohio. It was a marvelous prospect. He would recommend that Governor Dinwiddie use all his influence to have a fort established there before the French did it. And on the moment he felt rather hopeless about the Governor being able to do anything. England was in a bad way and slow to move. There were so many more problems and projects that made the American colonies appear insignificant, but Washington knew in his heart that anything concerning these American colonies and the unknown and unlimited possibilities beyond this frontier were certainly anything but insignificant. And then it came into his mind how for two years or more he had heard vague rumors and theories of the untameable younger generation of American colonists. He could not but feel that he was one of them and that he wanted this kind of a life—this free life—this opening up of the frontier and the inevitable empire in the making. He wanted to be something in that building, and therefore the thought of dissension among the younger colonists and a possible breaking away from the English rule would not leave his consciousness.

Soon the horses were safely across, and Washington and his men made ready to proceed on their journey down the river. They watched the traders paddle back toward the point at the Forks, and then they headed off the bank into the deep forest. Gist soon led into a broad trail, and Washington, catching up with him, said, "Gist, you've time now to tell me a lot I don't know. At home down in Virginia along the Potomac I knew the woods and the trees as well as my own plantation, but I am beginning to see trees that I don't know."

"Wal, that's the natural instincts of a woodsman," replied the frontiersman, "and it's most as interesting as knowledge of the wild birds and beasts. An Injun knows all the trees and the plants and how they can be used to sustain life in the wilderness, and that surely is a backwoodsman's business."

Before Washington was an hour older he had seen and made his own possession new and beautiful trees, among them the great broad-leafed sycamore with its opal-hued and spotted bark, the curly birch with its bronze bark and thin foliage, the shellbark hickory tree rising rough and straight to a goodly height with some brown leaves still lingering on the branches and hickory nuts clustering here and there, the white bark beech tree with its slender spreading limbs, and the elm rising with its round drooping branches to its dome-shaped top, the gray baked chestnut tree with some of its prickly nuts not yet fallen, the maple, the dogwood, the willow, and last the great white and black oaks. Gist said there were pine trees up on the high hills and forests of pine farther up the Allegheny.

"That's a buckeye tree," said Gist, pointing. "We Ohio frontiersmen make a lot of that tree."

Washington etched these various trees in his mind so well that he thought he would be able to recognize them even when they became full foliaged in the summertime. Washington saw flocks of wild turkeys and several buck deer with their skin already taking on the bluish tinge of winter and their antlers losing their velvet, but he did not want to delay travel by hunting. If he should see a bear he would shoot it because he had heard much about bear meat and then he would like to have a bear pelt. But though he saw several bear tracks in the wet trail, he did not see one animal. It grew to be slow travel, winding down and up galleys, crossing little stony streams, threading a tortuous way among jumbled sections of cliff and through portions of forest where the windfalls made travel almost impossible. Gist walked a good deal of the way on foot with an axe in his hand. He said there had been considerable travel down this trail since summer but none of it on horseback. There were sections of bank where Washington had to dismount and climb and deep slippery fords to negotiate, and altogether for some hours after midday it was plodding, laborious toil. But though Washington grew weary in limb, his mind stayed keenly interested in everything pertaining to this travel down river. Only once or twice during that long journey did he see the Ohio River. And he was amazed when Gist told him that despite all their travel they had come only a few miles in a straight line from the Forks.

The Delaware chieftains' encampment was a realization of one of Washington's boyhood dreams. On an open sunny bench high above the river, majestic at that point, there were located a number of wigwams arranged in a circle around a larger and more imposing wigwam. The few large white oaks grew as if they had been placed there for a picturesque setting. Campfires were burning; the pungent odor of wood smoke permeated the air, and lazy columns of blue floated aloft. When Washington rode out of the timber the scene was pastoral and lonely with hardly any moving object in sight, but Indian dogs soon barked alarm, and in a twinkling the encampment was alive with Indians. Weapons in the hands of several braves attested that the Delawares did not trust visitors. Gist had told Washington that the chief, Shingiss, had for the time being alienated himself from the main tribe because of his friendship with the whites. This encampment was composed of his relatives and followers. Gist rode forward into the camp after calling aloud and meeting the Indians; after a moment he turned to beckon Washington. The surprise of their arrival augured that Currin and Stewart had not yet arrived, and, in fact, that was the first thing that Gist announced to Washington, and he did it with some anxiety, for the two traders coming down river should have made the trip in one quarter of the time that it had taken the others.

Shingiss proved to be a swarthy Indian of medium stature not remarkable for any feature except his bow legs. He wore buckskin leggins and moccasins much the worse for wear, and he had a blanket over his shoulders. Washington felt the scrutiny of a pair of straight-gazing, intelligent eyes. He did not notice any cunning or deceit in the Delaware's countenance.

"Wal, Major, we're hyar, and just as I expected, welcome," said Gist. "Get down off your hawse and stretch your legs. The first leg of our journey is ended and we've been lucky. But I'm worried about the traders. I recken your eyes are as good at long distances as they are at short. Spose you take a squint up the river and see if you can locate our canoes."

It was some few rods to the bank, and, reaching a point under a big tree that grew on the edge, Washington surveyed the river. On the sloping grassy bank beneath him there were numerous birch bark canoes, paddles, bales, baskets, and other paraphernalia. The mighty Ohio was broad at that point, fully half a mile, and on its muddy and swirling breast it carried pieces of driftwood and other evidences of flood. A rather stiff breeze blew up the river, and that might have accounted for the nonarrival of his traders. Washington peered up the river. At first glance his sharp eyes picked up two dark moving objects which even at the distance of two miles or more he recognized as the canoes. And he was relieved. The traders were keeping close to the Pennsylvania shore, and that caused Washington to wonder if they had been alarmed by Indians on the opposite bank.

Through the French interpreter Washington made known to Shingiss the importance of his mission and made earnest request that the Delaware chieftain would accompany him to Logstown and use his influence with the great chief, Half King, in Washington's behalf. Shingiss readily consented to go, much to Washington's satisfaction. The rest of that day was spent in making camp with the Indians. About sunset Currin and Stewart arrived reporting that they had a stiff paddle against wind all the way. They had not seen any Indians on the Ohio bank. Washington went among the Indians and made presents to the children of knickknacks and baubles which he carried in his pockets. They were all friendly, these Delawares, and some of the younger squaws were prepossessing, but none of them could in any way compare with Winona.

On the following morning the traders were once more embarked in their canoes, and Washington, with his other followers and the Delaware chieftain, proceeded on the river trail for Logstown. It was only a score of miles or less, but with the bad going and the increasing cold it was a hard journey. They reached Logstown before sunset. The large building, not unlike a fort, and the surrounding log cabins had been built by the French as a trading post to deal with the Indians. It was evident that the French were far ahead of the English in the matter of winning the Indian tribes. There appeared to be a large number of lounging Indians and a number of white men, some of whom kept in the background and struck Washington as being renegades. After meeting Red Wolf and his comrades, Washington believed that he would not fail to recognize renegades. The welcome that had been accorded his party in the Monongahela and at Shingiss's encampment was wanting here at Logstown, but on the other hand, Washington's reception was not hostile. Having a vacant cabin assigned them, Washington's men unpacked and Washington made the mental reservation, after going inside the cabin, that unless it stormed he would sleep outside. The men were preparing supper when Gist came back from the post.

"Wal, good news so far," he announced. "Scarrooyaddy is hyar, and I sent for him. I forgot to tell you, besides being an Oneida chief he's also chief of these Logstown Shawnees. He's an Indian you will take to."

"Gist, that is good news indeed. But what about Half King?"

"He lives down the river a day's journey. There's an Indian interpreter hyar named Davidson. You should send him with a message to Half King, some tobacco, and a string of wampum, and another gift or two. Inform Half King that the English Governor has sent you to call on the Shechams of the Six Nations to advise them of your mission. Ask Half King and the chiefs to wait upon you hyar at Logstown. These Injuns are slow but I reckon Shingiss going with Davidson can fetch them back promptly."

That night in the light of a campfire Washington met Scarrooyaddy. The eagle eyes of this red friend of the white man and the clasp of his hand seemed to be to Washington the introduction to a great friendship. Scarrooyaddy could readily understand English, and he could converse fairly well without asking questions or talking about his mission into the French and hostile Indian country. Washington exerted himself to win the regard of this Indian. He sensed a good deal in the Shawnee that did not appear on the surface. He divined that here was a red man who was honest and generous, who would not break his word, who would always pay a debt whether it was one of friendship or hate, and that indeed he was a type of noble man not yet degraded by the whites.

Next day while Washington waited impatiently for word from Half King, canoes came up the river and landed at the mouth of the creek where Logstown was situated. They turned out to be ten Frenchmen who had come from an Indian town far up the creek. They were not particularly civil to Washington or Gist, but Vanbraam, by dint of wine and tobacco which luxuries they evidently had not had for long, shared the story of why they were there. Washington had coached his interpreter on what information to seek and how to use diplomacy in extracting it from the Frenchmen. They had been sent from New Orleans with canoeloads of provisions and supplies to meet other Frenchmen at this point and thereby be guided to a fort that was being built somewhere.

That evening Vanbraam, further ingratiating himself with these French travelers, learned that there were four forts between New Orleans and the Black Islands. These forts had upwards of forty soldiers and a few small pieces of cannon. At New Orleans they had thirty-five companies of soldiers containing the same number of men in each, and they had a well-built fort carrying eight large cannon. At the Black Islands they had several companies of soldiers and a fort with six guns. These Black Islands were several hundred miles above the mouth of the Ohio. There was also a fort on the Ohio about two hundred miles from the mouth, and lastly it developed that these ten Frenchmen had become deserters. They had two traders with them who were leading them to Philadelphia. When late that night this information had been given, Washington expressed himself gratefully to Vanbraam and urged him to leave nothing undone to learn all that these

Frenchmen knew about the movements of the French troops in Ohio.

On the following day the Half King came to Logstown with Scarrooyaddy and Davidson and a number of braves. In garb and manner he appeared to Washington to be wholly a king. Washington invited him to his cabin and, with Davidson as interpreter, explained his mission and inquired about the way to Fort Le Boeuf where the French commandant St. Pierre was located. The Half King informed Washington that a direct course to the fort was impossible owing to recent rains and much marshy land. It could be made, but he advised against it. The French were going into winter quarters, which would end their activities until spring. But it was imperative that Washington should go at once; he advised that the journey should be taken via Venango, a longer, but swifter, journey.

The Half King said that on his visit to the fort he had been received in a very stern manner by St. Pierre, who demanded to know the Indian's business. The Half King recited the speech that he had made to the French commandant and also the reply that was delivered. This reply of the French commandant, according to Washington's analysis, showed that he was bitter and hard toward the Half King and no doubt to all the other Indian chiefs who were friendly with the English. It did not augur well for the success of Washington's mission.

As soon as Half King's chiefs had arrived at Logstown, Major Washington called a conference in the Long House. He stood up before them, fully realizing the importance of the effect he might produce and with strong and earnest desire to be regarded favorably. He addressed them with all the force and eloquence he could muster.

"Brothers, I have called you together in council by order of your brother, the Governor of Virginia, to acquaint you, that I am sent, with all possible dispatch, to visit, and deliver a letter to the French Commandant, of very great importance to your brothers, the English; and I dare say, to you, their friends and allies.

"I was desired, brothers, by our brother the Governor, to call upon you, the Sachems of the Nations, to inform you of it, and to ask your advice and assistance to proceed to the nearest and best road to the French. You see, brothers, I have gotten thus far on my journey.

"His Honour likewise desired me to apply to you for some of your young men, to conduct and provide provisions for us on our way; and be a safeguard against those French Indians who have taken up the hatchet against us. I have spoken this particularly to you brothers, because his Honour our Governor treats you as good friends and allies; and holds you in great esteem. To confirm what I have said, I give you this string of wampum."

In silence and with a commanding dignity the Half King stepped forward and received the string of wampum from Washington's hands. And then, with slow and labored elocution, he delivered the following reply.

"Now, my brothers, in regard to what my brother the Governor has desired me, I return you this answer. I rely upon you as a brother ought to do, as you say we are brothers and one people: We shall put heart in hand; and you may depend that we will endeavor to be your guard.

"Brother, as you have asked my advice, I hope you will be ruled by it and stay till I can provide a company to go with you. The French speech-belt is not here; I have to go for it to my hunting cabin. Likewise the people whom I have ordered in are not yet come, nor cannot till the third night from this: till which time, brother, I must beg you to stay.

"I intend to send a guard of Mingos and Delawares, that our brothers may see the love and loyalty we bear them."

Washington hid his impatience at what necessarily meant delay. He dared not hurry these Indians. He rejoiced that he had made friends with Shingiss, had won over Scarrooyaddy and had struck fire from the Half King. As he regarded it, his mission was not only to carry word to the French commandant to leave the Ohio Valley or else incur the wrath of England but to win the regard of these Indian chiefs and to be the influence by which better relations could be maintained between the Americans and Indians. He felt that he was an American speaking to them, that there was much of English restraint and demands that he did not approve of, and that, after all, in the end the issue must be between the red men and the colonists. All day long off and on he talked with this chief and the Indians, with the honest purpose of showing them that he liked them, that he wanted to be an instrument of good for the tribe. Deep in his heart he felt dismay at the thought that Governor Dinwiddie or any other English official would not let him keep his promises. Therefore he must not make extravagant promises. At the end of that day, running over all that had been said and his reactions, he was astonished to find that he held a high opinion of these Indian chiefs. Scarrooyaddy particularly seemed true as steel, a red man who indeed would make a fine hunting companion, a friend in need, or a warrior to stand up beside him and fight.

On the following day Washington waited patiently. He had some discourse with Half King and that night made an entry in his diary:

> As I had Orders to make all possible Dispatch, and waiting here was very contrary to my inclinations, I thanked him in the most suitable Manner I could; and told him, that my Business required the greatest Expedition, and would not admit of that Delay. He was not well pleased that I should offer to go before the Time had been appointed, and told me, that he could not consent to our going without a Guard, for fear some Accident should befall us and draw a Reflection upon him. Besides, says he, this is a Matter of no small Moment, and must not be entered into without due Consideration: For now I intend to deliver up the French Speech-Belt, and make the Delawares do the same. And accordingly he gave orders to King Shingiss, who was present, to attend on Wednesday Night with the Wampum; and two Men of their Nation to be in Readiness to set-out with us next Morning. As I found it was impossible to get-off without affronting them in the most egregious Manner, I consented to stay.

Runners were dispatched at once for the chiefs that Half King wanted to consent in conference and he himself returned to his home to fetch the French speech-belt which was such an important adjunct to the conference. When Half King returned that night he sought council with Washington and through Davidson told that he had news which had arrived that day by runners. The Mingos and Delawares with their allies had congregated at Fort Venango and that it had been their purpose to travel down the river that fall, but, owing to the advance of cold water and the threatening ice, they felt they could not undertake it at that season and must wait till spring. They could assuredly be expected in larger numbers, and if they were interfered with they would unite all their forces against those who antagonized them. They frankly stated that they expected to fight the English and that even if it took years, they would conquer. This message, the Half King said, came to him through his runners from Captain Joncaire, who was a great chief in the French army.

Piece by piece, Washington was gathering knowledge of the activities among the French and Indians, and it boded ill for the English. The Half King and Shingiss besought Washington to stay one day more in spite of the fact that the other chiefs had not arrived, and if they did not come on the morrow they would send the important Wampum after them. They were very pressing in their requests, by which Washington inferred that the return of the Wampum meant the abolishment of an agreement. It later developed that Shingiss could not get the desired chiefs to come and that he could not come himself, which the Half King interpreted as meaning he was afraid of the French. Later there was a lengthy discussion among the chiefs about the sending of Wampum here and there and particularly of a very large string of black and white wampum which would be sent immediately to the Six Nations if the French refused to quit the Ohio Valley.

That night the great men of the Indian conference met in the Long House with Washington and discussed the journey to Fort Venango and particularly who was to go. The resulting decision of that conference was that only three of the chiefs and one of their best scouts should attempt the journey to take Washington to Venango. Half King asserted emphatically that to take more Indians would be sure to make the French suspicious. Therefore, they planned to send Washington, accompanied by the Half King, White Thunder, Jeskakate, and the Hunter scout.

Washington decided that, of course in any case, he would accompany the Indian chiefs, yet he was vastly concerned. After Half King and his brother chiefs had departed, Washington went into conference with Gist and Scarrooyaddy. The Indian assured him that he must go and take whatever risks that offered. Gist was disappointed that he could not accompany Washington and he spoke most forcibly. "Major, you gotta go with them redskins because it is an honor that they do you and proves Half King's trust and friendship. It will be tough going. On foot or hawseback these Injuns sure cover ground. Keep up with them if you have to crawl on your belly. You have impressed them by your sincerity, by seeing their side of the question. And now you gotta show them that a white man can keep up with an Injun by reason of his strength and endurance."

13 Washington Meets Daniel Boone

The arrangements for an early departure were retarded somewhat by Gist's reports to Washington that Scarrooyaddy was not going to go with them.

"Gist, I'm very sorry to hear that," replied Washington. "Did he give any reason?"

"No, but I reckon Yaddy has some reason for not going to Venango. He's sore at the French."

"I think I will talk to him," replied Washington.

Gist accompanied him to Scarrooyaddy and found the chief alone and evidently with something somber on his mind. Washington interrogated him and earnestly sought to change his mind, but the Oneida chief was not to be changed, and whatever had occurred he did not divulge. He fastened his dark, inscrutable eyes upon Washington. "Major, you will be coming back to the Ohio Valley. The English are going to war with the French, and I will be with you."

His assertion was solemn, and the grip he gave Washington's hand left no room for doubt. Washington assured him that whether there was going to be war or not he would return to the Ohio Valley and look forward to nothing as keenly as to renew his friendship with the chief. On the return to their cabin Washington admitted that Scarrooyaddy's decision not to go boded ill to the success of the trip. It was Gist's opinion that the Indian knew that the French would not leave the valley of their own accord and that it would be hard to drive them out.

Half King and his Indian companions had already set off on foot. Washington, leading the way for his comrades, trotting his horse up the trail, soon expected to catch up with their Indian guides, but it was a wrong reckoning. The moccasin tracks of the Indians showed in the wet trail, but the Indians continued out of sight. Gist, on the trip replacing Scarrooyaddy, said that they had better overtake the Half King and stay with him along the rest of the journey. This was much easier said than done. Parts of that rough trail were much easier to cover on foot than on horseback. After several hours of travel they at last had a glimpse of the Indians in the trail ahead of them. It proved to be a remarkable experience to try to keep these Indians in sight. They climbed the bad places at a swift walk and covered the few level stretches of trail at a jog trot. Washington remarked to his comrade Gist that they were evidently in for a strenuous trip, and Gist maintained silence.

What with toiling up and down gulleys on foot and urging the tired horses on the better stretches of trail, the hours passed swiftly. It was afternoon before Washington realized it. The thing uppermost in his mind was how to meet the French official at Fort Venango on the Allegheny and what was to be the nature of the speech he must make. But owing to the labor and worry of the journey, Washington's usual clear thinking was at fault. It was about all a man could do to urge his steed and pick out the best places, get off and walk and climb and proceed down hill, and mount into the saddle again to cross swift and muddy brooks and to keep those tireless Indians in sight.

It was late in the afternoon when Washington came out of the timber to the mouth of the Allegheny. To his surprise, the traders Stewart and Currin had already reached that point and had taken the loads of supplies and equipment to the other side and were now waiting for Washington's party. Half King and his three Indian companions were waiting by the riverside. At sight of Washington, the chief waved his hand and then, with the Indians, got in Currin's canoe. Washington had keener appreciation of what those canoes were capable of doing when he saw one of them in the water with the five men. The heavy load brought the gunwales pretty nearly level with the water. He wondered how they would manage to cross the swift Allegheny. Washington's comrades soon rode down the bank where they all dismounted and made ready to cross. Washington and Gist got in Stewart's canoe and led their horses into the water. Stewart pushed off; the horses plunged in to swim behind the canoe. Once or twice the two horses got close together and almost tangled up with each other, but Gist, by letting his horse drop back farther on a rope tied to the halter, obviated the danger. In midstream they passed Currin returning in his canoe. When they beached on the point of land between the two rivers, Half King and his comrades had picked out a campsite and had built fires. When Washington rode across the neck of land to see the Allegheny, he thought that he would not care to risk crossing there after dark. And as the sun had set, it would probably be dark by the time the other horses and men had been brought across.

And so it turned out to be. Night had come before Macguire and Jenkins called them to supper. It was a good warm meal and everybody was hungry, but it developed that everyone was also tired. And not talkative. With the treacherous Allegheny in flood to cross, with days on end of toilsome travel, there was need to get as much rest as possible. Washington had interest enough to watch the Indians roll in their blankets, feet first to the fire, and go to sleep as if by magic. He had exerted himself that afternoon and also had a jagged cut from a snag. These small things bothered him somewhat, but he slept at last, awakening twice during the night to notice that the Indians kept the fire burning brightly. Toward morning the weather grew bitterly cold. Washington arose to get warm, and as the Indians were stirring and dawn was at hand he did not go back to bed. There was ice along the edge of the river, and the water was bitterly cold.

"Traveling with these redskins is purty tough," grumbled Gist.

"They don't waste any time," agreed Washington.

After a hasty breakfast and two cups of coffee apiece, the men were packing to ascend the Allegheny. The canoes were hauled up under the trees to be left there until their return, and the supplies were packed on horses. Half King and his Indians led up a trail on the east side of the Allegheny for several miles until they came to a wide stretch which was evidently a ford. Each of the Indians, carrying a pack and gun, walked a hundred yards up the stream and then took to the water wading between the rocks and through the torturous channel. The swift water hurried their progress downstream and across at the same time. Near the other side where the water deepened, they held their guns and parcels above their heads and, turning in the water, swam on their backs to make the other shore almost in a line from where Washington sat watching the remarkable manifestation of the Indians' prowess.

"Now, men, let's all make the attempt together," said Washington. "And if one of us comes to disaster, the others can help. A couple of you will have to lead two horses behind you. I'll lead the way."

With that, Washington rode up to the point where the Indians had taken to the river. His horse, a big bay, had not particularly inspired Washington's admiration, and he wished for his favorite, Roger. Sighting an oblique line to the point down and across where the Indians had gotten out, Washington cheerily called his followers to come and waded his horse into the river. The water was shallow and did not reach the horse's haunches until he had covered half the distance. Glancing back, he saw that the men were coming all right with Gist in the rear. Near the opposite shore the deeper water running swiftly carried all the horses off their feet, and they had to swim. The cold water coming up to Washington's waist made his teeth chatter. His horse was the only one to make the point where the Indians had crossed. The others were carried downstream more or less, and Vanbraam was the only one to suffer disaster. He was rolled off his horse and forced to swim and then wade ashore. His horse came out some distance below.

Wet and bedraggled and numb with cold, the travelers followed the tracks of the Indians into the trail on the west bank of the Allegheny. The day was dark and lowering. It rained, and after a while the rain turned to snow. The trail left the river to avoid rough going leading through marshland where water and mud further obstructed travel. The hours passed with the riders bent and silent and miserable in their saddles. When that day's travel ended in a grove along the bank of the river, they were all well played out; Vanbraam was in bad shape. Here again a big fire welcomed them and, dismounting, they all trooped around it to warm their numb hands before attending to their tired horses. Gist was wet and cross, but he had not seemed to mind the strenuous travel.

"Major, hyar's a white man talking to Half King," said Gist, pointing to the other fire. "I recken I've seen him somewhere, but can't recollect the name."

The stranger, evidently a hunter, left the Indian's camp and strode over to that of the whites. He was a stalwart young man about Washington's age and about the same build. His broad shoulders and lithe body, however, did not have Washington's weight. He wore the buckskin garb of a frontiersman and carried a long rifle and the tomahawk, knife, and other accoutrements habitual with hunters.

"Stranger, reckon I've seen you before," said Gist. "Yes, it was at the Ohio Company settlement on the Monongahela. Forget your name."

"Howdy, Christopher Gist," responded the other in a deep pleasant voice. "Don't you remember Daniel Boone?"

"By George! I sure ought to. Howdy, Boone. This is Major George Washington and his party. We're on the way to Venango with a message to Pierre."

"Boone, I'm glad to meet you," said Washington, as he shook the hunter's hand. "I'd be glad to have you eat with us and talk and go on to Venango, if you will."

"Thanks, Major. I'll stay one night," replied Boone. "I'm on the way down river."

"Where are you bound, may I ask?" replied Washington, with interest.

"I'm on one of my roamin' trips," returned the other, "bound down the Ohio, I've no idea how far. The Indians have told me of a country far to the south across the Ohio. I want to see that country. And if it's what they tell me, I'll come back and persuade some of my Pennsylvania friends to go back with me and locate."

"Well, that's interesting. You're not the first hunter I've met with that idea in mind. It's been working in me for a couple of years. Did you ever know or hear of Ebenezer Zane? He's on his way across the Blue Ridge now. He has four brothers, and they're all going to locate on the Ohio. There's a beautiful island somewhere down the Ohio, I don't know how far from here, but Zane has already been there."

"I've been there," returned Boone. "It's Wheeling Island, the only big island I know of over in the Ohio. It belongs to Cornplanter. It's a pretty place and grand country all around, but the French will want it and then the English will want it from the French. I aim to go further south."

"Do you and the Pennsylvania friends you speak of complain of British rule?" asked Washington.

"Yes, we do. We want none of it," returned Boone shortly.

It turned out that Daniel Boone's trade, in addition to hunting, was that of a blacksmith. He heard Gist swearing about the loose shoes on Washington's horse's hoofs, and he offered to do the job. Gist eagerly consented, and Boone shoed the Major's horse in short order and made such a good job of it that Gist said he would have him shoe some of the other horses. Soon they had dinner, and that precluded conversation for the time being. Afterwards Washington engaged Boone in conversation and questioned him about Fort Venango and the French and the Indians. Boone was evidently well-informed but not a great talker. He knew a good deal more about the Indians that he did about the French. Some tribes were hostile and some were still friendly, but they would not remain friendly for long. Boone had a very high opinion of some Indian chiefs. He said the French had set their hearts upon the Ohio River Valley and that it would take fighting to dislodge them.

For his part, Washington informed Boone what his mission was to the French fort and that if Pierre did not give up the valley the English army would force him. "As soon as I deliver my message to the Commandant and get his answer, I will go back to Williamsburg and then will return to the Monongahela settlements either with another mission or on my own accord."

"Major Washington, then we will surely meet again," returned the hunter, with a smile on his keen brown face. "I'll be travelin' to and fro on these trails for several years, I imagine. It takes time to locate a settlement in this wilderness. Mr. Gist, how is your Ohio Company making out?"

"Wal, I'll tell you, Boone," returned Gist thoughtfully. "That Company was formed to start settlements for the English, but the only one so far is that one on the Monongahela."

"Gist, you know that the needful thing in this wilderness is roads to travel on," said Boone. "Hunters like me and this Ebenezer Zane you speak of can travel the wilderness alone and find rich and fertile country, but pioneers have to take things with them. They must have tools, household goods, grain to plant and plows to plow with, and that means wagons. The French have cut a few wagon roads into the wilderness, but they're bad and don't go in the direction we want to travel. Major Washington, if you come to have influence out here, it would be helpful for you to cut a road from somewhere on the Ohio clear through to what the Indians call Kan-tuck-ee."

"That's something to think of, Boone. I'll remember it."

Owing to extreme fatigue and staying up late, Washington slept well that night. The sun was rising clear when they had breakfast and the frost and snow would probably not remain long on the ground. At parting Boone shook hands with Washington, repeating his earnest conviction that they would meet again. Washington watched the stalwart hunter glide into the woods with the spring of a deer stalker in his stride, and long after Boone had disappeared Washington marveled at the man. Alone and self-sufficient in that wilderness! Here was another intrepid spirit that Washington had met and for whom he had instant regard. Captain Jack and the Zanes and Wetzels with this hunter Boone were the forerunners of the pioneer tide which Washington had vision to see would someday flow westward.

The sun did not stay out as long as it had promised. This day was again bitter. Snow and ice and muddy water, soft trails that ran through bogs, stretches of forest where windfalls made travel exceedingly slow and laborious; then higher ground where the rough way was more wearisome than the low lands, pieced together another disagreeable and arduous day that wore on the travelers' strength and spirit. They reached another camp. The Indians were, as usual, taciturn and reticent. That night Washington was too tired even to try to think. No sooner had his eyes glued shut than it seemed he was rudely awakened and they were on the trail again. That day and another passed.

The horses showed signs of wearing out before the men. The traders and Gist walked a good deal of the way, and at length Washington fell to the same habit. Back at Logstown the Indians had claimed it was seven sleeps to Venango, but Washington was sure it was more than that.

It was midday a week or more after Washington and his comrades had left Logstown that they followed their Indian guides out of the wilderness into a ghastly clearing where knarled and bleached dead trees surrounded the Indian town and French fort of Venango. The place was situated on French creek. The fort was inside a log stockade, and, rough as it was, it had a menacing look. The French colors were hoisted from a log house which Gist said had once been the property of a man named Frazier who had been driven out by the French. Washington told Gist to find some kind of quarters for them, and he immediately repaired to the log house where the flag showed that the Commandant resided. There was a sprinkling of Indians around, and they eyed Washington with suspicious curiosity. He dismounted in front of the house, and Vanbraam, who had followed him, laboriously fell off his horse, surely a bedraggled and spiritless traveler. The door was opened by a Frenchman who responded to Vanbraam's greeting, and they were ushered into a big room where a warm fire at least promised comfort. There were three French officers present, one of whom was Captain Joncaire, a thin-featured, sharp-eyed man of middle age, somewhat pompous and gaunt in his uniform. At the introduction, Captain Joncaire ceremoniously greeted Washington and inquired his mission, saying that he was in charge of the fort and that the Commandant Pierre was at another fort farther up the river.

"Captain Joncaire, I am the bearer of a message from the English Governor at Williamsburg," returned Washington. "And it is very urgent that I dispatch it to the Commandant at once."

"Major Washington, what is the nature of this urgent mission?"

"Governor Dinwiddie in the name of His Majesty the King instructs you French to leave the Ohio Valley at once."

Captain Joncaire received the information without showing surprise and bowed to Washington without comment. Then he invited Washington to have dinner with them which would be served immediately in an adjoining room. He led Washington and his interpreter into the dining room and seated them at the table with great politeness. Then he enquired about Washington's companions and did show surprise at the arrival of the of the well-known Half King. The other two French officers came in and seated themselves. Captain Joncaire then said Washington could take his message to Commandant Pierre on the following day. Wine began to flow, and Washington's example of partaking but little did not appertain to the French officers. They drank heavily, and soon they talked more freely and with less coldness. Joncaire said in substance that the French were quite aware the English could raise two soldiers for their one, but they were too slow to prevent the French from carrying out their design. He also said that the French had undoubted right to the river because of its discovery sixty years before by LaSalle.

"The French have absolute design of taking possession of the Ohio, and by God, they are going to do it!" concluded Joncaire, with great vehemence.

Washington made no reply to the speech, but he thought a good deal about it and, as he went on eating his dinner, told Vanbraam to remember all that was said. At the conclusion of the meal Washington made his excuses, saying he would have to return to his men and that he would plan to journey next day to deliver his message to the Commandant. He and Vanbraam then went out into the rain and gathering twilight presently to be accosted by Gist, who led them to their quarters, a cabin near the fort. The traders and the other two white men were there, but the Indians were not present. They went inside, and while Washington removed his wet coat and boots to stand before the fire, he told Gist about his reception by Captain Joncaire.

"Wal, Major, that's just what Boone said," returned the frontiersman. "He claimed we'd get scant courtesy hyar, and that if Half King and his Indians were friendly to us they might get themselves in trouble."

"Better hunt up Half King and have him and his Indians come here to eat. And now, Vanbraam, tell us the rest of that talk you heard among the Frenchmen."

According to the best intelligence that Vanbraam could translate, the French had had about fifteen hundred men between Venango and Fort Le Boeuf, but upon the death of their general, some of these soldiers were recalled and the rest were left to garrison three other forts besides Venango. It was about one hundred and twenty miles to Fort Presquile on Lake Erie, where the French stores came from Montreal. It was a four-week voyage from Montreal coming directly across the lake. Captain Joncaire expected more French soldiers to arrive at Venango before spring, and then the French were going to build their greatest fort on the Ohio.

"That surely will be on that splendid site between the Monongahela and the Allegheny where they form the Ohio."

"Wal, Major, you're sure right about that," responded Gist. "I reckon our job is to deliver that message to Pierre and then make tracks back to Monongahela, and then on to Williamsburg to inform Governor Dinwiddie that if he does not move quickly the French will build a dominating fort first."

"Gist, I am afraid that will be the case," said Washington ponderingly, "and it behooves me to lose no time in getting back with that news. Joncaire knows, of course, that Pierre will laugh at Governor Dinwiddie's demand. They have the advantage. With fifteen hundred soldiers here now and more coming they could put that fort up before I could bring any force to the Monongahela."

"Wal, Major, that's what we may expect, but fort or no fort, it won't change the main issue. The English army will drive the French out of the Ohio Valley no matter how many forts they build."

"Exactly," admitted Washington, with gravity. "But that means a big English army and it means war."

Half King and his Indians did not come to Washington's quarters for their supper. Gist went out to look for them but could not find them. The next day it developed that every possible stratagem was being employed to prevent Half King and his Indians from going on to the next fort with Washington. Davidson, the interpreter, could not get them to come to the cabin. He had been strictly ordered to remain in their presence. Finally Washington sent Gist to bring in the Indians. Washington decided that he had better not state his feelings at the moment, but he said they would leave at noon for Fort Le Boeuf. He had been so keen to start for the next fort that he had thought little of what the journey would be like. Gist informed him, not at all reassuringly, that a couple of Indian runners had been dispatched ahead of them, no doubt to tell Pierre of Washington's coming. Bad as the travel had been coming to Venango, it was nothing compared to this route to the next fort. French Creek was in flood, necessitating wide detours to get around the flooded land. It took them all the rest of that day to make Sugar Creek, and the next day they made twenty-five miles to Cussewago, an old Indian town. On the following day they could not cross French Creek and had to keep on up the west side. Gradually with rain and snow and flooded stream the journey became no less than a nightmare. At last they reached Fort Le Boeuf, a facsimile of the one at Venango, but it was minus some of the cabins and the numerous Indian habitations.

It was almost dark when Major Washington applied for audience with the Commandant and was finally conducted to him by the second officer in command. Legardeur De St. Pierre was an elderly gentleman of distinctive appearance and decided military bearing. He received Washington's papers and repaired to another apartment, evidently to have them translated. Presently the Commandant sent for Washington to have him enter with his interpreter and translate his message. Washington was allowed then to leave the office, and he took advantage of the time to make mental notes of the inside of the fort. He then went outside, accompanied by Vanbraam, and walked around the fort making minute observations of its location and character, especially of the portholes and cannon it mounted. Adjacent to the fort was a long section of cabin, evidently a barracks for soldiers. The yellow lights and loud voices attested that the barracks were occupied. At the moment Washington could not get any idea how many soldiers manned the fort. Afterwards, Washington and Vanbraam returned to Gist, glad to retreat from the rain. Gist reported that he had counted upwards of fifty birch bark canoes and over a hundred of pine. There were also canoes under construction.

No word was sent to Washington that night. When Gist came in the last time he said it was snowing hard and prospects for the return journey were bad. Whereupon Washington instructed him to dispatch Currin and two other men to take horses and hurry back to Venango. They were to wait there if in their opinion there was any prospect of the rivers freezing. If they did not freeze, they were to wait at the crossing of the Allegheny until Washington and his men returned.

"Major, I reckon we are going to miss Scarrooyaddy pretty bad," remarked Gist gloomily. "This Commandant Pierre is a smooth frog-eater and if I don't miss my guess, he's up to some dirty work. Yaddy can talk any Injun lingo, and he is certainly intelligent. He could get the lay of the land here much quicker than we can, and with winter coming on, delay for us is damn serious."

"Gist, I sense the undercurrent working of things here," replied Washington. "It can only have to do with one thing—to persuade or prevent our Indian guides from going back with us. That is what I'm afraid will happen. If it does, I will be mightily amazed at the Half King."

"The chief might go back on us if they get him drunk, but otherwise never. If Yaddy was hyar he could keep our Injuns from drinking too much."

"Well, we have no official answer from the Commandant as yet," returned the Major thoughtfully, "but you and I know that the French will not leave the Ohio Valley."

"Dead sartin sure!" ejaculated Gist. "Half King was afraid of it, and Yaddy knew it."

"We must have the wit to prevent the French from holding our Indians here, and we must get away soon. Pierre will hold back that official reply to Governor Dinwiddie. That is unfortunate because we will have to wait for it."

"Major, we will that."

"Get the men off early in the morning, Gist. Rain or shine, and now it certainly looks like snow. I would gladly brave the elements with them if it were possible."

Next morning it had cleared off, leaving a thin skin of snow on the ground, and it was colder. The men got away with the horses and the camp duffle and assured Washington they would wait for him either at Venango or the Forks of the Ohio. Following their departure Washington and Gist endeavored in every unobstructive way possible to find out the plot of the French and counteract it. The Half King informed Washington that he had offered the Wampum to Commandant Pierre, who made some excuse for not taking it. The chief said that the Frenchmen talked very fine and big, that he was all for love and friendship, and for peace with the Indians and the whites. As a proof of his good will he would send a canoeload of goods down the river to Logstown that very day.

Pierre made good his word, but as the several canoes embarked, Washington saw that they had a French officer with them; and then he divined that the Commandant's design probably had to do with traders he desired to seduce to their will. In this connection Washington was reminded that several English traders had been made prisoners, and he took occasion to inquire of Pierre by what authority he did this. The Commandant replied with suave and easy speech that all that country adjacent to the Ohio River belonged to France, that English men had no right to trade on those waters, and that he had orders to make prisoners of those who attempted it.

Washington made it plain, in terse reply, that the French were laboring under a misapprehension and that if they were not careful this would come home to them soon. Pierre evidently did not like this speech, but he preserved his deceitful diplomacy and assured Washington that his reply to Governor Dinwiddie, which would be ready soon, would make clear their stand in the Ohio Valley. Washington was irritated at the French officer's insincerity, and he wanted him to know that it did not fool anybody. He wanted to know where the Indians at this fort had procured the three fresh white men's scalps that he had observed. The Commandant's evasive reply was that he had no knowledge of where the white scalps came from. It then occurred to Washington that further discourse with Commandant Pierre would be futile. And he kept his own counsel.

That evening the Commandant's reply to Governor Dinwiddie was brought to them unsealed, and Washington considered it was his duty to read it. It was like Pierre's talk, grandiloquent and evasive. In part he said he regretted that Major Washington would not go to Canada with his message, which would be duly forwarded to the Marquis Duquesne. "As to the Summons you send me to retire," wrote St. Pierre, "I do not think myself obliged to obey it; whatever are your instructions I am here by virtue of the order of my General and I entreat you, sir, not to doubt one moment but I am determined to conform myself to them with all the exactness and resolution which can be expected from the commanding officer."

Washington read that passage to Gist, and the frontiersman swore lustily. "That is it, Major, in black and white! And if that doesn't make the English hot under the collar, I don't know my own blood. It's up to you to make a quick decision."

"I have made it," returned Washington grimly. "We must circumvent these Frenchmen; we must keep our Indians loyal and absolutely take them back with us because if the chiefs are kept here and propitiated by gifts, with their minds debased by rum, they will be like these other Indians on the French side when the war comes. And Gist—I have not the least doubt that this means war."

Gist replied forcibly that for the frontiersmen, the traders, and the colonists, not to speak of the English soldiers, the sooner the war was declared the better.

For hours thereafter, Major Washington paced the floor of the cabin until his men went to sleep and the fire died down, and before going to bed he jotted down in his notebook, "I can't say that ever in my Life I suffered so much anxiety as I did in this affair."

Next day canoes were placed at their disposal with a goodly supply of food and necessary blankets and much more liquor than was necessary or wanted. But Washington accepted everything with thanks. He assured the officers that he could not leave without his Indian guides. It developed then that every manner of overture was being made to Half King and the other chiefs to keep them at the fort. Washington went personally to the Half King who told him that the

Commandant would not let him depart until the next day. It was evident then that Half King had been plied with liquor. Washington went at once to the Commandant with a strong protest and claimed that the Frenchmen were keeping the Indians and himself and comrades there at the fort against their will. Pierre answered in a burst of surprise that he did not know of any cause of delay and certainly was not a party to it. But Washington, roused and angry now, carried the matter directly to his Indian comrades. He learned then that the cause of the delay was the promise of fine guns and equipment to the Indians if they would remain. The chiefs then pressed Washington very earnestly to remain another day, and finally Washington promised that if he did so nothing would prevent them from accompanying him on the morrow.

Next day the French lost neither opportunity nor invention to further their interest to keep Half King and his comrade chiefs at the fort. They made good the present of guns and then, evidently having exhausted the power of gifts, took to plying the Indians with liquor. Washington in desperation saw that he had to act quickly or the French would accomplish their design. He drew the Half King aside and, seeing that the intelligent chief was not yet under the influence of liquor, he addressed him with all the eloquence and wisdom and honesty which he could assume. He reminded him of the unfailing friendship of the American colonists for him and his people. He would not have made that long journey over the mountains to Logstown if he had not been assured that the Half King was a friend of the English. He told him how Scarrooyaddy had won his promise to stand by the Americans, that with the Half King's influence and the power of his tribe the French could never hold the Ohio River Valley. And at the conclusion of his brief and poignant appeal Washington said that he believed absolutely in the good faith and honor of the Half King and that if the Half King went back on his word it would rebound disastrously to Washington's mission in the valley and greatly prolong the coming war.

The Half King stood tall and straight and dark, with fixed gaze upon his American friend, and offering his hand he spoke sonorously: "The Half King keeps his word. He will return with the white chief and when war comes he and his great people will be against the French."

With intense relief and gratitude Washington made instant preparation to depart. His men loaded their few belongings into the canoes. Washington urged the Indians to take their places and presently the four canoes slid into the water. Washington made a brief and ceremonious speech to the French officer and conveyed his regret to Commandant Pierre. Then he took the front end of Gist's canoe and, picking up his paddle, gave the command to start. The canoes glided out into the swift yellow stream and very soon reached a turn in the creek. Washington looked back to see the French and Indians watching them from the fort. Then it passed out of sight, and Washington addressed himself to the serpentine stream ahead of him. Once in the current of the main creek, the four canoes shot downstream rapidly. The water had fallen a couple of feet but was still high from the recent flood.

Gist, like all traders and frontiersmen, was adept with the paddle. Washington, though having traveled in canoes, was far from being an expert. The creek was so crooked that Washington could not keep all the canoes in sight at any one time. And as the swift current flowed along at a six- or eight-mile speed they were soon far away from the fort. Washington hardly realized what he had feared. The French might not be above ambushing those canoes. The mode of travel could not help but be exhilarating, and they sped downstream for several hours without any mishap.

About noonday they came to the first rapids. After narrowly missing submerged rocks, Washington saw that they'd better follow the example of the canoes in front and, to avoid disaster, get out and wade over the shallows. This was a safe procedure, but the icy water gave them chills and cramps. In the afternoon, the creek, having enlarged by reason of tributaries, grew swifter and rougher as they progressed and finally grew so deep that they were unable to ford the numerous rapids and had to shoot them. Here Gist proved his skill with the paddle. But there were many times when Washington steered them aside from a crash by meeting a rock with his paddle and shoving the bow to one side.

At the bottom of one long rapid they could see the canoes ahead bobbing up and down through yellow curling waves which broke over the gunwales. When Washington's canoe hit this last slant of water the first big curling wave came over the bow and drenched him to his skin. But he was already so cold and numb that it did not matter. He was glad that he had taken the precaution of wrapping his papers in oilskin, which was buttoned inside his coat. The canoe was half full of water. Gist ran ashore where their companions had already gone, and, pulling the canoes up, they carried the contents up on the bank and then turned out the water.

As it was nearing sunset, Washington ordered camp right there. Frontiersmen were skilled in making campfires, but nothing compared to the Indians who soon had two hot fires blazing, putting a different aspect upon the situation. Stewart and Gist busied themselves at preparing a meal while Washington and the others dried things out before the fire. Before dark they were at least dry and warm once more, with the inner man satisfied. About dark, a fine misty rain set in again, very raw and cold, and soon turned to snow. Washington dispatched all hands to gather firewood, which was scarce at that point. Washington was amazed to see the Half King staggering into the camp firelight with the roots and the trunk of a tree on his brawny shoulders. And he reflected that this was another indication that the Indian was self-sufficient and that the Half King was a great chief.

It snowed all night. Washington slept, but he would awaken because one side was freezing and he had to turn that to the fire. Gray dawn came, bitter, raw, wet. The voyagers ate a scanty meal, had a hot drink, and then once more embarked.

That day magnified all the discomforts and hazards of the preceding day, and it was so full that it passed speedily.

Camp that night was made near a cliff face which sheltered them from the inclement weather and where they had plenty of firewood. Washington instructed Gist to give all hands some of the strong drink that Pierre had provided. Then the travelers lay down to sleep, turned over to keep warm, got up to replenish the fire, and so on through the endless, dismal hours of night till gray dawn broke.

There was ice on the water in the morning. One of the Indians shot a deer, and they had venison for breakfast. Once more they embarked on the creek that had grown to be a river, but this morning a welcome sun was shining. The stream was so swift that in many places it was not necessary to paddle, just guide the canoes in the proper direction. But that respite was short-lived. Soon the sky clouded over and a blustery wind and rain forced them from coming up the river, retarding their progress. There were more rapids to shoot and bad places so numerous that Washington forgot to take note of them.

That afternoon, wading and paddling and finally portaging the canoes through the woods over a long neck of land round which the creek was impassable made it imperative to camp and rest before proceeding. Washington had never been so exhausted in his life. Even the Indians were tired. The sturdy Gist was still strong, but he had frozen his feet and one of his hands and suffered great pain and inconvenience. Next morning they were off early, encouraged by Half King's word that they would soon reach Venango. But hour by hour of toilsome labor still found them in the wilderness. To cap the climax of that last day's torture, the canoes entered a rapid walled on each side by cliffs, and it was evident that no matter what lay ahead they had to go on. The creek ran so swiftly between these walls that the crest of the current in the middle was higher than on either side, but by dint of prodigious work and good luck, the canoes safely passed through except that at the bottom of the pass where the creek widened out again Gist's canoe ran squarely upon a submerged rock and, capsizing, threw the two men into the water. Fortunately the canoe did not turn upside down, and they were able to hang on to it and drift out of the current to shallow water where they waded out, almost utterly spent with exhaustion. But they could not tarry long and let the other canoes get too far ahead, so, weary and silent, numb with the icy water, they once more took to the canoe and paddled as hard as they could to catch up. Their strenuous work, however, exhausting as it was, once more made their turgid blood stir. When they were about done, Gist stopped paddling and, sniffing the cold air, exclaimed; "By God, I smell smoke!"

Washington smelled it too, and a few more moments rounding the curve his sharp gaze picked up the fort at Venango.

14 Sally Confronts Washington over the Indian Princess

Upon reaching Venango, Washington found that his party had arrived safely, though smitten by cold and weakened by labor. He learned to his amazement that four French canoes had left Le Boeuf ahead of them and that during the latter part of the journey these French canoeists waylaid the Indians and continued the scheme of trying to persuade the Half King and his associates to quit Washington. In the passage of a bad rapid, one of the French canoes capsized, and the Half King left them to make their way safely out of the rapids as well as they could. When Washington learned this, he was convinced that no further efforts by the French would succeed in alienating the Half King.

The horses were in too bad condition to attempt the trip down to Monongahela, but as there was no help for it, Washington had to take them and hope they would make the distance. Captain Joncaire, having received the Frenchmen from Le Boeuf, lost no time in approaching the Half King and the chiefs. It so happened that White Thunder had been lamed on the trip down and could not at once proceed on the journey. Half King and the others decided to remain with him. It was plain they were also in need of rest. Washington told the Half King that further efforts by the French to make him betray his friends must be expected, to which the chieftain replied, "My brother must not think anything of that. The Half King has learned to know the French too well. He will never engage himself in their behalf. He will send his young hunter with Washington and follow to Monongahela after one or two sleeps."

Washington rebutted Gist's advice that they stay a day or more at Venango. "No, we must go on. When the horses give out we will walk. We must not lose a single day in rushing our information to Governor Dinwiddie about the purpose of the French."

When it came time to saddle and pack for the return down the Allegheny, it turned out that the horses were so feeble and the baggage so heavy that they would have to walk and use their horses for pack animals. Thereupon Washington divested himself of his great coat, which had been more of an encumbrance than a help, and, clad in his buckskin suit and carrying his rifle and a small knapsack, he set out upon that return journey on foot. The frontiersman, Gist, was outfitted in the same manner except that he carried a larger knapsack. They headed into the trail down the Allegheny followed by their party and made camp at nightfall.

It stormed that night and all the next day. The cold increased and the snow became so deep in the wet trail that good travel was impossible. The horses grew so weak that they could not walk as fast as the men. At the end of the third day, which if anything was marked by worse weather and travel than any day yet, Washington decided that he and Gist would strike out ahead and leave the others to follow as best they could. Next morning Washington left Vanbraam in charge and supplied him with instructions and money. He was to slow down the travel, try to save the horses, and make the Monongahela settlements as soon as it was possible. Washington and Gist, with only their rifles and scant supply of provisions, headed down the river alone. They were both deerstalkers and addressed themselves to the trail with such energy that they made more mileage that day than the horses could have done in two. They had a dry night, but it was so bitterly cold that they could not sleep when the fire burned down and spent half the night replenishing it. The next morning they were off as soon as it was light enough to see. The snow was frozen, and they made good time. Some miles down the Allegheny the snow had thinned out. Washington's sharp eyes detected faint imprints of moccasin tracks, to which he called Gist's attention.

"Injuns, all right," muttered the frontiersman. "See how they toe inwards? When was these tracks made?"

"We'll find out," declared Washington, and plumping down on his knees he began the minute study of the faint tracks. A few paces distant Gist did likewise. Presently they arose to compare notes.

"What do you say, Major?"

"Well, from the looks of them I would say they were made yesterday, but the way they feel—the little particles of loosened snow which I couldn't see with my naked eye—indicates that they might have been made this morning."

"I reckon about the same. We'll take it that Injuns passed along hyar this morning."

Washington pondered deeply. "They wouldn't be traveling off the trail unless they had some design. It might be an ambush, but ambush or not, we *must* go on. You look on the right side while I look on the left. And don't miss anything."

With that, they proceeded along the trail, their pace slowed somewhat, but their movements stealthy and their vigilance keen. They did not come across any more Indian tracks. The snow continued to thin out until bare patches of ground showed. In the open stretches they traveled at a swifter pace, but when they came to heavy timber and wooded thickets, especially at turns in the trail, they exercised the most extreme caution. With Washington a little in advance they traveled on. Before rounding any turn in the trail they halted. It was still and cold in the woods, and the only sound was the distant rumble of the river. There was no movement of birds or beasts, but at length as he halted and Gist came alongside, Washington sensed danger. This faculty of Washington's, heightened by his long experience in the wilderness, was like an Indian's sense, and for a white man it was almost uncanny. He could not have said that he heard anything or that he had seen anything.

"Mebbe you can smell Injuns, Major," whispered Gist.

Washington held up his hand to warn Gist. He had seen a barely perceptible motion of something and then to his sensitively strained ears, low but clear in that still winter atmosphere, came the click of a gun lock.

"Down, Gist!" whispered Washington swiftly. Just as he ducked his head there came the ringing report of a rifle and a bullet zipped over his head to tear a hole through the sleeve of Gist's buckskin coat. In another instant both men had fired their rifles at a little cloud of smoke which appeared to the left of the trail in a thicket hardly fifty feet distant. The shots were followed by Indian yells, a report of another rifle, and then a commotion in the brush. Several Indians could be seen running back into the forest.

"There's one left, Gist!" exclaimed Washington. "You go one way. I'll go this. We'll head him off." Running fleetly, Washington got between the tree behind which he had seen an Indian hide and the place where the other Indians had disappeared in the woods. He headed off flight in that direction, and Gist, coming up speedily, came right upon the Indian and menaced him with a clubbed rifle. The Indian dropped the rifle he had evidently been reloading and drew his tomahawk to give battle. He was a young brave, a Huron, Washington thought, but at any rate he belonged to the Indians who hung around the French forts.

"Don't—hit—him," panted Washington, as he came up. "Gist, a live Indian—will be more valuable to us than a dead one."

"Wal, I kinda like to knock 'em on the head," admitted Gist, "but you're right, Major."

Keeping the captive Indian in front of them, they proceeded down the trail as rapidly as they could walk. They would be followed, of course, by the other Indians, but Washington believed that they would not be fired upon while they stayed close behind the prisoner. And he was right. During the long hours of the tramp through the forest Washington had a few glimpses of the pursuing savages. They could not make the young Indian talk. They kept him prisoner until an hour after dark, and then they let him go and proceeded on the trail. In some places they got off the trail but always succeeded in getting back on it, and they walked all night covering, according to Washington's figures, fifteen or twenty miles. The Indians would not try to trail them in the dark, but they would surely take the trail when daylight came. Washington thought they had a big enough start to insure safety. What little they had to eat that day they partook of while walking, and they kept up their steady progress until twilight came again and they came out upon a point that Gist said was a couple of miles above Shannapins. They made the disconcerting discovery that the Allegheny was full of floating ice. That accounted for the low rumbling roar that they had heard all day.

"Major, this ain't so good," said Gist gloomily. "Hyar it is almost dark, and how are we going to get across?"

"We can't until tomorrow," returned Washington. "Then we'll have to build a raft. If the ice runs out tonight or the worst of it, we can manage to get across. I think we can risk a fire long enough to cook something hot and get warm. Then we must extinguish it."

They spent that night taking turns at keeping watch. Washington refused to let the frontiersman stand more guard than he did himself.

In the morning they found the river still full of running ice, but the heavy masses and churning cakes had all passed by. Gist said it would be a job to make their hair stand up stiff, but that they could—they had to—accomplish it. With only one tomahawk, which Gist carried, they essayed to build a raft. They tied two thicknesses of logs together with pieces of tough bark and long vines. It took them nearly all day to build the raft.

"We better take an extra long-pole in case we lose or break one," advised Washington. "And now, let's push off, and may the good Lord help us!"

"Wal, we're gonna need him, all right," returned the frontiersman.

So they pushed off. The raft upheld them, but it was poor, and one end would submerge while the other stood up. Finally, by taking positions at opposite ends, the adventurers, kneeling so as not to be thrown off, managed to make some shift of navigation toward the other shore. It was a most precarious business, and kneeling, up to their knees in cold water which came aboard by every wave, soon benumbed them and retarded their efforts. The larger cakes of ice they managed to stave off with the poles.

Once in the middle of the stream where there were greater current and bigger waves, their plight became critical in the extreme. Once a big cake of ice came half aboard the raft, and the men almost came to disaster. Gist sprang to the forward end of the raft while Washington pushed off the ice floe just in the nick of time. The delay caused by this accident was the cause of their being surrounded by large cakes of ice, and presently they were jammed among them and could neither push them away nor dislodge the raft. Imprisoned on their frail craft, they were taken down the river. Every moment disaster threatened. The ice and the raft rose and fell on the waving bosom of the stream, and the men had to hold on to keep from being thrown into the water. Washington noted that as they proceeded down the river the mass of ice which held them was enlarged by additional floes. The excitement and the danger was so great that neither Washington nor Gist could make any note of the shoreline.

"Gist! Listen!" exclaimed Washington fearfully. "Do you hear anything?"

"Can't say I do, Major, 'cept anything but this grinding ice," returned the frontiersman.

"Well, I can. It's that rapid in the river above where we crossed. I recognize the hills too. We're not far from the Forks."

"Major, if our raft drifts into that rapid, we are gone."

Washington could not admit anything like that to his consciousness, but he did not voice any comment. The current of the river grew swifter. They turned a corner and saw ahead a long yellow slant of muddy water and dirty ice, frothy, surging, and fearful to behold. And beyond the rapid stood out the island that marked the near approach to the Forks. When they shot over the long gentle incline at the head of the rapid, the mass of ice that held the raft began to grind and disintegrate. Floe after floe loosened and slipped away on the current until finally once more the raft, pitching and tossing, furnished precarious footing. But though it twisted and turned and tipped, it did not capsize. The voyagers ran the rapid clear through to the foot where it grew rougher as the swollen river split around the island.

"Gist, we're going under," yelled the Major, as the raft slipped into a succession of high waves and broken fragments of ice, "but we'll make the island."

Gist made some unintelligible reply that might have meant that he did not share Washington's faith. Then the raft lunged and precipitated the men into the water, but they held on to the logs with one hand and their rifles in the other. Sometimes they were wholly submerged; at others they were almost dislodged by cakes of ice. Finally at the head of the island they came into shallow, very swift water, and, abandoning the raft, they waded, desperately fighting the current and upholding each other and made the shore, where they fell exhausted.

Again it was almost night. The sun was setting steely and cold in the west. Ice was already forming on their wet clothes. Presently when they had caught their breath they struggled up on the bank, and while Gist searched on the under side of logs for pieces of punk and dry slivers of wood that would burn, Washington got out his oilskin package inside of which he had taken the precaution to include flint and steel with his papers. They soon had a fire started and before dark were once more dry and warm and had eaten the last bits of bread and meat left in their knapsacks. They made camp on the island and had the first bearable night outdoors for a long time.

Next morning from the other end of the island they forded a way across. They were safe again and hurried onto Frazier's cabin. They ran right into a score of Indians who were stopping at Frazier's and who had informed the trader that up at a place on the river called Kunnaway they had found seven white people killed and scalped, one of whom was a young woman with very light hair. Others of the white people had been half eaten by hogs. The perpetrators of this dastardly tragedy, according to Frazier, were French Indians of the Ottawa nation, and it boded ill for all the white settlements.

While Gist arranged to get horses from Frazier and the necessary equipment and supplies, Washington took time to visit Queen Aliquippa who belonged to the main Delaware nation who were friendly to the whites, and she had told Frazier that Washington should have called upon her. He did so this day and was received with great courtesy and kindness for which he made return by giving her as a present his great match coat, which, despite its sad appearance, was received most gladly by the Indian Queen. Washington reflected that possibly some of her pleasure was owing to the presence of a bottle of rum in one of the pockets, which he had placed there with just this intent. He was glad to make friends with Queen Aliquippa, and he felt that she and the Delaware chief Shingiss would be valuable allies in the future.

It was New Year's Day when Washington left Frazier's with his comrade, and on the second of January they arrived at Monongahela, where Gist went to his home, there to attend to his regular business and await Washington's return.

"And, Major, when will that happy day be?" asked Gist.

"Winter or no winter," replied Washington seriously, "I will advise Governor Dinwiddie that he must erect a fort on the Ohio and do it at once or the French will, and that will be the first important step in the French war that is coming."

Leaving instructions with Gist to give Vanbraam and his outfit, Washington set out at once on a fresh horse to ride home to Mount Vernon and thence to Williamsburg. He was used to traveling alone and taking care of himself. The possession of a horse, however, and the need to feed it and keep it from straying complicated his travel. On the second day he met seventeen horses packed with materials and stores proceeding toward Monongahela and following that several pioneer families who were going out there to settle. They beleaguered Washington with their desire to know about the country where they were going to make their homes and what was the danger from the Indians. Washington did not tell them of the massacre of whites of which they would assuredly hear when they reached Monongahela. He regretted not having more time to spend with these good people, but he pressed on. The next day he arrived at Wills Creek, where he was besieged anew by the planters and farmers who had heard of the unrest in the Ohio River Valley. From the sixth of January until the eleventh, Washington traveled under most arduous conditions. It snowed or rained all the time, and he suffered intensely from the cold. Fires were difficult to build, but it was imperative that he succeed in building them for otherwise he would have been severely frozen.

Not until he arrived at Mount Vernon and was greeted by his mother with joy at his safe arrival, but horror at his appearance, did he think of himself or of the others that he left there at home or what they would think of his looks. He rested there all that day and the next night and resisted his mother's appeal that he visit Belvoir. Thought of Sally was sad and sweet and strangely seemed to remind him of the past that really was not far distant but seemed so.

Early the next morning he set out on his favorite horse, Roger, for Williamsburg and made the journey in record time, arriving there about midday on the fourteenth.

It was with no inconsiderable pride that Washington presented his papers to Governor Dinwiddie. The Governor hardly took time to greet him before reading the reply of the French Commandant Pierre to the important message that

Washington had carried. He slammed the letter down on his desk and betrayed immense surprise and humiliation. Then he grew red in the face and began to stamp around and fume with rage until he treated Washington to a magnificent exhibition of British wrath. In a few moments he wiped his red and sweaty face. "Major Washington, you will please excuse my outburst," he said, resuming his seat and motioning Washington to take the next one to him, "but that word from Pierre is bad. Recent news from England is very disturbing. And this is a very unfortunate period for us to become involved in war with the French. Yet I see no way to avoid it. . . . Now, will you please have a drink and enjoy one of my cigars and tell me in minute detail all that happened on your journey to the Ohio River Valley."

Washington presented his notes, but in the verbal account that Dinwiddie insisted upon he did not have to refer to them. He knew every incident, every sensation of that most exhausting and terrible journey. He avoided praising himself, but he did not stint in his credit to his white and Indian companions. At the conclusion of his narrative the Governor stroked his chin thoughtfully and looked intently at Washington with his little bright eyes, "Major Washington, your report is incredible, but I believe you implicitly. Lord Fairfax and the others who recommended you to me exercised a wisdom for which I am greatly indebted to them. You indeed have a future in America. Now I will account my debt to you the greater for advising me what *you* would do in this vexatious situation."

"Governor, I have been on the ground, and I know the French and have had ample time to think," returned Washington. His heart had leaped at the faith imposed in him and the opportunity that knocked at his door. "You must build a large fort at the Forks of the Ohio. Build it before the French!"

"Extraordinary!" exclaimed the Governor. "Build a large fort in winter?"

"Build it absolutely, despite weather or any other conditions."

"That is an utter impossibility before spring and even then—" The Governor broke off and shook his head.

"I am convinced that if you wait till spring you will find that the French will have already built it," returned Washington. This was his own personal opinion; he did not have anything but his own feeling and divination to substantiate it. "The French soldiers at Fort Le Boeuf are going into winter quarters and they are fifteen hundred strong."

"Major, I know the French, and if the winters are as severe there as I have heard, they are not likely to give up their fires and their wine until the warm weather begins."

"That is a natural conclusion. Probably it is right. But it is not mine."

"Suppose the French *do* build a big fort at the Forks of the Ohio?"

"Then they will have a strategic and formidable position from which they can only be dislodged by a large English army."

"From your report I gather that it will take a large English army anyhow to drive these pesky French out of Ohio, and it so happens that the English army cannot be produced by miracles. England is having troubles of her own without this little provincial war. How many soldiers would you require?"

"Governor Dinwiddie, I ought to have ten companies of soldiers, but I would undertake it with five," returned Washington eagerly.

The Governor laughed outright. "Major, you have done a man's job but you are certainly a boy yet. I can feel your enthusiasm, and I like it. The best I can promise you, and that not earlier than April, will be three companies of soldiers. I will have to send for them, and equipment and stores will be as hard to get as the men. . . . You have done well, and I shall recommend you to a higher office. Meanwhile, go home and wait."

Washington was impatient to get back home for other reasons besides his physical weariness, but as he had left his rifle and pistol with the gunsmith, he could not leave earlier than the next morning. Both his fine weapons had been nearly ruined by rust and sand, necessitating a complete overhauling. Added to that he had several errands, and he wanted particularly to inquire about the Zanes.

After diligent inquiry he found that the Zanes and the Wetzels had left Williamsburg early in the fall for parts unknown. Silas, however, had gone north to New York and Boston with the intention of returning in the spring and then joining his brothers. He had the good fortune to meet his former surveyor friend, James Genn, and the pleasure was mutual. Some of Genn's information was as startling as that which Washington had to impart. Captain Jack, the Black Hunter, had returned to his little plantation in the forest from a protracted hunt to find his cabin reduced to black ashes and the bodies of his murdered wife and children, terribly mutilated and scalped. It was reported that Captain Jack went insane. Genn could not confirm this, but he had met Indians who called Captain Jack the Wild Hunter instead of the Black Hunter, and it was certain that the new name would stick. Nothing had been seen or heard of Captain Jack in the settlements, and it was thought that he had gone on the relentless track of Indians. This called to Washington's mind all that he had been told about young Lewis Wetzel, who had given up his life to the tracking of savages. "What would I not give for hunters like these men to help me on my campaign in Ohio!" he mused.

That afternoon Washington renewed acquaintance with Williamsburg men and also met colonists just arrived from England. He heard disquieting gossip from both parties. It seemed that the burden imposed upon the colonists was having audible and bold representations. And the new colonists reported that anyplace, even the Indian-infested wilderness of Virginia, was preferable to England.

Washington went to bed early and upon awakening found that he had slept nearly twelve hours, and even then the comfortable bed was hard to leave. Securing his weapons and making all the purchases that he could conveniently pack, he set out for home. The three-day ride seemed short. And it was so because of his active mind. As the miles sped by under Roger's steady trot, Washington's thought was so profound that he did not notice the fleeting of the hour. And that thought was adequate to answer the wild and whirling questions with which he was assailed. How early in the spring would Governor Dinwiddie give him the three companies of soldiers? What was to be their equipment and how best could it be transported? How was he to build a fort? Would he be able to transport some heavy pieces of artillery? If, in the meantime, the French built the fort at the Forks, what then would be Washington's procedure? Fort or no fort, would not the issue be war? Yes, he thought a thousand times.

In due course, Washington reached home, and never had he been so glad to get there. He had lost more than a stone in weight, and his limbs were covered with cuts and bruises, his hands were blistered, and the long concentrated violent use of his muscles had rendered them sore and utterly weary. What he needed was rest, and, active as he had always been day in and day out, he found that sitting at home before the warm fire for days on end and sleeping the long nights through were things for which he was unutterably grateful. But his mind did not rest. His mother was so proud of his achievement, so glad at his promised commission, and so pleased with what she called his immeasurably improved look that she actually embarrassed him. All the news and all the gossip that had pertained to the colony during his absence his mother had gathered and now recounted to him. She was loud in her criticism of the government. And she asked him outright—what are we American colonists going to do about it?

In less than a week Washington was about, going over the estate and riding out to his farm. It was cold there in Virginia, but nothing compared to the weather he had encountered beyond the mountains. Snow fell occasionally, but it did not last, and the ground was dry enough to make riding easy. Usually at midday it was sunny and pleasant. It took a week or more for the news about Washington's return and the commission Governor Dinwiddie had given him to spread over the colony. Washington resisted riding over to Belvoir, but he very much wanted news of his old friends. Anne Fairfax was the first to call upon him at Mount Vernon. She was even more amazing and voluble than his mother. She plied him with a thousand questions and kept him talking incessantly for two hours.

After Anne had gone, Mary casually asked if she had said anything about Sally. When Washington replied in the negative, she asked even more casually, "Did she tell you anything about Martha?"

"Martha? No, she didn't. Martha who?"

"Oh, she is a friend of Sally's from Philadelphia. She visited Sally last fall."

Then Washington thought it would be incumbent upon him to go out and attack the woodpile to counteract a slight disturbance of mind as well as for the sake of old times. He found that he had lost none of his skill with the axe and that his strength had grown. William, his Negro slave, came by and remarked with great admiration, "Marse Gawge, you shore got powerful strong on that Injun hunt. You shore did."

Next day during the noon hours when the sun shone warm, Washington espied his friend Fairfax galloping down the road from Belvoir, and he ran out to meet him. That surely was a happy though rather tense meeting. Washington sent Fairfax's horse to the stable and, arm in arm with his old friend, he led him into the sitting room where, with wine to drink and comfortable chairs before the bright fire, they sat down to the old familiar pleasure of a long talk, only this one bade fair to be the most thrilling and poignant that they had ever indulged in.

"By jove, George! But you look great!" exclaimed Fairfax. And he repeated it. "I cannot get over how well you look. Brown and thin and hard, you've got something in your face you never had before. Sally will just about expire when she sees you." Here he broke into his old, pleasant laugh, which always made his handsome face shine. "Well, George, your news first. Mine can wait. Tell me all that happened to you on this trip to the Ohio Valley."

This was something that Washington could do without his usual reticence, and he spared nothing in the recital. At its conclusion, Fairfax stared at Washington with bright eyes and said, "Wonderful! Wonderful! Oh, how I would have reveled in being with you! That Indian princess Winona, that meeting with Red Wolf, that awful canoe ride down the French Creek—simply marvelous. George, you should have killed Red Burke. So he's become a renegade. . . . Now, about this commission we heard Governor Dinwiddie gave you."

Washington told him about that too, and Fairfax, receiving the news in silence, suddenly threw the stub of his cigar into the fire and, with flashing eyes and a ring in his voice, asserted, "George, you understand as well as I do that this means war!"

"Yes, it does," returned Washington simply.

"Dinwiddie could not have picked as good a man in all these colonies. That is a frontiersman's job. Perhaps you can draw to yourself enough frontiersmen, men like yourself, to offset the crude inexperience of these English soldiers. Why, in the woods with these savages the English soldiers would be lambs among wolves. . . . We have a great deal to talk about during these weeks you must wait. I can help you. I have a couple of books that will help you. I have been commissioned to bring you back to dinner, and if that is not convenient for you then come Sunday with your mother. As to that, you are to come Sunday as well as today."

"Well, Fairfax, I will wait until Sunday and come over with mother."

"All right. I'm sorry, and I'll certainly catch it from Sally. Now, you'll want to hear about her."

"Yes, indeed, it would be pleasant," returned Washington concernedly.

"See here, old fellow, you needn't take that tone with me," returned Fairfax, with a warm gaze on his friend. "I know about everything. First, we are all very well, Sally particularly, and I think more beautiful than ever since the baby came. It's a boy and we named him George which is jointly after you and me too. Sally worships the youngster and spoils him terribly. We are prosperous despite these new and unheard of taxes. I'll mention that later. But I want to give you a thought about—well, how to meet what otherwise might be an embarrassing situation for you."

"Now, Fairfax, here's where I return your admonition and tell *you* not to be constrained with me."

"Fine and deserved! Bluntly then, George, did you have a—an affair with an Indian girl over there?"

"Affair?" queried Washington. "With that pretty daughter of Black Hawk? Affair? You mean—"

"Yes. You know what I mean."

"Good heavens, no!" exclaimed Washington, with a laugh. "I met Winona once. She hardly spoke a word, and only once did she meet my eyes. That's the extent of the affair. How on earth did you hear such talk, if it were talk?"

"Red Burke wrote to Sally and some other old friend in Fredericksburg. Sally never mentioned it except to me and Anne, but the gossip spread from Fredericksburg. Coming from Burke it could easily be discounted, but Sally evidently took some stock in it. She was queer for a week. She lost her appetite. Finally Anne got it out of her, and the sum and substance of the whole thing was that she believed the story, and I guess it just about broke her heart."

"Why, Fairfax, of all the preposterous things!" exclaimed Washington, in amazement and anger. "That renegade Red Wolf better keep out of my way when I go back. . . . But, Sally—she didn't *believe* it?"

"Women are queer, George. Certainly she believed it. It's easy enough to believe, isn't it? With that Indian girl as pretty as Burke made out? Were all the young men on the frontier after her?"

"Yes, that was true, but she is very young, about sixteen, and her father is a dignified old chief, and he keeps the white fellows as well as the Indians away from her."

"To tell you the truth, George, the gossip tickled me," went on Fairfax. "I did not especially credit the story, but I knew it could have happened. I've seen one or two Indian girls that I could have fallen in love with if I had had a chance. Of course, you can conceive of that too."

"I can indeed," returned Washington dreamily as the image of Winona's dusky beauty came before him. "To men who have loved the wilderness as you and I, an Indian girl who typifies all the beauty and the primitive wildness of it would simply be irresistible if she was as innocent and good as she was beautiful. But fortunately for the whites, Indian maidens like that are few and far between. I saw several other good-looking Indian girls; none, however, who would compare with Winona. She was indescribable."

"Well, George, when you come to grips with Sally, you make sure that you do describe Winona adequately," went on Fairfax. "It will do Sally good. If you could stoop to the deceit of letting her believe that you did have an affair with this Indian girl, it would be just what she deserves, but, of course, you can't do that. Sally has always been in love with you. She has told me that many and many a time. She always said though that she loved me best, and I guess marrying me proved it. She is a perfect wife and mother, but that jealous twist in her nature, and I suppose it's common with a great many women, makes it hard for her to accept the fact that you could see any other woman but her. Now, when you come over to Belvoir, you be your old self. Don't mind Sally. She is liable to be as cold as Greenland's icy mountains, but if you apparently don't notice it, she will come round all right, and she is going to make overtures to you about this disturbing little Indian beauty. You rub it in thick."

And when he got to Belvoir, sure enough, that was the first thing Sally asked him. "What is this I hear about you and the Indian squaw!"

"Squaw!" echoed Washington, suddenly thrilled to his depths. She was wonderful then with that blaze in her magnificent eyes. "Oh, you mean the Indian princess Winona, the daughter of Black Hawk."

"Yes, that is who I mean."

"Why, Sally, when I saw her last she was quite well and happy."

"Winona! An Indian princess. . . . What is she like?"

"Sally, she is lovely, but, tell me, where did you hear anything about Winona?"

"I'll tell you presently. Now, I am intensely curious to hear if she is really as—as pretty as I was told."

"Pretty is not the word," responded Washington, tingling at this evidence of her jealousy. "But to describe Winona is quite beyond me. She is a woodland flower, a wild rose. She is about sixteen years old, slender in build but indeed a woman, she has a small regal head that is crowned by the most beautiful raven-black hair I ever saw. Her face is oval, not red at all, but a kind of dark golden tan, inexpressibly sweet, and her dusky eyes, not jet black nor brown, but just like the dusk after twilight, the shyest, deepest, most unfathomable eyes I ever looked into." And Washington went on warming in his praise, inspired by Sally's rapt attention, and he spoke of her lissome form, her picturesque buckskin garb, the bright beaded band she wore around her forehead, and the single eagle plume it held in place, and her wonderful hands, brown, graceful, yet strong as steel, and he concluded when he was both out of breath and out of eulogies.

"Major, you are quite poetic—for you," she replied bitterly. "I knew your Winona was all you say, only I wanted you to confirm it."

"How did you know, Sally?" asked Washington, and his heart began to fail him as he took her in from head to foot and noted the restless tapping of her slipper, the straight tension of her form, and the flutter of lace on her breast, and lastly, the look upon her face that was almost havoc.

"Red Burke wrote me from Monongahela," she replied. "I was surprised to get his letter and shocked—shocked that my old schoolmate, my boyish sweetheart, my *only* friend, had fallen to an affair with an Indian squaw."

"Sally, I lost the one love of my life," returned Washington sadly. "Can you begrudge me some little expression of joy—of my appreciation of beauty—even if it comes from an Indian girl out in the wilderness?"

"But, George, you are a Washington!" she returned passionately.

"Cannot you conceive that even for a Washington a lovely Indian maiden like Winona might bring something without which life would not be worth living?"

"No, I cannot conceive of that. I think it is terrible. I am shocked beyond words. What will your mother say? Oh, oh, that you could sink so low! You, the George Washington so superior to all his fellows! You, for whom your mother and Anne and I had reserved a great station in our American colonial life. I am horribly hurt."

"Sally, I'm sorry," returned Washington, deeply stirred. It was impossible to carry on any subterfuge with Sally. "Would you mind telling me just what you believe?"

"I *didn't* believe," she whispered low, and her eyes pierced him. "I wouldn't believe a word from Red Burke on his deathbed. I was tortured, waylaid by doubt and suspicion, human as any woman, but, I tell you, I didn't believe it . . . And, oh—now you have confirmed it."

"What have I confirmed?"

"Your relation to this Indian princess—this Indian *I* call a squaw," she retorted scornfully.

"Sally, you do me an injustice, and it is not the first time," rejoined Washington, unable to contain himself. "I never as much as held Winona's hand. She is as sweet and pure as you ever were in your life. That you could believe one single word from Red Burke is disgusting to me. I'm ashamed of you. You let your inordinate jealousy blind you—control you. It is little of you, to say the least. I didn't love Winona, I didn't have time. I can conceive of any man, no matter what the ties of blood were, if he were thrown with an Indian girl like her, he certainly would love her. Young McKnight, a fine fellow and friend I made in the Monongahela, was crazy about Winona. But what hurts me most, Sally, is this. That you didn't know me well enough to realize that if I loved Winona I would marry her."

Washington ended his direct and forceful speech with a heat he could not repel. It was always the same way in an argument with Sally. She always won it, not because it might be right, but because her emotional appeal was so tremendous that no man, much less himself, could deliberately make her suffer. Sally softened, she relaxed. She drooped her head and reached for him with trembling hands, and then she leaned her forehead against him, weeping. "I'm sorry," she whispered. "I was . . . always a jealous cat. It was despicable of me. You did right . . . to let me suffer. Oh, I know—you could have told me sooner. I should have known . . . that you are different. But men . . . are men, and you are human, but I never dreamed . . . that in case you . . . fell to care for an Indian girl . . . that you would marry her. Forgive me!"

"Sally, certainly I'll forgive you if there is anything to forgive," replied Washington.

"George, you horsewhipped Red Burke within an inch of his life on my account. I hope when your trails cross again—and I believe they will—I hope you will not let him off so easily next time."

"Sally, for that very reason I want to keep out of Red Wolf's way. He has become a renegade. He is a dissolute hanger-on about Indian camps. Let us hope I will never have the misfortune to have him try to injure me again. Forget it, Sally. And now, tell me about this Martha."

"Where did you hear about Martha?" she questioned quickly and stood away from him again wiping her flushed, tear-wet face. "Oh, of course, it was Fairfax. He was smitten with her himself."

"So I gathered. Tell me about her."

"George, she's the loveliest girl I ever knew," responded Sally. "An exact contrast to me! That doesn't seem complimentary to me, but she is dark where I am light. I often wonder why I did not think of Martha for you long ago. But I wanted you for myself. And when the inspiration came to me, it was too late. Only I didn't know it until after I had roused in her a strong interest in you. I wanted you to know her. You couldn't help loving her, and it meant so tremendously much to me that I should be the one to bring you two together—to make you happy. But hers was no romance. I suspect that Martha does not love Mr. Custis. Her family pressured her into marrying him, although he is much older. He's just a plain Englishman but very rich. I'm terribly sorry. I had set my heart upon it. But I will not give up, George. There must be another girl somewhere who will see in you what Anne and I see. I'll try to find her because—you big Injun!—it certainly won't be safe to allow you to roam that Ohio wilderness fancy-free and unattached."

15 Washington Sets Out for Fort Duquesne and Meets Red Burke

Washington found that ten days of resting and idleness with only a break here and there was all he could stand of inactivity. He began to gain weight, and he preferred to be lean and hard. Thereafter he attacked the woodpile, rode out to his plantation, built fences and did odd jobs in the meantime, and drove his mother over to Belvoir on Sundays—all the while waiting to hear from Governor Dinwiddie and particularly from Christopher Gist. The weeks passed without his getting word from either. The snow and bitter wind also passed, and as the sun grew higher the days became warmer, and at a distance the bare woodland took on a tinge of red and then of green.

At last came a communication from Wills Creek, much soiled by special messenger and addressed to him in Gist's crude handwriting. Washington tore it open in haste. He divined bad news and as usual was correct. Gist reported that a big force of Frenchmen had built a large fort at the Forks of the Ohio, which they called Fort Duquesne. A good-sized garrison already had been established; soldiers, supplies, and cannon were being transported from Montreal, across Lake Erie, overland to Fort Le Boeuf and thence down French Creek to the Allegheny. Gist said it was too late, of course, to build a fort on that most favorable site, but it was not too late to capture it with a goodly army. With the help of the Half King and Scarrooyaddy and their braves, Gist thought they might tackle the job of capturing the fort with five companies of soldiers. Gist went on to say that Washington could depend on him and a number of young backwoodsmen, and he urged Washington to hurry.

"Oh Lord!" groaned Washington. "It has turned out just as I feared. England is too slow. Dinwiddie will be furious when he hears it. He is liable to send a few soldiers in my charge to attack Fort Duquesne and expect miracles from it."

Washington rode over to see his friend Fairfax, and they talked until late. Sally certainly pouted that day for lack of attention, but as Washington left she searched his grave face with understanding eyes. Washington waited a few days in the hope of hearing from Dinwiddie and at the same time putting the affairs of the two plantations in order so that he could leave at once. Then, selecting his strongest horse, heavy enough to carry him and a small pack, he set out for Williamsburg. The roads had become dry, the early spring sun was pleasant, and the gray bareness of winter had given way to color.

When Governor Dinwiddie heard of the building of Fort Duquesne from Washington's lips and had read Gist's letter for corroboration, he burst into one of his rages. Recovering, he said that Washington would have to take an armed force to the Ohio Valley, pick out a place suitable to erect a fort, and there wait for reinforcements and cannon, with the purpose of capturing Fort Duquesne. The Ohio Valley belonged to England, and Dinwiddie vowed he would drive out the French and hold it no matter how long it took. The Governor deplored his government's dilatory attitude toward the American colonies, and he said he would undertake to make that government see the tremendous importance of beating the French.

Washington did not attempt to tell his chief the almost overwhelming obstacles presented and the fact that England would sustain more than one defeat out there on the Ohio before they made a conquest over France. But Washington admired Governor Dinwiddie for his force and determination and even for the hazardous purpose that would not brook thought of failure. Any day a ship might dock at Williamsburg to disembark troops, and meanwhile Washington was to start at once with what soldiers and equipment were available. Dinwiddie gave Washington two companies of foot soldiers under Captain Peter Hogg and Washington's own interpreter Vanbraam, whom he made a lieutenant, five subalterns, two sergeants, six corporals, one drummer, a hundred and twenty soldiers with a surgeon, and supply wagons with twenty-five soldier drivers in the charge of a sergeant. They were poorly equipped, lacking sufficient artillery, ammunition, horses, wagons, and even supplies. But Washington was given plenty of money to buy equipment on the way. And Dinwiddie's last injunction was for Washington to go ahead and prove again his influence with some of the Indian tribes. Dinwiddie had the keenness to see that if the English were to win this conquest over the Ohio, it had to be done through the Indians. The French had long been wise in this regard.

Before Washington started for Alexandria, information came from Captain Trent, who, with a small force, was proceeding from Cumberland to the Ohio, that he would have to have reinforcements or be stopped by the large body of French and Indians which his scouts reported.

Washington left with his detachment next day at noon and pitched camp that night at Cameron, which he had named from one of Lord Fairfax's titles.

Next day Washington moved his force on to Cresaps, the frontiersman who had his post near the mouth of the south branch of the Potomac. Here again Washington heard bad news. Captain Trent had never reached the Ohio and had been obliged to surrender to a thousand Frenchmen under Contrecouer. Further news was that the Indians on that side of the Ohio remained loyal to the colonists. Washington crossed the Blue Ridge at Vestal's Gap, a slow hard journey occasioned by the early spring and wet ground, then he went on to cross the Shenandoah, and thence to Winchester, and from there to Edward's Fort, and thence up to Wills Creek. This route gave Washington opportunity to buy more supplies and equipment of which he availed himself all that was possible. But he secured neither enough horses nor wagons nor supplies to reassure him. On the slow march the soldiers improved the road so that Washington's reinforcements would have much better travel.

At Wills Creek, Christopher Gist with the young colonist McKnight and a matured frontiersman named Tom Waggener and other woodsmen were awaiting him. For Washington the meeting with his old guide was certainly thrilling, if not reassuring. The moment he saw Gist's face he knew there was more bad news.

"Howdy, Major," was his greeting. "Hyar's your friend McKnight whom you met at Monongahela, and shake hands with Tom Waggener, Jerry Smith, Brad somethin-or-other, and Hank Oldham, all woodsmen I'll vouch for. The men we had with us on the trip to Venango are hyar at Wills Creek and available. Better take all the men you can get."

Washington greeted the newcomers and was especially glad to see young McKnight, and he assured all of them that he was most grateful for their willingness to accompany him to the Ohio. Tom Waggener had had even more experience on the frontier than Gist, and he would be very valuable.

"Major, is this hyar all the force you got?" asked Gist.

"Yes. Dinwiddie gave me all the men available and said he would send reinforcements."

"Wal, what are you gonna do with them while the reinforcements are coming?"

"We are to build a fort and remain there until I have a big enough army to attack the French."

"Humph! Have you figured out where you're gonna put up that fort?"

"I have, Gist. Great Meadows, on the Redstone, on the west side of the creek. I remember a high bank and plenty of timber off on the bluff. Logs can be cut and hauled down to the site very promptly, but if you know of a better place than Great Meadows, tell me about it."

"Wal, I reckon I don't. How about you, Waggener?"

"Major Washington, I know that country, and you could not have picked a better place for a fort. It's easy travel across the meadows to the Monongahela, and you can't be surprised at Great Meadows. The French travel in batteaux, but they can't get up the creek with heavy artillery."

"Well, that's settled," returned Washington. "Later I shall want to know all about this Fort Duquesne."

"Wal, that'll be a tough nut to crack," went on Gist. "But it is the backbone of this campaign, and sooner or later it's got to be done."

"Have you any news of the Half King and Scarrooyaddy?"

"No, I haven't. Sorry about that. It worries me. But I'll gamble on both them Indian chiefs. Won't you, Waggener?"

The sturdy frontiersman stroked his grizzled beard and nodded his shaggy head ponderously but did not give his assurance any verbal affirmation. Washington, quick to interpret these frontiersmen, received the thought that matters with the Indians might be at a serious point. He felt, however, that all he had to do was to get the ear of the Half King and Scarrooyaddy to win them to his campaign. Then Washington instructed his officers to go into camp and make ready to leave early in the morning.

But before that day was ended a messenger named Ward from Captain Trent arrived with two young Indians who brought messages for Major Washington. The Half King sent belts of wampum to the governors of Virginia and Pennsylvania and a message which said to them in part, "the bearer will let you understand in what manner the French have treated us. We have waited long thinking they would come to attack us, but we now see they have a mind to use us. We are now ready to fall upon them, waiting only your assistance." Half King's message to Washington was accompanied by a belt of wampum, and it was even more forceful and relieving than his message to the government.

That evening Washington called a council of war with several of his officers and the frontiersmen. Ward said that the Captain Trent had been forced to surrender in the face of a thousand French soldiers in possession of eighteen pieces of artillery, some of them nine-pounders. Washington, with his attachment of Virginia soldiers, was expected to go to the assistance of Captain Trent but would have arrived too late to be of any service. Washington thought it was impracticable to march against the French with his small force, and he decided to hold to his original idea and push on to the Great Meadows, building a road as they advanced and arriving at Great Meadows to erect a fortification on Redstone Creek. Both frontiersmen and officers approved of Washington's plan. Thereupon he gave orders for Ward and one of his young Mingo Indians to go on to Williamsburg with the message for Governor Dinwiddie and for him to acquaint the Governors of Maryland and Pennsylvania with news of the critical situation. Then Washington dispatched the other Mingo Indians to the Half King with a strong and persuasive message assuring the chief of Washington's greatest thanks and assurances of the greatest love and affection for him.

Next day began the laborious and momentous advance from Wills Creek toward Great Meadows. The building of the road necessarily slowed down travel. On the night of the third day out, Washington was surprised at the return of Ward and the Indian. They had come on fast horses with a message from Governor Dinwiddie. The Governor approved of Washington's proceedings, but he was considerably displeased with Captain Trent. He also informed Washington that a Captain Mackay with a company of one hundred men had arrived and would be sent on Washington's tracks and should be expected in due course.

The same night two Indian runners came from Wills Creek to Washington's camp. They had traveled from the Ohio country and told about the French troops building Fort Duquesne. The walls of the Fort were twelve feet thick, the logs being filled in with earth and stone. They had cut down all the timber around the prominent site between the two rivers.

According to the Indians, they were already eight hundred in number and expected sixteen hundred more soldiers and equipment very soon.

Washington agreed with Gist that the French would send out all possible news by the Indians to discountenance and discourage the English. Gist and Waggener took it with a grain of salt. "Major," said Gist, "you'll get the straight goods from Half King or Scarrooyaddy when we get over there."

It took all day to ford the swollen Redstone Creek. Next day Washington set up camp near the site he intended to fortify, and in company with Gist hastened here and there to see if his memory served him correctly. It seemed that he had been too conservative. The site for a fort was even better than he had remembered. Sufficient timbers for the fortifications were available less than a half-mile distant, most of which haul was downhill. Before the end of that day the several camps had been put shipshape, fires were burning, meals were being cooked, and Washington had his plans all drawn out and ready. At sunset he stood on the high bank and watched the swift creek of reddish water sweep on through the green meadows. The bleached grass waved in the breeze, rippling like a sea of gold in the sunset glare, the meadows rolled and waved away like a calm sea to the border of forest now decorated in light spring garb, meadowlarks and swamp blackbirds sang from the grass, there was a troop of deer across the creek, and the wide expanse of open country seemed too beautiful to be spoiled by the erection of a fortification.

A message from Half King told Washington that a French officer with soldiers had been sent out to take deserters. Washington sent Captain Stevens and twenty-five soldiers on a scouting trip to find the Half King and his Indians. If successful, they were to send him to Washington with a small guard. Then, happily, Washington learned that there was a detachment of soldiers at Winchester which would be sent out in a few days. There was also a possibility of three hundred and fifty men from Carolina and two hundred from

Maryland, and Pennsylvania had raised ten thousand pounds for the campaign, all hopeful possibilities which, however, could not benefit Washington in the immediate present.

Another message from Half King, conveyed by Captain Stevens, confirmed that a French army had set out to intercept Major George Washington's forces. They intended to kill any Englishmen they met and had already been on the march several days. Half King assured him that he and other chiefs would reach him soon to have a council. He was not able to say how many Indians he would bring. The young Indian who had accompanied Captain Stevens from the Half King imparted a good deal of information, the reliability of which Washington could not vouch for. The Indian said the French at the Forks were still hard at building their fort. On the land side, the fort was stoutly protected, but so far it was open on the water side. They had a number of small cannon, none of which was mounted. After thinking about this information, Washington decided not to pay much attention to it and to wait for Gist, who had been sent on a fact-finding mission to Monongahela, to return.

Washington broke camp that day and traveled as expediently as possible on to the mouth of Redstone Creek. Here he met an Indian trader who had come from the Monongahela settlement. He had met two Frenchmen the night before who reported that strong detachments were on the march, and this confirmed the advice from Half King and caused Washington to go into camp temporarily between two natural entrenchments. With that, he immediately sent out a scouting party on horseback to see if they could come upon the French forces and locate their number and equipment. These men returned late in the evening to report that they could find no trace of the French.

Matters were getting complicated and serious; Washington was in a quandary as to what to do. The next morning to his satisfaction, Gist returned from Monongahela. His report was brief and reliable as usual. The French officer La Force, with fifty soldiers, had been at his place on the Monongahela and had perpetrated some depredations there. Washington at once sent a detachment of sixty-five men under Captain Hogg to find and engage this French La Force. Gist said that the French he had encountered were very keen to locate the Half King and intended to kill him if they could not capture him.

Washington acquainted his several Indian runners with this information. These Indian runners, two of whom had reached Washington's camp that day, agreed to guide Washington to the French, and they assured Washington that if the Half King had been insulted, not to say killed, they would induce the whole Mingo tribe to fall upon the French. Washington at once dispatched two of these runners, one a Mingo and the other a Delaware, to bid the Half King to proceed with all haste to join Washington on the Redstone. Before dark that night a message from the Half King arrived, and it precipitated immediate action. The Mingo chief said that while on his way to join Washington he had come upon tracks which his Indian scouts followed to a ravine where they found the party of French in camp.

Washington had to make another swift decision, and he was equal to it. This might be a ruse on the part of the French to split his forces. It was an important if not a very grave decision to make. Fearing to be attacked by another French force while absent, Washington had his soldiers hide the ammunition and supplies while he selected Gist, Waggener, young McKnight, and forty seasoned soldiers to advance at once against the hidden Frenchmen. With the Mingo and Delaware as guides, this detachment set out at nightfall in a blinding rainstorm and through the darkness as black as pitch. Washington and his soldiers, sure of the Indian guides' instinct to take them as straight as an arrow to their quarry, had only to address themselves to the tremendous difficulties of the march. They tramped all night through the dense, wet, broken forest, and at daylight the rain ceased. They went on and presently came to an Indian encampment which proved to be that of the Half King, and, after eating and drinking, Washington had a conference with him. They both decided to attack the French camp at once. The probabilities were that La Force was waiting for reinforcements or for returning scouts.

"Gist, you go with this Mingo who knows where the French are hidden and get the lay of the land. If possible, see how many there are, though don't take any unnecessary risks."

After Washington's instructions, Gist and the Indians disappeared in the forest. They returned early in the afternoon. Gist's report said the Frenchmen were lolling around in their camp waiting and evidently were so securely hidden that they had not taken the precaution to put out guards. Washington asked particularly to have the location described to him. When that had been done in the frontiersman's graphic manner, Washington gave his orders. The Half King was to take his Indians and proceed to the far, or eastern, side of the ravine where the Frenchmen were hidden while Washington was to take his detachment and approach from the West. The attack was to be made Indian fashion. They were all to separate a little way from each other and to crawl to an advantageous position where a signal from the frontiersman was to be answered by the Half King. That was to begin the attack.

The whole party set off into the forest, and presently the Indians under Half King made a wide detour to the left. Gist led Washington's men, and he proceeded swiftly and silently through the forest for several miles, halting frequently, as was his way, to listen and to peer through the forest ahead. Presently as they came to rocky ground and a thinning out of the timber, Gist ceased his swift action and went forward slowly and cautiously. At length he halted and beckoned Washington and his men to surround him.

"The French are just ahead about a hundred yards," he whispered. "We'll spread out and crawl from hyar on and go slow."

"Men, keep within sight of each other and don't snap any twigs or rustle the brush," said Washington. "If our signals work we'll know when to fire, otherwise use your own judgment. But go slow, be careful not to make any noise. Remember this is Indian warfare!"

The attacking party spread out and got down softly to crawl. Gist was in advance of Washington, and he looked like a huge yellow worm slipping through the grass and brush. Waggener was on Washington's left and McKnight on his right. The heightened color and bright eyes of the young men betokened an intense excitement which recalled vividly to Washington his own sensations on his first Indian attack. Gist would crawl for a few feet and then rest. Every time he started up again he seemed to go more slowly and cautiously. At length he motioned for his followers to come on, and this time he waited until Washington had come abreast of him.

"The brink of that holler is only fifty feet further," he whispered.

"Waggener, pass the word along on your side, and McKnight you do likewise on your side," whispered Washington.

It was about midafternoon, hot and sultry in the forest. The melancholy notes of a hermit thrush permeated the forest. The leaves were still. From somewhere came the low melodious murmur of a running stream. From some distant treetop came the call of a crow. A bluejay began to squall somewhere near at hand. That would be a significant thing to Indian ears, but it remained to be seen whether or not the French would take note of it. A black snake glided from in front of Washington as he crawled noiselessly forward. He wormed his way through little aisles between the bushes, and he spread the ferns and the mayflowers with his left hand while with his right he did likewise with his rifle. Gist stopped the advancing line three times before they came out of heavier timber onto flat mossy rocks which formed the western embankment of the ravine. It ended abruptly a few yards ahead, and along the front there was a fringe of vines just high enough to conceal the attackers. Washington, rising on his knees, saw that most of his men were in position in line with him and that there were only a few yards more to crawl. It was a tense moment. All along that line sounded the slight metallic click of the rifles being cocked. With a sweep of his hand to the left and to the right, Washington started the last advance, and, crouching low, he made toward the clump of vines in front. The ravine was in the shade of tall oaks. Shafts of sunlight filtered through the foliage, and from below came the music of running water. Washington's keen ears caught the voices of Frenchmen and then a loud laugh. He thought grimly that the French would be laughing on the other side of their faces very soon.

The advancing line had almost reached the verge when suddenly a shrill piercing yell of an Indian rent the silence. The Frenchmen had an Indian scout down there, and he had been too clever to let the attacking party completely surprise the French. Rifle shots cracked from the opposite bank, and white puffs of smoke appeared against the green. Hoarse cries from men sounded below. Then Washington rose on his knee to peer through the top of the vine. He saw Frenchmen running everywhere on the flat green sward below, shouting and snatching up rifles, and then beginning to shoot into the green foliage from which the puffs of smoke arose. Rifles began to crack on Washington's side. Young McKnight was quick to fire, and then shooting began to crack on Washington's left. He noted that Waggener and Gist withheld their fire a moment, and, raising his rifle with clenched teeth, he thought grimly that as those old frontiersmen never wasted powder, neither must he. Then Washington fired, and well he knew that his bullet found its mark.

Pandemonium broke loose in the ravine below. The trapped Frenchmen yelled and fired their guns and rushed for cover. From the Half King's side of the ravine there came a volley of shots, seemingly from nowhere. A scattering fire ran all along Washington's side of the ravine. The engagement was short and fierce, lasting only a few minutes before some French officer yelled for mercy. Washington shouted for his own men to cease firing, but it was some moments before the Half King's Indians could assimilate the idea of surrender.

Washington, walking to the edge of the cliff, made a sweeping survey of the ravine and ascertained that the Frenchmen left alive had thrown down their guns. He shouted, "No, men! Reload, but hold your fire!"

Presently Washington followed Gist and Waggener down the declivity, calling on his men to come, and they were met by the Half King and his braves, whose powder-blackened faces attested to their participation in that short fray.

Washington took one grim glance at the first French officer to fall, and, noting where the bullet had entered his pallid forehead, he looked no more. There were nine other bodies of Frenchmen in sight. Whatever Indians had been with the Frenchmen had disappeared. Washington made twenty-one prisoners in all, among whom were Captain La Force and Major Drouillon. The Commandant of this small French force was De Jumonville, the dead Frenchman Washington had observed so grimly. He was surprised at the presence of this officer whose name was well known to the English. There was only one badly wounded among the French force.

Half King's Indians scalped all the dead and took their fire arms. Leaving the dead where they had fallen, Washington had his men surround the prisoners, and, with the Half King's Indians leading, they made their way back to the Indian encampment. Here they halted to eat and rest and made a hearty meal from the supplies taken from the French. Washington had counsel with Half King and informed him that the Governor wished to see him at Winchester. The Half King replied that it was impossible for him to go at the present time as his warriors were being harassed by the French, and his camp up the Allegheny had been menaced. Half King said he would send runners to all his Indian allies and tell them to take up the hatchet. The Half King sent the Frenchmen's scalps with his runners, and he promised Washington that having gotten his tribe in a safe place he would return and meet Washington at Great Meadows.

Next day Washington set out with his prisoners for his camp on Redstone creek. During that march a Frenchman informed him that this force had been sent to him with a summons to retire from the Ohio River Valley. Upon arriving at the Redstone camp, Washington sent the prisoners on to Winchester with a guard of twenty men under Lieutenant West. That done, Washington made plans to start erecting a fort immediately, making sure that the French would learn of the defeat of Commandant De Jumonville's forces and send a large army to attack him. Sitting around his camp fire with his frontiersmen, Washington could hardly believe that in such pleasant surroundings he was preparing for war. Right then he decided to get possession of some of that land when the war was over.

Next day he put his plan into operation. He sent one detachment of men to cut and trim logs, another to take horse and drag the logs down, and others to dig the trenches in which the log foundation was to be imbedded. He also sent the frontiersmen out to bring in what meat they could kill, and he spent his time walking to and fro superintending the work he had ordered. In the afternoon he was watching the diggers, and, as was his habit, he listened to the men and profited by their conversation. A loquacious Irishman resting on his shovel and wiping his red moist face, asked of his companion, "This deggin' is shore hard work. Wot the hell is that redskin huntin' boss of ours doin' it for?"

"Well, Pat, it shore ain't any harder than the work comin' over. There's lots of fishin' worms an' they may come in handy."

Washington stepped forward to answer Pat's question himself. "My good man, we are digging in of necessity."

The Irishman looked up with a twinkle in his blue eyes as he saluted Washington. "Major, if it's necessity that we're diggin' for, it's shore a good name for the fort."

"Fort Necessity! You've named it, Pat," returned Washington, and went on his way.

The day passed and another dawned. The work proceeded and as rapidly as it was done it did not satisfy Washington. Hourly he expected more Indian runners but they did not come. His apprehensions for the present were stilled. An impulsive idea occurred to him that night, and in the morning he spoke to Gist about it.

"Gist, the work is on the way," he said, "and while it is advancing, I think I'll take you and make a quick trip to Logstown. It might help a great deal if I had personal contact with our friend Scarrooyaddy."

"Major, reckon that's a good idea," approved Gist. "You can leave someone in charge hyar, and you and me can hit the woods and going straight as a crow flies, I reckon we can make Logstown in a couple of days or so. I'd sure be relieved myself to have a talk with our Injun friends."

To that end Washington wrote out his instructions, and, leaving Lieutenant Vanbraam in charge, he set out with Gist into the wilderness, heading straight west. They traveled light, carrying only their weapons and a pouch of dried meat, dried fruit, some parched corn, and a little salt, and they reached and crossed the Monongahela before dark that day. Gist was like an Indian for traveling through the forest, and the long-legged Washington was able to keep up with him. Washington had always reveled in this sort of wilderness travel, and now with so much at stake it afforded him vivid pleasure and deep satisfaction to make the miles pass as if by magic. As he had only to follow in the frontiersman's footsteps he was left free to indulge in his old familiar joy of the woodland. Trees and birds and animals and in open places a keen eye for possible Indian tracks and the many colorful vistas of the forest seemingly made the hours outrun his feet. They slept like Indians under the shelter of brush lean-tos, and Washington listened to the wilderness night sounds with all the joy and interpretation that had come to him as a woodsman.

To their amazement and vast concern, they found Logstown deserted. The French post and some of the cabins had been burned. There was not an Indian to be seen and only a stray dog or two. Marks of many canoes on the sand of the riverbank were thought-provoking, but they did not tell everything. Gist encircled the camp one way while Washington went the other. The red and white inhabitants of Logstown had left via the river. They took to the trail to Scarrooyaddy's camp, which had been some miles distant from Logstown. They found several young squaws there and some children and an old gray squaw who informed them that Scarrooyaddy had taken his braves and crossed the Ohio four sleeps ago. That was all the information she could give the men, but it was enough to alarm them. They took an Indian canoe and crossed the Ohio, found the trail of the Mingo chief and his braves, and followed it like hounds with their noses to the scent. The chief and his braves were heading straight west.

This was the Indian country and a total wilderness to all whites except a few renegades and frontiersmen like Daniel Boone or the Zanes. Gist did not know the country, but he assured Washington that they were all right so long as they were on the track of Scarrooyaddy, so they pressed on.

That night while they were snug under a sheltering rock where the remains of a campfire proved that the Indians had slept there, there was a heavy downpour of rain. In the morning almost every vestige of trail, even the one they had made themselves, had been washed out. Gist was disgruntled and Washington disappointed. There was nothing for them to do but return. Therefore, they turned their backs to the west and strode rapidly through the forest. It clouded over early, and the only way they could keep their direction was to go by the growth of moss on the north side of trees. Washington did not need to be told when Gist got lost. They sat down on a log in a glade and had a smoke. "Wal, Major, we're lost all right," said the frontiersman reflectively. "I've been lost a hundred times before, but never in this Ohio wilderness. I'd opine it would be all right if we wasn't in such a hurry. But it won't do for us to stay too long away from Fort Necessity."

"No," agreed Washington. "Let's eat a bite or two and then push on."

"I'll bet ten shillings we'll be running plumb into an Injun camp before we know it," said Gist. "And that would be all right too, if the Injuns only happened to be friendly. Most of our redskin friends, Major, are on the other side of the Ohio."

Gist marched on with Washington following, bearing toward the east as well as they could make out. Toward the afternoon the mist cleared off but the cloudy sky did not break. The several streams they crossed did not appear to run in the direction that they were traveling, and they believed that all streams in that part of Ohio should drain east into the big river. They crossed a couple of Indian trails widely separated with faint moccasin tracks pointing in the direction they did not want to take. They knew that the day was almost done when the forest began to get gloomy. They had hoped against hope that they would come out upon the Ohio River before this day was ended. Finally Gist halted and said solemnly that he was hopelessly lost.

"Well, so am I," replied Washington. "We've got to make the best of it."

"Man, how are you going to make the best of anything when there isn't any best?"

"I still believe our sense of direction hasn't been far wrong."

"Wal, hyar night is on us—what's that? Did you hear anything?"

They strained their ears listening.

"Gist, I didn't hear anything, but I smell smoke."

"Ahuh. So do I, now," said the frontiersman. "Let's don't be too sure. Sometimes damp vegetation, swampy ground, you know, smells like smoke. There! I heard it again. That's a dog bark. We're near an Injun camp."

"Gist, I had that figured," replied Washington, and he shot out a long arm to detain the frontiersman. "Wait, don't rush off. Let's think."

"Wal, what's there to think about?"

"We can't travel any more tonight. It will be dark soon. So if it is a friendly Indian camp we'd have to stay there all night. If it's a hostile camp it'd be just as well for us not to spend the night, in fact, not spend any time at all in it."

"Right you are, Major," nodded Gist. "You sure can think quicker and better on your feet than any man I ever traveled with. Let's camp right hyar."

They found a dry place in the shelter of a big log, and there they sat awhile munching their scant supper and then laid down side by side and went to sleep. Washington slept the night through. Gist, awakening him at daylight, said that he had not slept very well. As soon as the sun was up they started off in the direction in which they had heard the dog bark and presently came out into a trail. It led straight to an Indian encampment which was located in a park-like glade in the forest, and Gist said it was evidently a traveling bunch of Indians and not a permanent encampment. Barking dogs ran at them, snarling viciously; soon Indians leaving their campfires espied the white men and let out shrill yells. As Gist and Washington strode on toward them, the frontiersman said in a low voice, "Our bad luck sticks, George. These are Shawnee Indians, and they ain't very friendly. And I see a couple of white men standing in back."

Presently the travelers confronted a half circle of Indians. An old chief stepped forward, put up his hand in greeting, and said, "How."

Gist answered the greeting and informed the chief in the Mingo tongue and by signs that they were lost and wanted to be guided to the river. It was plain that the Indian did not believe Gist. He shook his head, eyed them with suspicious dark eyes, and spoke to an Indian beside him. Then he called out. At that, the circle opened to admit two white men dressed in buckskin garb. Washington was utterly amazed to recognize the first one as Red Wolf and the second one as one of the comrades he had seen with Wolf at Monongahela.

"Howdy, Gist," he said slowly, his swarthy unshaven face nothing if not cold, but his rolling eyes did not deceive Washington.

"Wal, if it ain't Red Wolf!" ejaculated Gist. "We come over hyar hunting for Scarrooyaddy. Do you know where he is?"

"No, I don't, but he's not likely to be on this side of the Ohio. Do you come from that new English army marching on Fort Duquesne?"

"Yes. We're building a fort at Great Meadows."

"I heard about it today when I crossed the river. There are a thousand Frenchmen and six hundred Indians already on the way up the Monongahela so if your fort is not built yet, you better be in a hurry."

"Thanks, Wolf, I reckon that's so. How far to the river?"

"About a day's travel, shortcut through the woods."

"Any trail?"

"No, not in the right direction."

"Can we hire an Injun to guide us? We want only one."

Red Wolf addressed the chief, and they conversed a little in Shawnee, which the renegade appeared to understand. Then he turned to Gist and shook his head. "No, the chief won't let you have a guide. But I'll be glad to guide you. I'd like to return good for evil to my old friend, George Washington." He spoke aloud with a sonorous roll in his voice, and he appeared sincere, but Washington did not fail to catch the glint in his eyes and he mistrusted him.

"That's decent of you, Red Wolf," returned Gist hesitatingly. "But it seems to me returning too much good for little evil. Can't one of your partners go?"

"They could, but they won't. You can take me or stay lost."

"Will you agree to get us to the Ohio River before dark?"

"Yes," replied Red Wolf.

"Come on then. You'll be well rewarded. Let's don't waste any time."

Red Wolf broke through the circle of Indians and could be seen making his way toward a tent where he was joined by two white comrades. They spoke low and then went into the tent.

"Major, I don't like this one damn bit," said Gist. "But that's the way it is. I wouldn't trust Red Wolf out of my sight for anything. But you're the boss. What do you say?"

"Gist, I don't like it any better than you, but we'll have to risk it. I believe that about the French on the way up the Monongahela River. We dare not lose any more time."

Red Wolf appeared, carrying a long rifle and slipping his powder horn and bullet pouch over his shoulder. Without more ado he motioned the frontiersmen to follow and strode across the clearing into the forest. Gist was soon at his heels, and Washington followed him. The morning was clear and the sun shone through the trees almost directly ahead of them. Washington calculated that the renegade had started out all right anyway. Washington looked back as he entered the forest to see the Indians and the white men standing in a group watching their departure. That did not surprise him because it was an unusual procedure. Washington would not have trusted Red Burke in any event, but that sudden, almost instantly vanishing glint in his eye had been a warning note that must not be disregarded. Despite the fact that Gist was between him and Wolf, he never took his eyes off that swiftly striding figure. Red Wolf did not travel in a straight line. He avoided thickets, logs, and bad places, but in the main he held toward the east.

After a few miles Gist relaxed his steady pace to step aside and whisper to Washington not to take his eye off the renegade. Then he stooped down evidently to fasten one of his leggins. Washington strode on until he almost could have prodded Red Wolf in the back with his rifle. He held his rifle before him with his thumb on the hammer ready instantly to cock and discharge the weapon.

Pretty soon he heard Gist coming along behind, and he thought he detected a singular alertness and a tenseness in the renegade. And Washington's supersensitive ears caught the slight click as Red Wolf cocked his rifle. Washington could have shot him in the back, but he forged ahead a stride swifter just as the renegade whirled with savage swiftness. And, as luck would have it, Washington tripped on a root which destroyed his poise for the instant. But he leaped forward to catch the muzzle of Red Wolf's rifle and thrust it up just as the weapon belched fire and smoke almost in

Washington's face. The malignant look on Red Wolf's face betokened murder. Washington dropped his own rifle and, still clinging to that of Red Wolf, he closed with him, and there was a swift and terrific struggle. Gist bellowed, "Let him go, Major!" But Washington would not let go. The instant he got hold of Wolf he knew he was the stronger. Washington's eyes dimmed with red. There was a righteous commotion within his breast. That hot, awful fury so seldom unleashed made of him as frenzied a savage as the renegade.

They whirled around with inconceivable rapidity. Gist yelled, "I can't shoot unless you let go." Washington heard him, but he did not intend to let loose of that ruffian. Nevertheless, when Red Wolf drew his tomahawk and lashed at Washington's head, it was necessary to let go with his right hand and still cling to the rifle with his left. He swung Red Wolf clear off his feet. But the renegade came down on his feet like a cat. Then Washington got his right hand on the rifle, adding so much to his tremendous strength that he threw Red Wolf with great force to the ground, and rushing up, whirling the renegade's rifle over his head, he was about to brain him when Gist interposed his burly form.

"Back, Major," he shouted harshly. "We don't want to kill him now . . . Red Wolf, you renegade, get up and turn your back. Now, lead off. Head for the Ohio River, and if you don't lead us there before dark, I'll kill you!"

Slowly the renegade got to his feet, his eyes rolling, his jaw wobbling, his face like ashes, and sheathing his tomahawk, he turned and led off through the woods. Gist kept at his heels with his rifle on the level. He yelled back, "Come, Major, we got this thing in hand now."

Whereupon Washington picked up his rifle and followed slowly, coming back to himself. That terrible passion receded like a wave of fire. He was wringing wet with sweat, his breast labored, his eyes were so dim that he had difficulty in following Gist, and presently, as intelligence and thought returned, he was appalled by the treachery of this renegade. What a fool he had been to trust him! And he remembered Sally Fairfax and how the woman, farsighted in her intuition, had told him not to let Burke off the next time.

The sun was setting behind Washington as he came out upon the broad Ohio River, shining green and gold. Gist stood facing the renegade. "Wolf," he grated out, "I ought to murder you as you tried to murder Washington. Now you git! And it'll be bad for you if you ever cross my trail again."

16

Washington Surrenders Fort Necessity

The two frontiersmen watched the renegade glide off to disappear in the forest, and it was Washington who disrupted the motionless watch to run down the bank and call Gist to follow.

"Gist, as sure as I'm alive, I saw an Indian," cried Washington tensely.

"Wal, Major, you've got sharp eyes, but this time you didn't beat me. Must have been this way. When Red Wolf went after his gun, he must have told some Injuns to trail us. Mebbe his white partners too."

"Yes, and they did not quite catch up with us because we traveled so swiftly that they couldn't get ahead of us to ambush us, so then Red Wolf made a desperate effort."

"Well, what'll we do? According to them hills on the other side, we are miles above where we cross from Logstown."

"We better not risk swimming across," replied Washington, his brow wrinkling thoughtfully, "and wc don't darc go down to find that canoe. If we can't find a good log we'll have to risk swimming."

"You might make it, George, but I could never swim that far."

"Let's run along the bank and look for a piece of driftwood. Hurry now. Of course, there was more than one Indian, and Wolf has joined them by now."

"Save your breath and keep your eyes peeled," returned the frontiersman.

They set off at a trot along the bank of the river. The water was at its low stage now, and there was pretty fair going except in the sandy spots that dragged their feet. They passed several pieces of driftwood that they did not consider good for their purpose. Meanwhile, the sun had gone down behind the forest and the calm river shone red and gold. Far below on the opposite side Washington recognized some hilltops that were not far from Logstown. As they hurried along through the willows they disturbed water snakes and turtles that slipped into the river. They also aroused wild fowl, which Washington thought might betray them to sharp-eyed Indians. Often he looked back over his shoulder. Owing to the brush and projecting bits of bank he could not see farther back than a hundred paces. Presently he spied a long dry log high up on the bank under the willows, and he halted to consult Gist. The log was heavy but easily rolled down the bank. When they rolled it into the water, they found to their great satisfaction that it floated readily with perhaps one quarter above water.

"Put your oilskin around your rifle," said Washington, as with swift fingers he performed that office for his own.

"I reckon you better sit astride the log and hold the rifles up so water won't run down the muzzle," said Gist. "Sure, you ought to be able to ride a log seein' how you can squeeze a horse with those long legs of yours. I'll take the rear end of the log and kick and paddle for all I'm worth. If we get a half hour leeway, we'll be out of range of them redskins."

They rolled the log over into the water, wading beyond their knees until they had the steady side upward. Gist held the log while Washington straddled it and held the two long rifles in front of him across his lap. This left his right hand free to paddle or hold on as the exigency of the action demanded. Gist pointed the log out in the stream, waded until he was up to his neck, and then with a shove he launched himself, and holding on with one hand, he paddled with the other and kicked vigorously.

"She's a grand bark, Major," called out the frontiersman cheerfully. "If only you can keep her from sliding out from under you."

"Save your breath, Gist," called Washington, looking back to see that they were already fifty feet from the shore. He scanned the shoreline furtively and then peered into the timber at the point opposite. He was reasonably sure that he could preserve his equilibrium, and he could see that Gist was propelling the log slowly but surely; they got beyond the slack water, and near shore the current caught them, and they glided downstream quartering across the river. Again Washington glanced back at the shore. A few more moments would make them safe. Then his keen eyes, so quick and sure in the forest, detected dark forms slipping from tree to tree on the bank. "Indians! Gist, there they come. They're running pell-mell down the bank into the water, and they're going to shoot. Double your efforts, but don't roll me off the log."

"Mebbe I'd better roll you off, 'cause them broad shoulders of yours sure make a big target."

Washington saw the Indians level their guns, he saw the flash and the belching of red and yellow. Bang! Bang! Two of the rifles went off almost simultaneously. One bullet spattered near Gist, another thudded into the log behind Washington, and the third whistled over his head to strike the water ahead.

"Lucky, but close shave," called Gist. "It'll take 'em a little time to reload. Aha!"

A fourth gun had been discharged from the bank, and this bullet tugged at Gist's shoulder and splashed water all over his face.

"That was a white man shooting. Major, while I hold the log steady, you slip off on the far side and hold with the rifles laying flat."

Washington was quick to act upon that suggestion and fortunately succeeded without losing either of the rifles. Then, with only his arm over the log holding the rifles in place and with his face just above water, he used his left arm to help propel the log along. Gist had exchanged his position to a similar one behind the log. Washington could tell that they were drifting with the current, yet making a little progress toward the opposite shore. In a moment more a volley of four rifle shots pealed out, and bullets spattered on the water all around them.

"Major, I reckon we're safe now. But don't stick your noggin up above the log to see."

Thus they held on, paddling steadily, and when the next rifle volley pealed out, the bullets fell wide of the mark and were spent. Washington did not anticipate any more shots after that, and he was right. They worked the log across the river, touching bottom at a shallow place perhaps a mile below where they had pushed off. There they abandoned their bark and waded ashore.

"I reckoned . . . that that derned Ohio . . . was wide, but not so terrible wide," panted Gist, as he took his rifle from Washington. "What you see?"

Washington shook his head in the negative. The lonely dark shoreline with its heavy timber looked as mysterious and menacing as ever, but the pursuers had vanished. Washington was wondering if that fourth rifle had not been picked up by the savages as they came along the trail. Far below where the river turned to the west, the sun had sunk low and was shining red and sinister on the watery horizon.

"Gist, we'll strike straight across country for the Monongahela and Great Meadows. I am worried now for fear that the detachment of French and Indians Red Wolf told us about will reach Fort Necessity before we do."

"Wal, Major, we'll sure have to make tracks," replied the frontiersman. "It's gonna be a clear night, and I can travel pretty straight by the stars. Drink your fill hyar and we'll eat the rest of our meat as we go along."

They climbed the bank where Gist stood a moment facing the river and the departing sun to get his bearings, and then he plunged into the forest, with Washington close at his heels. Twilight had already fallen in the woods and soon dusk followed and then night. Old woodsmen as they were, they could not travel fast except in the open places, which were few and far between, but they pressed on steadily and silently until sometime far in the night Gist suggested they get a couple hours' sleep. He soon had a fire burning by the light of which the two men cleaned and reloaded their rifles and dried their buckskin garments. Then they lay down to snatch a few hours' slumber.

They awoke in the gray of dawn and once more addressed themselves to their journey. All day and far into the night with only short and infrequent rests they pushed on until they came to the Monongahela River. In the night Gist could not tell just where they were, but he was certain they had come out upon the river downstream from where they had crossed several days before. The bank was dry and grassy, and Gist advised waiting till daylight to cross the river. So they composed themselves to sleep, but before that came to them they both at once heard sounds that brought them up transfixed and startled. The sounds came from down the river some distance. The men gazed at each other in the starlight and read each other's minds. Silently Gist got up and stole down the bank to reconnoiter or at least to see down the river. He was gone only a few moments, and while he was absent Washington had decided what the sounds had come from. Presently Gist returned to flop down beside Washington.

"Big campfires down the river. Injuns and soldiers! They've come up the river in bateaux. Them French frog-eaters are sure hell on boats. What'll we do?"

"Well, Gist, we'll sleep if we can. It's only a few hours until daylight. We'll cross the river before it's light and we'll wait to see how strong that force is, then strike a beeline for Fort Necessity."

No more was said. Gist fell asleep with his head on a log, and Washington sat beside him trying to sleep also but too greatly concerned to win slumber. The French coming up the river in boats meant that they would have artillery. Washington leaned there beside Gist thinking, pondering, while his senses were attuned to the occasional sounds from the camp below, disrupting the peace of the forest. The river flowed on almost silently with just a faint lap of water on the shore, with the occasional splash of a fish and the whir of a wild duck and the usual faint sounds of night birds and animals. The darkest hour passed, and when it began to get gray Washington awoke Gist and they got ready to cross the river. Some distance above where they had waded, they heard rippling water, which guided them to a shallow crossing which immediately gave Gist his bearings. "By golly, Major, these derned French came as far up the river as any boats could make it. We're at a point straight across from Fort Necessity and not so damn far either. It's pretty flat country, and the French with a couple of hundred soldiers clearing the way and hundreds of other soldiers to drag cannon along—why, I reckon, they can make it to Great Meadows in less than three days."

"That will give us time," returned Washington. "First we want to see how big a force it is and what equipment they have, and then we must reach Fort Necessity in time to prepare for defense."

They waded the river, only once getting up over their hips, and climbed the opposite bank at dawn.

"Now, Major, I've a suggestion," said Gist seriously. "We sure got a drill ahead of us. You must tie up your leggins and moccasins, or you'll be walking barefooted. I'll sneak downriver and find out just how much we're up against. I can tell by the boats and the canoes."

"All right. I don't need to warn you to be careful."

While Gist glided off into the gray gloom, Washington searched around for something with which to mend his torn leggins and moccasins. He was fortunate in finding a slippery elm tree. He peeled off strips of bark, and, removing the outer layer, he used the tough slippery inside strip to bind up his leggins and to fortify his moccasins. Every now and then he would stop to listen. Presently he heard sounds of an awakening camp. First the notes of a bugle, and then the ringing of an axe on hard wood, and presently the peace of the early morning was broken by long Indian yells. These sounds added to Washington's deep apprehension. When at length he heard a rustling in the brush he stood up and espied the frontiersman approaching under the trees. Just at that moment the sun burst out red in the east. Nothing could be discerned from the frontiersman's rugged visage. He sat down on a log and breathed heavily.

"Golly, I'd like to have a smoke most as well as a cup of coffee," he said.

"Well, Gist, out with it!" whispered Washington harshly.

"Well! Do you need to be told? Must be a thousand Frenchmen and Lord only knows how many redskins. Bet I saw a hundred canoes. And I saw cannon loaded on the bateaux. They were being beached and hauled up the bank. Major, if that force of men and arms ever git down on Fort Necessity, I reckon it'll be a massacre unless—"

"This was something I tried to prepare Dinwiddie for," declared Washington grimly. "Let's make tracks for the fort."

The frontiersmen set out on that last day's journey very much after the manner of Indian runners. They walked only in the bad places, which was the majority of the distance, and they ran through the open aisles of the forest and across the meadows, which were few and far between. Gist, who was leading, halted infrequently to rest and catch his breath, and Washington, not quite spent, would have been able to keep on but was glad for the respite. They had started just after dawn; at noonday the timber had begun to thin out, and by the middle of the afternoon the lay of the land showed they were nearing the flat country through which Redstone Creek meandered its lonely way. Two hours before sunset the frontiersmen burst out of the forest to come upon a wide area from which trees had been cut and hauled away. They had made the forest in less time than they had dared to hope. From the slope of the hill suddenly there burst upon their gladdened eyes a big motley structure of different colored logs. Washington stared. For all he could tell, except one section of roof, Fort Necessity had been erected. To his amazement he saw that the tents had disappeared and no doubt were inside the fort. A bunch of horses were feeding on the grass some distance away, surrounded by soldiers. The sound of hammers came to their ears.

"Gist, such a welcome sight made me forget the French army for a minute," declared Washington.

"Wal, sure they're not letting any grass grow under their feet."

"Something must have accelerated their movements," returned Washington, with a hard laugh. "That Irishman Pat who was curious about the digging—I'll wager he made an extra complaint about the labor being speeded up. I'll tell you, Gist, it strikes me that a messenger has arrived with bad news. Perhaps the identical news that we have to impart."

Now that the long and exhausting journey was at an end it was all the two frontiersmen could do to drag themselves down from the hill and across the meadow to the fort. Long before they arrived they were sighted by scouts. But owing to their ragged and disheveled appearance, they were not recognized until they were right upon the soldiers who held them up at the stockade gate. Then there was a great acclaim as officers and soldiers surrounded them.

"Captain Hogg, I congratulate you upon a remarkable job well done," declared Washington, interrupting the officer's alarm and solicitude about his appearance. "You've had cause? A messenger must have arrived with news?"

"Yes, Major Washington. It was the Mingo chief Scarrooyaddy who arrived the day after you left."

"Scarrooyaddy! That is good. What was his report?"

"A large force of French and Indians were leaving Fort Duquesne to stop our building the fort here."

"Ah! He was right indeed. Gist and I have seen that force. Did Scarrooyaddy bring any news of the Half King?"

"Yes. The Half King was hidden across the Ohio with his Indians awaiting our coming to attack Fort Duquesne."

"Captain Hogg, we passed the French force this morning on the Monongahela. They have at least a thousand soldiers and a big band of Indians. We don't know how many, but there were over a hundred canoes. Gist saw them dragging out artillery up the bank and it is our opinion that these guns will be used to reduce Fort Necessity. Have our reinforcements arrived?"

"Only the small detachment that Governor Dinwiddie sent."

"If the French have heavy guns and it seems best to assume that they have, we will be in a critical position here. Heavy cannon on the brow of the hill back there will make this fort untenable."

"How soon can the French get here?"

"That's a matter of conjecture. We can expect Indians tonight and the artillery sometime tomorrow, perhaps late. Meanwhile you must rush preparations for defense at once. Gist and I are half-dead from exhaustion and hunger. We will have to take advantage of the immediate hours to recuperate."

Inside the fort while Washington and Gist sat at table partaking of greatly needed nourishment, Lieutenant Vanbraam and McKnight sat with them, eager to hear about their adventures, and presently Tom Waggener came in with Scarrooyaddy.

"Yaddy, I am glad to see you!" exclaimed Washington gripping the chief's hand. "We found Logstown burned and heard that you had gone across the Ohio with all your Indians."

It developed that only the Shawnees at Logstown had gone back across the Ohio. Yaddy's band had joined the Half King, who had sent him and his runners to tell Washington that he was waiting to help him attack Fort Duquesne. Scarrooyaddy had discovered the force sent down to attack Fort Necessity, and he had hurried to inform Washington. Having eaten and drunk sparingly, Washington looked around the fortification, and, making his deduction and leaving instructions with Lieutenant Vanbraam, he finally sought a bed. He was too exhausted to remain awake that night, and the last thought that stayed before his consciousness was that his small force would have no chance against that French army, and he prayed for guidance.

Next day it was Gist who awakened Washington and who informed him that he had slept seventeen hours straight. Washington could hardly speak from hoarseness and his body ached as if it had been pounded. He forced himself to move about, to eat and drink again, and then to go out to see how the work was progressing. The soldiers, so many of them that they got in each other's way, were endeavoring to roof over the northern half of the block house. Before sunset that day Indians were observed on the brow of the hill. They did not indulge in their usual yelling or hostile demonstration but watched a while and then disappeared.

Waggener, the old frontiersman, shook his shaggy head and observed, "Reckon they don't need to make any bluff."

Washington regarded that significant remark of the frontiersman as quite in keeping with his own opinion. He called a council with his officers and the frontiersmen, and included the Oneida chief, and he asked for opinions as to the best procedure to meet the situation. They made varying reports, but not one of them suggested the advisability of surrendering the fort. The shrewd Oneida chieftain said something in his native tongue that Washington translated as being something akin to "he who runs away might live to fight another day." They were all eager and willing to fight, reinforcements were on the way, and one of Yaddy's swift runners could get word to the Half King in twenty-four hours. Washington had plenty of food supplies, rifles and ammunition, but no heavy guns. They could hold out there at Fort Necessity until help arrived, provided the French did not arrive with cannon. It seemed to Washington that the gist of the situation was whether the French had or had not the heavy guns. Washington reserved his decision. He knew what to do in either case. And he waited in anxious and profound gloom.

No runners arrived the next day, and not an Indian was to be seen. All Washington's force spent that night in dread apprehension. The scouts and sentries had nothing to report. About midmorning the French army suddenly stood silhouetted, dark and menacing on the brow of the denuded hill. The Indians made up this time for their silence of the day before. They yelled and screeched and ran to and fro like fiends. Long strings of soldiers dragged guns down the hill and across the meadow, halting just outside of rifle range. By early afternoon they had several heavy guns set up on timbers. There must have been several hundred Indians who finally settled down silent and watchful. The French officers could be seen strutting to and fro like turkey cocks. French flags were unfurled and raised on high. It was an oppressive moment. Washington looked for a messenger to be sent to the fort to dictate terms. Presently there was a leaping flame and bursting cloud of smoke from one of the cannon and a tremendous boom that awoke thundering echoes far and wide. The cannon ball went wide over the fort and crashed into the woods across the creek, tearing through the treetops.

"Major Washington, that was a nine-pounder," said one of the sergeants. "I've heard that kind of cannon before."

Washington had no answer for that. McKnight came running from one of the portholes to report, "Major, that gun was a signal for the Indians to approach, and they are crawling like snakes on their bellies." The rifles of the frontiersmen began to crack, and they were answered by shrill taunting yells by the savages. The soldiers had been ordered to withhold their fire. Another flash and gleam of bursting red and then a black puff of smoke, then another *Boom*! The missile from this cannon was also poorly aimed, striking the ground in front of the fort and then thudding into the foundation. Low down, the thick walls afforded protection.

Washington realized that once the French gunners got the range, they could reduce the fort in short time into shambles. Despite the protests of his officers, he kept watch out of one of the portholes, and when he sighted savages crawling in the long grass and behind the low bushes he gave orders for the soldiers to fire. Their heavy volley was heartening, but Washington failed to see any evidence of execution. Gist and

Waggener and his two traders could hit an Indian at that distance, but he doubted if the soldiers could.

Another cannon flashed and boomed. This time the ball struck the fort squarely in the middle and crashed through with a rending sound of broken and flying timbers. It went clear through the fort, and the falling and crying out of soldiers attested to the wounded. Washington saw that those hurt had been hit by flying pieces of timber and ordered the soldiers to that part of the fort which was still unroofed. The Indians, having crawled within range, began to fire their guns. Lead bullets pattered like hail on the walls of the fort. Some of the best aimed bullets came through the portholes. The shiny streaking of arrows and the thud of them striking logs attested that there were Indians without guns. The soldiers and the frontiersmen kept shooting.

The first cannon, having been reloaded again and once more vomiting fire and smoke, this time struck the left end of the fort and tore through a section of wall, splintering and knocking logs upon the huddled soldiers. When the two other cannons had been fired, one of which made a direct hit, Washington saw at once that his fears had been justified. Against heavy cannon, Fort Necessity was untenable. His mind was full then of whirling thoughts, not what kind of decision to make but how to make it. That question was answered for him. The firing ceased, and when a soldier appeared waving a white flag, Washington gave orders for his men to cease shooting. The messenger approached to within a short distance of the fort and shouted something in French. Washington instructed Lieutenant Vanbraam to go out to meet him.

All was silent within the fort while the lieutenant was let out to hurry toward that white-flagged messenger. Washington was relieved to have this unexpected turn of affairs. He anticipated what that messenger would have to say, and he had long known what his reply would be. Scarrooyaddy had suggested the right way to decide that terrible question. Washington wanted to save his men from needless death and agony. To hold out there longer in the face of these cannon was sheer madness. When Lieutenant Vanbraam returned to the fort, Washington sent him back with the word that his demand was accepted and that he himself would go out to meet the commanding officer. Then in a few moments Washington faced the Frenchman to find him an official-looking man, most ceremonious and courteous. Washington offered his sword and agreed to honorable surrender of the fort, and the Commandant, with an elaborate bow, returned Washington's sword to him and assured him that his request was granted but that his force should leave the fort at once, carrying their guns and baggage, but would not be permitted to remove any large guns. Washington bowed his thanks, and, returning to the fort, told Captain Hogg the terms of the surrender and told him to order evacuation at once.

While Washington was outside giving instructions to his officers to pack all supplies and equipment except the several pieces of light artillery which had not even been unpacked and to fetch in and harness the horses for immediate departure, the French Commandant sent men over to search Washington's effects and take any letters or official documents. When Washington went into the fort, he found it too late to save his papers, a great blow to him. He swallowed his chagrin and determined to make notes from memory at the very earliest opportunity. He was able to keep a supply of writing paper that had not been used, and he persuaded Scarrooyaddy to come with him and bring his runners to the first camp Washington would make after departing from Fort Necessity.

The final details of Washington's capitulations to the French Commandant were consummated that night, and that really was the cessation of hostilities. The French officer broke a bottle of wine for Washington in honor of the event. Next morning Washington's retinue left Fort Necessity. The event was gall and wormwood to Washington. He did not look back. In the depths of his secret heart, that still small voice which never spoke falsely to him told him that the time would come when he would retake Fort Necessity. His force crossed the Redstone Creek and made camp late that afternoon some fifteen miles down the road.

In camp, Washington wrote an important letter to the Half King. He addressed it to his brother and assured him of his regrets at the turn affairs had taken, that he had surrendered to save his soldiers, and that he would return with a larger and better equipped force and take both Fort Necessity and Fort Duquesne. If it took a whole English army to reduce these French fortifications, it would be done. Washington appealed to the Half King to take council with his chiefs and the chiefs of friendly tribes and tell them that the English were their friends, the French their enemies, and that this state of affairs could not last long. He read the message, to Scarrooyaddy and then dispatched him with his runner to make haste and deliver it as soon as possible consistent with the utmost care in avoiding the French and hostile Indians. When the Indians were gone, Washington relaxed and began slowly to reconstruct plans for the future. Any permanent failure for the English and the Americans could not lodge in Washington's consciousness.

Next day his small army resumed their travel. There were none of them who disapproved of his actions, and they sang and made merry on the way. Every step of the long road, which Washington had traversed when it was only a trail, was familiar to him.

Arriving in due course at Wills Creek he met reinforcements, a detachment of one hundred soldiers, which Dinwiddie had sent to him. Here he bade his frontiersmen goodbye and told them to wait patiently and be ready for his return. Gist said he would return to the Monongahela settlement and keep him posted on all frontier news. McKnight said he would remain at Wills Creek and await the happy day when Washington would return.

With the rest of his force, Washington returned to Williamsburg. He feared that Governor Dinwiddie would entertain some such disfavor which he had felt for Captain Trent. Therefore, Washington told him in detail what he had done, that he had taken the whole responsibility upon his own shoulders, that the men would have fought to the death for him, but his judgment was to retire until a more favorable time. To his intense relief, Governor Dinwiddie praised his common sense and vision, and the way the Governor stamped the floor and cursed the French boded ill to those in power on the frontier. "England is slow, but she is sure," he concluded, finally composing himself. "We will have to send you with that army either in command as you were on this campaign or as a lieutenant colonel. Go home and occupy yourself and be patient and wait. I need not tell you to keep in touch with your Indian friends."

Washington returned to Mount Vernon to his mother's happiness and to the great delight of Sally and Fairfax. He settled down to improving his plantation, making his large acreage productive, and raising and buying stock. He liked farming and especially grafting fruit trees. He resumed his old intimate association with the woodpile. On Sundays he would ride over to Belvoir where the conversation took on a pretty keen edge over the discontent of the American colonists. The weeks passed by pleasantly, and when autumn came and the forest foliage took on its many-colored beauty, Washington packed his rifle over the old trail. Sometimes he brought home a brace of wild turkey or a haunch of venison. Mostly, however, these long tramps were the return to old pleasant habits of solitude, and they brought a renewed and matured brooding over the war that would have to be fought with the French and then afterwards what his vision told him would be a revolt of the American colonists.

Late in the fall, Silas Zane returned from the East, and his dynamic, forceful personality and the things he reported about what was being thought in New York and Massachusetts played havoc with Washington's hope that England would cease putting the screws on the colonists and avert a revolution. Zane was particularly interested in Daniel Boone, and he claimed that his brother Ebenezer was a kindred spirit with Boone. Lastly Zane said that he would journey across the Blue Ridge before winter set in, spend the cold months with his brothers and the Wetzels, and return to Virginia in the spring.

At last a letter from Christopher Gist arrived, and seldom or never had Washington been as absorbed in any message. The French had made it very hard for the inhabitants of the Monongahela. It was the frontiersman's belief that the French were partly responsible for the hostility of some of the tribes to the settlers. As more and more colonists took to the wilderness, fighting both it and the Indians rather than living under the hard rule of the English government, so the border warfare between redskins and whites increased. Settlers building cabins in the woods and clearing ground always had a rifle at hand while they were using an axe, and while plowing the fields a rifle along with the reins. Massacres of settler families such as had driven Captain Jack insane and made Lewis Wetzel an implacable killer of Indians became less rare on the frontier, but Gist said nothing could keep back the tide that was flowing westward. When the French were subdued along with the Indians who would not be friendly, that vast Ohio wilderness would become a paradise for pioneers. Gist said that the Half King and Scarrooyaddy had gone into winter quarters in inaccessible flatnesses where they would wait for their white allies to come with an army.

That letter of Gist's was the outstanding hopeful feature of all these months of waiting. Washington made haste to answer it so that he could dispatch it across the mountains before the snow came. He gave Gist all the news that he had which he must tell to their friends, the chiefs, in due time, and he asked for a reply in the spring. Washington hoped that his favorite time, Indian Summer, would be prolonged, but winter came at last and then the less active months for Washington began. He did not let them be a waste of time, and for relaxation he visited the Fairfaxes and even allowed himself to be taken to several balls.

Spring came at last, and never had the warm sun, the fresh dank smell of earth, the red and green budding of the trees, the white blossoms of his orchard, and all the things of the outdoors that Washington loved so well given him such profound joy and faith in the things to come.

Washington's first excursion that spring was his trip to Williamsburg with his mother, Fairfax and his wife, Sally, and their old friend Richard Henry Lee who had just returned from England. The object of this trip was to see the play, *The Merchant of Venice*, with the English actor Lewis Hallam. On their way to Williamsburg they stopped at Hanover where they put up at Shelton's Inn. Washington met and took a fancy to the bartender at the Tavern, a young man named Patrick Henry, who appeared to be a fellow of most engaging and magnetic personality.

While waiting to be served, the party conversed. "A couple of years back," spoke up Fairfax, "the Massachusetts court prohibited stage plays of any kind."

"Look at Harvard College," replied Richard Henry Lee. "It was modeled after Oxford and Cambridge but didn't include playwriting in its curriculum."

"But in 1690," said Mary Washington, "there was a first play written by an American. His name was Gustavos Asa. That play was given by Harvard students behind locked doors."

"Well, indeed Virginia is coming to the front as a colony," interposed Washington. "It holds the honor of the first play in English."

"That was *Yebare and Ye Cubb*."

"Yes," continued Washington, "I remember the actors. Later the court found them not guilty."

"Tell me, if we are allowed to read Shakespeare, why is it against the law to hear it spoken?" asked Sally Fairfax.

"That is one of the enigmas of our present-day government," replied Fairfax. Then he rapped on the table and addressed the barkeeper, "Oh, I say, fellow. Don't stand there and gape at us. Give us some service. We are thirsty and hungry."

"Your brilliant repartee stirs me to think," returned Patrick Henry insolently. "I am Sir Oracle and when I open my lip, let no dog bark!"

Fairfax stared at the fellow in astonishment, and the incident added to Washington's interest. When Henry brought the drinks it was Lee who made a wry face and complained of poor quality.

"They love it that do buy it with too much care," retorted Patrick Henry.

Whereupon Mr. Sheldon, the keeper of the Tavern, approached to apologize for his too eloquent young bartender. "The fellow seems to have only two purposes in life. One is to rant speeches and the other is to marry my daughter."

Following the general laugh, Washington interposed in a kindly way to relieve young Henry's embarrassment. "Until a few days ago my birthday was on February eleventh, but now, according to more Government rules I find I was born on February the twenty-second."

"George, they can change the calendar but they cannot change that momentous day when you were born for me," spoke up his mother.

"It's a wise mother who knows her own child's birthday," said Patrick Henry.

"See here, you young scamp," threatened Sheldon, "stop wagging your tongue or I'll throw you out."

The fiery young orator rolled out sonorously, "You take my house when you take the props that do sustain my house. You take my life when you take the means whereby I live. When you halt my voice—"

"Mr. Sheldon," interposed Washington, as the proprietor was about to use force on Henry, "let the young man continue. He recited very well indeed. We are going to see *The Merchant of Venice*, and some good recitation would come in appropos."

Thus encouraged and prompted, Henry bowed and launched forth:

> The quality of mercy is not strain'd
> It droppeth as the gentle rain from heaven
> Upon the place beneath. It is twice bless'd;
> It blesseth him that gives and him that takes,
> 'Tis mightiest in the mightiest: it becomes
> The throned monarch better than the crown;

His scepter shows the force of temporal power.
The attribute to awe and majesty,
Wherein doth sit the dread and fear of kings;
But mercy is above this sceptred sway,
It is enthroned in the hearts of kings,
It is an attribute to God himself;
And earthly power doth then show likest God's,
When mercy seasons justice.

His voice was so ringing and seductive that his audience was spellbound when he concluded, and then they generously applauded him.

Sheldon spoke up to say, "What's more, young Patrick Henry can sing too."

"Very good, sir," replied Henry, evidently pleased. "I'll sing the Anacrenniti Song." This was almost as appealing as his recitation. The people at the adjoining tables stopped their drinking to hear him, and that action proved a good deal. Washington kept time with head and hand to the rhythm of the music.

"Very, good, young man," spoke up Fairfax, "that's the first time I ever heard that song."

"First for me too, Fairfax," rejoined Washington. "It should become very popular. Sally don't you think so too?"

Then as the company arose, Washington turned to the young singer and said, "Patrick Henry, my name is George Washington. I live at Mount Vernon. I would like to get better acquainted with you."

"Thank you, Major Washington. Oh, I know you," returned Henry, with his winning smile. "Whenever you come to Hanover be sure to see me. You'll find my speech for your private ear alone vastly more to your liking."

Washington eyed the flashing-eyed young man, and, recording in mind his significant words, he bowed, shook hands, and then followed his company.

They proceeded to Williamsburg and that night went to see *The Merchant of Venice*. Governor Dinwiddie was there, and he gave a special reception to Washington and his party and told Washington that he would have important news for him very soon. After the act in the play where the "quality of mercy" speech is spoken, Richard Henry Lee leaned over to Washington and whispered, "That actor Hallam did not speak nearly so well as the young Patrick Henry person."

"Indeed not," replied Washington. "That young Patrick Henry has a future, if not in plays then in some other way where his wonderful gift would inspire men. I must see more of him."

On the way back to their tavern, Sally slipped her hand into Washington's and whispered to him, "George, I haven't had a chance to tell you. I've heard from Martha, you know, the girl I picked out for you—too late. She wrote me on her birthday. She is only eighteen. She has heard about your exploits on the frontier, and she asked me to write all about you. What message may I send to her from you?"

"Martha? Oh, I have never forgotten, Sally. Tell her I am grateful for her remembrance."

"Well, George Washington!" cried Sally, in delight. "You're waxing really poetical! That frontier experience of yours—maybe your appreciation of the beautiful little Indian princess—has at last made you conscious of the fair sex."

17 Washington Takes a Commission under General Braddock

It was immediately following the visit to Williamsburg that news arrived at Mount Vernon which greatly distressed and hurt Washington. He had heard some little criticism from various parts of the colonies about his surrender of Fort Necessity, but when his private papers that had been taken away from him there were published in France and were sent back to America, they created a scandal. The French comment made upon them was wholly unjust, and some of the reports themselves had been garbled. In one instance, Lieutenant Vanbraam had used *assassination* instead of *killing*, and the consequent inference was wholly wrong. To those who did not know the facts as to the surrender of Fort Necessity, this amounted to dishonor and disgrace for Washington. To his proud and sensitive nature the gossip was exceedingly mortifying. His own men, Captain Hogg, Lieutenant Vanbraam, Gist, Waggener, and McKnight, came forward in earnest and passionate defense of Washington. Governor Dinwiddie had the right angle on the thing, and he assured Washington that sooner or later he would be completely exonerated of something that was unjust and despicable.

All this gossip and the growing dissatisfaction of the colonists were dwarfed by the arrival in Hampton Road of General Edward Braddock and his English army. At last they had arrived, and their purpose was to reduce Fort Duquesne and the other French forts in the Ohio Valley. For a time there was great excitement in the Virginia colony which even extended to Washington himself. He remembered the commission that Governor Dinwiddie had promised him, and he waited patiently, while his mother and Sally Fairfax made his life almost unendurable for him by their importunities.

By post and by travelers, Washington kept pretty well in touch with what was going on. What he did not learn himself, Fairfax was sure to inform him. Never had Virginia been so rife with conjecture and apprehension and certainly not all of the gossip could be credited. Fairfax happened to be in Fredericksburg when Benjamin Franklin arrived for conference with General Braddock. The general had not taken kindly to the long stage ride from Hampton Road and he was impatiently awaiting the agents he had sent into the interior of Maryland and Virginia to secure the large supply of horses and wagons that he needed.

"After I capture Fort Duquesne," General Braddock told Franklin, "I shall proceed to Niagara, and having reduced that fort, then go on to Frontenac. Duquesne can hardly detain me more than three or four days of attack after which I do not see anything to obstruct my march on to Niagara."

Benjamin Franklin thoughtfully regarded the pompous English general. He was a short, square-shouldered, heavy Englishman, ruddy-faced and gray-haired with blue eyes that flashed authoritatively. "The only danger I apprehend," replied Franklin, "is from the ambushes of the Indians. Your army line will necessarily be lengthened out for miles. That will expose them to attack. The Indians never show themselves when they attack, and these French Canadians have learned the waylay tactics of the Indians."

"These savages may be formidable to raw American militia, but upon the King's regular army troops, why, sir, to make an impression would be impossible," returned General Braddock tolerantly.

Franklin did not voice his wonder and his concern. The credulity of this English officer was hard to comprehend. He made no more suggestions. When that very day Braddock's agents returned to town having collected only twenty-five wagons, and all of those not fit to travel with heavy loads, the English officer snorted with disgust and uttered some unfavorable criticism of the American people, whom he had come across the ocean to save.

"General, every farmer and planter in Virginia or Pennsylvania has horses and at least one wagon. I can be of service to you here."

"Benjamin Franklin, I beg you will undertake it for me."

George Washington regarded his friend Fairfax in consternation. Slowly the red blood manned his tanned face, matching the color of his hair. Fairfax's expression too was not conducive to calmness. Washington's ever-ready temper was not controlled this time.

"Good heavens!" he burst out. "If that isn't just like an Englishman!"

"George, it's simply awful," returned Fairfax, breathing hard. "You and I can see right now what is going to happen to the great General Braddock's army."

The two friends locked into each other's eyes with frank and heated candor. They were both frontiersmen. They knew the Indians and the kind of warfare Indians carried on, and they knew the wilderness country. But, used to restraint, even among themselves, they swallowed their anger, and finally Fairfax spoke: "George, you will simply have to get a commission under General Braddock."

"What! Me solicit an officer's position? After all the calumny that my enemies have put upon me? No, I certainly will not."

"Forgive me for that, old friend, but this stirs me deeply. It is almost sure that Governor Dinwiddie will recommend you to Braddock, and you must accept."

"Why must I accept?" asked Washington in cold thoughtfulness.

"Because you are the one man who might save that campaign against Fort Duquesne. You have your powerful Indian allies, Gist and all the frontiersmen will flock to your call. You could take as many colonists as you wanted and with them you could meet those Indians and French halfway at their own game."

"Fairfax, it's an intriguing thought. In fact, it is hard to resist. But Braddock would not have these Indians and frontiersmen around his army."

"What makes you think that?" queried Fairfax quickly.

"I don't know. It wasn't a logical thought. It's intuitive."

"Well, that's your old mystic sense working. I have learned to respect it, but, George, even if Braddock would not have these frontiersmen and Indian chiefs, you could have them. And that would amount to the same thing. Really, it would be better to have these men under you."

"Fairfax, you disturb me. You are so stern and passionate about this. You are older in frontier experience than I am. What if I don't consider your proposition?"

"Braddock's army will be wiped off the face of this earth," retorted Fairfax, with ringing finality.

Washington went home much perturbed in mind. And it chanced that the following day he received an earnest solicitation from Governor Dinwiddie urging him to accept the post he had recommended General Braddock to give him. With that he was face to face with another far-reaching decision. For several days he was preoccupied and uncommunicative, and he took long, lonely walks into the woods. Finally he had to abandon these walks. The lonely trails, the deep forest, the silence and solitude called more strongly and eloquently to induce him to fight again for his country than any importunities which came to him at home. He knew his mother would be against this campaign, and when he confided in her, it turned out to be so. But her objection was caused by fear. Washington took another long walk into his forest. And that was the last straw. Wavering, troubled, surrendering, he went home and rode over to Belvoir. Fairfax had gone to Fredericksburg so he had to talk to Sally. He unburdened himself. He began by saying that he had resigned his army commission and that the shadow of Fort Necessity still darkened his name. Then he told her what his natural instinctive impulses were and, after that, about the disaster that was surely going to overtake General Braddock. Sally Fairfax was white of face and dark of eye when she answered him. The look of her was all that Washington could detect of women's fears. "George, you will have to go. I always shared your mother's belief in your future. It is your duty to America. Go!"

So with Sally joining the great forces which beset Washington, he went home and wrote to Governor Dinwiddie that he would accept the post under certain conditions. He received a reply by his own messenger, and he was told to expect a letter from General Braddock. When that came, also by special rider, it assured Washington that his motives in resigning from the army were understood and that Braddock would be glad to have him as a member of his official staff, and the commission was made out to Lieutenant Colonel George Washington.

Braddock requested him to come at once to Winchester. Not many hours after that, Washington, riding over the familiar road, caught up with numerous empty wagons, the drivers of which told Washington they were bound to join Braddock's forces. Arriving at Winchester, he was directed at once to General Braddock's headquarters and was accorded immediate reception. He found Braddock surrounded by several of his red-coated officers and that red color as much as the arrogant bearing and aristocratic air of these Englishmen struck him with a vivid reminder of Fairfax's prophecy for this army.

Washington was received courteously, served wine and cigars, and allowed to listen to the discourse of these officers and their general. His advice was not asked, and he was not consulted about the country or the Indians; he conceived that his duty to General Braddock was to be an aide and to ride hither and yon to carry messages from Braddock to his officers. Listening intently, Washington gathered that conditions in England were very bad. Washington heard that if his clash with Jumonville had made war possible between England and France, his losing battle at Fort Necessity had made it inevitable. The moment was recognized as a serious crisis in England and in France long before that time. England was very poorly governed. Up to this period hardly anything had been done to prevent the French aggression in the American country which England considered her own. Washington thought that while the French were making good their occupancy of the Ohio River Valley, building their forts, having their traders and coureurs de bois win the Indians with liquor and gifts and firearms, England was doing nothing but overtaxing the colonies and wrangling with them about it.

It was later disclosed that Braddock's campaign was almost hopelessly muddled. His two regiments had arrived in the same ship, but most of their equipment and especially cannon and ammunition were to follow on the next ship. This army was already on the way to Cumberland where it was to wait for its General. General Braddock had to depend on the American colonists not only for horses, wagons, and food supplies but also for finances to complete the campaign. This gave Washington an astounding shock. As if the colonists had not already been gouged to the limit! This shock was followed by another one, even more startling, and it was that General Braddock asked Washington to go to Governor Dinwiddie and solicit the funds so badly needed. Washington said he would go, and as soon as the general put his peremptory request on paper, Washington mounted his horse and started to Williamsburg.

Determined of will, Washington made that ride to Williamsburg in record time. He used up two horses. And when he delivered his message to Governor Dinwiddie, he was treated to the most magnificent exhibition of temper that he had ever heard the doughty Governor fall victim to. But he got the money and started back. Washington made the round trip short of seven days, a ride that was long remembered as remarkable and which more than confirmed Washington's fame as a horseman.

He found that during his absence Braddock's campaign bade fare to become a mess and that only a miracle could prevent a major disaster to English arms and prestige. Horses and wagons in abundance had arrived from the surrounding farms and towns. Braddock's officers loaded them with everything they could purchase in the way of food, grain, tools, bedding, and camp equipment. Washington made note that they did not purchase any powder and ball. On the second day a long, motley column of mounted horsemen, wagons, and pack animals started for Wills Creek.

Washington had lost considerable weight during his tenuous ride. He had not eaten properly nor half enough, and he contracted a bad cold. It did not grow any better on their journey to Wills Creek. Arriving there, Washington was glad indeed to be welcomed by his old comrades Christopher Gist and Waggener and McKnight. Waggener had a company of frontiersmen and colonists, some three score and more, which he had gotten together to serve in the campaign.

"Gist, I would be most happy to have you, but I haven't the authority," replied Washington. "Dinwiddie made me a colonel, but I am only Braddock's aide. I suggest that you see the general and make your offer."

Waggener snorted and Gist swore. Washington accompanied them to where Braddock was holding court and was present when the simple frontiersman offered his company of experienced American woodsmen and Indian fighters to the service of the campaign. Waggener said they would not want any pay and would consider it an honor to fight for Braddock and the colonies. Braddock bluntly refused the offer. The manner in which he briefly surveyed the frontiersmen in buckskin was arrogant and contemptuous. And it was manifest that he thought he would not need any help from that source.

Waggener was too struck by amazement and consternation to make any reply, and it was easy to see that Gist nearly burst with his feelings. When they turned away, Washington importuned Braddock to let him take along these frontiersmen as a company of his own, to help in whatever way woodsmen could be useful. General Braddock had always been courteous to Washington and he was so now, giving his consent for Washington to take along that backwoods riffraff if he so desired.

It was with conflicting tides of feeling that Washington turned away and sought his friends. They were glad indeed at the turn of affairs, and they repaired to the tavern to have a council. They planned to serve in this Braddock campaign under Washington, and McKnight was made a captain. There were a dozen men in the company who had worked for Washington, and as many more whom he knew personally. Then Gist and Waggener acquainted Washington with the change that had come over the frontier since his last visit. Indians of several tribes, surely instigated by the French, had been ravaging the frontier of Pennsylvania for months, massacring, scalping, burning their bloody way clear to the foothills of the Blue Ridge, and at the present time these numerous small bands of savages were making their way back to the Ohio laden with scalps, firearms, and all the plunder they could carry, and also a few white captives.

"These bloody devils will join together in the defense of Fort Duquesne and make one big band to fight under the French. And you can bet it will not be a fight defending the fort. I doubt that Braddock's army will ever see Fort Duquesne," Gist said scornfully.

"Men, the campaign has started disastrously," returned Washington. "Let us hope and pray that we can avert a complete rout. If Braddock's army ever does get under way from Cumberland it will make painfully slow progress on the way to the Ohio. It will drive us frontiersmen mad, but we must go, and if possible prevent an ambush of Braddock's army. It's a foregone conclusion."

"That French Commandant de Contrecoeur is pretty clever. And his Captain de Beaujeu is a French Canadian, more Indian than white. They'll rely on their Indians to stop Braddock's army long before it ever gets to Fort Duquesne."

Washington traveled to Cumberland, which seemed to be vastly removed from its sleepy status as a Maryland town to a bustling colorful, noisy encampment, poor for any army. The two companies of soldiers had arrived, and the wagon train of supplies and equipment and artillery was expected no one could say when. The town was full of Indians who camped on the outskirts, and what with them and the army and the many colonists and frontiersmen who had gathered there, there was a motley mob. Liquor flowed freely, and there was much drunkenness. The soldiers frequented the Indian camp and consorted with the squaws, and these conditions augmented while the army waited. There were sloe-eyed renegades in that crowd, dressed in buckskin or half-naked like the Indians, and only a frontiersman could tell the difference between them and the savages. Among them were spies for the French. Washington espied Frenchmen he took for coureur de bois. There were French traders openly selling rum to Indians and soldiers alike. At night the town was alive and vibrant with sound and movement. If Braddock made any effort to hold his soldiers in check, it was not evident.

Washington, fighting as best he could a fever that threatened to take hold of him, went here, there, and everywhere finding out all that he possibly could. What he could not discover for himself, his backwoods friends were sure to learn. Frontiersmen and colonists trooped to Cumberland on foot, on horseback, and in wagons. It had been a great joke among these Americans, the way General Braddock had ridden into Fort Cumberland. He had procured a lumbering and gaudy old chariot somewhere, and he reclined grandly in this vehicle with a body of light horse riders in red coats riding beside him. It was Washington's own private opinion that

Braddock was getting rid of some of his arrogant and English ideas. At any rate he had discovered the American wilderness to be a wild and inhospitable land with its dense forest and swift streams, all totally new to the English army.

The second in command under Braddock was Colonel Sir Peter Halket. He was a canny Scotsman and an old soldier and aristocrat. Washington found him to be a brave and sagacious officer and felt that if the two of them could have any authority it would be well for Braddock's army. Colonel Halket had his young son, a fine upstanding bright-faced young man, a captain, serving as his aide. The next in command was Colonel Dunbar and after him Major Orme and Lieutenant Sir John St. Clair. Another officer that Washington had met was Colonel Gage. They were all exceedingly irritated at the conditions there in Cumberland and at the tardy progress being made in the campaign.

At least a thousand soldiers of these companies consisted of Irish, Scots, and English who evidently were not seasoned veterans. Braddock had gathered together about seven hundred colonial soldiers, some of whom had not seen active service in the colonies. Then there were small bands of soldiers who came from New York, North and South Carolina, and Maryland. The whole force numbered over two thousand men, and they were divided into two brigades under Colonel Halket and Colonel Dunbar. This did not take into account the large number of nonmilitant teamsters, laborers, and hangers on, or the goodly number of women. This army with the horde of Indians and whites that the campaign drew to Cumberland made a congestion that was appalling. It required innumerable delays, an immense amount of labor, to get this army in any shape to travel. Not until June did they get the necessary number of wagons, horses, and tools and the provisions to get ready to start. Even then, some artillery had not arrived. To Washington and his advisors the delay was appalling.

Every day when Washington returned to his quarters, which consisted of tents shared by his frontiersmen, he always heard something new and disheartening.

"Colonel, what do you think?" asked Captain McKnight, with real concern not unmixed with disgust in his face. "Bright Lightning is here with her father. Been here for sometime."

"Bright Lightning? That must be an Indian girl," returned Washington. "I don't remember hearing the name."

"Bright Lightning is the name for the Indian princess we admired so much at Monongahela. Black Hawk's daughter, Winona, you called her. Remember?"

"McKnight, you don't say!" exclaimed the Colonel. "Remember Winona? Indeed I do. We were both sweet on her, and you had the advantage."

"That's what you say, Colonel," replied the young man, laughing. "I see her dancing and carrying on with soldiers. It's a shame judging by what she was when we knew her."

"But Black Hawk, that fine old Indian chief! He wouldn't let anybody near Winona."

"Colonel, that's two years ago and that's a whole age on this frontier. Black Hawk is drunk now most of the time, and Winona is not the same. It hurt me to see her. I advise you not to do so."

But that was advice that Washington did not heed. He did not go purposely in search of Winona, but when he did run across her at one of the dances in the fort, he did not avoid her. She had grown and indeed she had changed. She had the same dark beauty but her bloom and radiance were gone. This time her dusky eyes were not cast down. She remembered Washington very well, greeted him in English, and bestowed glances upon him which this time were not shy. Washington got out of the place murmuring to himself, "Black Hawk and all these Indians out here owe their degradation to the whites, mostly to the French." And straightway, because it gave him pain, he dismissed the Indian princess from his mind.

"Colonel, I've got some good news for you," said Gist to him that same day. "I'll wager you a new buckskin shirt to a pound of tobacco that I saw an old friend of yours today."

"Another! Don't tell me, Gist."

"Wal, I think I better," responded Gist. "You see it wouldn't do for you to meet up with this fellow without being prepared. I'm not sure but today I think I saw Red Wolf."

"That would not surprise me. All the renegades on the border are here, certainly all the Indians who are not afraid to come. And there are hostile Indians here."

"That French crowd at Fort Duquesne knows more about Braddock's army and movements than we know ourselves. Fact is, we can't know head nor tails of things hyar."

"We must be starting soon. If Braddock does not get under way, he had better abandon the campaign."

Another day Gist hunted up Washington and drew him aside from their quarter in a mysterious manner. "Another old friend to see you" was all he would say. On the outskirts of town where some frontiersmen were camping, Washington was confronted by a tall, dark-faced man whom he knew but could not place. He knew that face but could not account for the terrible strange evidences of havoc. They shook hands, and Gist said, "Colonel, this is Captain Jack, the Wild Hunter."

"Howdy, Colonel Washington, I'm glad to see you."

"Well, by all that's wonderful!" burst out Washington, "Captain Jack! Am I glad to see you! It seems so long ago, but I've heard of you, Captain, and I knew I would meet you again someday."

"Colonel, you're in for a bad time. This Braddock doesn't know what he's running into, but you ought to know. You must tell him."

Yes, Captain Jack, I know indeed. So does Gist, Waggener, and all of us. We can only hope that some light will penetrate this stubborn Englishman's brain before it's too late."

"I come direct from the Monongahela."

"Can you give me a report of the activities there?"

"Only what I figure out from what I saw. The Fort is ready. There's a big force of French soldiers and hordes of

Indians. They'll never let Braddock's army get within cannon shot of that fort."

"Gist and I share that conviction. Captain Jack, will you come with me?"

"Yes, Colonel Washington. I met two young hunters out here. They said they'll be in that fight."

"More good news. And who may these hunters be?"

"Jonathon Zane and Lew Wetzel."

"Captain Jack, you don't say!" exclaimed Washington eagerly. "By jove, that's great news. A few more of you Indian hunters and these French and Indians better look out!"

"I'll tell them you want to see them," said Captain Jack. And he strode away toward the woods, a dark striking figure, that Washington followed with his eyes until he was out of sight.

"Gist," he said thoughtfully, "they told me Captain Jack was hopelessly insane. It's my idea he's no more crazy than I am."

"Mebbe not. Mebbe he just gets crazy spells or more likely to my thinking he just pretends to be crazy for that makes the whites let him alone and the redskins scared of him."

"That's wonderful news about Jonathon Zane and Wetzel. Isaac Zane, you know, came along as a drummer boy. He's the youngest of the Zanes. I fished him out of the river near Williamsburg some years ago. We could use all the Zanes we could get."

"I only know what I've heard about them. Wetzel, of course, young as he is, 'pears about as well known as Captain Jack."

Washington rested in the shade of an oak and waited, hoping that Captain Jack would fetch the two young hunters to meet him. He was glad to get out of the turmoil in town. He hated to admit it, but he did not feel well. His head ached and there seemed to be a slow boil in his blood. He rather feared that a fever was overtaking him. Gist, Waggener, Captain McKnight, and others of his company came and went, each one of them imparting some bit of news from town. The last loads of artillery had been heard from a couple of days' journey from Cumberland, and that news was welcome because when they arrived Braddock might get his forces started on the way to Duquesne. Washington did not go into town until after supper and then, sickening of the revel, he turned back down the main street for the colonists' camp.

Washington had indeed never experienced anything the likes of this frontier town, Cumberland, on the eve of the first big battle in America. The wide street with its glaring yellow lights and the haze of smoke and dust and its heterogeneous streams of humanity passing up and down was a fascinating yet incredible sight. Within two main blocks, Washington calculated that he met at least a thousand soldiers in small and large groups. They were red-faced, merry, and more or less under the influence of rum. He saw white-faced, white-armed women whose haunting eyes roused Washington's pity yet repelled him. There were Indians everywhere, but for the most part they hung back quietly in the shadows of the buildings. He passed several places where discordant music offended his ears. An unseen singer somewhere, a woman whose voice was high-pitched and sweet, loud, vacant laughs, the shuffling tread of many feet, the metallic clink of drinking mugs that came from the open tavern doors—all these intermittent sounds, instead of breaking, intensified the low, steady, nameless roar of the town in its revelry. Washington soliloquized that another week of this—whatever it was—would make Braddock's campaign utterly futile if it did not actually prevent it.

In the park at the end of the street he saw several soldiers drinking with Indian girls. It was bad enough for white women to become camp followers but to see the young Indian girls, some of them not more than fifteen, was a sad spectacle for Washington. He liked the Indians. He believed that the bad in them, as far as intoxication and immorality was concerned, had been fostered upon them by the whites. And it angered him. Braddock's reported contempt for the red men was something Washington could not stomach. He could like to have told this Englishman that if his army was to be defeated it would be done by Indians and if they were to come out victorious the Indians would have much to do with it. He went back to his quarters and to bed, conscious that his illness had augmented his thoughts and perhaps had made him morbid.

18

Braddock Marches to Defeat

Next day he was better again, but he did not go into town except when it was necessary. Braddock's officers were putting the men to packing the wagons since there was an appalling congestion in the large open field at this end of town. Innumerable wagons and harnesses, piles of equipment and supplies and artillery littered the ground, and sweating, swearing soldiers, crowding each other, and all surrounded by a line of somber-eyed, silent Indians, further increased Washington's apprehensions of Braddock's campaign. He tried to fight the insidious thought, but it kept returning. He longed for the march to start toward Fort Duquesne.

When that momentous morning arrived, it was in time to save Washington from utter discouragement. The vanguard of troops went on foot, and the wagons got off in the early morning. Washington had taken orders from Braddock to some of his officers about the necessity of improving the rough road and especially building bridges over the creeks and washes. This would necessitate a slow dragging march. Washington's colonists and his frontiersmen could have taken the lead, and that would have been better for Braddock, but the order was that they should follow in the rear. Washington had the tents and equipment all packed ready to start at a moment's notice. As he was so ill he could not ride horseback, he had a bed made for himself in one of the open wagons. Gist, in examining Washington's wagon, observed that one of the wheels would have to be repaired, and he set out to find a blacksmith. Presently he returned with two men, one of whom was a tall fellow clad in buckskin and carrying a long rifle and a bag. Washington recognized that coonskin cap and the fine dark face beneath it. Gist said, "Colonel meet Mordecai Noah and another fellow I reckon you know."

Sitting up, Washington greeted Noah and then turned to the buckskin clad man who smiled warmly at Washington and dropped his bag upon the ground where it gave forth a metallic clatter.

"Daniel Boone!" exclaimed Washington. "Oh, I'd never forget you. You're the hunter who came to my camp one night several years ago and shod my horse."

"Yes, Colonel, I'm Boone," replied the other, extending a horny hand. "I'm right glad to meet you again. Noah and I want to go along with you fellows and take a hand in this fight."

"You are both mighty welcome," said Washington heartily. "My little company is growing, and it will be heard from. I'm down with fever, but it won't keep me down."

"Colonel, no fever can keep a frontiersman on his back, but you rest while you can. I've just come in on the Monongahela road. About two miles out Braddock's soldiers are building a bridge. That'll hold up the march. The army could cross that little wash without gettin' wet or sinking the wheels hub deep. But this general must have bridges. I don't think bridge buildin' is good. It makes so much easier for the enemy to follow you back, in case of retreat."

"Boone, our worthy general is building bridges to go *ahead*. There isn't going to be any retreat."

"Colonel Washington, there'll be one if there is any battle at all," replied Boone significantly.

Here Mordecai Noah intervened to say, "Dan, I'm not liking the way you said that."

"Well, Boone, me too," added Gist. "What is it that you woodsmen who live in the woods all the time know that we don't know?"

"Daniel Boone, tell us what's on your mind," spoke up Washington, his voice strong.

"I haven't so much on my mind," returned Boone, with a smile. "I reckon bridges won't be necessary because there won't be any retreat. If General Braddock's army goes on marchin' into Injun territory as I just saw them marchin', wearin' those bright uniforms—well, they'll make targets that even rum-soaked redskins wouldn't miss."

Here Noah spoke up severely, criticizing Boone for his outspokenness and advising him not to speak frankly like that again unless he was sure of his hearers.

"Boone, I'm afraid Noah is right," added Washington severely.

Here the tall frontiersman fastened with clear intent eyes upon Washington.

"I'm only a blacksmith and a hunter. You're Colonel George Washington. We both have been brought up in this American wilderness. You know you are not talking straight to me when you say what you did. No matter what this English general has in his mind—and I hear he expects to take Fort Duquesne in three days—he is absolutely stupid, not say more, in neglecting to send a scouting party of American frontiersmen ahead."

Washington, rising on his elbow, stirred by Boone's forceful speech, saw General Braddock riding up with two of his officers on one of his tours of inspection. "Boone, things work out strangely sometimes. Here comes General Braddock himself. You tell him what you told us."

Braddock reined in his horse beside Washington's wagon while his officers halted behind. "Colonel Washington, I trust you are feeling better," he said genially.

"Yes, thank you, General Braddock. I am better. I will follow a day or so along behind your vanguard, and I entreat you not to precipitate any action until I reach the front."

"Colonel, I'm glad you are so eager," rejoined Braddock. "This dratted wait is irksome for me too. I cannot promise to hold back the action, but that won't come for days, and meanwhile you will get well, and I am sure will be of great service to me."

"Thank you, General Braddock," returned Washington warmly. "I'll be sitting on my horse when the action starts. Let me introduce two of my men, Gist and Noah, and this is Daniel Boone. He is the most experienced frontiersman in the Ohio River Valley. He has a suggestion to make to you which I gladly endorse."

Braddock gave his attention to the frontiersmen and greeted them with a stiff bow.

"General Braddock, I am right glad to meet you," replied Boone simply. "Now, about this Injun campaign of yours. I am of the same opinion as all these frontiersmen. You ought to send a party of us ahead to scout this road and make sure you're not goin' to be ambushed. I offer my services as leader. Colonel Washington here will pick out some of his best frontiersmen. You'll excuse me, sir, for speakin' out boldly like this, but someone must tell you that these Frenchmen and redskins will not meet you out in the open and they will have to be fought in their own way."

"Boone," rolled out the General sonorously, with his florid face flushing, "if you Virginians, instead of offering advice had delivered to us the provisions contracted for, and if Benjamin Franklin had given us the wagons and horses promised, we would now be in Fort Duquesne and the British flag would be flying from the masthead."

Daniel Boone did not make any reply, and Washington saw that his expression did not change except for a slight darkening of his clear eyes. General Braddock after an impressive pause resumed, "The war is no different here from what it is in Europe or anywhere. I've been on many battlefields. My information is that the French and Indians are not now in large numbers at Fort Duquesne. They expect reinforcements, and we must capture the fort before they arrive.

Listen, Boone, for your edification and that of all you Virginians, a handful of French soldiers with all the Indians they can muster could not stand up against a thousand British regulars."

Whereupon Braddock with his officers wheeled their horses and rode away. Boone bent again over the wheel he had been repairing and in silence continued to work. His comrades also remained silent. Washington had been irked, and he broke out impatiently, "Boone, I don't like the way you shut your lips tight."

"Colonel, neither do I like the kind of silence around here," returned Boone, and then he looked up. "I'd feel more comfortable if there were a few shots being fired. Braddock is more thick-headed than I had supposed. Colonel, mark my words! Braddock is in for the surprise of his life. Like as not he'll march that army on to the Monongahela—if he ever gets that far—and find a silent and lonely woods suddenly burst into a roar of guns with Injuns and French everywhere but not one in sight."

Gist interposed in a husky voice, "Colonel, we have reckoned this might happen."

"Men, it does have a dreadful significance," returned Washington weakly, as overcome with excitement he lay back upon his bed in the wagon. "We can only do our best and pray for some miracle. But all you men of my company take only orders from me, and my orders are that you fight Indians in Indian fashion."

The four-mile line of troops, horses, and wagons took all day to leave Cumberland and wound slowly through the forest, the rear guard and Washington's company making camp a few miles out of town at the bridge which Boone had told them the soldiers were building. Washington was too sick to take much note of what was going on and lay in this wagon contending with the fever. The men of his company were attentive and solicitous. The next day he was better and sat up part of the time, aware of the tediously slow progress, trying to maintain his composure. He was aware of much of the talk among the frontiersmen around the campfire near his wagon, and that talk was not conducive to restful sleep. The third day his fever was worse, and he did not take much note of anything. About the only question he asked that night concerned the march of the army that day, and the reply disgusted him. If this sort of thing kept up, the French and Indians would have to come out along the road to speed up the battle, and that was just about what they were liable to do. The next day, more by reason of his tremendous will and spirit, he was on the mend, and he could sit up and partake of nourishment, convinced that if necessary he could soon take to the saddle again.

Another day assured Washington that he would be able to ride horseback when the action started, but he was unable to feel anything but disgust and doubt about the progress of this ill-sorted command. One day's march of the army did not exceed five miles and most of the time not half that many. Braddock was not satisfied with the old rough road. A new one had to be cut, bridges had to be built, marshes had to be crossed, and too often there was a steep hill to be surmounted. Boone or Gist or Washington himself could have chosen a much easier route. It was this fact that made Washington suspect the guide Braddock's officers had employed. Washington had not been able yet to see this guide, and he was intensely eager to. Gist called him a half-breed one time, and an Indian next, and finally he came out with a harsher term, calling him a renegade. That was because, no doubt, Gist had seen the renegade Red Wolf in the company of Nemacolin, the Indian guide. Waggener was even more outspoken than Gist. Boone, however, when interrogated only shook his head in silence. The heavy artillery was mostly responsible for the slow progress. Sometimes the mired wagons had to be hauled by a hundred soldiers. They did not have enough food, and they complained of what they had. In ten days of exceedingly hard travel the army was only twenty-four miles out of Cumberland. This would never do, and Washington risked telling Braddock's officers that they were being fatally tardy.

At last Washington's advice was heeded by the officers. It had become evident to them, and they convinced General Braddock, that Fort Duquesne must be reached before it was reinforced. The best of the army, traveling as light as possible, must push ahead with a selected train of artillery and pack horses for provisions and equipment. Colonel Dunbar was left behind with the rawest recruits, the heavy wagons, and the heaviest artillery and other baggage that could not be moved speedily. Even with this division and its consequent more rapid progress, Braddock did not enter Pennsylvania until the twenty-first of June, and it was the thirtieth when he crossed the Youghiogheny. Turtle Creek, the remaining difficult barrier, was yet to be traversed.

When on July seventh the army finally crossed Turtle Creek, General Braddock decided to wait there for Dunbar to come up. He was strongly advised to do this by Sir John St. Clair. But had not Braddock been prevailed upon by Washington to abandon this idea, the whole army would have been lost. Washington's scouts kept him daily informed of the condition and movement of the rear guard. Dunbar had lost so many horses from starvation and stealing by the Indians that he could only move half his wagons at a time. It developed that jealousies and hatreds had broken out among the officers. There were two of Braddock's brigade commanders to whom he refused to speak. The food was insufficient in quantity and poor in quality. Washington himself, despite his robust constitution, had begun to feel the effects of poor nutrition, and the fever laid hold of him again.

The succeeding days of slow travel and clouded mind were like another nightmare to Washington, but he could not give up. He divined what was going to happen. He knew that he and his men could help the campaign along if they could not save it. The army plodded on, making better time over better land. They forded the Monongahela and a few miles below forded it again. This was necessary to get around some high, rugged banks along the river which were insurmountable. At this time the army came out upon a broad river bottom land covered with a scattered growth of maple, walnut, and sycamore trees, and through there they made good progress coming out at length upon a grassy savannah.

It was pointed out to Braddock that the French and Indians were watching them in plain sight from the top of the high bluff, and General Braddock had an inspiration that he thought would effectually cast consternation and fear into the ranks of the enemy. While roads were being graded to allow the passage of artillery and their baggage wagons, he ordered the troops out on dress parade. One of the greatest shocks that Washington experienced on this campaign was to see soldiers come out in new uniforms with their shiny red coats and bright accoutrements. He marveled at Braddock packing all that mass of tawdry dress when there had not been enough provisions hauled. It must have been the English idea of intimidating the enemy.

Soon the rolling beat of drums and the swell of martial music broke the silence of that grassy plateau. Flags and colors were flown in the breeze, and the well-drilled troops marching impressively and joyfully glittering in their scarlet and gold were put through all their troop maneuvers with the order and precision that proved their military training. For over an hour this splendid parade went on, in full view of the French and Indians. Every moment the enemy lying on the bluff was augmented with new arrivals. Braddock's officer and soldiers felt that scene with undisguised pride and exultation. War was eminent, the enemy was in sight, and the fort close-by—in the minds of all there was only one thought, the speedy fall of Duquesne!

This splendid glittering spectacle, colorful and flashing under the blue sky and bright sun, wrenched from Colonel Washington a prophetic and sad heart, a reluctant tribute. It was a grand stirring spectacle. Afterwards he wrote that it was the most beautiful sight he had ever seen in his life. The broad river sliding along, the high gray bluff crowned with its dark horde of silent Indians and French, the broad savannah with its waving green grass and that gorgeous pageant of an English army on parade, marching proudly with rhythmic forceful stride to the inspiring war music made a picture so sublime that it would remain in his heart of hearts.

"March on! On to the Fort!" bawled General Braddock. His loud voice reached every soldier's ear and probably those of the enemy. It was not a ringing, inspired command. It was full of utter vainglory. The mind and heart of that man saw only his victory. The vanguard began to move forward four abreast, and long lines of soldiers were working to fall in behind.

"Look! That leader must be Nemacolin, the guide, and by the Lord Harry who is that man with him?" cried Gist, in sharp voice with his brown hand outstretched.

Washington had seen, and if he had spoken his thought it would have been far more forceful than Gist's. For the first time on this campaign he forgot that he should act on his own initiative, but the surge of his anger inhibited thought. Spurring his horse he rode toward the head of the column. He had no idea what he would do if that buckskin man with Nemacolin turned out to be Red Wolf. Before he reached the head of the column General Braddock came riding to intercept him.

"Colonel, ride back and tell Gage to fall in with his artillery as soon as this column gets by."

"General Braddock, I have my doubts about that Indian guide, and if the white man with him is who I think it is, we're being led into a trap."

"Washington you are here to carry out my orders and not to think," retorted Braddock harshly.

Without a word Washington, mortified and stifling his rage, galloped his horse down the meadow alongside the moving troops. Finding Gage, he delivered the order. Sir Peter Halket was with Gage, and when the latter rode away Halket turned to Washington. He asked Washington a direct question that was hard to answer, but Washington answered it forcibly and expressed his own opinion as to what he would have done if he had been in command.

"Sir!" exclaimed Sir Peter, aghast. "That is insubordination."

Washington's grim look emphasized by silence was evidently more of a shock to the English officer than had been Washington's bitter speech. Then Washington wheeled his horse away and rode back a few rods. He was hailed by a stripling of a drummer boy. It was his old friend Isaac Zane, the youngest of the Zanes.

"Colonel," spoke up the boy eagerly. "I've been wanting to see you. My brother Jonathon and Lew Wetzel are with us. They told me to tell you that the woods ahead will be full of Injuns."

"Well, Isaac, I'm glad to see you with us, and more than happy to know that your brother and Wetzel are here."

"Colonel, I saw them yesterday. They were marching along with us, keeping out of sight in the woods. There's goin' to be a hell of a mess. I'll chuck this drum for my rifle."

"That's good, Isaac. Drums are not needed here, and rifles surely will be. You stick close to Gist and Waggener and do what they tell you."

Washington rode back to his company where he was deeply delighted to see Scarrooyaddy and the Half King among his frontiersmen. They looked fierce and stern. Their greeting showed their loyalty to Washington and the dignity of Indian chiefs who were offering themselves singly to Washington.

Scarrooyaddy made one of his subtle gestures, having so much more meaning than just a mere point. His dark hand pointed to the bold bluff where a few moments before Washington had seen a long line of Indians and French watching the maneuvers. The bluff was now bare. Not a single dark figure was silhouetted against the sky. Washington saw in the chief's gleaming eyes and the Half King's hard red features all that his mounting fears had imagined.

It was early afternoon and the sun shone down hotly. The army crossed the savannah and was entering wooded country again. The rear of the long column had not entirely crossed the creek before the vanguard had reached higher ground. Colonel Gage with his pioneer woodchoppers and his three hundred videttes, engineers, captains, and light horse was followed closely by Sir John St. Clair's column and their brass six-pounders, ammunition tumbrels, and other wagons. The army had long since been led off the old road. Gage's axemen were cutting and clearing the way. As Washington understood it, General Braddock's orders were to march until mid-afternoon and make the stand before Fort Duquesne. English videttes flanked either side of Gage's column to ward off surprise, but it was Washington's calculation that they were not capable of handling the responsibility put upon them and that Braddock's army would never reach Fort Duquesne.

Washington distinctly heard the sound of axes ringing like knolls on the charged afternoon air. The boom of falling trees now and then broke the silence. The advance made rapid headway up the slowly sloping river bottom ending in a dark line of forested hills. Once through these low hills they encountered a heavily timbered flat where big trees here and there rose high above the thickets. Washington grimly agreed with Gist that they were marching into ideal cover for Indian fighters. There were patches of long grass and clumps of blossoming vines and long golden aisles between the trees.

"Colonel, you see them vine-cluttered ravines that head off this ridge?" inquired Gist, walking beside Washington with a hand on his saddle.

"Gist, I do indeed see them," returned Washington darkly. "And if I were not so damned scared I would be perfectly furious."

"Wal, there's one thing we can gamble on. Whatever's coming will come pretty quick."

Washington and his company of eighty, which he called his rangers, marched along beside the army column, his frontiersmen on his side and the colonists under Captain McKnight on the other. They were all to use their own judgment and for the most part kept out of the open broad land which had been cut by the advance. They came at length upon a sloping wooded plain; ravines like the ones Gist had observed bisected this plain. The one on the left was quite deep and in the bottom a small stream meandered. It ended in a swampy area which the army had to go round. Washington's all-pervading eyes observed a ravine on the right which was deeper than the one on the left and was chocked with fallen trees and vegetation. He thought as his eye ran along it that it was big enough to conceal thousands of Indians. And any moment now he was expecting to hear the crack of rifles and the screeching war cry of savages.

As fate would have it, according to the grim-thinking Washington, this wide road cut by the advance guard turned to go between these ravines and wound at right angles so that an army passing on this s-shaped road would have its advance and middle flanks exposed to the fire of hidden enemy within deadly range. Certainly not any of the British officers entertained such gloomy calculations as existed in the minds of Washington and his frontiersmen and his Indian chiefs, who knew what might happen and would be prepared for it. They would fight these savages in their own way. Presently, for some reason Washington thought he could guess, the vanguard halted, holding back the whole army which extended along the road for a mile or more to the rear.

"Gist, Waggener, Yaddy, keep out of sight and be ready for anything!" Washington ordered. "I'm going to see what's holding us up."

"Wait, Colonel," intervened Daniel Boone, hissing through clenched teeth. "Before you go, take a squint down this long aisle through the forest and you'll see what's holding up the advance."

Washington wheeled sharply to gaze in the direction indicated. Far down that aisle he espied a large body of French and Indians moving down the slope. They were far enough away to be indistinct except for movement and color. The naked, dark Indians gliding, stealing along, and the blue uniformed French marching not as soldiers but in small groups. Instinct with life and evil struck cold fear in Washington's heart, although it was what he had expected all the time. There were more than a thousand Indians and Frenchmen in this bunch, and the straggling ends of the company could not be seen for the trees. Washington and his frontiersmen were spellbound by the sight. When all at once that body of savages and soldiers halted, Gist emitted a grinding curse. Other frontiersmen expelled deep breaths. Washington was too fascinated to speak. When a French officer bounded to the fore like a dancing master, the sunlight glancing on his bright uniform and weapons and with his back to the watchers, he spread his arms wide to the right and left. "That's de Beaujeu, the French captain. He's half Indian himself, and he's a cunning devil. Look!"

Washington was looking with hard eyes, and what he saw was this big horde of savages and soldiers disintegrate like a spot of quicksilver. To the right and left the Indians glided like red phantoms and the Frenchmen danced away with equal speed. In a moment they had completely vanished as if by magic.

"That's it! And we sure wouldn't have known it if we hadn't seen it," said Waggener, low-voiced and tense.

"We can gamble that's not all of them," added Gist.

"They'll ambush the vanguard," said Washington huskily. "What can we do about it?"

"Colonel, we can't do anything to stop it," said Boone.

"Men, you'll advance and fight those devils in their own way," ordered Washington. "I'll have to ride up and down this road carrying orders, and I'll wager there'll be a hundred Braddock will command that cannot be obeyed. One of you slip through the column and find McKnight and his men and tell them what to expect."

Gist ran through the column of soldiers, halted with their muskets on the ground. Scarrooyaddy and Half King were the first to glide into the green foliage, then Waggener and Boone followed. Washington had a thrill as he saw Captain Jack advance from behind a tree to wave his hand at Washington and disappear. Young Zane passed with a smile on his bright face, carrying a rifle as long as himself.

Washington rode ahead in search of Braddock. He still felt giddy and weak in the saddle but excitement kept him up. Far ahead he found General Braddock in the midst of great confusion of troops, wagoneers, artillery, men, and horses all mixed together in a noisy throng. Braddock was yelling loud orders. Evidently he was trying to get the column lined up again. Washington joined him and asked for orders.

"This is most damn strange," shouted the general, almost foaming at the mouth. "What's halting us?"

"General, I think you will find out very quickly," answered Washington quietly. "But if you want I shall ride ahead and verify my suspicions."

"Suspicions?" rasped Braddock. "I ordered you not to think but to give me facts."

"General Braddock, the facts are that your army has been ambushed," retorted the Colonel, in ringing voice.

"Ambushed!" gasped Braddock. "How? Where? I don't hear the axes! There is no movement. What does this infernal silence mean?"

The gloomy forest could have answered that, but it was locked in the silence of the sultry summer afternoon. Deep in the forest Washington heard the melancholy call of a hermit thrush and then that poignant stillness was broken by the hideous screeching war cry of a savage. A rifle shot followed it closely, strangely like an echoing menace. Musket shots boomed out scattering and then a heavy volume of musket shots and distant hoarse shouts of men. The sounds energized the tired soldiers in the column, and they started up aghast, murmuring and gazing forcefully at one another.

"My God, Colonel, you are right," cried Braddock, leaping up in his saddle as if he had been stung. "The advance has been attacked. What can it mean? Ride forward and bring me back a report. Urge Burton to hurry forward with the vanguard while I get this artillery started. Order St. Clair and Gage to throw out flankers." While Washington turned to carry out this order, Braddock stormed at the congestion of troops before him. "Here! You infernal scoundrels of wagoners and cattle drivers, get out of the road with your rubbish. Get into the woods on either side. Let the troops and guns press on. Quick step! Don't dally."

And the last that Washington heard as he rode forward was the general berating the artillery men and ordering miracles that could not be accomplished. Washington urged his powerful roan off the road under the trees. Everywhere the road was choked up with artillery and soldiers all trying to move forward but unable to do so. He followed the zigzag course of the road and as he advanced the firing increased.

Soon he reached the head of that impasse. The army had been halted from further advance by the deep ravine which was crosswise. It was full of fallen trees and choked with thickets. From the opposite slope and from the level woods that thinned out into a plain there were white puffs of smoke rising here and there followed by the scattering ring of rifles. Washington did not look for an Indian or a Frenchman because he knew there would be none in sight. But the soldiers were firing their muskets at every puff of smoke. The vanguard had broken formation; some were huddled in groups along the road and others were running around like ants. Officers were riding to and fro. While Washington halted to look for Gage, St. Clair's company came surging on the vanguard. The steady crack of rifles continued, accompanied by weird yells of the savages, and here and there a soldier fell with loud cry of agony and the muskets of hundreds of soldiers began to boom.

The confusion increased until pandemonium reigned. Washington saw an officer shot from his horse, which neighed piercingly and, bolting into the woods, dragged his rider with him. Right in front of him Washington saw soldiers with bloody shirts and gory faces. It was then that Washington's eye of a woodsman detected dark floating forms of savages spreading from the ravine on each side to encircle this head of the army. After that quick glance around, Washington espied St. Clair and rode up to him. Sir John was mad with rage and roaring at the soldiers, to whom the orders meant little or nothing.

"Ho, Sir John," shouted Washington, as he came up. "What's all this disorder here? General Braddock orders you to halt there, throw flankers out, and hold your own no matter how hotly pressed. Burton with his troops will soon be here."

"Flankers out! Hold my own! Hell!" roared St. Clair.

"Tell me quickly what happened. I must report to Braddock."

"It's been incredible and as fierce as a furnace fire," replied Sir John. "Gordon was in front marking out the road on the plain yonder when he said he heard a rushing noise ahead and looking through the trees, he saw a big pack of French and Indians on the run. They came down across the plain with kangaroo leaps and they halted just over there. The French officer was gaily dressed and he had a silver gorget on his breast. This cursed Frencher stopped in his tracks and spread wide his arms and waved his plumed hat. Then his red devils scattered to the right and left, disappeared in the brush as if sunk into the very earth. Not a painted head nor hide to be seen, the skulking cowards! They began a hail of bullets and rifle fire, and the most horrid screeches and yells and infernal calls any mortal ever heard. I'm blessed, Colonel, if I can make heads nor tails of this kind of fighting. Our flankers, what's left of them, have come running in. Our carpenters and teamsters, what's left of them, are huddled down the road like so many sheep harried by wolves. You can see how the troops are appalled by these insane screeching demons."

"Yes, I see, Lieutenant, this is the Indian warfare which we frontiersmen tried to warn you against. Where's Colonel Gage?"

"There's Moore lying in the road. Half his face shot off. He was one of the first to fall. Gage has ridden back to hurry the reinforcements. Colonel, for God's sake, ride back and hurry Braddock up with the artillery! Tell him we've got the whole French and Indian army in front of us and that if we are to get to the Fort, we must fight our way step by step."

Washington did not need to ask any more questions. The evidence was already too shocking. He gave one glance at the prostrate form of Captain Moore lying inert at the side of the road, his indistinguishable face as gory as the color of his uniform, his outstretched hand still clutching his sword.

Washington's ear caught the whistle of bullets close to him. He made a fair target on his big horse. He wheeled off the road into the woods. His horse had not taken twenty strides before Washington espied the dark faces of Scarrooyaddy and the Half King peering from behind trees, rifles extended, their eyes like somber fire. "Hello there, Yaddy and King!" called Washington, halting. "You must get away from the road. Crawl into the woods and find where these devils are hiding. I'll ride to tell Braddock, and he will be here soon with his artillery. Maybe cannonball will have some effect on the enemy."

As Washington turned again to go his way, Captain Jack appeared from behind the next tree, wearing a sardonic grin on his dark face. At that moment, a bullet thudded through his coat, burning his shoulder.

"Ha, Colonel!" cried Captain Jack, and with incredible swiftness he fired his rifle. "That's what I've been waiting for. I've stood here for over a minute watching that skulking Shawnee, and a minute is too long to wait to kill another of these redskins. I figured that Shawnee would not let you pass without a shot. These Indians are fighting a cunning game. They've been drilled by the French, and if they have had rum, it wasn't enough to make them crazy. They're picking off the mounted officers. You look sharp for yourself. Keep moving or get into cover. The range is a little too far for Indians to shoot accurately. So there's a chance for a mounted officer if he keeps on the move or hides. Colonel, don't wonder about where I hit that Shawnee. Old black rifle is certain death. Hurry up the troops! We'll need them all and then there won't be enough. I haven't figured out how many French there are but there's a thousand Injuns creeping and gliding among these trees. Ha! Ha! There goes Yaddy's rifle. He's not wasting ammunition either. And this time it's another Frenchman."

"Keep up the good work, Captain Jack. Oh, if I only had a hundred men like you fellows!"

"Colonel, we'll lick 'em, anyhow. Ride on. I just heard a bullet whiz by you. You're a mark on that big horse."

Washington spurred down the edge of the road, everywhere passing the stupefied troops, crowded together, waiting for orders, fearful of the thundering din in front of them and not seeing anything at which to shoot. It was Washington's conjecture that Braddock would soon hurry them all forward to be massacred. The artillery would not do any good; cannon might scare the Indians, but when they found out that all that the cannonballs did was crash through the trees, they would screech only the louder and fight the harder. General Braddock had not waited for Washington's report, but had stormed through the rear guard of the army. Washington came upon Sir Peter Halket who informed him that Braddock had hurried forward eight hundred soldiers and the artillery and he had left Sir Peter in the rear with four hundred soldiers to protect the wagons.

"Sir Peter, you will soon be as exposed here as forward," replied Washington. "Already there are Indians this far down. Don't you see the puffs of rifle smoke?"

"Colonel, I do now that you call my attention to them," returned the Scotsman. "I am bewildered. There has been an appalling blunder. I didn't dare talk to Braddock. He swore at me. He was positively a madman. Brave? Why the man doesn't know what fear is. He rushed Burton ahead with the artillery and seemed to be furious with every trooper."

"Sir Peter, wouldn't it be wise to get your men a little off the road?" queried Washington. "The soldiers forward are being shot down without any chance whatever. They just stand and peer into the forest or run here and there until a bullet drops them."

"Colonel, I suggested that to Braddock, and that was why I didn't dare speak to him any more."

Washington crossed to the other side of the road and, working back at a fast trot, finally came upon Braddock who was driving a company of troopers to the front. His face was fairly aflame. Just as Washington caught up with the general, Burton's cannon filled the woods with a resounding roar. Following the crashing of the cannonball through the trees, a ringing English cheer pealed out at the front and ran through the column to the rear. They began to load and fire as fast as possible, but there was nothing at which to shoot.

Succeeding the rear of Burton's cannon, the deadly leaden hail that had been pattering through the forest working havoc among the troops now slackened until only a scattered rifle shot was heard here and there. The front of Burton's troops poured a hot fire into the quarter where the French soldiers had been found to be. Perhaps one bullet in a dozen might not have been wasted. As Burton's column advanced behind the roaring cannon, another tremendous volley burst upon them, coming from some unseen source which did not even leave a trace of smoke. Soldiers fell all around like dead leaves from the trees. But the thundering discharge of cannon had inspirited the bewildered troops, and they rallied again.

Behind a heavy storm of grapeshot and canister, the soldiers advanced again, pouring a tremendous fire of musketry into the forest. The trees were about the only living things to be seen. But Washington's sharp eyes detected that the English fire did reach its mark on occasion. And then he reflected that perhaps the Indians and French he saw fall had been picked off by his unerring frontiersmen. The savages, unused to the thunder of cannon and the crashing of heavy balls through the trees, wavered and broke from the slope of the ravine. It was then that they would be seen darting through the forest, and this sight was greeted by loud shots from the soldiers. Washington thought that a bayonet charge might have been effective at that time. It was soon evident, however, that the frightened Indians in front had been rallied by the French officers and that they had returned to the sides of the ravine to resume the battle.

At that moment a bullet struck Braddock's horse in the head, dropping him to the ground like a spent bullet. Braddock went plunging down to slide face forward in the dirt. Infuriated and desperate, the English general staggered to his feet and pulled his sword as if his foes were within reach. His eyes were aflame and his face one blur of vivid red as he glanced about to see his well-drilled veterans huddling without order, all shooting at random, some of them at the treetops as if the Indians were hidden there. Washington dispatched a soldier for another horse for the general. It was evident that Gage's vanguard had been annihilated or halted and that Burton's force even with cannon was wavering before a renewed merciless fire. Washington saw that the Indians had worked further down on the other side of the ravine and had slowed their fire, evidently yielding to the French officers' caution to make more sure of their shots.

Washington stayed within call of Braddock, but he took the precaution to keep his horse moving. He had seen mounted officer after officer fall, and he knew with absolute certainty that Braddock soon would meet a leaden messenger of death. General Braddock indeed had no sense of fear. He gave no indication of anything but bravery. He was heroic in his downfall. He had sensed catastrophe but would not let it stay before his consciousness. When the remainder of Colonel Burton's command came piling back down the road, crowding into Gage's and St. Clair's shattered columns, there was a terrible intermixing of soldiers and horses and wagons and artillery until Washington felt the situation had become awful. Here General Braddock had another horse shot from under him. He got to his hands and knees, and his red face splotched by dirt would have been ludicrous had it not been so tragic. He got up swaying and wagging his gray head, and about him in that moment there was something sublime.

"Bring me another mount," he bellowed to everyone in general and nobody in particular. And then in his striding and raging he encountered Colonel Gage coming back down the road.

"How's this, craven sir. Would ye so basely dishonor your King and the Duke. God's wrath! Is this the way you have been taught to fight! By the eternal, but I'll break your disgraced sword where you sit in saddle! Curses on you all for a set of white-livered cowards! You look more like a flock of silly sheep beset by hounds than drilled soldiers. For shame! Fall in ranks again, every mother's son of you! Come out from behind those trees! By the great God above us, men, but I'll cut down with my sword the first soldier, British or

American, who *dares* skulk behind a cover! Out with you cowards!"

Leaping from the roadside Braddock struck several soldiers who cowered behind trees and pushed them forward.

"General Braddock," sullenly expostulated Gage. "These insults are undeserved. How can we fight a foe who surrounds us on three sides but whom we cannot see? Our officers are falling. Our soldiers are panic-stricken. If you allow us to get behind trees and take to cover like the frontiersmen do, we may pick up heart and fight better when the enemy is actually found. Otherwise, all of us, soldiers and officers, will be killed!"

"Killed!" hoarsely roared Braddock, mounting the second horse that had been brought him. "And why not? Better die with naked front to the foe than blink and skulk like hares. Get behind trees! Oh, that I would live to hear a British officer and a nobleman's son give voice to such dastard words! Officers, I command you to separate your frightened mob! Advance the regimental colors! Set up rallying points! Tell the men off into platoons and hunt up the enemy that way!"

These military commands couched in the general's passionate speech seemed to Washington to be futile and meaningless in that forest. The men could not see what actually stared them in the face.

"Colonel Washington, bid the rest of the artillery advance and open with grape!"

"General," replied Washington quietly, in earnest tones hardly audible to the din, "since the enemy is evidently in great strength ahead and on either side of these ravines, would it not be a good idea to find out just where he is? If we could retire the troops a little—retreat a little out of fire—beat up these woods with a bayonet charge and reform—"

"Retire! Retire out of fire! And before a damn dastardly foe who dare not uncover himself," rasped the husky-voiced general. "Colonel Washington, you are my aide-de-camp to carry orders, not to give them. Retire is a well-picked word! It may suit your American militia, but, sir, it is a disgraceful word for an officer holding His Majesty's commission either to hear or speak. It was by retiring, as you so well call it, that Fort Necessity was given up by you last year to the French. Damn me, sir, it has been so much retiring that brings me and my army on this field!"

Washington, stung to the quick, grew scarlet at this stinging and wholly undeserved taunt, and that terrible temper of his halted just short of explosion. Seeing that Braddock was desperate and impossible and feeling sure in his prophetic soul that death would cut short his ranting, Washington turned away to hunt up the artillery.

Braddock waved his sword at the officers. "Tell off your men in small parties. Advance on a double quick and drive these damn skulking vagabonds from their hiding places."

And even as he finished his command, Colonel Gage was knocked off his horse by a bullet, St. Clair leaped from his saddle and bent over his brother officer slowly to raise his head and tell the general that Gage was mortally wounded. Braddock, shocked into gravity, gave orders for the officer to be carried to the rear.

Washington, trying to execute his order and extricate himself from the terrible confusion and at the same time preserve his own life, found it impossible on the moment to get to the artillery. The guns were hemmed in by a mob of troopers who, in their terrible shooting at random, might hit Washington. The whole thing was futile. He looked around for his frontiersmen, but they were hidden. He heard the bark of their rifles. The yelling savages having grown bolder, sure of victory, had advanced down on both sides of the road as well as keeping the advantage of the ravine and were pouring a murderous fire into the English ranks. Several officers, one of them St. Clair, driven by Braddock, put themselves at the head of small parties and with heroic courage marched into the forest to rout out the hidden foe. They never returned. Washington saw that the relentless attack was going to massacre the army or put it to rout.

The road, now gloomy in the shade of the western sun, was strewn with corpses, and under the thickets on each side crowded scores of terrorized soldiers, still shooting at nothing and in many instances killing their own comrades.

Washington saw all that in a single glance. In another he saw too that the Indians and French were growing bolder. Naked slippery red men would break from cover and run, and some of them were picked off by the frontiersmen. French soldiers, too, dared to show themselves, but in the main the screeching savages, now frenzied by bloodlust, kept up a continual fire of both bullet and buckshot in the exposed rank of the army. Washington saw one naked devil dart with incredible agility out from the brush to where Lieutenant St. Clair lay at the edge of the road, his white hair uncovered. At the instant when this savage, slowing his swift movement, bent over to scalp the officer, a frontiersmen's rifle cracked from somewhere and this bold Indian, a Shawnee, hideously painted and magnificent in his naked effrontery, started upright with a convulsive stiffening, spread wide one hand clutching a gory scalp and the other with a bloody knife and fell prostrate over his victim.

And then on the instant Washington was jerked out of his transfixed and thrilling horror by the tugging of a bullet through the sleeve of his coat. He swerved away from the spot into the woods. Despite the hot fury under which he almost suffocated, there came a cold sickening sinking of his heart. Well might he be the next victim! He rode forward toward the thickets of the fight, sure that his frontiersmen were on his side of the road and that he need not fear any menace from that quarter. He would try again to extricate the artillery and get it into action. As he galloped through a glade scarcely fifty feet from the road his horse stopped in midair as if he had struck a stone wall. Washington knew what had made that sodden little thud. He was thrown over the horse's head and when he got to his feet, breathless with a film of red over his sight, a lithe buckskin-clad form leaped out of the bushes and drew Washington under cover. It was Jonathon Zane. The right side of Washington's face was begrimed with burnt powder. A bloody welt ran across his forehead.

"Colonel Washington, are you all right?" Zane queried eagerly, feeling all over Washington's person.

"Yes, I guess so, Zane. I had a cropper. My horse must have been killed in the air."

"Well, the redskin that shot him got hit the same way," retorted Zane in deadly humor. "Lew here has been watching for that Shawnee. I saw him lean out from behind a tree to aim his rifle at you, and Lew shot him just as he pulled the trigger."

Then Washington became aware of another figure behind an adjoining tree. He knew of course that it was Wetzel, but he did not recognize him. The promise of Wetzel's youth had been more than fulfilled. Tall, built like a wedge with very broad shoulders and a striking dark face heavily pitted with smallpox, with glittering black eyes and long black hair that fell to his waist—he made a more wonderful presence than even Captain Jack. It had not taken him half a minute to reload his rifle, and when he looked up he gave Washington the full benefit of his singular features. He did not speak, but for a fleeting instant his relentless face changed to a smile which was more radiant than any movement of muscle. Then Wetzel left his tree and glided low and swift to the next one, from which he peered cautiously. Waggener appeared then with smoking rifle, and he had a word for Washington as he wiped his sweaty face and started to reload. Young Zane came hard upon his heels, and the boy had a bloody scarf around his head.

"Sonny, don't take such risks again," said Waggener. "Can't you copy Jonathon or Wetzel? This ain't a game, this is war and we're gettin hell licked out of us."

"Isaac, I hope you're not badly hurt," replied Washington solicitously.

"Hell, it's only a scratch," retorted the young man, "and you bet I killed the reddy that done it. Colonel, I see you were shot off your horse. Shall I run back and get you another one?"

"No, Isaac, I'll get one myself if there are any left. Waggener, look out for him, and Zane, you and Wetzel draw a bead on that French half-breed Captain. He wore a plumed hat and he had a silver horn or something around his neck."

"Well, I reckon we done hit him. Waggener, Jonathon, and Wetzel were shooting at the same Frenchy! So one of us hit that officer. And I'll tell you, Lew Wetzel can snuff out a candle at night one hundred yards away, and he could hit a squirrel in the eye in the top of the tallest white oak. So if Lew wanted to take the credit I reckon he could. Jonathon says he never saw Lew miss anything that he shot at."

"Zane, that must have been de Beaujeu, the French officer. Gist and I saw him. His death must have accounted for that little weakening of the Indians; I hope some of you draw a bead on other French officers. . . . Waggener, keep your men together as near as possible. Gist is on the other side of the road with forty of my rangers. He must be on the other side of the ravine so that the Indians are between him and the road. Gist's crowd must have given a good account of themselves, but I wish I knew."

"Wal, Colonel, we been talkin' back and forth with them with our guns," said Waggener. "Don't worry none about Gist or us either except maybe this crazy youngster we got with us. I reckon the day is not lost yet. No doubt you ought to have another horse to get from one place to another quick but you'd be safer on foot. I see there are three bullet holes in your coat."

"Yes, one of them burned my shoulder. I must have another horse. I'll keep back away from the road. Meanwhile you lay low and keep cool."

Washington hurried down alongside the road in search of another horse. The smoke and din of the battle diminished as he proceeded down the road, and there was not such panic among the troops. There were still some reserves to come forward with Captain Morris and Major Orme, but so far Washington did not sight them. He passed the zigzag part of the road where in several places it turned on itself and had furnished such a death trap for the soldiers. He calculated that fourteen or fifteen hundred soldiers, not including officers or teamsters, were back of him toward the front. Probably half of them had been already killed. He had not observed many wounded. He did not agree with Waggener that there was yet a chance for Braddock's army to escape defeat. That had been the frontiersman's fighting spirit. But Washington could not deceive himself. In his heart he knew that as the Indians grew bolder they would be more terrible in conflict. The main officers, except Braddock himself, had been killed. He was glad to get beyond the point where rifles were cracking all around and troopers were falling in the road and cowering under the bushes, knowing not where to turn or what to do. Turning down a curve in the road, Washington came upon the last division of reserves under Captain Morris. He was mounted and leading his soldiers in good formation.

He hailed Washington. "Colonel, how's the battle going ahead?" he asked eagerly.

"Captain Morris, I fear it has gone from bad to worse. Where is Major Orme?"

"Orme has been taken to the rear badly wounded but not fatally. How about the other officers?"

"Braddock is still raging like a lion up and down the road, bearing a charmed life. No one could question his courage. He's a grand fighter. The fatal thing was that he underestimated the French and Indians and could not get it through his thick head how to fight them. Gage is dead. Burton is dead. I saw St. Clair scalped. The under officers must all be killed. I have not seen Sir Peter and young Captain Halket."

"Merciful heavens, Colonel!" ejaculated Morris. "That is horrible news. I will quick-step my men forward. We have two brass six-pounders left, and some ammunition. There are extra saddle horses a mile or so back with the wagons."

Washington ran down the road as fast as he could, so preoccupied in gloomy thought that the distance seemed nothing. Coming to the last column where a number of soldiers were guarding the wagons, he hurried to choose and saddle a new mount, briefly answering the questions which were plied to him. Then he galloped back up the road, soon turning the corner to see ahead of him the rear guard of Braddock's army. Morris had almost reached the scene of the battle. Smoke and din once more crowded upon Washington's sense of perception. Washington passed the several disorganized columns to get into the thick of the conflict again. It was worse than any stage before. Colonel Halket with reinforcements had preceded Morris up the road, and at the turn of the road where wagons and horses and remnants of the two shattered columns of soldiers blocked the way, the fighting became fierce again. Fierce on the part of the Indians and the French and despairing on that of the English! What Braddock should have done at that hour, finding his depleted forces surrounded in a slaughter pen, was to have gotten his men in some kind of a formation and made bayonet charges down the ravine and through the forest. A company of provincials who had joined Braddock at Cumberland gave a good account of themselves until they were shattered. It was here that several of the sergeants and captains who had been forced by Braddock to beat their soldiers from under cover were shot by their own comrades.

At this most congested part of the battle where General Braddock was riding to and fro more furious than ever, it appeared to Washington that the red flashes of rifles, the little clouds of yellow smoke, and the sharp report so different from the heavy sound of musketry were coming as if by magic right out of the ground close at hand. Panic succeeded to demoralization. All this came to Washington as he pursued Braddock and, at last catching up with him, asked for orders. The general stormed at him. What were the use of orders that were not carried out? But he sent Washington back to urge Morris to rush his forces to the scene. Again Washington raced back down the road. He met Morris and gave him the general's orders and had no reply for Captain Morris's passionate outburst of profanity. Returning, Washington took to the woods and had just reached that zone of smoke and fire when his horse was shot. This time he was not thrown. The horse gave a groan and slowly heaved down. Washington slid off and with his pistol put the animal out of its misery. Then he hurried forward on foot. Gliding from tree to tree in the instinctive habit of a woodsman, keeping to cover himself while peering ahead. He came upon Boone and Gist who were likewise proceeding forward. In answer to Washington, Boone shook his dark head. His expression was fierce and sullen. His eyes darted to and fro with a quivering of a compass needle, but Gist, as always, talked. "Colonel, Braddock is taking a hell of a beating. And awful as it is, it serves him right. That company of colonists who joined at Cumberland are about wiped out. Your ranger company, Colonel, is still intact. Not a man dead or even wounded bad that I could see. It was getting hotter than hell on the other side of the road. I led my rangers out of it, and they crossed the road just above hyar. We've killed an all-fired lot of redskins."

"Colonel, you're gonna find yourself in charge of what English forces are left," spoke up Boone tersely.

"Boone, that thought crossed my mind more than once. It's a miracle that Braddock and Halket have not been killed long ago. I've had two horses shot from under me and three bullet holes through my clothes."

"Wal, I reckon I count four, Colonel," responded Gist dryly. "Where'd you last see Waggener and Captain Jack? And Yaddy and the Half King?"

"Not far forward here on this side of the road. I believe Wetzel killed the French captain."

"Boone has done for some Frenchies, but my luck has been to see only Injuns. My bullet pouch is almost empty! Colonel, you better stick with us."

"No, Gist, I'll work out here to the road. You and Boone go forward and pass the word among my rangers to work close together in case I will need them in a body."

As Washington proceeded cautiously toward the road again, the woods echoed to the thunder of cannon. The swishing and crashing of cannonball through the trees now brought only screeching, mocking yells from the Indians. They were lying flat somewhere, peering over logs or through the brush, and cannonballs had ceased to intimidate them. The musket fire had grown scattered and intermittent. The fire from the French and Indians had slowed down till there were no volleys, only steady firing in front and along the road to the left. Washington could not hear how far. He came abruptly to the side of the road where he encountered Sir Peter Halket dismounted, leaning paled and weary against a huge oak tree, the bridle of his horse in his hand. There was some little evidence of blood upon his uniform. There were soldiers to one side under the tree, and in the road both up and down were broken troops kneeling, lying flat, standing, all firing or reloading their muskets.

"Sir Peter, I trust you are not badly hurt?" asked Washington seriously.

"Na, na, Geordie; but I'se gotten eneuch," answered the Scotsman. " 'Tis joost aboon my baldric. What culd luke to go thro' siccan an awsome day wi'out scaur or scaith. I ha'e fear Ise ta'en a strong grippit o' death. I am sair forfoughten, but never fear, mon, but wha' the auld Sir Peter will e'er present a heckle to his foes."

"Oh, 'tis not so bad as that, Colonel," said Washington. "We are receiving our baptism of fire. 'Tis a gory field and the end is not yet."

"D'ye mind, Colonel, the 'secon-sight' I tauld ye of yestreen and the vision of bluid? Said I not recht? But ha'e ye seen Jamie, laddie?"

"I have, Sir Peter; here he comes, and unhurt."

" 'Tis strange, verra strange. 'Tis the bairn Francis, and not James that's hurt and ta'en to the rear, alang wi' Sir John Sinclair, Colonel Burton, Gladwin, and mony ithers. Oh, but this is a sorra day! Braddock's just lost his fourth horse. The fule carle thinks he's fightin on the broad plains o' Flanders. 'Tis eneuch amaist to drive one distraught to see him trying to wheel and manoeuvre a whail army, shoulter to shoulter, in a twal-fut road. I ha'e beggit him to let his men tak to the woods, but the dour deevil wi' not. He's clean daft, Geordie, clean daft."

"Well, Sir Peter," returned Washington. "It's useless to discuss General Braddock now. You are wounded and need immediate attention. You must go to the rear. . . . Captain

Halket, get a couple of soldiers and take your father back for medical attention."

"Oh, Colonel!" exclaimed the young man. "Is Father hurt? He was all right a little while back."

Before Washington had time to reply, a bullet from an unseen foe in the ravine struck Sir Peter straight through the heart. The old man staggered against the tree, his pallid face changing from weary to surprised and then fixing somberly. He would have fallen if his son James had not rushed forward to catch him.

"Oh, Father, Father!" cried out the young man, in poignant agony. "Are you hurt badly? Where did it hit you? Ah, my God! Colonel Washington! Look! He's—he's—help me, oh, help me!"

Washington, overcome with pity and with no thought of rescuing himself, stepped forward to lend whatever assistance he could, but another bullet hissed by him from that ravine and struck young Halket in the breast. He uttered a mortal cry, and, clutching his father's arms, he slowly bent his corded, tragic face till it hid on his father's breast. Then his whole frame twitched convulsively. Young Halket died on his feet as his father had done, and, clasped in each other's arms, dead, they fell away from the tree, into a little hollow among the leaves and ferns. Washington gave them one more horrified look, and, snatching up the bridle of Sir Peter's horse, he hurriedly led him away under the trees and then turned forward in the direction his frontiersmen had taken. The first man he espied was Captain Jack. His face was all begrimed with black powder out of which his eyes gleamed demoniacally.

"Howdy, Colonel," he called, through his clenched teeth. "I've been chased from tree to tree by some Ottawa Indians. I saw them kill the Halkets, and the next will be you if you're not careful. There were eight or ten of them, but I got them down to less than half that number. Send one of your men back to help me. I'd like to have that Wetzel or Dan Boone."

"No, Captain Jack, you come with me. The Ottawas will follow, and somewhere ahead of us we'll meet some of my men."

In less than a hundred cautious steps, Washington and Captain Jack surmounted a little bench above the road where back, hidden from below, they found Gist, Boone, Yaddy, and other of the frontiersmen.

Waggener rose to meet them. "Colonel, Captain Jack, just in time! We've found out something. Wetzel is here just a little ways up. He located a mob of redskins behind those two big logs you see lying halfway up the other side of the ravine there. Once the place was pointed out, we seen that there were hundreds of Indians hidden there. We can sneak around a ways and charge those logs, kill a good many Indians and chase the rest away. Boone and Gist agree. What do you think of the plan?"

"Waggener!" exclaimed Captain Jack. "It's a crying shame that all these soldiers were forced to stay there in the road and be butchered for the mad ideas of a man who may be as brave as a lion but crazy as a loon. If we don't do something to rout these Indians we'll get the same as Braddock's men."

Once more Washington was confronted with a terrible responsibility. If he gave his consent, his rangers would charge the ambush of the Indians, and, wonderful as they were, some of them would get killed. But now he was a frontiersman again, and he was not actuated by his duty as General Braddock's aide.

He gave a stern assent and advised a bit of caution, which he knew was not necessary to those frontiersmen.

"Colonel, that's what should have been done long ago," returned Waggener, "and Captain Jack, Old Hickory, I'm with you on that charge even if it means death. But I think we can do it and get away. I will round up all our men and get them back here in a jiffy."

When he glided into the forest Washington once more turned his attention to the battle below, the thickest point of which was down the road perhaps a hundred paces to the right. Up and down, ahead and below the two brass six-pounders, Morris's fresh troops were making a valiant stand, but it was just as useless as all the other attempts. He espied

Braddock coming tearing up the road, his charger leaping over dead bodies on the ground. He was bare-headed, and his red face blazed in the sun, the hue of his coat. He was waving his sword around his head.

Washington wondered what use it would be to ride down and tell him of the plan of his rangers, and he decided against it. Braddock could not see that kind of fighting. Washington marveled anew that this English general had not been long ago laid low. He watched the battle, waiting. In twos and threes, the frontiersmen began collecting back of the little rise of ground. Then his colonial rangers, whom he had put under Captain McKnight and Gist, arrived in a body. His Indian friends, the chiefs Scarrooyaddy and Half King, came together gliding under the trees. Washington watched them, hoping that he was big enough to appreciate their greatness. They were savages, red-colored and lean-bodied, just the same in nature as the red devils they were fighting, but they were indeed the embodiment of all that was noble in the Indian. They were brothers to the white men. There was blood on Yaddy, and the Half King's close-cropped head showed where a glancing bullet had streaked across his scalp.

Boone was there kneeling close above the brink of the bank peering through the vines, studying the lay of the land and the ambush of the French and Indians which the cunning Wetzel had discovered. He was nodding his head in approval of Captain Jack's plan. Young Isaac Zane came running up with a frontiersman named Bill Williams. The lad was as wild as any of the Indians and as bold as any white man. Washington's trader friends, Currin and Stewart, came next and then Jonathon Zane. Wetzel was the last to come up, running easily, his keen dark face bent toward the ravine and his black hair waving down his shoulders. He was loading his rifle as he ran. All these men of the forest were terribly dear to Washington's heart, but it was Captain Jack, Daniel Boone, Jonathon Zane, and Lew Wetzel, all simply Indian hunters and nothing else, which made Washington's breast heave and his eyes glisten. Then Waggener called on all to come close around him. Washington joined the circle, leaving his horse tied to a sapling.

"Men, now listen. Wetzel got a line on one of the main bunches of redskins, and Captain Jack has come forward with an idea. It's to charge that mob hidden behind those fallen trees and all back of them. Colonel Washington approves. We'll cross the road just below here, head the ravine, slip up on the opposite side and make a run for it all stretched out in a line but close together and when one man shoots, the one next to him will withhold his fire while the other reloads. When the reddies break and run, as you can bet your life they will, we'll charge down that ravine hot as hell."

A low-spoken but deadly voiced accord came from the most of the eighty rangers.

"Now some of you sling yourselves around trees and stick out your head or cap to draw the fire from that ambush across there."

A dozen of the rangers crawled toward the brow of the little hill. Washington crawled to a vantage point from which he could make his observation. Waggener was on one side of him and Boone on the other. The balance of the rangers waited eagerly. Waggener's ruse drew a volley from the ambush. From all along those two huge logs and from the stumps and the windfalls farther up the ravine and from the bow of the slope where the woods began there puffed up a continuous line of rifle smoke.

"Come back, men, That's all we want. We'll make a run for it. It'll take us mebbe two minutes to get over there. Then we'll spread out in a line and rush these damn redskins."

Washington drew his pistol, and, taking another from the saddle of Sir Peter's horse, he joined the frontiersmen. They ran to the right and down across the road with the rangers following. They broke through the column of bewildered soldiers and were under cover of the forest in a very few moments. And, according to Washington's excited calculations, in less than the two minutes, given, they had run through the forest to the opposite side of that ravine which had been such a fatal ambush for Braddock's army.

"Now, men," called Waggener, his voice ringing sharp, "spread along in a line and keep back under cover till they run. If we don't have something to boast of this day, my name's not Tom Waggener. You frontiersmen spread along ahead and you rangers spread along here below.... Aha! Hear Wetzel's rifle ping! That fellow can see through wood. Look! Look, Jack. Look, Colonel. And Boone, d'ye see the painted devils slipping and wiggling away!" Here Waggener raised his voice to a stentorian roar. "Shoot! We've got 'em running. Make every pop count. Quick! Don't let a damn redskin get away. Now up springs the whole bunch! Now, all of you fire."

A tremendous volley from nearly eighty rifles burst as one gun to roar through the forest. Washington saw the whole raft of Indians break cover and come out in the open, and as they could not run downhill on account of the wind falls, they had to run up the slope and they could not run fast. Washington, half-rising beside Waggener, still keeping under cover, began to shoot into that wiggling red of Indians. Almost before the long echo of that volley had faded away in the forest the swift frontiersmen had reloaded and then another deadly hail of bullets mowed down the Indians as if from a giant scythe. Captain Jack's sortie turned out to be a great success. The Indians at the top of the slope fled back into the forest, and those in the open who had not been killed ran every whither like frightened quail, abandoning their guns and thinking only of flight.

"Ho! Ho!" yelled Captain Jack, springing out into the open and reloading his rifle with nimble fingers. "One more volley like that, boys, and we'll have scalps enough to buy a farm a piece. Hurrah! Load up fast. Let's charge. We've got a hundred of them cornered."

In short order, and before the Indians could effect an escape, all of the frontiersmen and some of the rangers had reloaded, and led on by Captain Jack's wild whoop, they charged down the slope and killed the majority of the Indians left and routed the rest. Washington, watching, saw the frontiersmen club their rifles and crack the skulls of Indians who had been wounded.

"Men," shouted Waggener. "There were some French in that bunch, and now they're dead Frenchmen. Let's hurry below now. If we find another ambush like this one, by the Lord Harry, we'll change the tide of this battle into victory. Hurry there, rangers, forward. And all of you behind, come on!"

Washington, elated and thrilled, fell in with the frontiersmen as they came running, and they all fell in behind the fifty or more rangers who had bunched at Waggener's order. In a body, they hurried down the slope of the ravine to a point below where it was possible to cross, and they climbed out to the road. When they had collected on the road and were moving down toward Morris's column, suddenly there came a loud blast of musketry. It drowned all the scattered rifle fire, and to Washington's horror, he saw at least forty of his eighty rangers fall dead or wounded in the road in front. They had been shot by the British soldiers. After a single instant of petrification such a yell rose from the lusty-throated frontiersmen that even the crazed soldiers realized their blunder.

"My God," gasped Captain Jack, when the frenzied yell had stopped. "Colonel Washington, we've been shot at by our own men. As I'm a living sinner, we have. Oh, by heaven, worse than murder! The day is lost when British soldiers can slaughter their betters."

"Men come out of your stupification," commanded Washington. "It's horrible, but some of us are alive. Run back to our bank above the road."

"Come on, Waggener, Gist, Bill, and the rest of you. Here, Captain McKnight, I see you're wounded. Let me help you. . . . There's more shooting. Damn me, if our own soldiers are not at it again! Run for your lives!" shouted Captain Jack.

Washington recognized, as did all of his men who were left, that the thing to do was scatter and run. As he gazed around, panting from his exertion, Washington noted that the two Indian chiefs, the Zanes and Wetzel, and Boone had all disappeared as if by magic. They were the ones who knew how to survive. Plunging across the road, jumping over dead soldiers, Washington saw Captain Morris lying scalped beside his horse that was heaving and shaking in its death throe. If Washington had had a shot left he would have ended the horse's pain.

He rushed up the bank through the brush and came out on the little hilltop and ran for his horse. He rested a moment, panting laboriously, feeling the hot sweat run down his breast and gazing about him with fearful eyes. He had heard so many bullets, he had seen so much death, that he had no hope for himself. But, as he caught his breath, that temper of his mounted like a fiery flag and once more made a lion of him. He mounted and rode down the hill and kept to the right of the road until he came abreast of the remnant of Morris's soldiers, and there he galloped out in the open to find General Braddock.

The firing had lessened volume because of that routing of the French and Indians in the main ambush, but there was still firing from three sides that was anything but desultory. Washington spied General Braddock down the road and spurred his horse to reach him. The general was inactive for the moment. Hatless, his red coat slashed into ribbons by bullets, blood stains in his gray hair, he gazed about him with eyes that were like dying furnace fires. Washington meant to tell him that the day was lost, that he must retreat to save himself and the few of his army that were left, but the words stiffened on Washington's lips. The general was knocked off his horse by a heavy bullet. He had been standing on a rise of ground a little above the road, apparently at the end of his rope. It was indeed the end. Washington leaped off his horse, and at a single glance ascertained that Braddock's moments were numbered. He was not shot through the heart but higher, through the lungs. Blood stained his lips. His eyes rolled, and he muttered indistinctly. Washington looked up to see where he could get someone to help him carry Braddock toward the rear, and he espied Captain Stewart, the Virginian officer of the body guard of light horse, riding up post haste. He too dismounted and looked at Washington before he glanced down at the fallen general.

"Captain Stewart, Braddock is done for. He won't last long."

"Colonel Washington, here comes Orme behind me. He's wounded but he wouldn't stay in the rear. We will take charge of the general. And carry him back until we can get help."

Major Orme rode up, his face ghastly but with an unquenchable spirit in his eyes. He took in the situation at a glance and painfully clambered out of his saddle, showing that he was stiff and weak. Bloody bandages showed under his coat. "Colonel Washington, you are in command," he said. "You may save the last of our army." Whereupon he knelt by Braddock and searching inside his coat found the scarlet sash interwoven with silk and net work which was the custom of every English officer to carry about him to be used in case he was wounded or killed.

Washington mounted and rode into the midst of the soldiers. Repeatedly he gave the command to retreat and presently came upon a bugler and a drummer along the edge of the road. He ordered them to sound the retreat. They abandoned guns, knapsacks, artillery, and wagons and broke pell mell down the road. When Washington had got that herd in motion, he rode back up the road and to the hill where he expected to find his frontiersmen. He soon saw some of them, and yells brought the others—Gist and the two traders, Bill Williams, in one group, the Indian chiefs came at Washington's call, and then Boone, Captain Jack, the Zane brothers, and at last Wetzel. When Washington turned back with them, he found all that was left of his rangers collected with the frontiersmen.

"Men, the battle is lost," he said. "I've sounded the retreat, and the soldiers are running wild down the road. I want you to cover that retreat. Split into two parties, keep the road close under cover, and stop the red devils from pursuing us while I ride ahead and try to bring some order out of chaos."

Washington rode down the hill into the road. A whistling bullet passing near his ear reminded him that Providence had indeed saved him so far but he must remember not to be reckless. The road was littered with soldiers, and Washington did not see any wounded. He passed one of the brass six-pounders over which a gunner hung, limp and dead. The other six-pounder had been turned over into the ravine. Ammunition wagons were hard by with horses dead in the harness. All along the road each vista was more ghastly than the one behind. At the turn of the road Washington halted to look back. Far back he saw dark gliding savages in the road. Then he saw an agile redskin run into the road and bend over to scalp a soldier.

Then the ping of a rifle came to Washington's ears, striking and significant above the other scattered gunshots by reason of its peculiar ring. The sound came from a long-barreled small bore squirrel rifle which had been expertly loaded with small charge. He thought grimly with a cold thrill up his spine that he knew whose rifle had given forth that ping.

He remained there long enough to see that the pursuing savages were shot or driven into the forest by his frontiersmen slowly coming down the road to cover the retreat. Then he rode on, passing wagons, gun carriages, ammunition carts, dead and wounded horses, artillery, military chests, personal baggage littered everywhere. The ground was littered with muskets and knapsacks, soldiers' caps, and everywhere dead troopers. Washington found that wounded soldiers had been left on the road. He halted once and again by the side of a stricken soldier and then he rode on, furious sick, feeling how helpless he was to follow the dictate of humanity.

Washington came up with the rear guard of the retreat, and, though moving without order, the soldiers were moving fast. All up and down that mile of road which Washington traversed, everything that had to be carried had been abandoned. Farther on he came to a stream of wagons loaded with provisions and wounded soldiers. He counted twenty-two of them. He rode on forward until he found Captain Stewart, who was riding beside a covered wagon in which were General Braddock, still living, Major Orme, and several other wounded officers. Washington told Stewart that he expected the retreating army to be pursued until possibly they came upon Colonel Dunbar's forces still somewhere down the road. Then Washington galloped back clear to the end of the retreating column. Far up the road he saw a band of Indians, at least fifty in number, who were approaching but were kept back by the fire of the frontiersmen. It was Washington's judgment that they would not keep up the pursuit. There was too much plunder and too many scalps to collect.

His calculations proved to be correct. The mob of fugitive troopers made all possible speed down to the ford of the Monongahela. In the narrow passage leading to the ford, the savages who pursued the rear end of the retreat tomahawked some of the wounded and exhausted until a short, sharp conflict between them and the frontiersmen drove them back minus half their number. That ended the pursuit, though Washington still feared it. Soon they came upon Dunbar's forces in an incredibly wild confusion and terror occasioned by the arrival of wagoners who told of Braddock's defeat, whereupon Dunbar's forces, abandoning everything but a few wagons of food, two of which had to be hauled by soldiers, joined in the retreat.

Toward sunset, approaching Fort Necessity—which had been abandoned by the French for the time being, probably because of Braddock's march on Duquesne—Washington halted his forlorn, crippled, and terrorized troopers and ordered camp. They could not march any farther. Wounds had to be dressed, and food had to be partaken of. Giving these orders, Washington sought the wagon where General Braddock lay mortally hurt. He found Major Orme sitting up, looking pallid but cheerful, and he assured Washington that his wound was not serious. The several other officers were spread upon canvases on the ground and were being attended to, but General Braddock was dying. When Washington arrived, it was evident that Braddock could last but little longer. Captain Stewart and Washington lingered beside him, hoping that he would break his bitter silence. It would have been better had he died on the battlefield. Approaching the end he rallied and softly spoke to himself over and over, "Who would have thought it? We shall know better—how to deal with them—another time." With these words General Braddock expired.

Early the next morning Washington had Braddock's grave dug in the middle of the road so that the wagons could be passed over the grave and obliterate it and render futile any French or Indian marauders who might come along after the retreat had passed. Washington read the funeral service over General Braddock's grave and spoke generously and fittingly of the great qualities that the stout-hearted English officer had possessed.

After the funeral, the wagons were driven over Braddock's grave and the troopers followed, and the retreat, by reason of rest and food, grew less of a tragic one. At the Redstone camp there came the first disintegration of Washington's frontiersmen. The Wetzels and the Zanes departed unobtrusively, as was their strange habit. Only the youngest Zane, Isaac, who had conceived an affection for Washington, came to bid him goodbye. He told Washington that they were going to make for their camp on the west side of the Blue Ridge and that some day, if Washington journeyed down the Ohio River, he would find their settlement at Wheeling Island. His oldest brother Ebenezer was going to buy that island from Cornplanter for a keg of whiskey. Washington remembered the lad's words and stored away in his mind the thought that indeed he would see the Zanes and Wetzel again. Morning disclosed the fact that Scarrooyaddy and Half King had left during the night, but Boone approached Washington to say farewell, to assure him that had he been at the head of Braddock's army, Fort Duquesne would have fallen. All he asked of Washington was the replenishing of his powder and ball, a sack of salt and another of dried fruit. At parting, Washington could only squeeze this great woodsman's hand and leave unsaid what was in his heart.

The retreat of that army along the road the soldiers had built in cheerful anticipation of defeating the French and their

Indian allies was traveled more swiftly than during its making. Washington again succumbed to his fever and lay in the bottom of a wagon, sick and hopeless, until the army arrived at Cumberland. Here there was a larger separation of those left in Braddock's defeat. Washington and his frontiersmen proceeded on to Wills Creek and there, after a day's rest, nourishment and medicine that gave him considerable improvement, Washington set out on his lonely, melancholy ride back to Mount Vernon.

19

Washington Meets Martha Custis

News traveled swiftly ahead of Washington, and that night as he stopped at a tavern he fell victim to a weary amazement when he was applauded by a group of men eager to learn more about Braddock's defeat. His brief bitter replies were not those of a returning hero. Sick as he was from fever and exhaustion and not caring about anything except to get home, he could not ponder on why he should be acclaimed. To be sure he remembered at Cumberland and at Wills Creek that Captain McKnight and Gist were loud in their praises of him, but it was all so hopeless. Next morning he packed food for himself and grain for his horse and set out intending to keep to the trails and even the wilderness to avoid meeting another crowd. And that day as the fever and wracking pain clamped down on him his mind gave way to all except the sense of testimony that was so impossible to stand against. He kept his directions by instinct rather than by any roads or signposts. There were nights and days of torture when he could not rest or sleep and could hardly keep his seat in his saddle.

It was dusk when at last he reached Mount Vernon. His joy at the end of the long journey as well as the end to all his military ambitions was so great that it upheld him so that he did not fall off his horse and have to crawl in the house. William must have taken him for an apparition, and his mother screamed at sight of him. She called him a ragamuffin. He must have been a spectacle for her to behold. He had not shaved for a week nor washed the travel stain from him for days. His uniform was ragged, black from powder stain, full of bullet holes. He could only smile wanly at her, tell her that he was only exhausted and starved and sick with fever. He begged her not to spread the news of his homecoming just yet and to make William keep it secret. Then weakness and faintness overcame him.

Washington was ill in bed for several days. Then the fever left him and the irrational cloud lifted from his mind. He would rather have continued to be out of his head, because with the return of memory his torture began. He felt the forces of his strength begin to renew. His robust constitution had not been undermined, and it rebounded whether he wanted it to or not. And despite his morbid languid desires to lie there and forget, the spiritual strength of him awoke and almost unconsciously began battle with his mental and physical wakening.

He did not try to understand what was going on within him. The horror of that bloody battle darkened his sleeping and waking hours. The futility of that sacrifice—how terrible to see in all its ghastly detail! And even in the dark hours when he reproached himself for not having done more to avert it, even in his bitter sorrow over the tragedy of Braddock and his brave officers, he would remember his heroic frontiersmen and the Indian chiefs and feel his heart beat and his vein throb at the memory.

His mother tried to draw him from his morbid obsession. She claimed it was only the physical and mental exhaustion and the horror of that battle. But Washington knew that he would find out presently that it was more. But to please his mother he got out of bed and moved about and went downstairs to the sitting room where he soon sought the couch. He tried to fortify himself against what was inevitable—that his friends and neighbors would learn he was home and come flocking to Mount Vernon. It was an ordeal that he dreaded. Not only had Braddock failed, but he felt that he had failed just as signally. And when his intelligence tried to pierce his morbid brooding and asked why and how he had failed, he could not answer. He did not want to think about such things.

The only peace he got was in thinking about the trails in the forest and in longing once more to be able to take to them, to the solitude of the wilderness, and therein find the only solace that was left to him. But another day and another found him growing stronger in spite of himself and having a regurgitation of troubled thought when all he wanted was to lie or sit alone, yielding to his despair.

One afternoon when he was lying on the couch in the sitting room dozing and for the time being oblivious to his mental inhibitions, his mother came in greatly excited.

"Oh, George, they've found out—they've come," she cried, in mingled joy and dread. "It's all over the country that you're home—that you've been sick. William or some of the servants must have disobeyed. But surely, dear, you cannot go forever lying here alone, a prey to something I can feel but cannot understand. Please see them."

"Mother, how you carry on! Who's come to see me?"

"Why, Fairfax, Sally, and Anne, and—"

"Well, and who?" he interposed gently.

"Sally's friend, Martha Custis."

"Martha! I remember. Sally used to talk about Martha. It seems so long ago, and so—so—. Bring Sally and Martha in. Ask Fairfax and Anne to wait. They will tear me to pieces."

His mother left him and went out. Washington lay there trying to remember something, dreading being seen and being compelled to talk, and yet vaguely pleased. Outside he heard Sally's gay voice and the throb of its contralto melody struck some dull chord within him. Then his mother entered, followed by Sally, who was leading someone by the hand.

Sally's sweet face blurred in his sight, and he could not see it distinctly. His mother murmured something, then hastily retreated. Sally came to his couch still leading the other visitor who apparently hung back a little. Then Sally bent over him. She squeezed his hands. She kissed his cheek with tremulous lips. "Oh, George! Thank God you're here safe and getting along well again. I had frightful pictures in my mind of you. But, Sir Colonel, hero of Braddock's Field, you are almost your old self again. Almost, but not quite. I cannot tell—"

"Hello, Sally Fairfax," responded Washington deeply. "Now you are here, I'm glad to see you. I didn't want to see anyone. I've been ill—distraught. And is this Mrs. Custis hiding behind you? Your old friend and schoolmate—about whom you told me so much?"

"Yes, George, this is Martha," replied Sally, sweet richness in her voice. "I've been a long time in keeping my word. . . . Martha, come here."

Then Washington looked up with clearing eyes to see a tall and lovely young woman. She was dressed in black and her black hair made a striking contrast to her white beautiful face. Dark eyes, dilated and misty, bent intent and soft gaze upon him.

"Colonel Washington, I'm glad to meet you—at last," she said, and her voice was strangely compelling and rich like Sally's. "Welcome back to Virginia. It is so wonderfully good to know you are here and well."

"Mrs. Custis!" he ejaculated, striving for his habitual dignity. "So I have met you at last—at last in the flesh!"

"Yes," she murmured simply.

"But you are all in black!" exclaimed Washington.

"I am a widow."

Sally interposed gaily with a triumphant little laugh. "George, I think I'd like to leave you and Martha alone for a little. It'll take more than your mother to hold back Anne and Fairfax till you and Martha get acquainted. But don't waste time. You're not strangers and, well—Martha will tell you. . . . Here, Martha, sit down on the couch beside him."

Sally gave Martha a small push and again, uttering that strange little thrilling laugh, stood back and gazed down upon them with wonderful eyes. She was treating her heart to something long cherished, but she was as coquettish as ever and full of a devilish little audacity, as one possessed of knowledge that she could have divulged if she had wanted to. Then she ran out of the room to scream at Fairfax, who bellowed, "But he's my friend, too." But he was dragged back from the half-opened door, then somebody closed it.

"Colonel, this surprise was planned by Sally," Martha said hurriedly. "I did not approve of it. I wanted word to be sent to you, but you know imperious Sally. Still, as it is done, let us get around it. You are indeed no stranger to me. Did your mother tell you I had been here several times?"

"You have! Well, indeed that is fine. Mother never breathed a word about it. It is—a surprise. A little too much for me. I deplore the embarrassment to you, but Sally is a devil. I do appreciate meeting you. I thank you for coming."

Washington sat up and arranged the pillows so that he could lean comfortably back, and this done he looked directly at her, stirringly aware of her nearness and her charm. There was no evidence of confusion about her. She was a marvelous contrast to Sally in her vivid dark loveliness. Their eyes locked in one long earnest gaze.

"Your mother told us a little about this strange mood that possesses you. Tell me. I can see the havoc in your face. It must have been a dreadful ordeal. But it is over, Colonel Washington."

"Please wait a little for that," he implored. "I want to get things straight. I haven't had a rational thought for a long time. You are a widow? A lovely one, surely. And you so young—already known suffering."

"Yes, Colonel. I have had trouble," she replied. "Captain Custis died last year, leaving me with two babies. It was a blow, though not such a one as you might imagine. He was twice my age, the marriage was a family arrangement as is the custom these days. I looked up to him—was fond of him, but ours was not a love marriage."

"Ah, I'm sorry," replied Washington simply. "It makes me see that the world does not revolve about me and my little troubles. A widow with two babies—yet you cannot be more than twenty. You are visiting Sally for a while?"

"I'm staying at Belvoir indefinitely."

"That is fine. How nice for Sally! I'm glad. I—we must—"

Washington faltered here as the excitement under which he labored subsided to let him see his true self again, and he dropped his eyes and sighed. He did not divine what had been working in him, but it was too late. "I—I must tell you, Mrs. Custis, that I have returned home from Braddock's defeat a broken man. I'll never recover from the horror of that—and for my failure. It haunts me even in my dreams."

"Colonel Washington, I do not need to be told what you have suffered," she replied softly, and she took his calloused hands in hers. "But you are home safe, and you will get well, you have your mother and all your old friends, Sally—and me. Having returned ill and distraught, denying yourself to everyone, it's possible that you do not know that you are not a failure. Everyone in Virginia knows of your heroism on Braddock's Field. You are a hero!"

"Nonsense!" ejaculated Washington, staring at her, transfixed and thrilling. "What are you saying? That is the way mother tries to talk. Spare me please, Mrs. Custis."

"You are wrong, Colonel," she replied earnestly. "I speak the truth. Your comrades have spread it to the four winds. You saved the remnants of Braddock's scattered army from annihilation. Virginia honors you. America will need you in the trying times ahead."

"Mrs. Custis, you impress me as an intelligent, sincere young woman," returned Washington huskily. "Yours is not the language of compliment. You must believe what you say."

"I know it. I understand you. I can feel to what depth you have sunk, but you are all wrong. You must pull yourself out of this slough of despondency, this thing—whatever it is—has crept over your mind like poison lichen. Dispel it! I—"

Her soft compelling voice was disrupted by a pounding on the door, and Fairfax called to be let in. It was evident someone was holding him from entering.

"Mrs. Custis—you make me hope—feel new life again!" burst out Washington, surrendering to his emotions, and he clasped the little hands that held his. The commotion in his breast almost prohibited speech. "Oh, it will come back—that black horrible spell—when you are gone."

"Then I shall come back," she whispered softly with a radiant smile, rising from the couch.

"Mrs. Custis—Martha—make it soon, please. I'll try—"

"Tomorrow."

Then the door burst open, and Fairfax and Anne entered abreast and rushing to him, the two of them overwhelmed him as he had predicted. But Anne's kisses and the hard clasp of Fairfax's hands were so amazingly sweet to Washington, who never dreamed such sensations would come to him again.

"You old Injun fighter!" burst out Fairfax. "Oh, but it's great to see you. I could have murdered Sally out there. Swore you and Martha had secrets. . . . George, I'll come to myself in a minute. Let me get it out. We've been hearing rumors for weeks. Then days ago—it seems longer—the news came by way of Winchester. Father was there when Captain McKnight arrived. Did he cover you with glory? You were supposed to be on the way home, but you had left Wills Creek in bad shape. We were distressed. Then when the news came this morning that you were actually home—that you had been home for days—why, we were crazy with gladness. And here we are, old friend!"

"Fairfax—you'll excuse me—if I'm ovcrwrought by all this," said Washington, brokenly. "I have been ill. I spent myself in that march and fight. I was down with fever part of the time, then some terrible cloud darkened my mind. . . . I'll overcome it. Believe me, if one thousandth part of all that Sally looked—and Martha said—and Anne and you have dinned into my ears is true, I have been terribly wrong."

"George, you've been wrong, all right," returned Fairfax heartily. "You were always one to disparage yourself—to see what you have done as little. But that stand of yours, in spite of Braddock's blindness and hate of us provincials, that saving the army from massacre, that, old friend, made you the biggest man in the American Colonies. You've no idea what that means, you Englishman! You're like your father. But we're in *America*, George! My father and I have come to see the handwriting on the wall. When it comes—well, whatever is coming—you will be forced to some great position in America."

They were gone at last. Washington fell back upon his couch, spent, strangely shattered, unable to see at once what it was that had happened. The warmth of Fairfax's greeting and the outburst of joy of the usually quiet Anne, the haunting radiance of Sally's face, the mocking sweetness of her voice, the mystery in her eyes, and lastly, the incredible and devastating presence of Martha Custis—these for long dominated his mind and kept aloof those phantoms of doubt and despair. His mother came in and called him to supper. She was unusually smiling and happy and she too had a mysterious air. He was used to volubility but tonight, though very solicitous and sweet, she did not talk unless he addressed her.

"Mother, that girl Martha Custis told me she had been here," he said, at length, trying to be casual.

"Yes, indeed she has, George. Three times and one afternoon she came alone and stayed a long time with me. Isn't she just lovely?"

"Yes I did observe that she was quite pretty," replied Washington, looking down at his plate. "It was good of her to be so—so friendly. I must thank her."

"Martha told me that you had asked her to come tomorrow," said his mother.

Washington felt the hot blood come to his cheeks. Then he changed the subject, speaking of Anne and Sally and lastly of Fairfax. He told his mother all that Fairfax had said about how he was regarded in Virginia. He hoped she would refute it in some measure, but she enlarged upon it. What was more, she had not been surprised in the least. She had always known he would do unusual and noble things. And she concluded, inexplicably to Washington, her old motherly psychic nonsense about predestination.

Washington went to bed early and, as always since he had been a young boy, dropped at once into a slumber, but as always, too, when he had his sleep out, he awakened sometime during the night. In the darkness and silence he fell victim to the old morbid phantasms. His demons came out of the blackness and beset him, and the hours wore on interminably. As long as it was dark and his spirit was at low ebb, he could not combat this spell that bordered upon irrationality.

When daylight came and the sun arose he shook the spell off somewhat, and during the morning the periods of his depression broke only to one thought and that was of Martha Custis. He held her in his mind as long as he could. He could not understand why she influenced him so strongly. But he remembered her beauty, that pearly whiteness of her lovely face crowned by the black waving tresses, the charm of her manner, the lithesomeness of her form, and lastly, her unforgettable eyes.

But when his wracked brain again went off on its evil tangent his despair was worse than ever. His mother and these good friends were blinded by their affection for him. They could not see what he knew—that he had failed to avert Braddock's defeat. And he knew absolutely without any doubt that if he could have gotten under the skin of that irascible bullheaded old general, he could not only have saved the day but have been at the fall of Fort Duquesne. It was the perfidious guide or guides that led Braddock's army into ambush that had been their downfall. There had really not been such a great force of Indians and French. It had been the way they fought. England, like a bulldog, would never let go. Another army would be sent over to attack the

French and Indians. It would be the same as the last one. It would meet the same doom. Washington thought how terrible it would be to be importuned again to accept office under a commander and be subjected again to the same insult and ridicule. What tortured him was the useless sacrifice of life. If he could not have absolute command, he would never accept another commission.

And when that feeling of freedom came over him he thought again of the wilderness and of those roving spirits like the Zanes and Wetzel, of Daniel Boone and Captain Jack. Theirs was the life he longed to live. There were times when he succumbed to the temptation and when he turned himself over to a moment of melancholy happiness, dreaming of the wonderful Ohio River Valley, the intrepid frontiersmen and the red men who would do unto white men as they were done by, the dusky eyes of Indian maidens like Winona, there came a strange nameless call to his spirit, as if voices unknown to him were whispering how impossible it was for him to accept the freedom that had been fostered in his nature by his years in the wilderness in conflict with another kind of freedom, perhaps the unconscious call of his countrymen to lend his strength, his spirit, his genius to make them free. And here there came a deadlock in his mind. Emotion and thought gave way to the encroachment of his evil doubts and fears.

Washington began the day rather restless and nervous and found that walking as of old was good for him. He went out to see the horses and almost yielded to getting into the saddle again. He longed to take the river trail and spend the day in the woods. But all the time he remembered that he was to have company, and he could not run away from what he dreaded yet desired very much. He was in the sitting room after lunch reading when his friends came, and this time Fairfax was the first to get to him.

"Hello, George, how are you today?" said Fairfax cheerfully, shaking hands with Washington. "Say, you look different today. Not so moody! And your hand has got life in it. Yesterday it was like a dead fish."

"Hello, yourself, Fairfax," replied Washington, just as warmly. "I confess to feeling very much better, and of course that credit goes to you and the girls. Did they come with you?"

"Yes, they're out with your mother. I claimed your attention first today because I knew if I didn't I wouldn't get it. Something very particular to talk to you about which I couldn't divulge yesterday. But—how did you like Martha?"

"Very much indeed, Fairfax. She's charming," returned Washington too casually.

"Oh, is that all," returned Fairfax, in a disappointed tone. "Sally and I expected you to lose your head at once."

"Well, if I had," said Washington, laughing, "I'd be rather inclined to hide it for a while."

"George, didn't Sally's behavior strike you rather significantly?"

"No, it didn't. She may have been a little more joyful and mysterious than I remember her, but that of course was because she brought Martha."

"Sometimes you are very obtuse or else you are pretending. Now, point blank, Sally and Martha are bent on your subjugation and you haven't a ghost of a chance."

"Fairfax, I expect it would be wise for me to take that as your usual exaggeration. But at any rate you flatter me."

"Well, in the face of other important things, I've done my duty in preparing you. If you want my advice, here it is. I'd gracefully capitulate."

"Fairfax, I can't wave a white flag before I've been asked to surrender, but tell me, what else is on your mind?"

"Father left for Fredericksburg this morning. From there he is going to Williamsburg. There's something going on that everybody knows except you. Virginia is going to raise fifteen or twenty companies of colonist soldiers, and you will be given the command."

Washington sustained a violent break in his pleasant thought and felt his breath had suddenly caved in. "For heaven's sake, Fairfax. Where did you hear that? Who started it? Why? What is it being done for?"

"George, it shouldn't surprise you. Fort Necessity and Braddock's Field will have to be avenged. Will you accept the command?"

"I! It's so sudden. I'd made up my mind I was through with the military. I don't want to live through any more such experiences. If the command is offered to me I will refuse it."

"George, I urge you to reconsider. You've been ill. You're just recovering. Think what you could do with twenty companies of Virginians—all hunters and frontiersmen!"

Washington tried to check the leap of his thoughts but he was failing when Sally and Martha burst into the room. They wore riding habits and to Washington appeared particularly stunning. They were gay, rosy-faced and bright-eyed, and bent on conquest or mischief, perhaps both.

"Good afternoon, George," said Sally, as she gave him her hand. "We rode over horseback. Martha's horses came. You should see them. As a great rider and lover of horse flesh I should think you would never be happy until you had got possession of them and also their—"

Martha interposed here, quite as gay though somewhat confused by the audacious Sally. Her greeting was low and rather indistinct, and Washington, very glad to see them, replied to their greetings in like manner and said he would like to see Martha's horses. Whereupon they went outside and he took quite a time in appraising the thoroughbreds, after which he congratulated Martha upon possession of three magnificent animals. In the conversation that ensued he gathered from Fairfax that Martha owned a stable of such fine animals, and he could only assume that the young widow was wealthy. They wanted Washington to ride on horseback, but he declined and promised that he would some other time, perhaps soon. Fairfax went somewhere with William, and Washington repaired with the girls to the house. They did not want to go in. They walked up and down the veranda, the young women each taking one of Washington's arms, and he sensed that there was something afoot. It amused him to remember that wherever Sally turned up there was sure to be interest or conflict, something out of the ordinary.

"Fairfax told you about the call for volunteers?" queried Sally.

"Yes, he did. I was pretty much surprised."

"But you shouldn't have been. It is a wonderful thing for Virginia to do. You will accept of course?"

"Sally, I think not. I am through with soldiering."

"No Virginian can be through with soldiering these days. Until the French are driven out and peace made with the Indian tribes and until the colonies are free."

"Free! Sally, what are you saying?" exclaimed Washington incredulously.

"George, I am saying just that. But I don't want to precipitate an argument now. You will want to talk with Martha. And so I will ride around with Fairfax for a while."

"But, Sally, aren't you hurrying away?" queried Washington blankly.

"I am. I'm always hurrying, even without such a good reason as I have now. These are hurrying times. I do not know to what end unless it is, as I said, to be free."

"I see, Sally. Fairfax and his father are weaning you from England."

"It didn't require much persuasion. . . . Martha, I will leave him with you. Do not be awed by the fact that he is Colonel Washington, a great Virginian. He is vulnerable on his primitive side. . . . I love you, dear friends and I remind you that time is fleeting. Make the best of it." Sally gave then the benefit of her lovely eyes intent on them together, solemn, full of hope and prophecy. Then, with a radiant smile, she lifted her skirts and tripped away.

Washington watched her go, conscious of the old tingling sensation and that he would like to have been alone to think, to prepare himself for something that he defined as beyond his control. The pressure of Martha's gloved hand on his arm seemed like a magnet. He turned to her and found that she was looking up at him.

"Let us walk down to the summer house," she suggested.

"That will be nice. I haven't been down there for a long time," returned Washington as he led her off the porch. The path led winding among the trees down a gentle slope toward the river. It was lined with tall goldenrods beginning to bloom, and along the river the green of the willows and the sycamores had been touched with gold. Washington waited for Martha to speak, which she did not until they had reached the summer house and she had seated herself upon the railing.

"George, you have heard Sally and, of course, Fairfax told you before, our particular news."

"Yes, it was indeed a surprise. I hate to think of it. I have not yet recovered from my last trial at arms."

"You must not think of yourself," she rejoined earnestly. "Virginia has roused. She has awakened as a colony. Consider what may come of this. After the French and Indians have been conquered."

"Martha you are intimating something similar to what Sally said?" he queried.

"I'm not hinting but affirming. It may take long, but the future of the American colonies is in uniting. I do not want to lose my inheritance. I have children to raise. Fairfax and his father and Sally have gradually turned against the existing government. It cannot grow better. It must grow worse. But this rousing of Virginia to take upon herself aggression that England failed in—that should be tremendously significant to you. And that you should be expected to lead this colonist army—it is a tribute to which you cannot be deaf. Virginia is vindicating Fort Necessity and Braddock's Field. You are the one chosen."

"Martha, you put it so—so clearly that you make me ashamed," replied Washington, with emotion. "But I am sick of soldiering. That massacre before Fort Duquesne was horrible. Why, it was only yesterday—since I met you—and was so tremendously attracted to you—that I have lost partly the gloom and despair of my morbid thoughts."

"I am very happy if my coming has helped you," she said simply.

"Martha, I feel that I have known you long. I—it's hard to explain. If there is any man who could be morbid and sick in your lovely and gracious presence, I certainly am not he. To go away now—when I have just met you—when I feel there is a promise of so much, it would be cruel."

"But as I understand it, there is no immediate need of your leaving Mount Vernon. The gathering together of twenty companies of fit young men cannot be done very quickly. If our being together is anything like as wonderful to you as it would be to me, why, let us be together. Every day! You must get out in the sun, you must ride, you must work to get back your strength. I will see you anytime—go with you anywhere—I would love to ride your wilderness trails. Oh, I know so much about you from Sally, from Fairfax, and from your mother. I know what you care for. I know what you need. Your weakness, if you have one, George, lies in thinking so poorly of yourself, of your capabilities. I can help you there. I can influence you to think right. I can make you forget all this morbidness."

"How do you know so much about me?" asked Washington curiously.

"Sally and I became intimate at school in Philadelphia when we were just mere girls. I know all about you as a boy. I know what Sally thought of you as a boy with Sally and Fairfax and Dickey Lee, and as we grew older she did not break that habit of confidence. She told me what she could not tell anyone else. How she loved Fairfax and how she loved you. That she wanted you both. And those confidences were only broken when we left school and did not see each other again for long. Then she was engaged to Fairfax, she was terribly distressed as well as wickedly glad that you loved her still—that you loved her not as a brother but as a lover—too late! It was then she had to try to win me to think—to feel—in fact to take her place. How little she guessed how much she made me care for you, but too late again! But my father meant me for Captain Custis. . . . Well, things work out strangely. I am here in Virginia. I am having my possessions transported here. I am going to make a home here, and before you came back I met your mother. She is a lovely woman. We became attached to each other at once. And what Sally did not tell me about you, your mother did. So you see, Colonel Washington, I know you very well, perhaps better than you know yourself."

"Martha, I am now utterly grateful for all this," returned Washington huskily. He took her gloved hand in his and pressed it while he looked out through the trees upon the shining river. The first dreamy langourous touch of autumn had fallen upon the land and at a season which had always meant most to Washington, had called most poignantly to him, divined that he had been confronted with love again. "I feel that I do not deserve what may be possible for us. I appreciate that you see my duty to Virginia much more clearly than I do. My mother is that way too. But the hard fact comes clear to me now. I have met you. It seems that it might be my great good fortune to be with you, see you every day. And I do not want to give it up. I do not want to leave you."

"But, Colonel Washington, I will be here when you come back," she said softly.

"How well I know, and I only, that I might never come back," he replied bitterly. "Or I might return crippled."

"Those things are possible, but they are not probable."

"Why are they not?"

"Because the facts of your life seem to have ordained something other than sacrifice. Your mother always knew this since your childhood. I feel it too, and I want you to take command of this Virginia army."

Washington had succumbed to her beauty and charm, but all his intelligence and selfish longing for what he had never had fought against her sense of duty, her ideal for him, her woman's intuition and vision. He met her clear reasoning with passion and vehemence and with every argument at his command except the cardinal fact that he loved her. He did not tell her that. It was too new, too wonderful. He wanted to live with it a while, and so they talked on and on for hours, living in that time months or even years of ordinary association. He found more and more in her of depth, of intelligence, of rich womanly generosity and noble sentiments, and he unburdened himself as he had never done in his life before. And when at last the sun was setting and Fairfax had called them from above, they started up the path hand in hand, sweeping through the scented goldenrod. For Washington, the air seemed charged with blissful portent. There was a glow on the land, an amber golden light, that could not altogether have come from elemental things. He knew that she knew he loved her, but his mind halted and his tongue went to the roof of his mouth when he tried to ask her a momentous question—at the moment too daring and preposterous for him to voice.

The horses had been brought around to the front of the house. Fairfax was there, and he made facetious and sentimental remarks. Sally looked at them with wonderful understanding and gladness in her eyes, but she had no word for them. When they were mounted and goodbyes had been given, Washington looked up to Martha and said, "I will take a short ride with you tomorrow. I'd better not ride one of your spirited horses until I have become used to the saddle again."

Washington and Martha rode down the river toward Belvoir. He thought at first that he could not have been very talkative in any event at least very soon, but the fact that he was up on his favorite, Roger, for the first time since long before his Indian campaign wakened so many associations that he hardly spoke at all. His companion stole sideways glances at him and smiled as if she understood and did not break his reverie.

The horses and saddle brought back vividly the never-to-be-forgotten scene of Braddock's defeat. When that memory had its way with him, he did not see how any Virginian, let alone an Englishman, could lay aside the memory of Braddock's Field and abide it unchallenged. The old call of the wilderness pealed out to him. The green winding trails called again to him. They always called to him, but this time it was a martial thing and not the old longing for the loneliness and solitude of the woods. He came to himself presently, brought back suddenly by the thought of why he had set out upon this ride with Martha. And the unfrequented branch that led off the main road up to the familiar oak grove spurred and inspired him to learn of fate that he could not believe would be unhappy.

"Martha, let us turn off here," he said. "You will like the view from on top."

"It is very pretty in any way that you look," she replied. "I love Virginia, and I have not seen any part that is more beautiful than here at Mount Vernon and Belvoir."

It was only a short ride to the summit of the low hill, and Washington halted under the great gnarled oak tree with not only the past knocking at his heart but some divination of a glorious future. It was the waning of afternoon in an early autumn day. The fences zigzagged gray and old out of the straggling lines of goldenrod. The river wound away in the distance like a golden ribbon losing itself in the dim haze of the forest. There was a faint blue haze in the hollow. The woods were drowsy with summer heat. For a moment there was silence, then the old familiar birds he knew so well emphasized that dreamy silence. In the call of a crow from a distant hill and the lonely melancholy song of a hermit thrush he felt something that had been his all his life and which had grown and grown now to unfold its meaning.

"George, haven't I ridden here before?" cried Martha. "It is a lovely place and so familiar, but, no, neither Fairfax nor Sally ever led me off the main road. That great old branching oak tree—why, I know it. I have been here before."

"Martha, that is hardly possible. If Fairfax and Sally never led you off the main road."

"But I tell you, I know this place," she cried, her voice ringing. "Oh, oh, I remember. This is where you met Sally that day long ago—that day she confessed she broke your heart."

"Yes, Martha, this is the place, and I have come to it instinctively. I don't know why, but I have ridden here so many times alone. You know that is a habit of mine, always to go back to places that are dear to me."

"Oh, it was wonderful of you to bring me here!" she exclaimed with her great dark eyes shining upon him. "Oh, if only what you have to say to me is—"

"Martha, of all places in the world I love, this is the one to tell you," returned Washington. And, dismounting, he went quickly to her side and put his arms around her. "Let me lift you down. But wait a moment," he went on unsteadily, as she put her hands on his shoulders and leaned towards him, "I can say better what I have to say—while you are here."

"George, it's a rather precarious position in more ways than one," she murmured with a little rich laugh. "Let me get my foot out of the stirrup. There! If Prince bolts—at least you will have me."

"Martha, I wonder—I wonder if I dare believe—I'll ever have you?"

"Sir, I do not see how I could give you any more encouragement," she whispered roguishly.

Then Washington burst out with a flood of words. "Martha! I've fallen terribly in love with you. I don't know when—yesterday or long ago, but it's now. I love you madly. I think you are the most wonderful girl—you have everything that I revere in a woman. I knew last night. I could not sleep, and here I am telling you—I love you. I must be mad, I think, to be influenced by Sally and Fairfax. I must be mad to think you could care for me so soon. Two days, but oh, such splendid days of sweetness and promise! Martha, tell me, am I right in my instincts? Dare I hope that you might return my passion in some little measure?"

"George, I have loved you for ten years," she replied, with her arms slipping around his neck. "You have been my hero all that time and now, having known you only two days, I find you all I had dreamed of."

"Martha! Darling, that is too sweet—too wonderful to be true," cried Washington hoarsely. "But you are here so close—almost in my arms. I would see it in your lovely eyes if you never said a word. . . . Martha, will you marry me?"

With an inarticulate cry of relief and rapture she slipped out of the saddle into his arms. Washington held her closer and closer, bending with dim eyes to her lovely face, his heart seemingly about to burst, and then their lips met, and in that charged moment all that Washington had ever dreamed of and longed for of beauty and bliss seemed lavished upon him. He surrendered to the trenchant call of love, and the feel of her clinging arms and her dusky hair that blinded his sight and the kisses of fire that could not have been just born of the moment. It seemed long when he let her down to the ground and stood holding her while she gazed up at him with flushed face and dim eyes.

"Martha, it must be true! Bless you. Once in my life a dream come true, and my most glorious dream. . . . But you have not told me—you have not spoken. Will you marry me?"

"George, I will marry you—when you come back from Fort Duquesne."

20

Washington Takes Command

It was just ten weeks after Braddock's defeat that Washington led his sixteen companies of colonials into Fort Cumberland. He had recruited these colonials in and around Fredericksburg and Alexandria and out among the frontiersmen that he knew so well. He hoped that a like force of troops from Pennsylvania would meet him there, but the hope was vain. Whereupon he left Cumberland and marched on to the frontier to learn what the situation was, how the Virginia rangers were posted, and how best troops might be disposed of for the defense of the country. He did not risk going into the Ohio River Valley yet. There were a few settlements on a line between Fort Dinwiddie and Cumberland. He saw where additional forts would have to be put up whenever he could raise the money and the men to do it.

As the weeks passed he grew discouraged. He had not fully recovered from the illness he had contracted during the Braddock campaign. He wrote to a friend that "no man can gain any honor by conducting our forces at this time but will rather lose his reputation." But nothing could stop him, nothing could blind him to his vision of the future. Once having started out on this adventurous and hazardous campaign he would not give it up because the morale and condition of his troops hardly justified it.

He left Fort Dinwiddie and traveled on. He marched back to Fredericksburg to Williamsburg to report to Governor Dinwiddie; he received a message from his frontiersmen that hostile Indians had broken out on the war path again, murdering and burning their homes along the south branch of the Potomac. He turned back, collected his troops at Fredericksburg and Winchester, and rushed to the scene of the hostile acts. He stopped the depredations on the south branch.

Among his many trials during the months of his command of this Virginia company, he was greatly embarrassed and harassed by one of his men, Captain John Dagworthy, who had held a commission in Canada. Dagworthy claimed that he outranked Colonel Washington and caused him all kinds of inconvenience and annoyance. At length Washington could not stand it any longer. Wherefore he left his troops at Fort Cumberland and set out for Boston to lay his case before the commander-in-chief of the British forces. On this trip he showed remarkable endurance and skill as a horseman. From Philadelphia he rode the ninety miles to New York in two days and covered the distance to Boston at the same average. He laid his case before General Shirley, who decided the question of the command in his favor. Then, elated at his success, he set out once more for Virginia. He was detained at the Governor's house by men like John Adams, and he made a deep impression on this gentleman by telling of conditions on the frontier. He gathered from Adams that in the vague and distant future of the colonists he would be called upon. Then Colonel Washington rode back to Williamsburg, and, having delivered his good news, he was free to hunt up his friends the Zanes and Patrick Henry. But he could not locate them; Ebenezer Zane was on one of his mysterious missions to New York and Boston.

Washington left Williamsburg for Winchester, where he found the frontier worse than when he had left. The Indians had broken out again. He could not do anything at the time because he could not engage enough troops and equipment. He kept sending to Williamsburg for money, for soldiers, for authority to give him control over the militia. Everywhere he met a wall of discouragement, hopelessness, and even disapproval. It was the most disheartening period of his life. He had committed himself, and now failure stared him in the face from every direction. A diversity dogged his footsteps. He had trials and tribulations that daunted him, but he did not give up, and always his marvelous store of experience and his judgment of men and circumstance were being stored up as if fate intended some gigantic problem for him in the future.

That autumn Washington undertook a bolder and more hazardous enterprise. The boldest of the marauding Indians spread from the Potomac River to the North Carolina line, and he set out to establish a line of forts along the frontier between these points. Once more he recruited troops, many of them his old frontiersmen who had worked for nothing, and he drew upon what finances he could obtain and set out to build those forts. And he succeeded in doing it. This feat established his status as a military engineer.

Returning to Virginia from North Carolina, he once more undertook to enlist men to fight the Indians now growing bolder and more murderous than ever, but only a few of his frontier friends came at his call. So, for weeks on end, Washington traveled from one place to another, praying for the time to come when soldiers and funds and equipment would be given to him, and fighting his longing to give up. Always in his mind, however, was the wonderful reward which was coming to him when he returned from the fall of Fort Duquesne.

At long last his fortunes changed for the better, and, indefatigable and indomitable, he found himself once more at Fort Cumberland with a large force of troops, many of whom were colonists and faithful frontiersmen who had been with him before. There Washington was to meet another brave Scotsman, General John Forbes, who marched to Cumberland with a large force. He had thirteen hundred Scottish highlanders and a large number of Pennsylvania colonists. They had equipment and supplies. When Colonel Washington joined General Forbes with his Virginia force, he felt that at last the doom of Fort Duquesne had been foreshadowed.

The march toward Fort Duquesne along the Braddock army road was a poignant one for Washington. Even after the intervening time since the massacre of Braddock's army, there was still left old wheels and wagon tongues and dilapidated wagons; even skeletons along the road for miles. Washington sent his frontiersmen scouts, one of whom was the faithful Gist, ahead to reconnoiter. It was well that Washington took the precaution to do this. General Forbes sent two thousand men to occupy a point, and part of this company, some eight hundred troops under Major Grant, approached to a point almost under the walls of Fort Duquesne. Grant's vanity and carelessness came near repeating the former disaster to British arms. The French and Indians streamed out of the fort and, flanking Grant's company on both sides, were working to a position which was their old favorite maneuver, an ambush. But Washington's frontiersmen circumvented this daring enterprise. Washington moved up with his provincials and saved Grant from utter annihilation. There ensued a fierce and deadly battle. The highlanders came up, and, incensed by the atrocious butchery by the Indians, they added their fierce attack to that of the provincials. The French and Indians were treated to something similar to what they had done to Braddock's army. Their ambushes availed nothing. They were packed off by the frontier marksmen and cut down by the Scottish highlanders. They fled to the Fort while Forbes was massing his troops again, set fire to the Fort, and, abandoning it, escaped down the river in their boats.

This triumph of the provincial made General Forbes's campaign a decisive battle. It ruined the French. They fell back down the river and were deserted by the Indians.

It was dusk when the frontier scouts informed Washington that the enemy had escaped down the river. The next day Washington visited the site of Fort Duquesne and saw with mingled feelings the blackened charred mass and the thirty standing stone chimneys. That was the end of Fort Duquesne. General Forbes left a company of his men there to erect a new fort which was to be succeeded the following year by a large commodious fort to be named Fort Pitt. Washington, happy at last, vindicated even to his own meticulous satisfaction, returned to Virginia to find that, whatever doubts he had entertained before, he was indeed a hero. And once more he gave up his commission, and Martha Custis and he settled down to what he hoped would be a happy and busy plantation life.

The weeks and months and seasons passed so fleetingly that Washington took little account of them. He was so happy that even the wilderness did not call to him. The presence of Martha and of her adorable children was all that Washington needed to make life infinitely full for him. He added to and improved his land. The cultivation of the soil had always appealed to him, and now it became his work. Only seldom did he go to Belvoir. The balls and parties given from time to time, which Martha and his friends found such pleasure in, he let go by for the serene content of his home. The pattering of feet of the children and their merry voices echoing through the halls of Mount Vernon gave him as much pleasure as he had ever had in his life, and it lent a haunting sweetness at the thought of the time when he would have children of his own.

The seasons had a way of multiplying into years. Washington and Martha, having so much property and the means to cultivate it, prospered while many Virginians grew worse off. He did not turn a deaf ear to the discontent of the times but neither did he let the bitter dissatisfaction of his friends linger in his mind. He hoped and believed that time would cure the evils of the colonies and now as always he was in favor of careful judgment and a conciliatory attitude.

Nevertheless, as the troubles of the colonists increased, Washington was not able to keep them from touching him. From time to time men who were interested politically in the future of America called on him or wrote to him and in that way he was kept abreast of the times. England's new king, George III, began to show the cloven hoof. At the end of the Seven Years' War, England's resources were drained, and this new king pressured the colonies for more economic support. The Stamp Act aroused the colonists to anger and to uniform resentment as had nothing else. Washington heard it as the first rumbling of a mighty storm, and for the first time his optimism suffered a blight. So fiercely did the colonists resent this act that it was revoked at the end of the year. But that did not still the unrest, and the levy of future taxes to make up for the repealing of the Stamp Act made matters just as bad for the colonists and therefore made their anger permanent.

Ebenezer Zane visited Washington again and told of his talks with leaders of the opposition in Boston and Philadelphia, and this time his pessimism about the future had augmented to a direct and prophetic revolt. Washington heard him in dismay and was eagerly receptive when Zane told about how his frontiersmen brothers with the Wetzels and the McCullochs and other intrepid men of the time had penetrated further down the Ohio River Valley toward the objective old Ebenezer Zane had decided years before. Washington renewed his desire to go down the Ohio River Valley and decided that he would do so when these troublesome times were past.

But these troublesome times did not pass. They grew worse. They were like spreading black clouds on the horizon, and with the Boston Tea Party and especially the closing of the port of Boston, the low rumblings became thunder. Washington belonged to the Virginia assembly and had attended to listen and sit silent. But after these two great and unjust blunders of the English Government he got up in the assembly and in a ringing voice addressed his associates.

"I will raise one thousand men, subsist them at my own expense, and march them to the relief of Boston!"

This first impassioned utterance of Virginia's greatest man was indeed a proof of the uniting of the colonies.

Patrick Henry and Edmund Pendleton on their way to the First Continental Congress at Philadelphia stopped off at Mount Vernon to visit Colonel Washington. In the grave discussion that ensued not only about the Congress but what Washington would or would not have to say to it, Washington's wife Martha exerted a great deal of influence. When she spoke it was not only with the spirit of a Virginia colonist but with the wisdom of one who saw through the density of the thing.

"Yes," said Patrick Henry in his high-pitched voice, referring again to the Boston Massacre, "it started while we were celebrating your birthday a while back. A dozen unarmed men and boys were shot and killed by the regulars!"

"I imagine they were shot down without warning by Preston's regulars just as you were sitting down to dinner," said Pendleton.

Washington gazed ponderingly at his fiery visitors. "Henry, you speak very forcibly and that without full detail of what actually might have happened. You have lost your temper and your head. Is that any reason for me to lose my temper and my head?"

"Colonel, no matter how you may soften the incident, the fact is that the soldiers of King George fired upon the subjects of King George and these subjects were unarmed and were killed without warning. As far as I am concerned, the revolution has already started, and His Majesty fired the first shot."

"I regret that I have to agree with you that in a certain sense the revolution has started. Gunshots cannot be denied, but it can be mediated. We can hold back the hotheads."

"Colonel Washington, I can see what you are getting at, and I am sure Patrick does too," interposed Pendleton. "You are on the conservative side. You would have us go slow. But the tremendous question with us here, Colonel, is this.

If these hotheads like Patrick Henry do gain control and start a revolution of the American Colonists, where will you stand?"

"No man should hesitate a moment to use arms in defense of freedom," replied Washington quietly.

"And here is what I am going to say in Philadelphia," rang out Patrick Henry. "British oppression has effaced the boundaries between the several Colonies. I am not a Virginian—I am an American!"

That was one of the fiery orator's remarkable statements. Washington heard it as the voice of colonists who had actually awakened. He could imagine Martha speaking like that. It was powerfully thought-provoking, and he was prepared for the impression it made upon the congress.

But it did not move the congress as a body. They held back, inhibited by nameless fear, and it was practically the same at the Virginia convention at Richmond. Members got up and made long or short speeches, undecided, leaning toward pacific methods, trying to hold back catastrophe.

Then like a thunderbolt out of a clear sky Patrick Henry leaped up, white of face, piercing eye, to peal out his wonderful voice: *"Sir, we have done everything that could be done to avert the storm which is now coming on. We have petitioned, we have remonstrated, we have supplicated . . . We have been spurned with contempt . . .*

"The war has actually begun . . . Is life so dear or peace so sweet as to be purchased at the price of chains or slavery? Forbid it Almighty God! I know not what course others may take; but, as for me, give me liberty, or give me Death."

Long after that clarion voice had ceased, the audience sat spellbound in an absolute stunned silence. Perhaps every listener was hearing the reverberations of his conscience. George Washington's reaction was profound. He remembered the first time he ever heard Patrick Henry speak. There had been a meaning in it then. Henry's had been a subtle growth, and now he had burst with lightning stroke upon his comrades, blasting weakness and vacillation from their hands and uplifting them to the vision that he saw afar.

* * *

George Washington was ready for the next sequence in this drama. As much as he had pondered over it, when it came it was far-removed from his calculation. It had to do with a lone horseman and a wonderful night ride. When Washington sat in his study under his bright light with his wife's sweet face and earnest eyes on him and read the news of this ride, he was transfixed. Thrill on thrill coursed through him. His first reaction came through the physical—his love of fast horses, his many and many perilous rides, and lastly, the thundering up and down Braddock's Road, carrying useless messages, riding to bring order out of chaos to have bullet after bullet tear through his coat and have two horses killed under him. He was reading of a ride by a lone horseman whom he would have liked to have been. Then, following swiftly upon his primitive reaction, flashed a singular and great meaning. On through the black night that horseman rode pounding on doors and windows yelling to the startled inhabitants, *"To arms! To arms! The British are coming!"* On through the dark night that horseman rode, through town, out into the countryside, flashing by the hamlets, awakening the colonists, inspiring them by his trenchant call, *"To arms! To arms! The British are coming!"*

On from Boston through the murky night thundered that horseman—Paul Revere!

"Paul Revere," whispered Washington, reading aloud to his startled wife, and though he did not tell her, he knew that days before this fateful news could arrive the American colonists had fired their first shots in the revolution.

It was only a short while after that in actual time, though long and far-reaching judged by pondering thought, that Washington stood facing the Second Continental Congress in Independence Hall and listened to the trumpet calls of his colleagues. He was nominated by John Adams, and that nomination was seconded by Samuel Adams for the greatest honor that could be conferred in that troubled and fateful hour. And as he listened he heard, too, the strange whispers that had come to him on lonely trails, in the conference hours when he chose to win the friendship of the noble red men, in the perilous journeys with his frontiersmen comrades—these whispers became clear in this hour as well as his miraculous preservation! He heard too the mystic voice of his mother when he was a child and Sally's girlish eulogies and Martha's mature love and judgment. These women had a sixth sense. They knew what they could not explain. Their intuitions and their spirits were divine, and here at last Washington accepted them, gratefully, reverently, as ones guided by unseen powers. Gravely he accepted, too, the tremendous responsibility thrust upon him by the members of this Congress: *General George Washington, Commander-in-Chief of the Army of the United Colonies.*

Editor's Notes

p. 2. Halley's comet, of course, did not come around in the year 1732, in which George Washington was born. Edmund Halley was an English astronomer, mathematician, and the first to calculate the orbit of a comet. He published a work in 1705 that included his calculations showing that the comets observed in 1531, 1607, and 1682, were actually one comet. He predicted its return in 1758, and the comet came late that year. *The New Encyclopedia Britannica*, vol. 5 (Chicago: Encyclopedia Britannica Inc., 1989), 644–45. Grey could conceivably have been describing the meteor showers that occur twice every year from the debris left behind in the wake of the comet.

p. 2. Bridge Creek Plantation. According to Paul Wilstach, *Mount Vernon: Washington's Home and the Nation's Shrine* (Indianapolis: Bobbs-Merrill, 1930), 9–10, the Bridge Creek Plantation was developed in 1658 by John Washington, George's great-grandfather, at the point where Bridge Creek meets the Potomac. George Washington was born at Bridge Creek Plantation in February 1732. In the old style (Julian) calendar, Washington's birthday was February 11. In 1582 Pope Gregory XIII reformed the calendar; however, since England was a Protestant country by that time, it did not adhere to the Gregorian reforms. When the American colonies started they too were under the old Julian system. It was not until 1752 that England decided to accept the Gregorian reforms. One consequence of that acceptance was that George Washington's birthday shot forward from 11 February 1731 to 22 February 1732. See Daniel J. Boorstin, *The Discoverers* (New York: Random House, 1983), 9.

p. . Mary Washington (maiden name: Mary Ball) was of English descent. Mary became Augustine's second wife on 6 March 1730. Augustine had four children by his first wife, of whom two survived. George was the first child of the second marriage and had an affectionate relationship with his mother. After the death of Augustine, Mary was left with five children to raise. She took over the care of the estate and the education of her children. While George was in the army, Mary managed the home alone. She had simple virtues and a humble dignity which she passed on to her loving son. *American Women, 1500 Biographies*, vol. 2 (Detroit: Gale Research Company, 1973), 751.

p. 17. While it is true that Grey depicted much Indian violence and brutality throughout the thousands of pages he wrote, he always emphasized that ill treatment by the white man was instrumental in turning many of them into savages. Grey himself claimed Indian blood through his great grandmother, Elizabeth, wife of Ebenezer Zane.

p. 19. Mount Vernon was built by Lawrence Washington, George's half-brother. It was named for Admiral Edward Vernon, under whom Lawrence had served in an expedition against the Spaniards in the West Indies. See Wilstach, 17. It was Admiral Vernon who in 1740 ordered his sailors to take rum and water on a daily basis to prevent scurvy. Since Vernon wore a "grogram" coat, the sailors began to call him "Old Grog," and the rum became known simply as "grog." See Stuart Berg Flexner, *Listening to America* (New York: Simon and Schuster, 1982), 171.

p. 19. Belvoir. "The Fairfax Estate was a long peninsula of nearly three thousand acres on the west side of Dogue Creek and it was one of the finest set of estates on the Potomac River. On the glorious promontory overlooking the river, William Fairfax built Belvoir, a great house destined to be the scene of much that was significant in the lives of both Lawrence Washington and his younger brother George." Wilstach, 12. The estate had nearly ten miles of waterfront, and only one mile of fence on the north side was needed to enclose it.

Lord Fairfax. Born Thomas Fairfax, he was an English nobleman who was proprietor of the Northern Neck of Virginia. He visited his land in Virginia from 1735 to 1737 to solidify his claims and later moved to the colony in 1745 and retained George as his surveyor. Fairfax was the only English nobleman in the colonies during the American Revolution. *Encyclopedia Americana*, vol. 10 (Danbury: Grolier Inc., 1990), 837.

Anne Fairfax. Married to Lawrence Washington, she was the daughter of Colonel William Fairfax, cousin and agent of Lord Fairfax, one of the chief proprietors of the area. Anne was a charming, graceful, and cultured woman. After his father's death, George lived with Lawrence and Anne. He also spent time with his half-brother Augustine, called Austin. Among others, Lawrence and Anne helped shape the development of George's mind and manners. *New Encyclopedia Britannica*, vol. 29, 716.

p. 19. Despite claims to the contrary, it seems that Abner Doubleday was not actually the inventor of American baseball. Two ancient English games, criquett and rounders, require that the ball be hit to accomplish scoring. During the colonial period rounders had several different names: one hold catapult or "one old cat," and if more than one person played the game, "two old cats." In one hold catapult the game's progress depended mostly on the batter, and its object was to hit the ball and run to a stake that was posted in the ground. The runner had to go back "home" without being "soaked," that is, being hit by the ball. The same person remained at bat until being soaked or until someone caught his fly ball, at which time the fielder took the batter's place at home. Of course, these procedures sound very much like modern-day English cricket, and it may be argued that the American game of baseball descended through English cricket. See Harold Seymour, *Baseball: The Early Years* (New York: Oxford University Press, 1960), 5; and Victor Salvatore, "The Many Who Didn't Invent Baseball," *American Heritage*, vol. 34 (June/July, 1983), 66. Zane Grey himself was an ardent baseball fan and in his earlier years had pitched for several semiprofessional teams. In fact, he attended the University of Pennsylvania on a baseball scholarship. Some of his more successful baseball stories were *The Redheaded Outfield and Other Stories* (Harper, 1920); *The Short Stop* (Harper, 1909); and *The Young Pitcher* (Harper, 1911).

p. 21. Richard Henry Lee. Lee became the American political leader who presented the Continental Congress with a proposal calling for independence of the American colonies from Britain on 7 June 1776. He was educated in England and returned to Virginia in 1758 when he entered the house of Burgesses. From this point on, he and Patrick Henry led the opposition to British colonial measures. Lee was a "polished orator" and was called the "Virginia Cicero." *Encyclopedia Americana*, vol. 17, 154.

p. 38. George did not seem to relish farm life; thus he was agreeable to his brother Lawrence and the elder Fairfax's proposals that he have a career at sea. He viewed it as romantic, and Lawrence hoped that as soon as George gained some naval experience he could receive a commission into the Royal Navy. Washington's mother was against his going to sea and apparently in real life she played much more of a role in dissuading him than Grey credits her in this novel. See Wilstach, 26–27. Also Francis Rufus Bellamy, *The Private Life of George Washington* (New York; Thomas Y. Crowell, Co., 1951), 33–34.

p. 46. George Washington's relationship with Sally Fairfax is still debated. It seems clear, however, that Lucy Grimes might have inspired him to poetry, since he proposed to her one time. She later married Richard Henry Lee and became the mother of "Light Horse Harry" Lee. See Wilstach, 46. Michael "Red" Burke was probably a composite of evil men who roamed the colonial frontiers. Grey was adept at creating such characters for his western novels.

p. 53. Washington evidently did catch smallpox while in the Barbados because he was allowed to return to Virginia only after he had been released from quarantine "imposed on him by an attack of smallpox." Wilstach, 33.

p. 59. The "renewed travel" Grey speaks of was probably by the Scotch-Irish. These people came in substantial numbers, first to New England, and then to Pennsylvania. Around the 1740s they began westward moves out of Lancaster County, Pennsylvania, which took hundreds of them over the mountains into Kentucky and Tennessee. The British government took no real steps to curtail the arrival of the Scotch-Irish from Ulster because they were good fighters against England's enemy, France, and the Indians. It was not until just before the American Revolution that Parliament tried to restrict Scotch-Irish movements, but by that time, of course, it was too late.

p. 60. James Genn was the county surveyor of Prince William County, Virginia. Washington worked under him as a surveyor on the frontier.

p. 61. The Zane mentioned on this page was Ebenezer Zane, great-grandfather of Zane Grey. Ebenezer's daughter, Betty, figured prominently in saving Fort Henry (Wheeling, West Virginia) by running through a hail of bullets and arrows to get much-needed gunpowder. Zane Grey's first published novel was *Betty Zane*, and it told not only of Betty's heroic dash but also of Ebenezer's taking "tomahawk rights" of many places in the Ohio Valley. Ebenezer married Elizabeth, who was part Indian, and it was through his great-grandmother that Zane Grey claimed to have Indian blood flowing through his veins. Ebenezer founded the town of Zanesville, Ohio, where Zane Grey was born on 31 January 1872.

One of Ebenezer's sons, Jonathon, figured prominently in two other Zane Grey novels, *Spirit of the Border* and *The Last Trail*. In these books, Jonathon Zane was joined by Lewis Wetzel (who actually existed), and the two of them considerably cleared the frontier of hostile Indians and white outlaws and renegades. *Betty Zane, Spirit of the Border*, and *The Last Trail*, make up Zane Grey's Ohio River trilogy. In fact, *George Washington, Frontiersman* antedated all the events of these three novels, and thus becomes their foundation.

p. 63. Washington's sighting of the majestic eagle soaring over the bountiful land, and his conviction that it was a symbol of freedom, point toward his future greatness as president of the United States.

p. 64. In Grey's own day (1872–1939) it was commonplace to speak of black people as "darkies" and "niggers" and also to refer to the American Indian as "Injun" and "redskin." These terms are, of course, unacceptable today; they are slurs against these two American minorities. However, to maintain the authenticity of Grey's work, the editor decided to keep Grey's words and sentences as much to the original as possible. Certainly no offense is intended to those minorities by either editor or publisher.

p. 64. The Scotch-Irish too were enchanted by the beauty of the Blue Ridge Mountains. Several diarists rhapsodized on the mountains. One, Sally Hastings, said they "sank into insignificance all the works of art" she had ever seen.

p. 66. Thomas Cresap helped Nemacolin, a Delaware Indian guide, build "Nemacolin's Path" or wagon road into the frontier areas over the Allegheny Mountains. Cresap was a colonel in the Virginia militia. See Charles Henry Ambler, *George Washington and the West* (Chapel Hill: University of North Carolina Press, 1936), 33.

p. 75. Though the conversation on this page between Sally and Washington may have been fictional, her reference to his diary one day becoming a "precious document" was certainly borne out.

p. 79. Isaac Zane, in Grey's novel *Betty Zane* (1903), was captured by the Wyandottes, and he became engaged to one of their princesses, Myeerah. He was called "White Eagle" by the Indians. Once, at least, in Grey's novel, Isaac was captured by Cornplanter, the Seneca chief. While imprisoned by the Senecas, Isaac met the notorious frontier renegade, Simon Girty (who actually existed), who told him about impending Indian conflicts.

p. 81. There is no historical evidence that George Washington ever met Ebenezer Zane.

p. 85. In addition to founding the "Island of Wheeling," and Zanesville, Ohio, Ebenezer Zane also laid out the road from Wheeling to Maysville, Kentucky, known as Zane's Trace. It later became a part of the National Road. See Hugh Cleland, *George Washington in the Ohio Valley*. (Pittsburgh: University of Pittsburgh Press, 1955), 252.

p. 85. The Ebenezer Zane on this page was the great-grandfather of Zane Grey. Jonathon Zane played a leading role in Grey's Ohio River trilogy, particularly *The Last Trail*. Elizabeth, or Betty, later became famous for saving Fort Henry (Wheeling, West Virginia) during an Indian attack.

p. 85. Lewis Wetzel was a historical character. He was a "professional" killer of Indians because his family had been wiped out in an Indian raid. He was known to the Indians by various names: some were "Deathwind," "Longknife," "Destroyer," "Le ven de la Mort," and "Atelang." See Carlton Jackson, *Zane Grey*. (Boston: Twayne Publishers, 1973; revised edition, 1989), 23—28.

p. 94. It is probable that George Washington never kissed Sally Fairfax, at least not in public as Grey here describes. There is no evidence that George's and Sally's relationship ever got beyond a "chaste flirtation," as Rufus Bellamy put it. See Bellamy, 56, 149—50.

p. 107. Grey liked to create characters who played tricks on other people. He was around cowboys for a good part of his life, and he became, like many of them, a practical joker. It fits Grey's style, but not perhaps Washington's characterization, to have George try to fool Sally in this way.

p. 122. Ashby's Gap in Virginia is named after the Ashby mentioned on this page. See Ambler, 21. Captain Jack the Black Hunter actually existed. He was later involved in the fight that led to General Edward Braddock's defeat. He pulled his men out of Braddock's forces because he thought Braddock was abusing them. Ambler, 102.

p. 132. Besides Lawrence, George Washington's brothers were Austine or Austin (half-brother), Charles, Samuel, and John Augustine. His sisters were Elizabeth and Mildred.

p. 138. Governor Robert Dinwiddie was lieutenant governor of Virginia and was acting as governor since the actual governor was "sinecure." He sent Washington in 1753 to western Pennsylvania to confront the French who were impeding upon the land claims of the Ohio Company. The following year the French-Indian War broke out. After Braddock's defeat in 1755, Dinwiddie was left with the responsibility of protecting Virginia's frontier settlements that were exposed. In 1757 he requested leave from England's Prime Minister, William Pitt, and returned to his home country in 1758 to retirement. *New Encyclopedia Britannica*, vol. 4, 104.

p. 141. Washington refers to Vanbraam in a journal entry of 31 October 1753. Vanbraam was a French interpreter. The name is spelled many different ways: Vanvraam, Vanbraam, Van Braam, van Vraam, etc. Washington, in his diary, spelled it Vanbraam.

p. 141. Wills Creek is a tributary of the Potomac, just north of the Pennsylvania border. Barnaby Currin and John Macguire were Indian traders who met Washington at Wills Creek in 1753. See Cleland, 3.

p. 142. Christopher Gist. Christopher Gist met George Washington at Wills Creek in the autumn of 1753. He led Washington's group out of the area. Cleland, 3.

p. 145. Washington entered the Ohio Valley in the fall of 1753. Most of his expeditions were in the upper valley, which is now Pennsylvania.

p. 152. There is no historical evidence of Washington ever meeting an Indian maiden named Winona. The name means "first born if it is a girl."

p. 155. Cornplanter was the chief of the Senecas. In 1753 the Miamis sided with the French. At the Council of Six Nations, the Mingoes were suspected of being spies. The Oneidas were from New York, one of the tribes of the Iroquois. The name means "large standing rock." The Wyandottes were originally the Hurons. Wyandotte was the name of a type of chicken in the colonial period in New York and Massachusetts. Pontise, the Ottowa chief, could possibly be

Pontiac, who led a rebellion in the early 1760s in Pennsylvania, primarily against the Scotch-Irish. The Chippewa, who lived in the Great Lakes District, were said originally to be cannibals who rarely came into contact with the white man. The Senecas were Mohegan people who lived around Seneca Lake in northwest New York. They were a part of the Iroquois nation. The Tuscaroras lived in areas of North Carolina; many of them were removed to New York state.

p. 156. Frazier was an Indian trading post on the Monongahela near Pittsburgh. Washington and Gist went there for the first time on 22 November 1753.

p. 157. Half King was an Indian chieftain who met Washington at Logstown in 1753 for the Council of Six Nations.

p. 158. Shingiss was chief of the Delawares and was at Logstown for the Council of the Six Nations. The Delawares were considered "uncles" of the Six Nations.

p. 164. Council of Six Nations: The Iroquois Indians were a powerful group in eastern America that played an important military role in the colonial struggles. The original league, or five nations, were the Mohawk, Onondaga, Oneida, Seneca, and Cayuga; in 1722 the Tuscarora joined, thus bringing their number to six. Most of the league sided with the British against the French, yet there were persons from the Mohawk and Onondaga tribes who converted to Catholicism and sided with the French. The Council met to discuss the impending war and the role they would play. *Encyclopedia Americana*, vol. 15, 468–69.

p. 165. In 1753 Half King, chief of the Oneidas, was also at Logstown, a place just north of Fort Duquesne.

p. 166. In November 1753, Washington found four French deserters who explained that France had four small forts on the Mississippi River from New Orleans to "Illinois." Illinois translated into Black Islands. Vanbraam translated for Washington on this occasion.

p. 169. Jeskakake and White Thunder were elderly Indian chiefs who, according to Washington, were friendly with the French.

p. 175. While both Washington and Boone served under General Braddock during his 1755 attempt to push the French out of the territory claimed by Virginia, they probably did not meet at this time, as Washington was part of Braddock's staff and Boone was a blacksmith traveling at the rear of the wagontrain. See Reuben Thwaites, *Daniel Boone* (New York: D. Appleton and Company, 1902), 21. Washington and Boone probably met in Culpeper County, Virginia around 1758 when Boone moved his family there to escape a Cherokee uprising. See John Bakeless, *Daniel Boone* (New York: William Morrow & Company, 1939), 30—31.

p. 179. Captain Phillipe Thomas Joincaire. This is the name by which he was known to Indian traders. He was a son of a Seneca woman and a French officer. In 1753 he was forty-six years old.

p. 181. French Creek is a tributary of the Allegheny River. It leads to Fort Le Beouf. Washington ventured up French Creek in 1753—54.

p. 181. Legarder de St. Pierre. Was a principal French officer. He assumed control of the French army in the Ohio Valley a week or so before Washington's arrival in 1753. St. Pierre had been visiting the Ohio Valley since 1739, when he had fought the Chickasaws. He had once been on an exploring mission which took him "almost" to the Rocky Mountains.

p. 195. Perhaps "Shannapins" was an old spelling of Shawnee? See Cleland, 43.

p. 198. Queen Aliquippa of the Delawares was a friend of George Washington. She and her tribe lived near Frazier's Store. Washington went to visit her in 1753 because she complained that he had not done so for some time. He took a matchcoat with him, and also a bottle of rum. Queen Aliquippa liked the rum better than the coat.

p. 199. In Europe, Britain and Prussia were allied against France, Austria, and Russia. When Frederick of Prussia invaded Saxony, the Seven Years' War (1756—1763) began. See William B. Willcox and Walter L. Arnstein's *The Age of Aristocracy; 1688–1830* (D. C. Heath and Co., 1983), 117.

p. 210. It is not likely that Sally brought George and Martha together since Martha was a stranger to the social set at Mount Vernon. See Wilstach, 63. However, this situation changed, and Martha did become familiar to the "society" people in the area, especially at Belvoir, the Fairfax Estate. Though Sally and Martha were always friendly with each other, there is no evidence to show that they were as close as Grey here depicts them. See Bellamy, 149–50.

p. 213. Peter Hogg was a militia captain. He was in charge of the Virginia rangers at Braddock's defeat. He had also served under Washington before as a commander of foot soldiers. See Ambler, 60, 100.

p. 214. Captain Claude Pierre Pecardy, sieur de Contrecouer, commanded a French force of about one thousand men on the Ohio Valley frontier. He had almost decided to surrender Fort Duquesne to Braddock before the skirmish broke out between Braddock and de Beaujeu. Ambler, 105.

p. 216. Wampum was a string of shell beads used by Indians throughout the northeastern part of America as a medium of exchange. The beads also came to be symbols of wealth and position. A religious aura was attached to wampum, which added to the solemnity of a ceremony. *Encyclopedia Americana*, vol. 28, 316.

p. 216. Washington arrived at Great Meadows with the first artillery to cross the Allegheny Mountains, and here Fort Necessity was built. The site was one of the relatively low and open places in an area of virgin forest. Redstone was a fort built on the Monongahela near the site of present day Brownsville, Pennsylvania. Washington directed the building of a road to this fort in the 1750s, just before the French and Indian War. Ambler, 63, 76, 77, 87.

p. 219. Captain La Force was a French officer on the frontier who spoke Indian languages and escorted Washington's party in various visits to French military officers. He was captured at the skirmish of Laurel Mountain on 28 May 1754. Ambler, 44, 62, 64, 70.

p. 225. Joseph Coulon de Jumonville was the commander of the French forces at Laurel Mountain. He was caught and scalped by the Half King. Ambler, 64.

p. 249. Marion Geisinger, *Plays, Players, and Playwrights* (updated by Peggy Marks; New York: Hart Publishing Co., 1975), 300, says that "young Lt. George Washington may have been a member of that audience for he had developed a taste for theatricals in the West Indies. Certainly he was to see the younger Lewis Hallam in many of his performances in later years." Lewis Hallam sailed for America in 1752 with twenty-four plays in his repertoire. Four were by Shakespeare and five by George Farquhar. He came to Williamsburg, Virginia, where he converted an unused storehouse into a theatre. His first performance there was *The Merchant of Venice*. After some time in Williamsburg, where performances were given each Monday, Wednesday, and Friday, Hallam's show went on the road to Annapolis, New York, and Philadelphia. Some of the more popular plays they performed were *Love for Love, The Conscious Lover,* and *Damon and Phillida*.

p. 252. The "Anacrennatic song" referred to was "Anacreon in Heaven," a British drinking song, long favored in pubs. Later, in the War of 1812, Francis Scott Key wrote some lyrics one night while marooned on a British ship in the harbor at Fort McHenry, Maryland. He put these lyrics to the tune of "Anacreon in Heaven," and this song later (1931) became our national anthem, "The Star Spangled Banner."

p. 255. General Edward Braddock was born in Ireland, though he was English. He was a forty-three-year veteran of the British army when he commanded the forces in the Ohio Valley. He was a strict disciplinarian. Evidently Braddock liked Washington, and the feeling was mutual, though they had serious disagreements about strategy in facing the Indians and the French. Braddock was well-known for his condescending attitude toward the American colonists. Ambler, 97–99.

p. 275. Colonel Thomas Dunbar followed Sir Peter Halket a few days later, leading a regiment. His troops were literally destroyed at Braddock's defeat. Major Robert Orme helped Washington arrange his affairs so he could join Braddock's staff. Sir John St. Clair was an engineer in the royal army. He was wounded at Braddock's defeat but recovered. Ambler, 108, 128. Colonel Gage was in command of the artillery at Braddock's battle.

p. 281. Captain de Beaujeu was a commander of a force of approximately six hundred French and Indian fighters that met Braddock's force to start the Battle of Monongahela. Ambler, 105.

p. 295. Daniel Boone was at this battle. Sir Peter Halket was killed at Braddock's battle. He commanded the 44th Regiment and was the first to leave Alexandria for Fort Cumberland. Ambler, 100. There is no mention in the various sources of his son.

p. 302. Washington's men were gunned down by panic-stricken English soldiers as he was trying to take them on a flanking maneuver that might have saved the day. Ambler, 107.

p. 308. Braddock was indeed buried in the middle of the road, which later became the National Road. Washington read the Anglican burial rites over Braddock's body.

p. 330. Captain John Dagworthy was in command of Maryland troops at Fort Cumberland. He refused to obey Washington or give him troops or supplies. Ambler, 115–16. General Shirley was the governor of Massachusetts and commander in chief of all British forces in America. His son was killed at Braddock's defeat.

p. 333. General John Forbes built "Forbes Road," which ran from Raystown, Pennsylvania, to Fort Duquesne. He had a very low opinion of Virginians; hence he would not take Washington into his confidence. Ambler, 126–27. Major James Grant led a group of Scottish Highlanders in a premature attack on Fort Duquesne. Over eight hundred men attacked in what should have been a successful undertaking, but Grant's desire for glory caused it to fail; three hundred men were killed in the attack. He, along with several other officers, was taken prisoner. Ambler, 128–29.